A SPARK IN ASHES

ANNABELLE MCCORMACK

Published by Annabelle McCormack

Cover by Patrick Knowles

All images used from Shutterstock with permission.

www.annabellemccormack.com

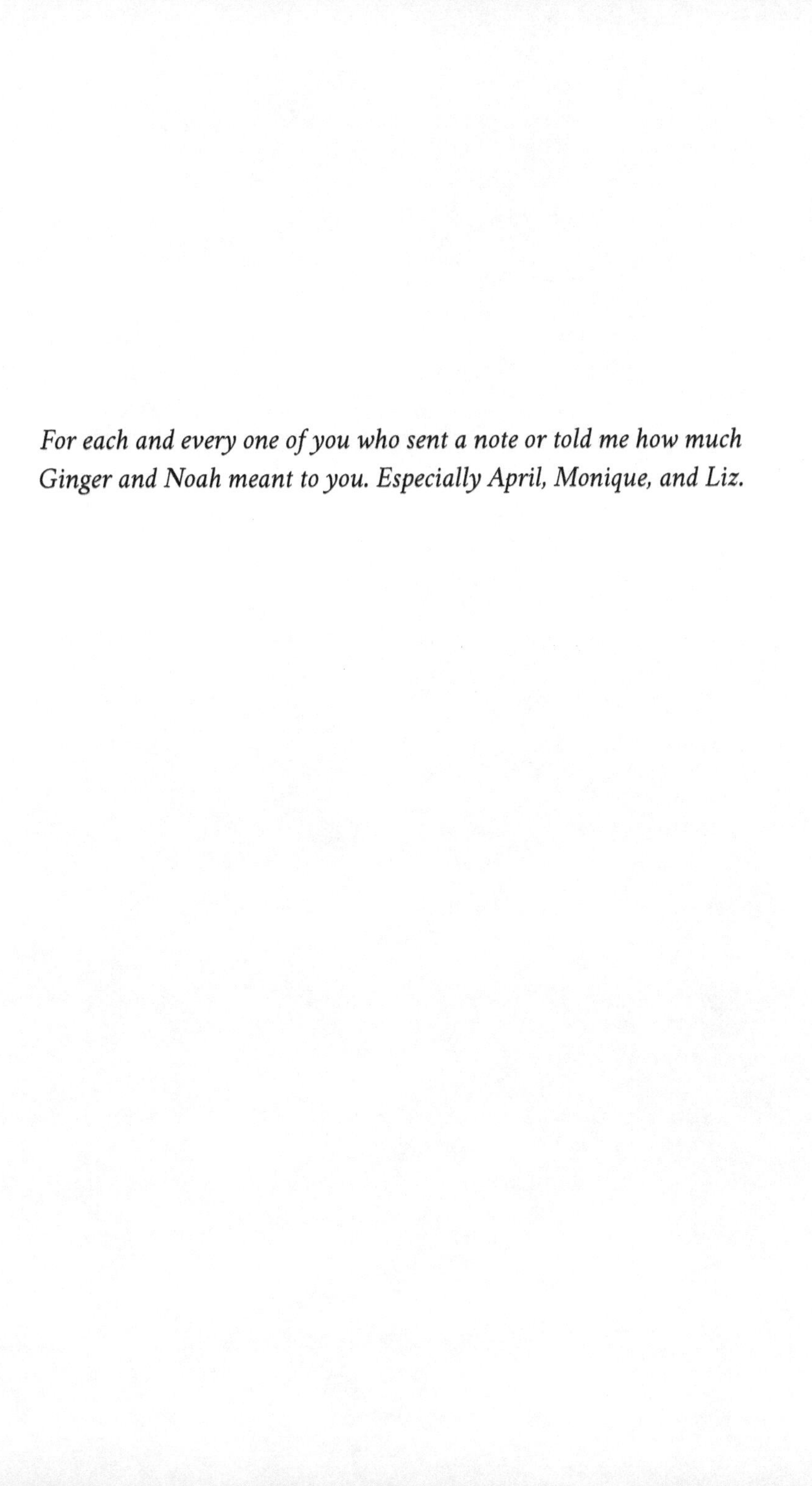

For each and every one of you who sent a note or told me how much Ginger and Noah meant to you. Especially April, Monique, and Liz.

A SPARK IN ASHES

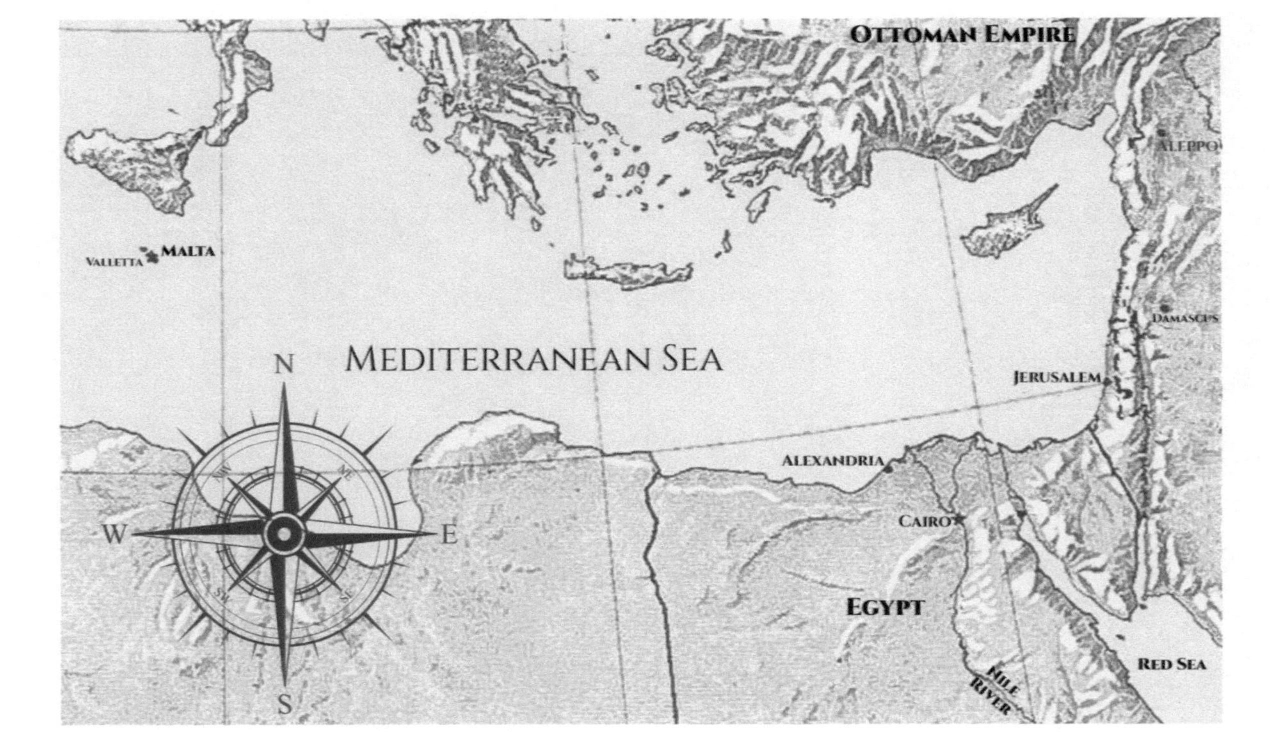
OTTOMAN EMPIRE
ALEPPO
DAMASCUS
VALLETTA
MALTA
MEDITERRANEAN SEA
JERUSALEM
ALEXANDRIA
CAIRO
EGYPT
NILE RIVER
RED SEA
N
W
E
S

PREFACE

The Great War has ended. The Ottoman Empire, which for centuries ruled the Middle East, lies in ruins. Britain and France, victors on the battlefield, quickly move to secure the spoils. Yet beneath the triumph is a tangled web of promises and betrayals.

During the war, Britain pledged support to the Hashemite leader Sharif Hussein of Mecca, assuring him of an independent Arab kingdom in exchange for the Arab Revolt against the Ottomans. At the same time, under the secret Sykes–Picot Agreement of 1916, Britain and France had already agreed to carve the region into spheres of influence. The following year, the 1917 Balfour Declaration offered still another promise: support for a Jewish national home in Palestine. These contradictory commitments would ignite decades of tension.

By the early 1920s, the Hashemites found themselves sidelined. France expelled Hussein's son Faisal from Damascus and claimed Syria for itself. In compensation, Britain placed Faisal on the throne of Iraq and another son, Abdullah, in Transjordan. Meanwhile, Palestine became a British Mandate under the

League of Nations, with London tasked to administer the land while facilitating Jewish immigration. To the Arabs of Palestine, this mandate looked less like stewardship and more like dispossession. Violence simmered and erupted throughout the 1920s and 1930s, as Arabs resisted both British authority and the growing Zionist movement.

Across the Mediterranean, a different battle was brewing. In Britain, concern turned toward the rise of fascism in Europe. The Security Service, known as MI5, had been founded in 1909 under Vernon Kell to counter German espionage. By the 1930s, the service's focus shifted to a new and more dangerous threat: Adolf Hitler's Nazi regime. Kell and his officers worked tirelessly to infiltrate far-right groups at home and to track Nazi subversion abroad. Among his agents was the eccentric but brilliant Captain Maxwell Knight, whose network of informants penetrated fascist movements within Britain.

German ambitions, however, were not confined to Europe. Berlin sought allies in the Arab world, exploiting resentment against Britain and France. Nazi propaganda began to circulate in the Middle East, promising liberation from colonial powers. For nationalist leaders disillusioned by broken promises after the war, these overtures were tempting. The seeds were sown for a contest of influence that would stretch from London to Jerusalem, from the cafés of Cairo to the deserts of Iraq.

The 1930s would become a decade of uneasy bargains, clashing empires, and shadow wars—where intelligence officers and agitators moved quietly in the margins, while the world edged closer to a second, even more devastating conflict.

CHAPTER ONE

JACK

Kharga Oasis, Egypt
February 1934

The desert didn't want him there, but it hadn't quite killed him yet.

Jack Darby stepped out from the shaded ruin that passed for shelter, the air brittle and dry. The first light of dawn crept over the horizon, casting a golden hue upon the sandstone walls of Qasr al-Ghueita. The temple walls rose around him, half buried in deep sand drifts—columns chipped by time, a lintel etched with a name the sands had nearly devoured. Amun. Or what was left of him.

Even here, the cool morning breeze carried the scent of date palms and humanity in the oasis as it stirred—smoke rising from hearths, the distant bray of donkeys—the slow, remote life of a desert people untouched by the chaos of the outside world.

He sipped from his canteen, the water warm but refreshing.

The tranquility of the morning was welcome. Here, amidst the ruins and the vastness of the desert, he could almost pretend the world was still whole, that someone hadn't scribbled over it in broken promises and barbed wire.

That his heart hadn't nearly bled out in the process.

He swigged again and spat onto the sand beside his booted feet, rinsing away the stale taste before the memories could rise.

The soft hum of an engine reached him. Then a slow-moving shadow stretched over the dunes, coming his way.

A biplane.

Jack's gut tightened. No one flew over Kharga without a reason.

Goddammit.

He should have known it was a bad sign when the local boy, Fadi, hadn't returned with supplies last night.

Fadi wasn't always consistent with the food he brought—he'd substituted pigeon meat for chicken on more than one occasion—which Jack might've accepted if the pigeons didn't taste like sandal. But Fadi *was* punctual. Once a week, the boy would make his way up from the village with the supplies Jack requested. Other than that, Jack didn't see or speak to anyone.

The miserable police outpost stationed near the village was mostly symbolic, a leftover from when the Metropolitan Museum of Art had conducted excavations in the area. Winlock's team had moved out almost two years ago, though. Now officials were happy to look the other way and leave Jack in peace in exchange for a few bank notes when they decided to remember he was still here.

As the biplane drew closer, Jack moved back into the makeshift shelter and knelt by a locked box below his cot. From it he removed his extra pistol—he always kept one at the holster at his waist anyway, mostly for snakes. He tucked the spare one under his waistband behind his back.

The noise from the engine grew deafening.

Whoever had come for him wasn't trying to hide it, at least. So much for quiet regrets and dying in peace.

He left the shelter once again, stepping out into the lee of the temple wall. The biplane had landed nearby, propellors still spinning grit into the air. Both the pilot and the passenger were outfitted with goggles and aviator hats, giving Jack little insight into their identity.

For good measure, he pulled the pistol out from the holster at his waist.

Can't hurt to be ready for anything.

The engine died, dispersing the scent of fuel in the air. Jack raised his chin, beard itchy. He kept it for convenience now, not like in the war, when it had been a disguise. Back then, he'd thought a beard could help him move around without being noticed.

In the time since, he'd learned the trick to not being found was picking a hiding place no one wanted to visit.

Which made the biplane's arrival even more ominous.

The pilot remained in his seat but the passenger shifted, then climbed out from the aircraft. He jumped to the ground, landing in a low crouch, then stood to his full height—tall, thin, and disturbingly familiar.

As the man removed his goggles and cap, Jack's empty hand clenched at his side. The face, a ghost from his past, once handsome, now lined with age.

Prescott Federline.

The man who'd stolen his sister, Alice. The father of the first woman Jack had really loved, and who'd been such a menace to them both that Kit had fled and crushed Jack's heart.

And taken a good portion of Jack's will to live.

Son of a bitch.

Prescott strode across the sand toward him, a perfectly

straight smile at his mouth. His hair had turned white since the last time Jack had the misfortune of seeing him. But those ice-blue eyes? As cold and sharp as ever.

A cold, slick sweat broke out across the back of Jack's neck, then he lifted his pistol, aiming it lazily. "Funny, I was just wondering what to use for target practice," Jack said with a confidence he didn't entirely feel.

Prescott wasn't a man to falter in his steps, even at the threat of a pistol.

"Good to see you haven't lost your flair for the theatrical, Darby." He stopped a few feet from Jack and his eyes flicked lazily toward the temple behind him. "Still shacking up with desert fleas, I see."

Jack gritted his teeth. *How the hell did he find me? And why?*

Deep down, he knew Prescott wasn't here to kill him.

Prescott would have done that a long time ago if he'd wanted to. Part of the reason Jack had been so infuriated when Alice had started working for the man's organization was that Jack had known it was Prescott's way of controlling him. Of keeping him under his thumb.

So he'd put an ocean between Alice and himself. Not only to protect her but to minimize the influence Prescott could have on him.

It was the best lesson Kit had taught him when she'd fled from the United States and assumed a new identity.

Jack swallowed the lump rising in his throat. Even though Prescott had aged considerably over the last twenty years, Jack still saw a reflection of Kit's features in her father's face. The first woman he'd loved—and lost—wasn't someone he wanted to remember now. Kit's death during the war had nearly destroyed him.

"What do you want?" Jack lowered the pistol but kept it in his hand.

"Is that the sort of welcome I get? Do you have any idea the trouble I went to find you?"

"If you were smart, you'd understand I don't want to be found—and especially not by you. And, yet, here you are, defying logic as usual."

Prescott released a chuckle. "Aren't we beyond all this? It's been twenty years, Jack."

Jack narrowed his eyes at him. "My parents are dead because of you. No amount of time will ever undo that."

Prescott sighed, pulling out a handkerchief from his pocket. He wiped his brow despite the cool morning temperature. The Kharga nights were damn near chilly. But during the day in February? Perfection.

"Jack—I've always been a busy man. I didn't come here to waste my time on squabbles."

Jack crossed his arms, vaguely aware of the sweat stains that would likely show under his armpits. "Then why are you here?"

Prescott folded his hands in front of him. "What else? I'm here about Alice. She's missing."

Missing?

Jack's mouth went dry.

A dull ring started in his ears as Prescott went on. "She's been embedded with Leonard Woolley's team at the Royal Tombs of Ur the last two years. Her task was one of a sensitive nature. But about a month ago, she and another member of our organization went out on assignment to Baghdad and never returned."

Alice … in Iraq?

The idea that his younger sister had been on this side of the world—relatively close to him, for all intents and purposes—disturbed Jack in a way he didn't know how to verbalize. And working with Leonard Woolley, a fellow archeologist Jack knew on a first-name basis.

But the truth was, what did he really know of Alice now? He'd spent more time out of her life than in it at this point. That thought made his chest ache.

He met Prescott's gaze. "And what do you want from me?" Somehow, he doubted Prescott had come all this way to simply give him bad news.

"To find her. Of course." Prescott gave him a thin-lipped smile. "She was in possession of information I need. Information we went to great trouble to obtain."

Of course.

Jack glared. "And why not put your lackeys to the challenge? I don't work for you, Prescott."

"It goes without saying that my men are scouring the area for any trace of her. But, Jack, surely you have a vested interest in finding your own sister—don't you?"

Something wasn't adding up.

Prescott's presence here wasn't a sign of goodwill—it was a sign of desperation. That something had gone terribly wrong. Something out of Prescott's control. If his vast network of informants and operatives couldn't find Alice ... *Alice may not want to be found.*

Or she was dead.

"What makes you think that I can find her when you can't?"

"You're her brother. You know how she thinks better than anyone. And you still have friends in British Intelligence—people who can help you move around out here. I've heard high praise of your exploits during the war and the mess that followed in Syria and Palestine."

The idea that Prescott had been keeping an eye on him wasn't surprising, but it didn't disturb him any less. He'd come here to get lost from the world—to spend his time chasing puzzles that didn't need urgent solving, to show anyone who'd ever wanted him dead that he was no threat. He just wanted to be left alone.

And yet, Prescott still felt the need to track him.

He'd vowed never to work for Prescott. Not for money. Not for revenge.

But for Alice?

This was why he'd tried so hard to put distance between them.

And he knew Prescott. No such thing as one job. *Not when there are favors to call in and lives to ruin.*

Goose bumps pebbled on his arms, and he shook his head slowly. "I'm not your man. And I don't know her anymore. Sorry you came all this way for nothing."

He turned away, acid biting his throat as he started back toward the temple.

Nothing could compel him to help Prescott.

Nothing.

Prescott's voice carried in the wind. "The other operative Alice vanished with?"

Against his better judgment, Jack glanced over his shoulder back at him.

Prescott gave a knowing smile. "It was Kit."

Jack's heart stilled. *Kit.* The only ghost worse than Prescott.

Cold spread through his chest like desert nightfall.

Now Prescott had his attention. And the man damn well knew it.

CHAPTER TWO

JACK

Cairo, Egypt

The hiss of steam filled the air beside the train as Jack stepped off onto the platform in Cairo, squinting into the crowd. Porters in red fezzes darted between travelers with crates and luggage trunks, calling in Arabic over the cacophony of voices and footsteps, while young boys darted between the arriving passengers, offering their services in exchange for *baksheesh*.

Jack adjusted the strap of his satchel over his shoulder, then met the gaze of a young man leaning against a far wall watching him with dark, solemn eyes.

The hint of a smile tugged at the young man's mouth, then he straightened, sweeping the long black hair from his forehead. He was clean-shaven and thin but well-groomed, sharply dressed, and even conventionally handsome. Little remained of the scraggly Bedouin boy who'd once been such a useful little spy—and only the wooden prosthetic in the place of his left hand remained as a heartbreaking souvenir from those days.

Jack breathed out a sigh of relief and started toward him. "And here I was worried Alastair hadn't gotten my message," Jack said when he reached him. "You're a sight for sore eyes, Khalib."

Khalib chuckled and gave Jack a skeptical once-over. "I'm not certain I can say the same." His English was nearly flawless, only the slightest hint of an Arabic accent and spoken with a British intonation. "Alastair may insist on de-licing you before he lets you stay."

Jack scratched his beard and offered a grim smile. "I might take him up on it."

They started through the train station, and Jack checked over his shoulder. Sure enough, the man who'd been following him since Luxor was there. He didn't bother hanging by the shadows or acting with any pretense. No doubt one of Prescott's men.

This was what life had been like when he was a younger man living in America, having to watch his back and wondering when Prescott Federline might decide Jack was enough of a threat to get rid of him. Those who knew about the Blackwell Society usually worked for it—for Prescott. Most others didn't live long after finding out the truth.

Jack was an exception to that—only because of Kit and, later, Alice. Kit had done everything to protect Jack from her father, and she was the only one who'd held any sway with him. After she'd fled, trying to escape the wide net of control Prescott cast, Prescott had recruited Alice to Blackwell. He'd had the audacity to call it a favor to Jack.

Jack knew the truth though. He'd tried to convince Alice of it too. The only reason Prescott wanted Alice to work for him was so he could keep some measure of control of Jack. By keeping Jack's beloved sister under his thumb, Prescott bought himself the security of Jack's silence about Blackwell.

But now, twenty years after Jack thought he'd left all that behind, here Prescott was, pulling those puppet strings again.

"You have a shadow," Khalib said, interrupting Jack's thoughts.

Jack tore his gaze away and looked forward again as they exited the train station. "Why do you think I called Alastair?" Outside the station, the mild February weather was a relief, but that's where the calm ended—the wide palm-lined boulevards were jammed with motorcars and carriages, horses clopping, and horns honking, the scents of dust, spice, and sweat mixing on the bustling streets.

Too much noise.

Too many people.

A perfect place for spies to mingle with British colonial officers, tourists to blend with wary-eyed Egyptian nationalists, and smugglers to hide amongst antique and trinket shops. The constant simmering of unrest only fed into the thrum of disquiet inside Jack, and the belt that had existed around his chest for years on end now tightened like a vise around his lungs.

I hate Cairo.

The thought persisted as Khalib led him to a waiting motorcar, then continued as they turned away from the European-inspired building façades toward the narrower and older streets of Old Cairo. His friend, Alastair Taylor, had found both peace and freedom by settling here rather than in Anglo Cairo, where most English and Europeans made their homes.

As the streets gave way to narrow, dizzying alleyways that Khalib handled with impressive expertise, Jack looked over his shoulder. Knowing Khalib, he likely had a better route in mind than Jack did if Prescott's tail had managed to follow. He'd trained for this sort of thing extensively with Alastair, who gave all the orphaned Egyptian boys he took in not only a fine education but also skills that might help any endeavor they wanted to pursue.

In Khalib's case, those skills had all been in clandestine work. He'd idolized Noah Benson, Jack's closest friend and a gifted wartime spy. Noah's decision to settle in England permanently with his wife, Ginger, had been difficult for Khalib. And though Noah and Ginger came to Egypt during the winter season every few years, Jack sensed the young man's continued sense of loss at the closeness he'd once shared with Noah, despite Alastair stepping in to raise Khalib.

Then again, Jack felt the same loss—perhaps even more. His friendship with Noah had mostly recovered since the war's end, but neither of them could completely forget that Jack had married Ginger when Noah had gone missing in order to save Ginger from destitution and to help her raise her and Noah's son, Alexander.

Or the fact that Jack had fallen in love with Ginger during that time.

He'd been emotionally unbalanced, still reeling after Kit's death and Noah's disappearance, and what he'd found with Ginger had been unexpected and profoundly deep.

But he'd lost her once Noah returned—not that he could blame her.

And now ... to think the possibility existed that he'd mourned in vain for Kit too.

Jack clenched his jaw, the threat of a headache pulsing behind his burning eyelids.

A sharp turn threw his stomach in a nauseating way, and he grimaced as Khalib stopped the car suddenly, then backed up straight into a pile of crates stacked near a building. The crates collapsed with a crash, banging to the ground around them, bouncing off the sides of the car—and they pulled into what appeared to be an old horse barn.

As Khalib killed the engine, a few boys appeared from the shadows near them, then slammed a wooden gate shut over the entrance they'd crashed through.

Jack stared at the gate, his heart thudding. He hadn't missed this. "Was the tail that close behind us?"

Khalib nodded grimly, then set a steady hand on Jack's shoulder and squeezed. "But he won't find us now."

"You certainly still know how to make an entrance, Jack."

Alastair's voice came from Jack's left and he turned, squinting deeper into the dark. Alastair emerged a moment later—the picture of a polished English gentleman, a pipe in one hand. More grey at the temples than the last time Jack had seen him though, and his dark curly hair was trim, like the moustache he sported. He grinned at Jack, the sweet scent of pipe tobacco filling the air between them.

"And you still have more tricks up your sleeve than anyone I've ever met." Jack offered a smile, then opened the door and swung his legs out of the car and stood. He'd only taken one step forward when he saw Alastair's eyes flick over him with uncertainty, a frown in his expression.

"The desert wasn't kind to you this time. Did you find what you were looking for at last?"

"Not yet. But something found me. *Someone.*" Jack tossed a wary gaze around them. He wouldn't talk about Prescott in front of Khalib, no matter how trustworthy he was. For his own safety.

Alastair was one thing—Jack's friendship with him ran long and deep. And Alastair traded secrets almost as skillfully as Blackwell did. On a much smaller scale, of course. Alastair had narrowed his level of expertise and contacts almost exclusively to Egypt, with a few closely placed connections throughout

Arabia. The difference was that Alastair did his best to ensure the information ended up in the hands of the worthiest cause.

If anyone could help Jack find Kit and Alice while avoiding being tracked by Prescott Federline, it was Alastair. But Alastair risked exposing his own contacts and allies in the process.

Alastair gave one nod, then gestured toward a darker area of the barn. "We can follow this tunnel to my house. Have some tea."

They didn't speak any further until Jack was seated in Alastair's sitting room. If there was a more secure place in Cairo, Jack didn't know of it. Alastair had more than one safe house, some of them connected by tunnels. His own personal residence, though, was known to only a handful of people, Jack being one of them.

He stretched his legs in front of him, sitting back on the sofa. "How's the wife?" Jack asked Alastair with a tired smile.

Alastair handed him a teacup, then sat at an armchair across from Jack. "Useful. Busy with all the excessive nonsense the wives of the diplomats adore. We see each other every few weeks, but I expect it might be more soon. Unrest seems to be stirring everywhere."

Jack nodded absentmindedly. Normally, he'd be interested in Alastair's take on the political changes in Europe and elsewhere, but he had too much to worry about to divert the conversation to that topic or to be genuinely interested in Alastair's wife. That Alastair had married at all had been a shock to his closest friends—especially considering whom he'd married: Lucy Whitman, Ginger's often snobbish younger sister.

After the initial surprise of Alastair's nuptials had worn away, their reasons for the match became clearer—it wasn't about love, for either of them. He had wealth and position here in Cairo—something Lucy wanted—and they were both willing to grant each other the freedom to do whatever they wanted. Love whomever they wanted. *Discreetly.*

London society had rejected the scandalous divorcée—she had been briefly married to a distant cousin who had inherited her father's earldom—but Alastair had helped her find social standing in Cairo once again. And, in exchange for that, Lucy provided Alastair with yet another source of information. A useful one, at that. Lucy had always excelled at schmoozing with the upper crust.

Alastair crossed one ankle over his knee and sipped from his own teacup. "Do I dare ask who was following you here from Luxor?"

"Alice has gone missing," Jack said, pinching the bridge of his nose. "Prescott Federline had her working in Ur with Woolley's team—or that was her cover anyway—and now Prescott can't find her."

Alastair grimaced. "Alice? In Iraq?"

Jack nodded.

"Did you know she was in this part of the world?"

Jack shook his head.

Alastair's teacup clinked against its saucer. "That's unfortunate."

Staring at the teacup in his own hands, Jack drew a slow breath. Maybe he should let himself be more affected by the news of Alice than he'd been by the news of Kit, but the fact was, he'd spent a lot longer mourning the loss of that relationship. Seven years younger than him, Alice had followed him around everywhere as a child. Adored him.

But all that had ended a few years after Prescott had come into their lives. Somehow Prescott had wormed his way in, become the "father she'd never had." Which wasn't difficult because their own father, Frank, had been a drunk and gambler who'd died when they were young.

Jack squeezed his eyes shut for a moment, then set the cup to the side on a small end table. "The bigger news is that he claims Kit is alive. That Kit was with Alice when she vanished."

Alastair raised a brow. "*Your* Kit?"

The words were ironic. *His.* As though Kit had ever really been his. They'd had their moments. And for a few short weeks after they'd reconnected during the war, Jack had let himself be deluded by the idea that they might finally have a chance.

But he'd been there when she'd been killed—or so he'd thought.

And if she hadn't died, how could she have possibly gone back to work for Prescott? She'd sworn she never would. Changed her name. Broken Jack's heart. All to escape her father.

When Jack didn't answer, Alastair frowned. "How did Federline find you?"

"I don't know."

"I'm assuming he wants you to find Alice and Kit."

"Something like that." Jack leaned back and popped his elbow on the armrest, then rested his head against his fist. "Kit's the only one who ever ran from him successfully. He won't say as much, but my guess is that he's desperate if he's coming to me. He offered me Kit's field notes as evidence that she's alive—and because I think he wants me to decode them."

"But?"

Jack leveled his gaze at Alastair. "But I won't work for *him.* No matter what the prize is."

Alastair gave him a sympathetic nod. "That's a rather vexing dilemma. Those field notes might be the best chance you have. Though I applaud your morality, however much I may disagree with your methods. Wouldn't it be better to take his offerings and cut your ties with him once you've found the girls?"

Jack laughed bitterly. Trust Alastair to speak so plainly. He was right, of course. Working with Prescott, getting those field notes—and any other information Prescott might have—was the easiest way for him to try to start a search for Alice and Kit. "I won't do it," he said simply. He gave Alastair a pleading look. "That's why I'm here. I need your help. You have a few contacts in Iraq, don't you? Or Syria. I know things are tense in Iraq since they got their independence, but I'm sure there are still some British officers you're friendly with—"

"British government officials will be of no use to you. Do you know how many times they've hounded me for your information? Surely you know how much they want you, Jack. Noah too. They won't give you an ounce of help without expecting something in return."

He'd been afraid of that. Jack flexed his sun-roughened knuckles. "The State Department has done their best to recruit me too."

Alastair nodded, clearly unsurprised. "It's a pity you don't think of pulling Noah into this, come to think of it. He might be more useful to you than I am in this case. He spent a good deal of time in Iraq during the war. Likely still has contacts there. And he's friendly with Woolley from their time in the Arab Bureau."

"Ginger would kill me. But I'll admit that's crossed my mind." Jack removed the hat from his head and set it on his knee. "But Prescott's watching me. He knows that I'll be looking even if I won't do it for him. That's why he came to me in the first place."

"Could you go directly to Woolley? He may be able to assist you."

"Maybe—I haven't ruled it out yet. But I'm sure whatever he knows he's already told Prescott. And if Prescott came up short, then I might not have much better luck."

A few beats of silence passed between the two men, then Alastair sighed. "If that's the case, then you need to consider the potential consequences. Maybe Kit—and Alice—don't *want* to be found. Or whatever information they have is so dangerous that it cost them their freedom or their lives. It could cost you yours too, Jack."

Jack held his gaze. "I've already thought of that."

Alastair nodded. "I wouldn't be your friend if I didn't warn you." He reached into his breast pocket and pulled out a notepad and a pencil. He scribbled something, tore the sheet from the notepad, then folded it in half.

He paused, then gave Jack a once-over. "You should think of going to a tailor. Or at least getting a new suit. That one looks almost twenty years old."

"It *is* twenty years old," Jack grumbled. He'd lost so much weight in the desert that none of his older suits fit him.

"Well, you may want to fix that. If you're going to be a part of society again—even if it's just while you search for Alice— you'd best be trying to blend in."

Standing, Alastair crossed the room toward him and held out the paper. "There's a man named Alain Roche. French official, born in Palestine from an influential Catholic family, and he's very friendly with British espionage personnel. Stays at Shepheard's. Give him this paper and he'll talk to you. He has deep connections in Syria and Iraq."

Jack reached for the paper, but Alastair held it back. Jack raised a brow. "What?"

"Just … be careful, old friend. I said he was well connected— *not* that I trusted him."

Jack snatched the note. "Trust never was your strong suit."

Alastair smiled. "And that's why I'm still alive. Never forget that fact. Good luck."

CHAPTER THREE

JACK

Twilight fell like silk over the desert, cooling the stone beneath the colonnades of the Mena House Hotel as Jack made his way toward the outside terrace. Lanterns swayed in the breeze, carrying the heady scents of jasmine and sand. Their warm light fell across the mosaic tiles that held the echo of footsteps of so many who had come and gone—adventurers, diplomats, royals who'd once used this as their hunting lodge— and yet the feeling here remained the same. And in the distance the pyramids kept watch like silent sentinels who took in all secrets and buried them deeply.

Egypt had been "independent" for over a decade now, and yet Cairo still served as the empire's living room. Diplomats and British officers still took their tea on the verandah of Shepheard's Hotel or ruled the interior of the exclusive Gezira Club. The resentment of the nationalists was understandable at this point.

Jack sighed as he slipped into a chair, scanning the exterior. He didn't have the heart to worry about any of that right now. Alain Roche had directed him to meet him here tonight. It was a start, at least. But he was sure he'd seen Prescott's man pick up his tail again after he'd checked into Shepheard's. Not that he hadn't expected that. If he looked hard enough, he was sure he'd find someone watching right now.

He tugged at the collar of his shirt, which he'd bought in the afternoon. Alastair had directed him to a shop to buy ready-made clothes that would be suitable for the upper-class settings of Anglo Cairo. But he felt uncomfortable and awkward in his clothes, which was a new development, since he'd never struggled in a suit before.

A young Egyptian man in a galabeyah came by his table, bowing as he filled a glass of water. Jack pulled out his bifold wallet, making a deliberate show of plucking a bill from a thick stack. He slid it across the table. "Alain Roche?" he asked in a low murmur.

The Egyptian paused for a moment, eyeing the money. A regretful look came into his face. He shook his head, ever so slightly. "He's not here yet, *effendi*. I will tell you when he arrives."

Jack thanked him, then ordered a whisky. *Damn.* He'd hoped to observe the man first. Size him up. From what he'd heard at Shepheard's, Roche spent most of his time in Cairo at the lounge here. They were meant to meet in the smoking lounge in a half hour.

So much for that.

Jack sat back in the rattan chair, which squeaked under his weight, and removed his hat, then set it on the table. Fact of the matter was, he felt old and out of practice with anything that involved stealth and secrets. What his wild youth hadn't done to kill his sense of adventure, the war had.

He was forty-one and had all the money he could want but not a single thing to show for his time on this planet. Nothing that really mattered, anyway.

What would he say to Kit if she was alive?

To Alice?

The last time he'd seen his sister, they'd argued and said the worst things to each other.

How could Prescott think he really knew her now?

A shadow fell over his table and he looked up, expecting his drink. Instead, a pretty young woman stood there, blond hair swept back and under a bucket hat. Her blue eyes sparkled as she took the seat across from his without bothering to introduce herself, a hint of a smirk under her red lipstick.

Jack gave her a bold stare, his lips twitching. She had an unusual fire in her eyes, a look of determination that intrigued him. After what felt like an eternity, she leaned forward. "Roche is nine tables over, next to the oud player," she murmured silkily.

His eyes darted in the direction she'd mentioned.

"No. Don't look. You don't want to give me away, do you?"

Jack frowned, then gave her a closer look. The hint of dimples showed under her high cheekbones. Who *was* she? Her accent was clearly English. "What's it to you?"

She grinned, then leaned back in her seat as the waiter arrived with his whisky. "Thanks, sweetheart," she said, taking the whisky. "Can you get one more?"

As the waiter hurried away, she tilted her head. "Ruby Wilkerson," she said with a grin. "Journalist."

He might have known.

She motioned to a nearby table, where a young man that resembled her closely was seated. She lowered her voice to a whisper. "I was having drinks with my brother Theo when I heard you ask for Roche." She winked at Theo, who shook his head, then looked down at the book in front of him.

"I didn't ask that loudly."

"For the terrace? You may as well have been shouting." She sipped the whisky. "What do you want with Roche?"

Jack chuckled. "You think I'd tell a journalist anything? This isn't my first time in Cairo."

She bit her lip. "I'm just curious—"

"What do *you* want with Roche?" Jack asked, giving her a suspicious look.

"I don't care about Roche. I'm interested in the man who followed you in here tonight." Ruby took another sip of whisky, but this time Jack noticed a slight tremor to her fingertips. Not of fear. *Excitement, maybe?* "Six tables back. Don't look."

Jack didn't have to. She had to mean Prescott's man. He sighed. "So I can't look this way or that. Guess I'm stuck looking at you." The waiter arrived again and Jack accepted the drink, then gave her a tight-lipped smile and swallowed some back. It burned the back of his throat, the warmth of it welcome. He rarely had fine English spirits in the desert.

He adjusted his collar again, and Ruby's perceptive gaze went to his throat. "New clothes?" She leaned forward on the table a bit. "Let me guess. You're fresh off the boat. Come to Egypt for adventure and treasure hunting—a little late in the season, though."

He repressed a chuckle. Though she'd guessed about his clothes well enough. He must look like new money on the prowl. Not exactly Alastair's intent when he'd suggested Jack blend in. Though it didn't help that he was being followed.

Why did Ruby want to know about Prescott's man?

"You know the man following me?" he asked, flicking a glance in the direction she'd said Alain Roche was seated. Sure enough, a well-dressed man in a Panama hat was there, smoking a cigarette and drinking a glass of red wine.

"Gerard Bailey?" Then she frowned, a cautious look coming into her face. "Friend of yours, Mr. ...?"

"Not exactly." He cleared his throat. "Darby. But you can call me Jack."

Her light eyebrows drew together for a moment. "Darby ... why do I know—" Then she stopped, her eyes widening. She stared at him, blinking. "Oh!" Then she finished her drink and stood. "Well, it was a pleasure, Mr. Darby. Thanks for the drink."

What the hell?

"Wait." Jack's hand shot out, and he grabbed her by the wrist.

She turned, a panicked expression on her face.

"I—"

Jack stood, stepping closer to her.

What about his name had made her react that way? This whole introduction had been beyond baffling, raising dozens of questions—none of them coherent enough for Jack to verbalize. "You know, usually when I buy a woman a drink, I like to pretend she won't take off at the sound of my name. What the hell is going on?"

She winced, pulling her wrist out of his grasp. "I'm sorry, I shouldn't have—"

"You shouldn't have what?" He searched her eyes. Why was there genuine fear there?

She held his gaze for another moment, pupils dark and wide, then she turned, hurrying back to her table.

Other guests were watching him now.

Jack's breath deepened as he considered storming over to Ruby's table and demanding an explanation. But he'd already drawn too much attention to himself.

He glanced back toward Roche.

The table was empty.

As he felt the energy drain from his limbs, he frowned and searched the terrace. Then he saw the glimpse of a man in a Panama hat, going around the corner.

Roche.

If Jack had been aiming for discretion, Ruby had blown that plan to shreds. She also appeared to be leaving the terrace … but he couldn't worry about that or her right now. Roche had specified that he wanted their meeting to be discreet, and if he was heading out into the lawn rather than the lounge, he might be irritated.

Jack moved quickly, tossing some money onto the table, and hurrying after Roche. Stepping off the terrace onto the lawn, he scanned the horizon. Dusk was falling rapidly. While limited light came from the terrace and the interior of the hotel, most of the exterior was quickly fading into shadow that Roche could disappear into.

For a moment, Jack thought he had lost him but then he saw Roche's silhouette in the light near the stables. Even from here the scent of the animals carried in the wind, and Jack hastened his steps, tempted to call out to Roche as he slipped into the stables.

He was clearly leaving.

Dammit.

He never should have entertained Ruby for even a moment. He knew better than to let pretty girls distract him when he was in the middle of something serious and clandestine. But he was rusty, and being rude to women when necessary didn't come naturally to him anymore.

Jack entered the building using the same entrance that Roche had used. The stables held on to the heat of the day, the air staler being trapped under the warm wood that surrounded him. He peered into the darkness, his senses more alert in the relative silence here.

The soft sound of his rapid breath marked the stillness as he moved further in.

Not even footsteps.

"Roche?" he asked softly.

The soft groan of a gate came, not too far from where Jack squinted, his heartbeat slowing.

He turned toward the noise in time to see the man in the Panama hat emerge from the darkness, a pistol in his hand.

Jack held his hands up, reflexively, but relaxed. "I didn't mean to alarm you."

The corner of the man's smile, dim in the limited light, turned up. "I don't think you understand the situation, my good fellow."

Then the shuffle of a step in the darkness.

Jack whirled around to see Ruby and her brother only a few feet behind him. Her brother also held a pistol. "Hi, sugar," Ruby said with a wink. She came closer. "Empty your pockets. Now."

Seriously?

The hard dig of the barrel of the pistol into his back made it clear just how serious the situation was. Jack drew in a breath through clenched teeth, his body going rigid. "And here I thought you were a respectable journalist."

Ruby smirked, her bright-red lips showing off perfectly straight teeth. "Who says I'm not?" She edged even closer, then set her hands on his chest. She slid her hand into his breast pocket and pulled out the slim leather bifold located there.

He hadn't really known what to think of her—but petty thief hadn't been the first thing that crossed his mind.

You're a damn fool, Darby. One day back in Cairo and this? Walked right into it.

Jack held her gaze as she handed it back toward her brother. "Anything else?" she asked. "I'll want that wristwatch too." The English accent was gone, but he couldn't quite make out what accent she used now. Something American Southern? Her fingertips ran over his shirt and then felt around his waist.

"Normally I save that for after the second drink together," he said with a scowl.

Her hand landed on the butt of his pistol tucked into his waistband, and she raised a finely arched brow. Pulling out the pistol, she lifted her chin calmly. "And here I thought you were excited to see me."

He almost laughed. "I take it the fellow behind me isn't Roche. What about the other one? That your brother?"

"Quite the detective, aren't you? Sadly, I don't like sharing details on the first date." She held her hand out. "Wristwatch."

He gritted his teeth, then removed it and handed it over to her. "Takes a bold woman to stalk the Mena House Hotel for victims. I'll make sure you'll never be able to show your face here again."

"Sure you will." She winked and stepped back, handing his pistol to the man behind her. "Pleasure doing business with you, Jack."

She turned to go, the man behind her following her lead. The pressure of the pistol at his back didn't abate, and Jack watched her through narrowed eyes as she kept moving, her svelte body swaying with a confidence he envied.

As soon as she and her companion had slipped back outside, Jack cleared his throat. "I get to walk out of here free, right?" They hadn't bothered to try to hide their faces, which worried Jack.

"Yeah, mate. Whatever you say," the man behind him said gruffly. The gun lowered a few inches.

That was enough.

Jack might have been robbed blind, but he wasn't about to let them all walk away—nor did he trust the man behind him not to shoot.

Jack pivoted sharply and struck, slamming the heel of his hand against the man's windpipe. As the man fell back, choking and gagging, Jack kicked the pistol from his hand, and it went clattering against the dusty ground. He dove for it, snatching it seconds later.

As Jack steadied himself, he aimed the gun toward his assailant, who tore into the darkness, still coughing and rasping. Jack cocked his head to the side. *Huh.* With a frown, he spun the barrel of the pistol, then stopped and shook his head.

Empty.

He'd been robbed with an unloaded pistol.

Jack pinched the bridge of his nose and sighed.

How could I have been so foolish? Something about him had clearly screamed "easy target" to these thieves.

Maybe coming back to the world wasn't as easy as dressing the part and pretending he fit in.

He checked his bare wrist then gritted his teeth, remembering how Ruby had taken his watch. *If that's even her name.* It probably wasn't. He should go, though. By now, the real Roche was probably waiting in the lounge.

And this time he wouldn't let himself fall prey to any pretty faces.

CHAPTER FOUR

JACK

The air was thick with cigarette smoke as Jack leaned back in his chair, staring across the small card table at Alain Roche. Ironically, the *real* Alain Roche was as stylishly dressed as the imposter Ruby had claimed was Roche. No Panama hat but a nicely tailored suit and elegant white bowtie and dinner jacket. He kept a silver cigarette case on the table from which he'd pulled the cigarette he was currently smoking. The wrinkles around his lips, hidden only slightly by a trim black moustache, spoke to a tobacco habit.

Roche sipped on the glass of red wine he'd just been delivered and frowned at Jack. "Are you certain you don't care for a drink?" His French accent mixed with the finesse that the Levantine people seemed to give the language.

Jack gave a tight-lipped smile. He wasn't about to admit to Roche that he didn't have a cent on him—or that he'd just been robbed. Neither gave the semblance of competence. "I'm fine, thank you."

Roche raised a brow. "You're not in America now, *monsieur*. You can drink freely here."

This time Jack did smile. "I'm not a fan of temperance either. Just need to keep a clear head tonight."

"I see." Roche sniffed, then settled further into his seat. "Well, how can I help you, Mr. Darby? I've heard a great deal about you. You have quite the reputation in Cairo, it seems."

"Maybe I did once. I only visit Cairo to see friends now."

Roche's smile didn't quite meet his eyes. "Ah, yes—Captain Noah Benson, correct? I was told you still frequent his house in Cairo during the winter season."

"Sometimes." Jack shifted in his seat. Apparently, he hadn't been the only one trying to find information on the other for this meeting tonight. And Roche had been far more successful than Jack had been at accomplishing his goal.

"But not this winter."

Jack flattened his palms over his thighs, feeling unsettled. Being robbed likely had a good deal to do with that. Not to mention the reason he was seeking out Roche in the first place.

Focus.

"Not this winter," he said. "Captain Benson and his wife were unable to come to Egypt this year."

"Pity." The corners of Roche's mouth lifted. "I've heard stories of Captain Benson's wife. She's described as being quite beautiful. A shame I could not meet the English rose myself."

Jack's throat clenched. He didn't have to overthink Roche's line of questioning. The implication was clear enough. He'd heard of the scandal surrounding Ginger and Jack's divorce.

Whatever reason Roche had for informing him just how much he'd learned, Jack was familiar enough with this sort of man to understand the subtle warning: Roche had access to information. And that could be used against Jack, if necessary.

"She's more than beautiful," Jack said gruffly. "She's a doctor and surgeon. And she runs a private hospital in the country, which makes it difficult for the Bensons to leave England. Maybe next year."

"Indeed." Roche held the stem of his glass in his fingertips, swirling the wine gently. "But I interrupted you, of course. I assume you didn't call me here to discuss Captain Benson and his wife. Forgive my curiosity."

"No apology necessary." Jack's breath slowed. "I was given your name as someone who might have contacts in Iraq."

Roche nodded, his eyes glittering. "That's true."

"I'm looking for information—discreetly—on two women who went missing in Iraq. And I'll pay for that information, if necessary."

"Two women?" Roche leaned closer. "Friends of yours?"

"My sister. And ... her friend."

"Do you know where they were last seen?"

Jack hesitated. How much information was safe? He did a quick survey of the room. The smoking room may have been a better, more private place for a meeting, but it wasn't hard to get a good sense of who gathered nearby. The wood-paneled walls seemed to absorb the golden-hued electric light, the scent of beeswax drifting from their reflective polish. Voices here were low and muffled, the constant reminder of polite society that restrained its laughter—and its emotion.

"They were working at the dig in Ur," he said at last.

Roche nodded. "Fascinating site. I've been there several times."

One of Jack's least favorite aspects of modern archeology— the transformation of digs into major tourist attractions. He kept his face blank and nodded. "I don't have a lot of information to go on—either about the extent of their involvement with the excavation or where they were last seen. But that's where I was hoping you might come in."

"My condolences of course. This must be a ... *difficult* time for you." Roche swallowed some wine, then shifted in his seat. "Unfortunately, I have a situation I must confess to you. I'm unable to help you at the moment."

Jack's eyes narrowed at him. *Unable?* "You can't or you won't?"

Roche cleared his throat. "Surely you remember Captain Maxwell Knight? He believes you'll remember him, at least."

Jack nearly groaned.

Knight? The man was a menace. An intelligence agent for Britain's MI5, he'd contacted Jack several times over the last couple of years, requesting a meeting. When Jack had finally met with him, he'd made it clear that British Intelligence wanted Jack back in service—especially with the rise of socialism everywhere.

The US State Department had done the same thing but less aggressively. At least they seemed to take no for an answer. *For now, anyway.*

But what could Knight possibly have to do with Roche? Or this?

"I know him, yes."

Roche offered an apologetic smile. "It seems that Captain Knight feels it necessary that those of us with ... *connections* should refer you to him before assisting you with any inquiries."

Jack's jaw nearly dropped. *What the hell?* "He wants what?"

"Regretfully, he's requested that you speak to him before I lend you my aid."

Hands clenching into fists, Jack's head spun. Knight had made it clear when they'd last spoken that if he wouldn't help him in intelligence work he wouldn't tolerate his participation in it. *"I'll be keeping a close watch on you, then. If you're not with us, you're against us."*

But *this?*

"I didn't know you were beholden to the British government," Jack snapped, his irritation flaring.

The tips of Roche's teeth showed, stained red with wine. "Careful. You wouldn't want to discourage me from helping you later, would you?" Taking a drag from his cigarette, he went on. "Besides. You must understand my position. There are certain individuals I must keep content. Captain Knight has made it clear there are consequences for those who cooperate without his blessing."

Like he gave a damn about insulting Roche.

"So that's it, then. You won't help me unless Knight gives permission? What do I have to do, exactly, to get this permission?"

"He thought you might ask." A plume of smoke came from his lips. "He's asked that I travel with you to London. Come to a resolution." He gave Jack an eagle-eyed look. "But you should know—the greater the favor you ask, the more he's going to expect. And you're not nearly as valuable to Knight as your friend Benson."

A deep, sudden pressure pushed in against Jack's chest, sudden understanding dawning.

Of course.

Captain Knight had intimated as much when they'd talked. He wanted Jack's help at MI5—but Jack was American. And Knight knew the Americans wanted him. He would be willing to let Jack go and defer to the wishes of his allies.

But Noah?

Noah was British. Brilliant too. A polyglot who could blend seamlessly into a variety of cultures, and a veteran with hard-boiled experience. And while Jack had politely declined Knight's proposals, Noah had been less congenial.

Knight wouldn't just ask for Jack to help him this time—he'd try to leverage Jack's need for help and information to find a way to pull Noah back into this.

Jack's anger coursed through his veins, hot and unfiltered. The room felt smaller, the air thicker and suffocating.

"I don't speak for Noah," he said with a glare. Then he stood. "And you're not the only person who has connections in Iraq, Roche."

As he turned to go, Roche said, "I'm afraid you'll find a similar result anywhere you turn, Jack. Captain Knight has made certain of that."

Jack shook his head. "I'm willing to take my chances."

"Are you?" Roche gave a skeptical look. "I thought this was about your sister. A loved one. Perhaps … her welfare is of less concern than I assumed."

His words landed straight on target.

Alice.

Kit.

Maybe Prescott had lied. Or maybe they were out there in the dangerous desert right now … captive or *worse*.

He couldn't think about that.

But did he really have time to waste? Jack heard his pulse hammering in his ears, unable to take a full, deep breath to ease the choking feeling. "And if Knight permits it, then you can help me?"

This time, Roche's smile showed delight. "You were referred to me for a reason. Help can always be arranged—for a price. You just have to decide what you're willing to lose."

CHAPTER FIVE

GINGER

Somerset, England
March 1934

Ginger Benson turned off the engine to the motorcar and climbed down from the driver's seat, shivering as she stepped into the blustery winter air. She hadn't taken the time to grab more than a shawl on her way out the door from the hospital.

And she wouldn't have rushed over here, either, if it wasn't for the fact that *this time* he'd pilfered her favorite artery clamps.

She scanned the exterior of the small farmhouse she'd shared with her family for the first five years of life here after the war, heartstrings tugging at the darkened windows that had once been such a source of light and life for her. But as Alexander and Clara had gotten older, they'd all outgrown the two-bedroom cottage. It had been silly to consider staying here when the residential side of the estate had more than enough bedrooms for them all—even if it meant moving back to her family's ancestral home, where the ghosts of her past stalked every corridor.

But she wasn't the only one who missed the farmhouse.

The tracks in the snow led straight for the front door and Ginger followed them, then paused at the doorway. She opened it a crack. "Alexander?"

Silence.

She sighed and opened it more widely. "Alex."

A grunt answered from the kitchen, followed by the unmistakable *snap* of an electric discharge.

Swearing under her breath, she hurried into the house, surprised to find it warm. A fire glowed from the woodstove in the empty living room, a cot beside it with neatly stacked books at the foot.

Apparently, Alex had decided to make this his hideaway for some time now.

She rounded the corner and found her fifteen-year-old son at the kitchen counter hunched over a mess of wire, batteries, a coiled bit of copper tubing—and something that looked suspiciously like the foot pedal from her operating table.

He didn't look up, his dark head bent with concentration. "Don't touch the gap; it's still live."

She sighed. "Is that my surgical clamp holding the—"

"It was the best conductor I could find," he said absently, twisting a knob made from a sardine tin lid. "And your glass slides make excellent capacitors. They're only cracked a little."

A crackle lit up the makeshift transmitter. Alex's face glowed —not from the sparks but from sheer satisfaction. "I just sent a 'CQD' in Morse. If there's a ham operator within ten miles, they'll pick it up."

She pinched the bridge of her nose. "You're going to burn the farm down. Or, worse, attract someone in a uniform with more questions than patience."

He finally looked at her and grinned. "Well, if they show up, at least I'll know it works."

Ginger shot him her sternest glare, doing her best to suppress the smile tugging at her mouth. "Shut it down—if that's possible. Put out the fire and lock up. We'll discuss your blatant thievery at home. I'll be out in the motorcar waiting for you."

A look of consternation crossed his handsome young face and she turned away, hurrying to the motorcar before sentiment got the best of her. He'd always been too intelligent for his own good. She didn't even know what in God's name he was building now.

And Noah, who'd lost his own father at a young age, had responded to that trauma by being the opposite of a disciplinarian with his children. Her husband would likely encourage Alexander in his exploits. Buy him another damn book on mechanics.

But stealing from the hospital crossed a line. Funds were painfully low since the Slump, and Ginger had fought tooth and nail to keep the hospital and mother-and-child home afloat. They'd had to turn so many impoverished women away, though, and that had been devastating.

She ground her teeth as she reached the motorcar, restarted the engine, then settled into the driver's seat. Alexander soon emerged, a canvas satchel slung over his shoulder. He trudged toward the vehicle and climbed in beside her wordlessly, frustration still written in his stormy blue eyes.

Ginger suppressed the urge to soothe him, then pulled out of the snow-covered drive. Fortunately, it had only been a light dusting—enough for her to be able to track her son's footsteps —but not so much that she hadn't been able to drive here to collect him. The walk back to the hospital would have only taken fifteen minutes, but she hadn't wanted to do it in the cold.

Tense, thick silence hung between them, making her miss the days when he'd been an angelic—if incorrigible—toddler who'd wrap his arms around her neck, rather than a serious adolescent who thought himself smarter than her. Which he probably was.

Not that he needs to know that.

But he already did speak as many languages as Noah. Clara was also proficient in at least four languages, since Noah had tutored them both. And sometimes Ginger envied that bond between the three of them—the time she'd given over to Noah to spend with them while she worked in the hospital.

"What on earth were you building anyway?" she asked at last, glancing at him.

"A spark-gap transmitter, of course." He frowned, one hand tightening on the strap of his satchel.

A what?

She looked back at the road, hoping he wouldn't see the blankness in her face. "Is it legal?"

He didn't answer, sighing instead and turning his gaze out the window.

"Why are you so much like your father?" she muttered, gloved fingers tightening around the wheel.

"Were you hoping I'd scrub in with you like Clara or Ivy? Sorry—I'm not that kind of prodigy."

He said it matter-of-factly, as though he'd considered the matter before. "No, I wasn't saying I was hoping for ..." Ginger shook her head, unable to complete the thought due to her own frustration. "I'm not trying to encourage you to be anything other than what you aspire to be, Alex. But the stealing has got to stop. Even Papa won't be on your side with this one. My supplies are strictly off limits for your experiments."

"I was *borrowing*."

"Well, you should have asked."

"Most of the things I used were sitting in a dusty old cabinet—"

"And yet they're still not yours to take."

"Fine," he gritted out.

That tone was enough to boil her blood. She clenched her teeth to keep herself from saying anything she shouldn't, then focused on the estate looming in front of them. The house that —rightfully speaking—belonged to Alexander. A fact he didn't know. And one that she was increasingly worried of telling him about.

Jack Darby had bought the estate from her former brother-in-law, the last earl of Braddock, after the man went bankrupt. At the time, Ginger and Jack were still married—she'd thought Noah dead, and Jack had wanted to raise Alexander as his own.

When Noah returned, she divorced Jack and chose the man she'd never stopped loving. But instead of selling the estate, Jack quietly put it in Alexander's name. Then he left—first for America, then later Egypt. Every so often he'd turn up at Penmore, and the children loved it when he did—Uncle Jack was their favorite person.

And when Noah had become restless at home and Ginger had agreed his plan to winter occasionally in Egypt for the archeological season, they saw Jack there as well. She was never able to stay in Egypt as long as the rest of her family—she could only be away from the hospital for a limited period—but both Alexander and Clara always came back brimming with stories about Jack.

Her feelings about Jack were much more complex.

Falling in love with him when she'd thought Noah was dead

had been surprisingly easy. Not that her love for him compared to the love she had with Noah—and now the life they'd built together—but a part of her would always love Jack.

But marriages didn't function well when a wife still loved her husband's closest friend, so she'd put distance between herself and Jack. Was never alone with him. Didn't write.

The space was necessary. She'd created a mess by getting involved with Jack in the first place—one that she still feared the repercussions of, especially when Alex would learn someday that the estate belonged to him.

She pulled into the courtyard and parked beside an unfamiliar motorcar. Not that it was unusual for unfamiliar cars to be here—it was a hospital, after all. The work here was endless, the days long and sometimes unbearable, though she rarely admitted that out loud.

Alex's hand shot toward the latch to open the door, and she reached across, setting her hand on his forearm. "I'm proud of you for your experiments. Truly. But next time, just ask me. If I can give you the supplies—if they're really not being used—I will."

He held her gaze for a split second before nodding and looking away. Then he was gone, hurrying out of the car and heading into the house.

Ginger adjusted her shawl, then followed him, her heart unusually heavy. She'd started the morning performing a hysterectomy for a poor woman with fibroids, then gone immediately into an emergency surgery for a local farmhand whose arm had been mangled from a thresher. She'd worked for hours stitching torn muscle and staunching blood with the help of her nurses, all the while hearing the health inspector's voice from last month, *"Patients under the panel must go to approved physicians, Dr. Benson. You've no authority to treat them here."*

Maybe the back-to-back surgeries had got the day off on the

wrong foot. Or it was the unrelenting bone-deep weariness she never seemed to shake.

For twelve years she had begged, borrowed, and bent the rules to keep the hospital alive. Donations dwindled each season. The county association ignored her letters. Still, she carried on—stitching wounds, setting bones, coaxing babies into the world—all while her male colleagues dismissed her as a curiosity and closed the paths for funding and payment.

Sometimes, she wondered whether the fight itself was killing her more quickly than the work.

By the time she reached the foyer, Alex had vanished from sight. They'd had to renovate several parts of the estate house to make it suitable as both a hospital and a residential home, but certain spaces still retained their former glory, like the main foyer and grand staircase. The right wing now served for medical purposes, and the left wing was for residents.

When Ginger and Noah had moved back into the estate, they'd converted one area for their family alone, but they still shared most of the common areas with the women and children they provided housing for, including Victoria Everill and her daughter, Ivy, who'd grown up with Alexander and Clara like a sister.

Funny how Victoria had once been practically Ginger's rival —and now she was one of her closest friends. Ginger didn't know how she'd run everything at Penmore without her.

Ginger hung her shawl at a rack near the door, the sound of male voices drifting from the library nearby. Maybe the owner of the motorcar parked in the front?

But if they were in the library, it wasn't a patient. That room was for the Bensons' exclusive use—by necessity. More than one book had gone missing after they'd opened their doors to others. Ginger frowned, then headed toward the library.

She caught sight of Noah from the open doorway as he

leaned near the fireplace, arms crossed. Even after sixteen years of marriage, her heart still stumbled when she looked at him. He'd always been the handsomest man she'd met, of course, but it went much further than that—he was the one person with whom she could be utterly, completely herself.

As though he knew she was staring, he glanced up and caught her gaze, then straightened. "Here's Ginger now, actually."

She crossed the threshold into the library, then stopped short. Three more men were in the room—two of which were strangers.

The third was Jack.

Her breath caught, guilt blooming in her chest—ridiculous but reflexive. As though somehow thinking about Jack had summoned him.

The three men stood and Jack stepped away from them, a wan smile on his face. He appeared thinner than she remembered and much more tanned—though it seemed he'd recently shaved a beard from his face, as the skin on his cheeks and strong jawline were lighter there.

"Hello, Red," Jack said as he stepped closer to her. He pressed a light kiss to her cheek, moving away just as quickly.

Ginger smiled warmly. He'd latched onto that moniker shortly after meeting her because of her bright-red hair. "Jack—what a surprise. You should have let us know you were coming. We would have planned a special dinner."

"It was a last-minute plan," Jack said, glancing at the two other men. "Ginger, may I present Alain Roche and Captain Maxwell Knight? Gentlemen, this is Dr. Virginia Benson."

She glanced between them, a knot of tension forming in her gut. Alain Roche she'd never heard of, but Maxwell Knight was a different story. The genteel-looking dapper man with a clean-shaven face and neatly parted hair had a keenly penetrating gaze and a still, poised demeanor. He was an intelligence man—and had been trying unsuccessfully to recruit Noah for several years now.

Before he could speak, Alain Roche, a tall man who appeared to be in his late forties with jet-black hair, olive skin, and a trim moustache, stepped forward. "Ah, the famed Dr. Virginia Dar—er, Benson." He smiled, a twinkle in his brown eyes. "Pardon. I was reading through your file this morning. You're a very modern woman, Mrs. Benson. Operating a country hospital named after your ex-husband."

Her heart ticked faster at the slip.

Not a chance he'd done that by mistake. He'd meant to unsettle her not only by calling her Virginia Darby—a name she'd never really used, even when married to Jack—and make a vaguely nasty insinuation about the hospital being named after Jack.

And what did he mean by her *file*? Was Roche an intelligence man too?

Ginger stiffened, then joined Noah by the fireplace, calling on all the manners and composure she'd been taught in finishing school years ago as she sat on the unoccupied sofa. She was accustomed to men dismissing or outright insulting her. Being a lady doctor was bad enough to most of them—but a "divorced" one? *Scandalous.* She'd even heard of patients refusing their wives and children to come to her hospital because of it.

But starting off an acquaintance with rudeness? Even the spymasters used to offer tea first. Very un-British. As was Mr. Roche's accent—which had the soft lilt of French.

"I suppose I am. But if you've read my file, Mr. Roche, you should know I don't tolerate being underestimated. Not by men in suits and certainly not by men with smirks." She set her hands in her lap. "Please do be seated, gentlemen."

Relief filled her as Noah sat beside her. She didn't have to meet his eyes or hear him speak to guess what he was thinking—or that he was likely as concerned as she was.

"A nurse turned spy turned formidable suffragette and lady doctor," Roche said with a grim smile to Jack. "No wonder you and Benson nearly fell out trying to claim her."

Insufferable bastard.

"I think that's quite enough probing into my personal business," Ginger snapped, glaring at him.

Roche exchanged a glance with Captain Knight. "To be honest, Mrs. Benson, we came to speak to your husband—"

"Anything you have to say to me can be said in front of my wife," Noah said in a curt tone.

"Not when it's a matter of national security, unfortunately," Captain Knight said pleasantly, his eyes locked firmly on Ginger now. He was dismissing her just as quickly as she'd come. "Your husband may have left the army and his espionage work years ago, Dr. Benson, but I assure you we're not quite as finished with *him* as he might be with us."

Ginger frowned, her gaze flicking toward Jack.

She was always glad to see him—*but what in the world is going on?* Men—even military ones—never spoke so openly about Noah's former line of work during the war. Even Ginger and Noah rarely spoke of it, especially because they hadn't quite decided what they needed to share with their children and what needed to remain concealed for their innocence and safety.

Jack avoided her eyes.

Noah leaned forward on the sofa. "Sadly, gentlemen, I'm no longer in the business of national security. Or of caring what the army wants from me. So I'd urge caution in including *me* in the conversation, if that's the concern."

"Come now, Major Benson," Captain Knight said smoothly, "you may have walked away from the military, but your country still needs you—now more than ever, I'd say, now that the Nazi party has taken power in Germany. Though I agree with Major Benson, Alain. Mrs. Benson has clearly shown her chops in intelligence. We shouldn't discount the service she gave our country during the war."

Ginger tilted her chin, giving him a thoughtful look. Noah had met with Knight on more than one occasion—usually in London—but this was the first time the man had come out to Penmore. She had a feeling the reason for his presence at this meeting had everything to do with recruiting Noah back into intelligence.

But had they managed to rope Jack into it already? Both Jack and Noah had sworn they'd never set foot in that river again. And though Noah rarely spoke of his experiences during the war, Ginger knew how much that part of his life still affected him. He often woke with nightmares.

Noah straightened. "I won't speak for my wife, Captain—or waste your time. My position on the matter remains unchanged. While I can appreciate the lengths you've gone to in bringing Jack here to persuade me, none of it will make a difference."

Jack met Noah's stare, his face softening. "I wouldn't have brought them here if it wasn't absolutely necessary. It's about Alice."

Alice? The air thinned, and Ginger felt Noah shift beside her. Jack rarely spoke of his estranged sister.

A creak, so soft that Ginger barely heard it, caught her attention.

But it was also familiar. She'd grown up in this house. Knew its creaks and groans.

Her eyes shot to the hidden doorway by one of the book-cases—the one that she and her brother Henry had often used as children and now led directly to her family's private quarters.

The barest hint of a crack there confirmed her suspicion: someone was there, listening.

Alexander.

She struggled for a breath.

Just what had he heard? And how long would it take before he asked the wrong question?

CHAPTER SIX

NOAH

Noah stretched, watching from the sofa as his twelve-year-old daughter, Clara, suppressed a yawn as she moved a chess piece while sitting across from Jack.

She wouldn't win, but that didn't matter to her. She was as stubborn as her mother. Ginger's spitting image too, with red hair more auburn than fiery.

Jack was taking it easy on her, of course—Noah had seen him demolish opponents in a handful of moves—but it was late, and Noah had spent most of the day waiting for the opportunity to catch Jack alone, once the children were asleep. Ginger had retired after dinner, but she'd rouse for conversation once Noah came to bed.

And when Ivy had seen Alex wander off, nose in a book, she'd mumbled some excuse to go help Victoria with inventory at the hospital. Noah had always anticipated that Ivy's childhood crush on Alex might one day be more obvious to his son, but, for now, Alex remained oblivious.

Maybe purposefully so.

Which left Clara. She was putting up a valiant fight—not

only to win but to stay awake—but it was time. Noah met Jack's gaze, then gave a subtle tap to his wristwatch. He caught the hint of a smile at Jack's mouth as he gave a barely distinct nod.

Jack moved a knight, then Clara sat up straighter.

"That was foolish." She reached for her rook, then happily took Jack's knight … and stopped short. Her eyes narrowed, then she looked from Jack to her father, then back at Jack. "Are you trying to throw the game, Uncle Jack?"

He feigned an innocent look, lifting his hands. "Not a chance. I just messed up. Must be tired. Speaking of which—we should probably wrap this up in the next few minutes. I have a bed waiting for me."

Clara groaned, then replaced the knight with a scowl. "If you wanted to end the game, you could have just told me." She sighed and stood. "You owe me a new game tomorrow."

Jack cringed, clearly chagrined. "I will, I will."

She went to his side and kissed his cheek. "Promise?"

"Always, kid."

She smiled, then scooted over toward Noah. "Good night, Papa." She gave him an equally enthusiastic kiss, then hurried out of the room.

"She's sweet, that one," Jack said, watching as the door closed behind her. "Smart. But sweet."

"Better than smart but surly?" Noah chuckled and stood. Alex already occupied that position, of course. "Scotch?" he asked, going over to a decanter on a table near his desk.

"God, yes. I've been drinking Bedouin moonshine for the last six months." Jack palmed his face, then sat back in his chair, loosening his tie. The distress etched into his face said enough. Once upon a time, Jack's dark-brown eyes would have found a way to light with humor, even in the worst of situations.

That humor had all but gone dry now.

While Roche and Knight had still been here, Jack had

explained that his sister, Alice, had gone missing while working with Woolley's team at Ur. That he needed Noah's help to locate her and that—of course—required clearance and assistance from British officials.

But Noah was certain Jack had much more to tell him.

Noah poured the amber liquid into a glass, then took it over to his friend, sitting in the seat Clara had just vacated. "So are you going to tell me what really brought you to my doorstep this afternoon?"

Jack sipped his drink, then held Noah's eyes. "The whole situation is a nightmare, Noah. I'm sorry I'm here at all." He sighed, swirling the whisky in his glass. "Alice is still working for Prescott, you know. He's the one with his foot to my throat. And I thought I was prepared for it. I spent my whole goddamned life waiting for him to turn up and try to use Alice against me like he did—but he was smarter. Three steps ahead of me, as usual."

Jack took another swallow, then sat back. "Prescott says Kit was working with Alice."

Noah stilled, then reached for a pawn, thinking for a moment before he responded.

If Kit was alive, it changed everything for Jack.

"Didn't you say Kit was dead?" He didn't know the particulars. Jack never spoke of his first love, and Noah had never met her. But one time in Egypt, a few years earlier, Jack had confessed that Kit had died during the war. That he'd *seen* her die.

Jack nodded.

"So is Prescott lying?" He rolled the pawn in his palms. That would be the logical thing—that he was manipulating Jack with that hope. "She left America to escape him, didn't she? Why would she suddenly be working for him now?"

"He swears it's true. That she didn't die and came back to

work for him." Jack avoided his gaze. "I'm not sure if I believe it. But if she's alive and I didn't save her … what does that make me?"

"But your curiosity's been piqued. And now it's not just about Alice anymore, either." Noah had to admit there was a mad bit of genius to Prescott's claims. True or false, Jack couldn't do *nothing*.

"Right." Jack finished his drink, then set it down. "And, God, I could have punched him. He stole my own damned sister from me and then has the gall to come to me and say, 'But, Jack, surely you have a vested interest in finding your own sister— don't you?'" Jack imitated Prescott's voice with disgust. "And then he flaunts Kit at me? I felt so … helpless."

The pain etched into Jack's features said as much. Noah flexed his arms, muscles bunching with tension. He hated to see Jack so desperate. "So you agreed to help."

"Sort of. I agreed to see what I could do and went to Roche. According to Alastair, he knows more about Syria and Iraq than anyone—spent years there working for both the French and the Brits. But Knight got to him first. He's put a dossier out on certain individuals. He doesn't want anyone in his network aiding or even speaking to them without his sign-off. I'm on that list. So are you."

"And Roche directed you to Knight."

"Basically. And Knight agreed to help me, if and only if I got him you."

Noah clenched his jaw, his palm closing around the pawn. "Of course."

"He's been after you for a while, hasn't he?"

Noah nodded.

Jack cracked a smile. "I think he may be in love with you."

Noah didn't return his grin. He'd heard enough about Knight's purported proclivities that it wasn't completely outside the realm of possibility, however discomforting the thought might be. But that didn't bother him as much as the fact that Knight had played his hand in all this well: he knew Noah *just might be swayed* if Jack needed it.

And Ginger would hate every second of it if he said yes.

"He wants me for a section of MI5 he's created to infiltrate subversives," Noah admitted, releasing the pawn. It had left a crescent in his palm—small, but sharp enough to linger.

"Well, he would. You're good at that. A natural choice, despite your Irish and Egyptian blood and your fondness for nationalists."

Noah set the pawn down quietly, then rubbed his burning eyelids. "Is it too much to ask to be left alone to live my life in peace?"

He'd fought hard for this quiet life. For his children, for Ginger. For normalcy. And now here he was, being asked to enter into a world where the consequences of even minor missteps could destroy everything he'd built.

Jack chuckled. "Believe me, I understand. I was hiding in a half-buried temple in the Kharga when Prescott came for me." Jack released a long, slow, guttural sigh. "We'll be paying for the sins of our youth for the rest of our lives, it seems. We had the audacity to survive the war with mostly interior scars."

Noah rubbed the stubble of his chin. "They're after all of us. Last time I saw Lawrence when I was in Dorset, he had the same complaint. The man turned his back on it all, changed his damn name—and they still can't leave him alone."

"You're right. They want all of us. You think Woolley isn't still involved somehow? Not a chance. The fact that Alice was there makes that clear enough. You know what Prescott's organization does."

Noah peered at him. Jack had never gotten into the specifics, but Noah could assume the basics. "Maybe it's time you give me a better idea of it, Jack. There's no use in trying to protect me from the man. If he's the menace you've always claimed, he's well aware of me by now."

With a sigh that sounded more like a groan, Jack stretched back and rolled his shoulders, then looked around the room. "It's always felt like such a risk to speak of it, but you're right. You should know what you're up against if you're going to help me." He drummed his fingers against the table, his thumb settling into a scarred groove that Alex had placed there as a child.

Noah watched him intently, waiting for him to continue. Prescott Federline and his daughter, Kit, had shaped Jack's youth in many ways. The man was to blame for the death of Jack's father and he'd eventually recruited Alice to work for him —Noah knew that much.

"Prescott's organization—Blackwell—they're … a global mercenary network of operatives," Jack said slowly, his eyes dark and troubled. "They specialize in collecting intelligence or covert, unsanctioned operations. Assassinations. When governments want something done but don't want to get their hands dirty or be implicated—they call Blackwell."

Noah had suspected as much. "What's his goal?"

"Goal? Power. Money. Influence." Jack gave a bitter chuckle. "People want to believe they're truly free because their government tells them they are—all the while, the ones with the real power are tightening the nooses, playing with them like puppets on strings. Bigwigs like Prescott, organizations like Blackwell—they're the ones that are really calling the shots. And then they throw their weight behind agendas that suit them … like suppressing the peoples and races they hate."

The bitterness in Jack's words ran deep—and Noah understood it all too well. Like Jack, he'd once been a naïve young man who believed that if he joined the cause of his country, he could do something to truly help humanity.

And then he'd watched humans murder each other in the most savage ways imaginable.

Noah had been more fortunate than Jack, though. In the arms of his wife, Noah had been able to rediscover love and family—the only real goodness in the world. But that was only because, after everything they'd been through during the war, Ginger had picked Noah over Jack. Despite loving Jack.

Noah swallowed hard, the memory of it something he could barely think of without feeling as though he'd choked down a mouthful of glass. Forcing himself to move away from those thoughts, he gritted out, "How does Blackwell present itself to the public then? A humanitarian organization?"

"Yes. They involve themselves in charity work and Prescott is beloved as a philanthropist. But the people on the inside— they know the truth. The information they collect and the work they do is sold to the highest bidder and they're willing to work for anyone and any cause if the price is right. It's an elite group and Prescott has no problem eliminating anyone who he thinks is a threat or will expose him."

Noah held Jack's gaze, outwardly calm despite the depth of unease he felt knowing his family was known to such a monster. "How does Prescott recruit if he tries to remain covert?"

"He approaches men and women whom he has been tracking—offers them a position. He doesn't attempt to recruit unless he's already convinced he'll be successful. But he's not above manipulation either, though he likes to keep his people happy and wealthy. And once you're one of his people—you have his protection too. He tattoos a triskelion on the under-side of his operatives' right wrist, where it can be easily covered by a bracelet or something. A basic triskelion means you're on the outermost layer of the organization. If the center of the triskelion is filled, you're second rank. One with a circle threading through it—those are his closest, most experienced operatives."

That seems foolish.

Noah frowned, glancing down at his own left wrist, where he'd received a scorpion brand from an Egyptian nationalist organization during the war. More than once, that brand had exposed him to the further scrutiny of anyone who recognized it. He'd allowed it to happen while undercover, but the consequences had haunted him.

"Wouldn't that be a risk?"

Jack shook his head. "No. If someone knows that symbol, they know to keep their distance. Prescott will go to any lengths to protect one of his own. Or to get revenge on someone that harms them."

No wonder Jack had done his best to stay away from Prescott for so long. But the fact that the man had resurfaced now, asking for Jack's help was disturbing. "And why is Prescott coming to you, then? If his reach is so extensive, why involve you at all?"

"I'm not sure, and it's part of what is bothering me so much. Clearly, he's not telling me everything. And if I do manage to find Alice and Kit, the last thing I want to do is lead Prescott to them—especially without talking to them first."

"Any possibility Knight is collaborating with Prescott to get to us both?" Noah asked wearily.

"I considered that, but I don't think so. It's too convoluted and expensive a route for Knight. Prescott's favors aren't cheap, and Knight would be a fool to indebt himself to him for either of us. There are younger, smarter men out there now to take our place. We're not worth it."

Probably true.

"So what's Knight's plan, then? Give you the necessary clearance, and I agree to work for him?"

"After you help me. And then I'll owe him too."

Noah reset the chessboard, keeping his face blank.

Despite his best efforts, the idea lit a fire he hadn't felt in years.

A sense of listlessness had been slowly creeping over him the last couple of years, especially with the news from the Eastern part of the world, where Fascism, socialism, and Communism all seemed to be spreading.

After the Slump that had gripped England in economic hardship for years, socialism had made inroads here too. Noah had watched it all with quiet concern, but after Germany had elected a new chancellor—Adolf Hitler—and he'd taken office the year before, the speed of the changes seemed electrified. Maybe not to those who were more worried about where their next meal might come from but to anyone keeping a wary eye on the situation.

And that was just Europe and the Orient. For Noah, the situation that had been unfolding in Palestine, Syria, and the surrounding lands was just as worrisome.

But when he'd resigned from the military after the war, he'd given up with it the idea that he could effect change. That had been a naïve, youthful ambition. Now he knew better. Letting himself get seduced by that lie once again would be foolish.

"How long do I have to decide?" he asked at last.

"As long as necessary. But every day that passes, the trail is growing colder, I'm sure. You know how it works. I am considering damning the official channels and going looking on my own, though."

"But you made the mistake of talking to the officials first—which means they'll be warned."

"Exactly." The legs of Jack's chair grunted against the hardwood floor as he pushed it back and stood. The fire popped quietly behind them, echoing the silence that seemed to emphasize the need for action. Choices to be made, here and now.

Noah hesitated. He shouldn't offer without speaking to Ginger first, but this was Jack, after all. Jack would do anything for him. "If you do decide to take that route—I might be willing to help with that too. In fact, we might want to try that first."

Jack's eyes darted to his. "Are you serious?"

Noah held his gaze, then nodded as he stood. "Between you, me, and Alastair, we might know enough people that Knight doesn't know. But we'd have to move quickly. Knight's likely to be watching."

Something that looked like relief relaxed Jack's features. "And here I was thinking you might not help."

This time Noah smiled. "You wouldn't be here if you thought that. But maybe you just thought I wouldn't be interested in breaking the law with you again?"

Jack chuckled. "Maybe."

"We'll leave after everyone goes to bed tomorrow. I'll think of a way of getting out of here without being seen, and we can discuss the details during the day. In the meantime—I have a harder job to face first."

Their eyes met.

"Ginger," they said simultaneously. And for the first time in a long time, they laughed together.

CHAPTER SEVEN

JACK

The door to Jack's bedroom creaked open before dawn.

Always a light sleeper, Jack roused, then rolled over in the bed to glance at the doorway.

Alexander had already crept in and was busy closing the door silently when Jack sat up. "Alex?" he asked, his voice rough with sleep.

The boy glanced over his shoulder, then stood straighter. "Sorry. I didn't mean to wake you."

"I'm going to go out on a limb and say that's probably not true, considering the fact that you're here." Jack ran his fingers through his hair, then swung his legs off the side of the bed and stood. "Something wrong?"

Alex's lips pursed. Oddly enough, even though everyone always compared Alex to Noah, Jack had known Noah long enough to be able to spot the differences. Whereas Noah had been aloof and reserved as a child, Alex was shy and anxious. Noah held his cards close to his chest, the master of a blank poker face. Alex, on the other hand, wore his worries in his expressive eyes.

"Couldn't sleep," Alex mumbled at last, then crossed the room toward the curtains. He peeked outside, then shut them just as quickly.

Jack raised a brow. "All right, now I have to know. What's going on?"

"I thought I saw someone out there earlier. Watching from the tree line." Alex turned and settled against the wall, hands behind his back. "It's something to do with those men who came with you, isn't it?"

Dammit.

Could be someone left by Knight to keep watch.

But more likely it was someone working for Prescott. Blackwell had operatives everywhere—and Prescott had been fairly quiet since Jack had left Egypt with Roche a week earlier. Fact was, Jack was surprised that Prescott hadn't interfered with him more.

But he would. That much Jack knew. The fact that he'd kept someone watching over him in Cairo had made it clear enough: Prescott wasn't done with him yet. He was smart and patient— like a mountain lion hunting its prey. He'd wait until the right moment, then pounce in and make his kill.

He wanted Alice and Kit. Wanted Jack to be looking for them.

But why? What does he think he'll gain by having me be the one to search for them?

He just hoped Prescott would stay far away from Noah's family.

Jack reached for his shirt and shrugged it on. He joined Alex by the window, then peeked out himself. How Alex had been able to see anything was beyond him—darkness stared back at him. "How'd you see out there?"

Alex stiffened. "I found an old war glass in my father's trunk in the attic. On a moonlit night, it seems to amplify the light." Then he turned his chin sharply. "You won't tell him, will you?"

The idea that Alex had been digging around Noah's old supplies wasn't surprising—but hopefully Noah had the good sense to get rid of or better conceal anything truly dangerous. Jack would be shocked if he hadn't.

Jack grimaced. "I'm not usually in favor of keeping secrets from your dad." He leaned over and set a comforting hand on Alex's shoulder. "But this one can probably stay between us. And there's nothing to worry about, I'm sure. You just probably saw an animal moving around."

"Nocturnal animals have eyeshine." Alex frowned, then released an exaggerated sigh. "Anyway, it's not likely he's my papa after all, is it?"

Jack's gut dropped. *What the hell?*

He lowered his hand from Alex's shoulder slowly. "What are you talking about?"

"The man here today—he said Mama was married to you first. So I went through her cabinet, the one she keeps locked in her office."

A low hum of panic buzzed in Jack's ears as the confession seemed to bubble out of Alex. "I found the divorce certificate first. You were married to her from 1918 until 1921. Her medical degrees have Virginia Darby written on them. And then …" Alex's eyes flared, the quiet devastation of his gaze the only betrayal of his true inner turmoil. "I saw my birth certificate. Mama and Papa always told me my birthday was in September 1918, but that's not true, is it? I was born in November. Nine months after you and Mama married."

Oh goddammit.

Jack's mouth went stale and dry as he felt the weight of Alex's perceptive gaze, caught between the strongest rock and hardest place he'd ever been. That was all true. And missing from the paperwork would be the certificate of Ginger and Noah's original marriage in November of 1917, which had gone down in a shipwreck, or the truth about Alex's birthdate, which was that Ginger's friend who had delivered Alex had altered the date on his birth certificate.

This was not a conversation Alex needed to have with him. His parents should be the ones to do it.

And Noah may murder me if I say the wrong thing.

To be fair to Noah and Ginger, Alex was only fifteen—they probably believed he was too young to share the messy past with. Maybe they'd even hoped he'd never find out. That was what Jack would have hoped for if he was in their shoes.

But the fact that Alex had come to him also gave insight into how betrayed by them he probably felt right now.

No wonder the boy hadn't been able to sleep.

What a way to start the morning.

Jack sighed, then moved away. He lifted his belt from the chair beside the bed, then slipped it into the waistband of his pants. "The facts aren't as straightforward as you think, Alex. Your mom was already pregnant with you before I married her."

Alex made an expression of disbelief. "I know science. How things work. I look enough like you for it to be true." The brittle matter-of-factness in his tone suggested that Jack risked pushing him away if he wasn't careful enough.

And yet, underneath that stoic veneer, Jack recognized an innocent boy on the brink of manhood, one who was also less ready for the cruelty of the world than he thought he was.

Jack turned toward him and sat on the bed, giving him a thoughtful glance. The light was dim enough to mostly obscure his features. If there were tears in those eyes, Jack couldn't see them. But he didn't think there were either.

Alex was the son of Noah Benson and Ginger Whitman. He wasn't built to fall apart easily.

Instead, he'd take on too much, ruminate on it until it ate away at him, shrug his shoulders in that too-big-for-his-britches personality, and suffer silently until he found the right person to share it with.

But Jack couldn't be that person. He'd risked too much of his friendship with Noah in the past. In some ways, one of the biggest surprises of Jack's life was how effortlessly and fully Noah had thrown himself into fatherhood.

Jack would never interfere with that.

"I'm not your father, if that's what you're thinking. Noah is. And your birthday *is* in September. I was there for it, actually. I swear that's all true." He sighed. "But it's not my place to give you any of the other details. Your father and I have always had a resemblance—people used to think we were brothers—and while I'm happy to believe someone might mistake me for your uncle, there's no question that you're your father's spitting image. Suffice it to say, you need to talk to your parents."

Instantly, Alex's posture closed off to him, the disappointment in his demeanor visceral.

"I see," he said. "Sorry to disturb you, Uncle Jack." He started for the door.

"Alex—"

The boy didn't slow or stop. Instead, he slipped out the door as quietly as he'd come, closing it behind him.

Jack stared at the closed door, the guilt settling like sand in his throat.

Fantastic.

Jack scrubbed his face with his hands, groaning softly. This wasn't a mess he was equipped to untangle. But he'd brought it to their door. He stood.

Better to find Noah and deal with it quickly than give his friends more chaos to sort.

He donned his shoes, then left the room and walked down the hallway toward the room Noah and Ginger shared. He tapped at it.

No one answered.

He gave another light tap.

"They're both already up," a soft, girlish voice said.

Jack suppressed a startle, looking up to see Victoria's daughter, Ivy, standing in the hallway, several feet away. She'd snuck up on him almost soundlessly and, like Alex, she was already fully dressed.

Does everyone get up before dawn around here?

Ivy crept out of the shadows, coming closer. She was a beautiful girl, even at fifteen, with rich-chocolate-brown tresses and grey eyes that reminded Jack of someone he couldn't quite name. For a long time, many people had gossiped that Ivy was Noah's secret daughter—and anyone from society who'd known Victoria, Noah, and Ginger in Egypt had been only further scandalized when Victoria had sought shelter with them after the death of her husband, Stephen Fisher.

Ivy was also Stephen's only legal child and heir, and that was precisely why Victoria had come to Penmore—to get Ivy out of the Fisher family's grasp. When Stephen had died, there had been whispers that circulated, saying that Stephen's parents intended to take Ivy from Victoria permanently. Stephen, in one final act of villainy, had been trying to commit Victoria to an asylum, when he'd been killed.

Fortunately, the simultaneous death of Victoria's wealthy father, Lord Reginald Helton, had given Victoria the financial means to escape the Lord and Lady Fisher.

Why Victoria had come here didn't quite make sense to Jack,

but he was glad to see Victoria and Ivy doing well—and finally free.

He snapped back to the present and straightened, then tilted his head toward Noah and Ginger's door. "Did you see them leave?"

She nodded. "I don't know where Uncle Noah went. But Aunt Ginger is in her office at the hospital. She starts her mornings at four."

Jack thanked her, then left the hallway, heading toward the hospital. If Ginger was the easier one to talk to right now, so be it. But who knew what sort of mood she'd be in when she saw Jack? Noah had been worried enough last night.

He found the door to Ginger's office open, yellow electric light spilling from it into the hallway. She was at her desk, writing, her head bent in concentration, a teacup on a saucer beside her.

Jack paused a few feet away.

Not just because he dreaded having to bring up another unpleasant topic but the sight of her always reminded him of what he'd lost. Took his breath away a bit.

He wasn't in love with her still—though he would always love her, deeply—but when their marriage had ended, so had any hope of ever finding someone else to love. He'd only loved twice, and deeply, and he couldn't go through it again.

The loss of love wasn't worth the pleasure of it. Love always ended in heartbreak inevitably. Death made sure of that.

He cleared his throat, then moved toward the door. "Morning."

Ginger raised her head, then met his gaze. She stared at him for a moment, then looked back down at her writing. "I'm not sure if I should return the greeting or find something to beat you with, Jack Darby."

He cringed.

"I'm sorry, Red."

She finished whatever she was writing, then set down her pen and stood. "Don't feign some half-hearted apology." She sighed. "I'm not angry, per se. Just … worried. Less about the legality of whatever it is you and Noah are up to and more about the enthusiasm I haven't seen in Noah's eyes for a long time."

She lifted a book and then moved out from behind her desk, going over toward a bookshelf. "He's been reading the newspapers from start to finish before breakfast lately. As many as he can get his hands on. Exchanging more letters with Fahad and Alastair too. It's as though he's already on patrol, scouring for potential threats. Restless."

He didn't answer, leaning against the door frame as she stepped closer. He understood Noah better than most. And for someone like him, the only thing worse than watching the world burn was feeling helpless to stop it.

Ginger turned away from the shelf and toward him with an arched brow. "Well? You didn't just come here to stare at me, did you?"

He cracked a smile. "I was letting you finish."

This time the smile she gave him actually met her eyes. "I'm finished."

He crossed his arms. "Unfortunately, I have a different problem to bring you this morning. It seems that Alex was eavesdropping yesterday. Heard something about our marriage, then went scouring your files for evidence. He was in my room first thing, looking for answers. Thinks I'm his father."

Ginger's face fell. "Dammit." She rubbed her temple. "I knew he'd heard something. I told Noah last night." She came closer. "What did you tell him?"

"That I'm not his father—Noah is. And that he needed to talk to you."

"Thank you for that," she murmured, looking away. She shook her head. "I always knew we'd have to tell him something … but he's so young still. Waiting felt logical." She met his eyes again. "He must be hurt. It pains me so much to know he's found out this way."

She pressed a hand to her chest as though trying to ease the ache there.

"He is. But I doubt he'll admit it. And since I didn't provide the information he wanted, he's probably angrier now too. If it were me, I'd give him some time to cool down and think a bit. He's a smart kid. He'll come around if you're honest and explain why you didn't say anything sooner."

"I'm not so sure." Ginger frowned. "But thank you for telling me."

Jack turned to go, then paused, an unsettled feeling passing through him. He glanced at Ginger. "Also—does Noah know Alex has been poking through his old trunks? He mentioned something about a spyglass he'd taken from him."

Ginger's lips pursed, irritation flaring in her eyes. "Alex has a penchant for *borrowing* anything he thinks might serve as a good tool for his experiments. That's not surprising, but I'll have Noah go through his trunks and ensure nothing concerning is in there."

Jack grimaced, then added, "You also might want to know that he thought he saw someone watching the estate from the tree line."

A tired expression crossed her face. "You really are the bearer of bad news this morning, aren't you?" She took another step toward him. "Tell me the truth: Is my family in danger now? The men you brought here are dangerous."

Jack held her gaze. He should tell her about Kit—about the truth of her. *The whole truth.*

About Prescott Federline.

But he'd already brought enough turmoil for one day. "You could be," he said instead. It was true. *And far simpler of an answer.* "Just keep your eyes open, and don't trust anyone who comes poking around. You know the drill."

Ginger bit her lip. "I was afraid of that."

"I really am sorry, Red."

And this time he truly meant it.

CHAPTER EIGHT

GINGER

Ginger stood in front of the bed, her heart growing heavier with every pistol and magazine of bullets that Noah slipped into his bags.

Why does it feel as though I've traveled back in time?

She sighed and came up behind him, slipping her arms around his waist as he tied one bag shut. Resting her cheek against his back, she inhaled deeply, relishing the scent of him. "Do you really have to go?" she murmured, closing her eyes.

He chuckled and turned, then slipped his arms around her, pulling her against his chest. She looked up, lifting her mouth to receive his kiss, which lingered as his lips melted against hers, warm and pliant. His tongue dipped against hers, and she gave a throaty moan of pleasure.

I love this man so deeply.

He smiled and pulled back. "You know, we might have time before I leave …"

She grinned and stood on the tips of her toes to kiss him, more gently, but she shook her head. "It's not the best time of the month. If my estimates are right, I'm likely fertile right now.

And you're not leaving me with child before you go on a dangerous mission again, Noah Benson."

He pulled her closer, undeterred, then nipped her earlobe, dragging his lips to her neck. "There are other things we can do," he whispered huskily.

She laughed and wiggled out of his arms. "I'm not giving you a sendoff, you rascal. You didn't even have the decency to ask what I wanted before you agreed to this adventure. Consider this your punishment."

He grimaced apologetically. "If it helps, it's the only way I could think of to help Jack *and* avoid being recruited by Captain Knight. The man is a menace."

"*You're* a menace," she returned with a mock glare. "And now you're leaving me to deal with this whole mess with Alexander all on my own too. I'm worried that he didn't turn up at supper. He's been out at that farmhouse all day—is he intending to sleep there? It's frigid tonight. And he must be starving."

"Take him a blanket and a meal and leave it at his doorstep. Who knows? He may even see it as a peace offering."

"I'm not fine with him sleeping down there by himself, Noah." She set her hands on her hips.

"What harm is it going to do? He's a boy. Those adventures are good for him. By the time I was his age, I'd slept in caves and trees and spent full weeks out in the wilderness with Neal."

She didn't need to point out the fact that he was an orphan by Alex's age. "Yes, but as you said, you weren't alone, you had your brother with you." She sighed. "I regret not having a third child for that reason alone. Who knows. It might have been another son. Someone for him to traipse around with."

Noah tipped a smirk at her. "Or it could have been another daughter, and then he'd be surrounded by *three* females." He stepped closer. "You know, there still is time to remedy the matter—"

She shooed him away with a roll of her eyes. "You're relentless, Noah Benson."

He caught her in his arms regardless and kissed her softly. "I'll miss you," he whispered as he pulled away.

Ginger's throat clenched, and they held each other for another moment. No words came, despite her best effort. She didn't want to cry. Didn't want to guilt him either. Jack's friendship had saved them both in the past, and she didn't have to question why he was going. And it wasn't as though Jack ever asked for much. If he was here, it was because he truly needed Noah's help.

That doesn't mean I have to be happy about it though.

She released him, watching as he left her and lifted his bags. She hadn't asked for details about where he was going or how he'd get there—information was a dangerous commodity, and she'd learned well enough not to ask unnecessary questions.

He started for the door to their bedroom, and she followed. Pausing at the doorway, he glanced back. "I love you, *rohi.*"

"I love you too. Just try to come back in one piece, yes?"

He smiled gently, then was gone.

As the door closed, Ginger stared into the space he'd vacated.

Despite her best efforts, tears stung her eyes and a lump rose in her throat. She sniffled, wiping her wet lashes with the backs of her fingers.

God, please don't let anything happen to him.

This wasn't anything like when they'd been separated at the end of the war. She needed to be logical. And they'd spent time apart when he and the children wintered in Egypt.

But this *felt* different too. More ominous.

She glanced back toward her wardrobe, considering just changing and going to bed, but with Alex still out there, sleep wouldn't be possible.

Maybe she'd take Noah's advice, get Alex some supplies, then drop them off at the farmhouse.

She left the room, then headed toward the kitchen. Just twenty years ago, this had been a fully functioning estate, with maids, a housekeeper, footmen, butlers, and underbutlers. The war had changed all that. When she'd started the hospital and home, she'd been able to hire many of the former staff to work in new jobs, which had helped the villagers as well.

But the one thing that hadn't changed?

The kitchen staff.

Ginger's kitchen skills were pitiful, and with patients and residents to feed, they needed a full kitchen staff still. The cook, Mrs. Grimes, had been working at Penmore since 1906. In some ways Ginger felt a special closeness to her now. She was one of the few threads to her former life. When her mother visited from London, even she seemed to feel that bond and always asked to see her.

But Mrs. Grimes would already have retired for the evening. Noah and Jack had purposely waited until everyone would be in their rooms to leave the house.

Ginger slipped into the darkened kitchen, then startled. Clara was at the main table, holding a bottle of milk.

Her daughter looked up, eyes widening. "I-I … didn't know you were still up."

Ginger smiled. "I might say the same." She crossed the kitchen toward her. "Don't worry, you're not going to be scolded for helping yourself to a glass of milk. Couldn't sleep?"

Clara nodded solemnly. "I'm worried about Papa. I don't understand why he has to leave so suddenly. Where's he going, anyway?"

"I'm not sure. Jack didn't say." Ginger went over to the cupboard and fetched a glass for herself. She sidled up beside

Clara, then poured herself some milk too. "Would you like some sugar toast?"

Clara smiled. "All right."

Ginger went over to the bread box and pulled out a loaf, then hunted around for a knife. At least she knew her way around the kitchen now—before the war, she hadn't even known how to boil a kettle. "When I was a little girl, if I happened to come down to the kitchen before Mrs. Grimes had gone to bed, she'd make me a slice of sugar toast too. Sometimes with cinnamon."

"Alex says you used to make it for him when we lived in the farmhouse." Clara's voice was soft as she settled onto a stool near the counter.

Ginger didn't look back at her and turned the toaster on. But guilt bit like acid at her throat. Their lives at the cottage had been more cohesive as a family, to be sure. No cooks, no staff, no residents. Occasionally one of the nighttime nurses or order-lies would come flying down the path from the house toward the cottage to fetch Ginger for an emergency, but other than that, life had been tranquil.

And Alexander doesn't like change.

"I always thought it helped me sleep better. Or at least Mrs. Grimes convinced me it would." As the warm scent of toasted bread wafted through the air, the coils of the toaster glowing, Ginger turned back to face Clara. She hesitated a beat, then managed, "Speaking of Alex—did he say anything to you today?"

Clara furrowed her brow innocently. "Say anything?"

Some of the tension in her chest uncoiled. If Alex had told Clara, she would be asking questions by now. She wasn't a very gifted liar either. "I-I just haven't seen him all day."

Clara twisted one of the ribbons of her nightgown around her fingertip. "Actually, I haven't seen him either."

"I think he went to the farmhouse. That's where I found him

yesterday, anyway. Maybe I'll ask Ivy in the morning. See if he spoke to her." In some ways, Alex was closer to Ivy than he was to his own sister. They were closer in age, and Noah often gave them lessons together.

Clara frowned. "Come to think of it, I didn't see Ivy today either. And she wasn't in our room."

The weight of her words seemed to thin the air around Ginger. Since they'd moved back to the estate, Clara and Ivy had insisted on sharing a bedroom. They were best friends, and the idea had thrilled them both.

But why wouldn't Ivy be in her room? It was well past bedtime.

Though it might be entirely innocent, if she was with Alex, it wouldn't be appropriate. Both Alex and Ivy were growing up. Their days of shared adventures were coming to an end—especially since Victoria planned to send her to Roedean for the Michaelmas term in autumn—a fact that she'd shared only with Ginger and Noah. As the heiress to the Fisher fortune, Ivy had a more settled path to follow.

And Victoria needed to keep the Fisher family content. Lord and Lady Fisher still kept a close eye on Ivy and Victoria kept them happy with quarterly visits and letters from Ivy. To Victoria's dismay, Ivy adored her aunt, Angelica Fisher, often trying to copy her sense of taste and fashion. But Ginger was certain that also was because Angelica indulged Ivy's every whim, since she had no children of her own to lavish attention on.

Ginger kept a calm demeanor as she turned back toward the toaster.

Maybe I'm worried without reason. Ivy could be with Victoria.

She set the toast on a plate, then buttered it and sprinkled it with sugar before carrying it back to Clara. "Here you go," she said with a smile. Leaning forward, she kissed Clara on the forehead. "Now take your treats and straight to bed."

Clara grinned and slipped off the stool. "Good night, Mama."

Ginger waited until she'd scampered off, then poured her own milk down the drain. Her stomach was already too tight to drink it.

Hurrying out of the kitchen, she followed the hallway that led to the staircase used by the residents to reach a smaller kitchen—once the butler's pantry—that had been set up for their use. She took the stairs two at a time, lifting her skirt as she went.

Calm down. There's no reason for alarm.

She reached Victoria's bedroom within a few minutes. She knocked softly on the door, then hugged her arms to her chest, nervous energy sparking through her.

Footsteps sounded on the other side of the door, then Victoria opened it, dressed in her nightgown. The raven-haired beauty sobered at the sight of her. "Is there an emergency with a patient?"

"No." Ginger forced herself to sound less worried than she felt. "Is Ivy with you, though?"

Victoria's delicate brows furrowed. "No … why?"

"Clara says she's not in their room. That she hasn't seen her all day. And … I haven't seen Alex either. I think he's in the farmhouse."

"I—" Alarm filled Victoria's eyes, her lashes flaring. "I didn't see her either. I assumed she was with you or the other children." Victoria opened her door more widely. She left the doorway, then hurried to her wardrobe and pulled out a coat. She gave Ginger a worried glance. "You don't think there's anything … she follows him around like a puppy."

Ginger bit her lip, understanding her concern. The truth was that while Alex might not currently even be aware of Ivy's crush on him, everyone else could see it. And Ivy had started to develop into a young woman rapidly the last few months. It was part of Victoria's urgency to get her to boarding school.

"I doubt there's anything untoward. But we should probably make a visit to the farmhouse."

Victoria nodded, then donned the coat. She closed the door to her room and locked it, then followed Ginger down the hallway.

Within minutes, they were in the motorcar and had started toward the farmhouse.

Ginger tried to keep her teeth from chattering as they drove in tense silence, the headlamps of the car brightly illuminating the path toward the farmhouse. Somewhere out there, Noah and Jack were already on their way away from here.

She wished she had a means to reach Noah now, ask him to delay his trip and help her handle this whole situation with Alex.

Stop being a ninny.

But as they drew closer to the farmhouse, Ginger felt the cold fingers of fear grip her heart more tightly. The windows were dark. Not a single light inside.

She left the car running as she parked and jumped out, Victoria at her heels.

The door was locked; she knocked on it. "Alex! Ivy!" she called.

Nothing.

Victoria knocked hard on the closest window. "Ivy Leah Fisher. Open this door right now!"

She ground her teeth, then went over to a window box and fished around inside it. After finding a key in the dirt, she wiped it on her skirt, then put the key into the lock, fingers trembling.

She opened it. The silence was worse than Ginger had feared. The air was cold, the stove unlit. "Alex?"

No one answered.

Ginger and Victoria stepped inside regardless, then separated as they searched the house, finding each corner as empty as the last.

They weren't here.

Victoria's voice trembled as they came together in the living room once again. "It's dark, Ginger. Where would they go?"

Ginger's heart clenched tightly. Somewhere out there, their children were missing—and she had no idea where to start looking.

CHAPTER NINE

JACK

"We're being watched," Noah said as he slid closed the door to the sleeping compartment.

A cold ripple shot down Jack's spine. He'd known this run of luck couldn't last. Not with Prescott in the game.

Jack looked up from the newspaper he'd been attempting to read, his eyes locking with Noah's as the soft thumping of the tracks filled the quiet. From the moment they'd boarded the train in Paris, he'd been worried about this.

"Are you sure?"

Noah nodded and sat on the bed on the other side of the compact space. "I only saw one man. But I'm sure."

Damn.

"Terrific. I was just thinking this trip was going too well."

The trip from Penmore had been smooth enough: they'd left the town traveling along the coast via fishing boat until reaching a town where Noah kept a motorcar with a local miller—then driven to Dover and caught the ferry to Calais, where they caught a train to Paris. That Noah had a planned escape route didn't surprise Jack—*old habits*—but maybe Jack had let himself get a little too comfortable with the ease of it all.

Maybe they'd been spotted at the Gare de Lyon.

Jack released a slow breath, his fist flexing and unflexing. "It's got to be Prescott. If he knew I was in England, he probably expected me to turn up at one of the major travel routes."

They should have rested in Paris and taken the day train rather than the night train. There were more people in the station during the day, making it easier to blend in.

"We'll be able to slip away once we get to Egypt. I'm not concerned." Noah removed his jacket and rolled his shoulders back, an old habit that Jack knew he'd acquired after being shot in the shoulder during the war.

"Spoken with every ounce of confidence I don't have," Jack said with a half-smile. He shook his head. "Did I tell you I was robbed in Cairo? Pretty blonde con artist—took me for a chump. Guess I was a chump, though, considering she got me good. Stole every last penny I had on me and my watch. First night back in Cairo, and I'm relieved of my cash by a slip of a girl with better street sense than I had. My life is really on an upswing."

Another woman he hadn't seen coming. His fist curled, thinking of how easily he'd let his guard slip.

Noah raised a brow. "Where did this happen?"

"Mena House Hotel, if you can believe it. Guess they thought I was a rich tourist."

"That's bold. What did the hotel staff say?"

Jack cringed. "I didn't report it. My pride didn't allow it."

Noah chuckled but said nothing further. Loosening the button of his collar, he stifled a yawn. "If you were twenty years younger, your pride would be suggesting we jump from this train in the middle of the night to rid ourselves of any shadow."

"Thank God I'm older and wiser now, right? And have far

less enthusiasm for broken bones." Jack cracked a smile, then ran his fingers through his hair with a heavy sigh. "How did we end up here again, Noah? Midnight trains, spies everywhere. There's not even a war going on right now."

Noah murmured as he nodded and lay back against the pillow of his narrow bed. "Not yet, anyway. The changes in Germany worry me. And the situation in Egypt and Palestine—which is bound to get worse with what I'm hearing from some of my German friends. Fahad wrote to me last month. Said the tension in Jerusalem is palpable. Zionist-Arab relations have only worsened since 1929, and the number of Jews seeking refuge in Palestine is quickly growing."

Jack met his gaze. The new German chancellor had shown he had a taste for violence and a talent for deception. Noah was right to be worried. The noose on peace was coiling tighter.

"Not that I would wish the administration of that area on anyone, but I'm not sure the British have any idea what they're doing there anymore," Jack said wearily.

"Agreed. Though, now more than ever, I'm convinced the people who call that land home and bled for it are the only ones qualified to make decisions for it."

Spoken like the true Irish Egyptian he was. Jack almost smirked. Noah presented to everyone the face of a blue-blooded Englishman—his wealthy English uncle and aunt had raised him when he'd been left an orphan as a boy—but he shared the opinion of most nationalists.

The Levant and Arabia had always been an area of interest to them both, since they'd come out that way before the war as young, eager archeologists, woefully unprepared for the reality of life for the desert peoples who had been bleeding and battling over their lands for centuries.

Jack grimaced. Empires loved making promises they

couldn't keep—and men like him usually ended up cleaning up the mess.

Unfortunately, when the Ottoman Empire had crumbled at the end of the war, the absence of a ruling government had led to the British and French administrating more colonies, areas that the Arabs who'd joined Lawrence in the Arab uprising had been promised the freedom to rule themselves, like Syria, the Transjordan, and Palestine. The Arabs—Muslims, Christians, and Jews alike—were understandably furious, especially as the Zionists advocated for statehood in Jerusalem on the grounds of the conflicting promises made through the Balfour Declaration.

The result: a powder keg that was being roasted like a pig on an open spit.

As the men lapsed into comfortable silence, Jack folded the newspaper and started to put it away, glancing at the name emblazoned on the front—*The Manchester Guardian*, which Noah favored. As he did, a name on the cover caught his eye under a headline: Gretchen Herbert.

He froze.

A memory, long sealed in his brain, floated to the surface.

The last night he'd spent with Kit, they'd been in a quaint hotel room, lying in bed.

"You know, you might have picked an alias I would be able to use to find you a bit easier," Jack had teased, pressing a kiss against the soft curve of her throat.

She smiled and rolled her eyes. "You weren't supposed to find me, Jack. And even if you had, you weren't supposed to come into my life like this again."

"And after this? We both know this won't last forever. America is in the war now—I can't live with myself if I don't join in. Where do you go after here?"

She shrugged, her gaze traveling away from him and focusing on the ceiling overhead. "I could find you a role in the State Department, I'm sure. My contact—"

"I don't want one. I've had enough of rubbing elbows with my enemies while calling them friends. I'd rather just meet them face-to-face."

"I don't know any other way at this point," she murmured, her body tensing in his arms. "Once upon a time, maybe. Before I married. I thought that dream of being a housewife with an armful of children might even appeal. But Paul killed that dream."

Jack's throat clenched at the thought. What she'd gone through with that man—Jack hated him for it. Hated that he hadn't been able to protect her. But she was resilient. Smart. Hadn't really needed his help or protection.

Whatever else Kit was, she was first and foremost a survivor.

"Well, then, promise me this." He rolled onto his side so he could hold her gaze. "No matter what happens, where we go, you'll give me a way to find you in the future." He reached for her hand, interlacing their fingertips. "Maybe starting with an alias I already know."

"Jack—"

"I'm serious. Promise me. I'm yours, Kit. You know that. I don't need rings or vows or anything else. I'm never going to marry anyone else. Wherever I am in the world, I'll be waiting for you."

For a breathless moment, Jack feared she would refuse. That she would vanish again into the shadows he couldn't chase.

She swallowed hard, her blue eyes glistening with tears. At last she nodded, then leaned forward and whispered, "All right. I promise." She kissed his lips gently then sniffled. "Gretchen. Gretchen Herbert. That's the next alias I'll use."

He chuckled. "Already have one lined up?"

She grinned. "My father will keep looking for me—and I can't use the one I had anymore. Gretchen was my grandmother's name. And Herbert was the name of the first horse my father bought me."

Now he arched a brow. "Herbert is an awful name for a horse."

"I was seven," she said, *looping her arms around his neck.*

"Doesn't make it any better," he said, *kissing her as she dissolved into laughter.*

Jack blinked hard, his heart squeezing even tighter as the memory faded and he focused on the name staring back at him from the byline.

Gretchen Herbert.

It *had* to be a coincidence—didn't it?

He peered closer at the headline.

Attacks on Assyrians Continue: Terror Tactics Increase

His throat clenched. Whoever this journalist was, she appeared to be a foreign correspondent. Reporting on *Iraq*, of all places.

He let out a slow breath, loud enough that Noah stirred. He shot him a questioning gaze.

"You ever see this name before?" Jack asked, crossing the space and thrusting the paper in Noah's face.

Noah frowned as he focused on the name in question, then he nodded. "She's the foreign correspondent for that whole region. Probably working out of Baghdad."

If there was one thing he could count on, it was Noah's nearly perfect recall of anything he read. And he noticed things like that—names of journalists in bylines that everyone else seemed to ignore. His obsession for detail had always made it easy for Jack to rely on him, considering he was far less interested in the minute.

Noah gave Jack an alert, penetrating gaze with his dark-blue eyes. "What is it?"

"It's … *her.*" Jack cleared his throat, his brain buzzing. "Kit. S-she told me that was the next alias she'd use."

"Gretchen Herbert?" Noah asked with a skeptical look. "Are you certain?"

"I'm certain that's the alias she said she'd use." Jack pulled the paper back. "What's the date on this paper?" He'd brought it and several others from Noah and Ginger's house to catch up on some of the news he'd missed over the last few months.

"I think that's from a week ago."

A week. Jack stared at the date on the paper. A week would mean the article, if it had been a cable dispatch from Baghdad, might have been sent three days before it was published.

His heart raced. "This …" He tried to formulate the words. "This means—if it is her—that she might have been alive and maybe even in Baghdad ten days ago." *She's probably lived in Baghdad for a while if she's a correspondent there.*

Noah nodded. "It's a good possible starting point. Checking in with my contacts in Baghdad will easily confirm if Gretchen Herbert has been working from there. If you're right about that being her."

Jack's gut burned. He gripped the paper hard enough to crumple it. Was he dredging up ghosts pointlessly—or had Kit just reached out to him across the years, across a continent, in ink and print? This *had* to be more than just a coincidence.

But up until this, a part of Jack had still rejected the idea that she could be alive. If she was, then Noah needed more information—the part of the story he'd never been ready to talk about.

"There's something I need to tell you." Jack stashed the paper away and paced for a moment. He glanced out the darkened window of the train, looking out into the inky blackness of the French countryside at night. "About Kit and who she was. Something I should have told you fifteen years ago."

The tips of Noah's mouth curved into a grim smile. "I think I already know, Jack. I suspected it when I saw you together. I just didn't ask, because I knew if you weren't telling me, it was for her safety—or because of what it could cost you."

Jack paused, his words catching in his throat. *When I saw you together.* Then Noah *did* know. Because, otherwise, he wouldn't be pretending he'd ever met Kit. Of course Noah knew. He was too smart, too perceptive not to figure it out. "Then—"

"Besides the fact that you're my friend and I owe you more than I can say, I'll admit I joined you on this for selfish reasons. If Kit is alive, then the news is bound to have an impact on Ginger. And it raises a lot of questions."

Jack's lips pursed. He should have told both Noah and Ginger more about Kit during those brief days when they'd met her. But Kit had asked him not to reveal her true identity to anyone, and his loyalty to her had stopped him.

The two men stared at each other, the air between them rife with the tension of so much unspoken. Of a time that neither of them wanted to revisit or remember. The most painful years of both their lives.

Their friendship had been formed as innocent youths and had been tested by fire. The end of the war had put them through hell and back and—somehow—they'd survived still seeing each other as brothers.

Jack nodded wordlessly, his attention drawn to something else. The train had slowed, but they weren't expected at the next station for hours.

Noah stood, his gaze darting to the door. He crossed toward it, checked the lock, and Jack groaned.

"You think it's for us?"

Noah turned back toward him. "Could be something innocuous, like cattle wandering over the tracks, but chances are it's not. And if it's not, we don't have a lot of time."

"Prescott has a lot of sway, but I doubt he has the authority to stop a train." Jack went over to the bed and began pulling his bags from the storage rack overhead.

"My thoughts exactly. It's probably Knight. He would be able to manage it with the clearance he has and cooperation from the French." Noah cleared his throat. "Which is why I'm going to stay here. Give you time to get away."

Jack's jaw slackened. "Noah, don't—"

Noah's expression was resolute. "I'll be fine. Knight will be satisfied with bringing me in. I'll join you in Cairo if I can. But if I'm not there in four days, go to Jerusalem and find Fahad. He'll help. And contact Hayyan al-Khaliq Arif in Baghdad about 'Gretchen.'" He went over to the window and pushed it open. "In the meantime, this is your chance to get there without further interference." He held out his hand.

Jack stared at him, dimly aware of the sound of the wheels screeching. "You don't have to offer yourself as bait," Jack rasped.

"I do. Because if he's tracked us this far, he won't quit. And there's far more at stake for you if you continue to be delayed, Jack. If necessary, I'll negotiate for you with Knight. Make sure that the risk you took coming for my help wasn't in vain. But go. Now. Before it's too late."

"I can't let you do this—"

Noah chuckled. "This isn't the end of the line for us—just for you. Good-bye, Jack." Before Jack could protest further, Noah pushed one of Jack's bags out of the window.

"You sunnofa—" Jack shook his head. "You really know how to make a man feel welcome."

"You'd better go get it."

He'd be lucky to find the bag in one piece.

With one final grunt, Jack grabbed his other bag and swung his legs into the window well. He held his breath, taking one last glance back at his friend. So many debts between them—ones that could never be repaid. And now Noah was taking on one more.

Jack's gut twisted with guilt. But there was no time to dwell on it.

He jumped.

CHAPTER TEN

NOAH

Noah rested his head back against the wooden chair where he'd been sitting for hours, barely able to stay awake. The French police who'd taken him to the local gendarmerie and dumped him in a small room hadn't returned —but they hadn't bound him either. His detainment had been rather civil, as Noah had willingly surrendered. Their expressions when he'd explained they must have been mistaken about a traveling companion had been grim, though.

How long had it been? Five hours? Maybe more. The room was windowless, barely large enough to be a closet. Paint peeled from the plaster walls, and only a single bulb provided warm electric light that had been his companion and disturbed his attempts to sleep.

He shifted, his leg starting to ache from an old war wound that had left him with a limp for years.

Maybe he should have jumped with Jack. Of course, he wasn't as young as he'd once been, and the truth was that he'd been anticipating this. Knight was bright. Keen on recruiting Noah. His tactics thus far had been friendly *enough*.

Noah hated to muse about what tactics Knight might turn to if Noah continued to refuse him.

A rustle outside the door drew his attention, and Noah held a breath as the knob turned. Then the door opened and Alain Roche entered, a stranger trailing behind him.

Tall and blond, with an angular jaw and a broad torso made of muscle, the stranger sat in the only other chair in the room, directly across from Noah. In his hands he held a leather folio. The temperature in the room seemed to increase, the air thicker with the heat of three bodies inside such a crowded space.

"So this is the infamous Noah Benson I've heard so much about," the man said, his accent English. He tossed some of the hair back from his wide forehead. A deep scar crisscrossed his left temple—likely a war wound of some type. Many of their generation had that in common.

"And you are?" Noah asked.

The man leaned forward, revealing a mildly crooked smile. "Clive Hower. Knight sent me."

"I thought as much." Noah bored his gaze into Hower's. "As far as I know, it's not a crime to take a holiday, Mr. Hower. We might start with that."

Hower nodded. "That would normally be true, Captain Benson—but, as it turns out, the French have seen fit to revoke your transit visa. You're a known anti-colonial and have ties to both the Arab and Irish nationalists." He crossed one ankle over the opposite knee. "You can see the concern."

Noah ground his teeth. *Of course.* That would be Knight's first tactic. Cut off his feet. His ability to travel. Going through France had been a risk, but Noah's contact at the border had come through with the paperwork. Had that been where they'd taken a misstep?

If so, it gave an alarming insight into just how large a net MI5 had begun to cast through Europe.

"And, yet, I've been traveling through France without issue the last decade."

Roche cleared his throat. "The French government was recently made aware of your political leanings, Captain Benson. Do you deny them?"

Noah flicked his gaze toward Roche. Alastair had sent Jack to the man, which meant on some level—even the most basic—there had to be something about him worthy enough to make it onto a list of people Alastair would see fit to contact. But a vast gulf existed between outright villainy and so-called "goodness" and Roche's background intrigued Noah. Jack had told him he was Levantine, born in Palestine—but a Catholic, not Moslem, with clear ties to the French government. His loyalties would be interesting to test.

"What would you like me to say, Roche?" Noah replied smoothly. "That the empire isn't bleeding at the seams? From India to Ireland, unrest shadows the lands. Six weeks of riots followed the last clashes of the British authorities with the nationalists in Palestine. Hundreds were injured." He locked his eyes on Roche. The man didn't flinch, giving little away. "I merely observe the changes. But you'd be grasping at straws to make the claim that I've done anything to aid a single nationalist movement."

"Regardless, I'm certain you can see why the French would want to be cautious with someone of your level of notoriety, Benson." Hower pulled out a pair of glasses from his breast pocket and set them on his nose, then opened the folio. "You went absent without leave during the war—did you not?"

Noah shifted in his seat. "Everything in my file has been corrected to reflect what actually happened during the war. Yes —I went absent. But my superior officer was a spy working for the Germans who attempted to frame me for his crimes. Nearly succeeded too." His eyes narrowed at Hower. "I had to do what was necessary to survive and was honorably discharged."

Hower held Noah's gaze. After a beat, he glanced back at Roche. "Leave us."

Roche nodded, then exited quickly.

As the door clicked shut, Hower closed the folio, then assessed Noah with a piercing gaze. "Let's start with the basics. Where did Jack Darby run off to?"

"Why are you assuming I know anything of Jack's current whereabouts?"

"He was with you on the train, wasn't he?"

"If he was, I certainly wouldn't know where he is now, would I? I've been here for hours, Mr. Hower. Jack's a resourceful man. And, more importantly, I don't think you or Knight really care *where* he is, do you? That's not the point of this exercise, is it? The French revoking my visa is about as subtle a threat as a blow with a hammer."

Hower ducked his chin, his eyes simmering.

At least Noah had spelled it out clearly enough. He wouldn't play games. He had no time for them. *God help me if I choose wrong—and Ginger never forgives me.*

After he'd returned from the war, they'd made promises to each other—promises he would never break. No more secrets. No more lies. He would never embark again on any mission like he'd been forced to resort to when he'd needed to clear his name after Stephen Fisher had done his best to destroy him during the war—at least, without telling her, anyway. Noah had nearly broken their marriage, lost her and Alexander as a result. He would never risk her and his family. *Ever.*

A few beats sounded before Hower cleared his throat. "Work for us, Benson. We don't want to make life difficult for you." His face softened. "And you'd be doing your country a great service. You may not believe it, but we're all on the same side here."

Noah raised a brow. "And what side would that be?"

"The one opposing tyranny. You're a father, Benson. A husband. You may feel safe and unthreatened in the countryside of England, but I promise you, there are spies everywhere. We must find out what we can about who our enemies are before we find ourselves in the midst of yet another conflict. You were a young man in the last war. Another one might very well threaten your children."

Ice splashed through Noah's chest, his gut coiling with tension. The idea of Alexander facing any of the horrors he himself had faced was enough to make him sick.

But Clara—sweet, innocent Clara, so like her mother with such an enormous heart for every sick and injured creature she came across—she would suffer too.

She'd once cried for days, as a young girl of six, when a lamb she'd been nursing to health had died overnight in the barn. She'd blamed herself. She'd sobbed into Noah's neck, "If you'd only let me stay with him at night, Papa ..."

More worrisome, though, was the fact that Hower had *mentioned* his children—almost in the same breath that he'd made a vague threat. Noah's jaw clenched as he stared into the man's face. "What is it you want?"

The hint of a smile in Hower's eyes told Noah that the man felt his message had been received. "Colonel Vernon Kell has dispatched us to put eyes and ears in necessary groups. Groups that need surveillance. Knight had hoped that with your subversive background you might make a valuable asset for us within the Communist circles in London—but I've since changed his mind."

Noah tilted his head, taking a closer look at him. Just who was Hower? He must be someone of influence if he had access to two men of such rank within MI5. "I'm not a Communist," Noah said in a flat tone.

"No, we know that." He said it with a confidence that nearly made Noah shiver. "But it wouldn't take much for you to convince others that you are, and that's what matters. But—as I said—I have other plans for you, Benson. We need reliable men and women in Arabia, Palestine, and Egypt. If we are to maintain any level of superiority in the air or at sea, that region of the world is vital to us."

Noah held his gaze. Hower wasn't saying anything Noah didn't already know. The Royal Air Force was growing rapidly. The Suez Canal was an indispensable area for British sea vessels. Vessels and aircraft that needed petrol. "Men and women for *what* exactly?"

"To befriend the locals. Procure invitations to meetings and gatherings with groups of interest to us."

But a gap in logic still existed when it came to Hower's plans for Noah. "I live in England."

"But you travel to Egypt for the winter season occasionally. And are still involved with archeological pursuits, yes?"

Noah's lips turned in a sardonic twist. "You apparently know quite a bit about me, Hower—who am I to dispute the facts of my life?"

Hower gave him a patient smile. "We've created the cover of a dig in Khirbet Qeiyafa—just outside of Jerusalem. The sooner, the better. Chancellor Hitler has been sending envoys to the Arabs. We need men there that we can trust. We can, of course, move your family to Egypt if it helps. But as you're already away from home and have no current employment, we'd prefer for you to go immediately."

"I'm employed with educating my children." Noah tried not to allow the comment to bother him. Then, for the sole purpose of seeming less informed than he was, he asked, "Are you suggesting our alliances with the Arabs are failing?"

Hower studied him. "Surely, you know the answer to that,

Benson. The Arabs are difficult to pacify—nothing but a bunch of warring, uncivilized tribesmen as far as I'm concerned. Even Faisal Hussein and his brothers, who made such a big show of supporting us during the Arab Revolt and in posing for pictures with T.E. Lawrence—were already in the process of exploring alliances with the Germans before the war's end. They can barely agree on anything amongst themselves."

Noah didn't answer. Hower wasn't entirely wrong about any of it, though the broad strokes of his prejudice clouded the tone of his answer. The Arab tribes, particularly the Hashemites under the Hussein family and the people united under Ibn Saud in the peninsula, had different visions of a united Arabia— mostly due to differences in their worship.

And at the heart of it all, a swath of *promised land* along the coast of the Levant that no one seemed to be able to agree what to do with—and Jerusalem, a beating heart of three global religions. Add the lure of oil fields, and the entire Middle East was a breeding ground for conflict.

Noah crossed his arms, choosing not to tell Hower any more about what he knew of the region. "I've already told Knight I have no desire to return to the intelligence world. Nothing has changed my mind, Hower."

Hower leaned forward, the tips of his incisors showing under his upper lip, giving him a ruthless, menacing look. "Come now, Benson. You might be able to use that line of reasoning with some, but I know better. Your record during the war speaks of a man who was a finely tuned instrument. Effective. And willing to take risks. That sort of spark doesn't just die because you've settled down. And you have even more you're willing to protect now than you did then."

There was that not-so-subtle threat toward his family again. Noah's breathing grew shallow. "Then I suppose I had better not risk them in the first place."

"Do you think your son would feel the same way? I understand the lad has … quite an aptitude for the clandestine, just like his father. A handful of years from now and I'm certain we could find a place for—"

"Enough." Noah's tone was more of a full-throated growl now. He curled his fingers into his palm. "My family is not to enter this discussion. Otherwise you will not find me receptive to your overtures."

"But that's the problem, isn't it, Benson?" Hower sighed and drummed his thumb against the top of the folio. "You always knew the ghosts of your past would come haunting. They never have stopped, have they? And you knew better than to leave yourself vulnerable to attack by surrounding yourself with so many innocent targets—but you couldn't help yourself. Not when you found such a pretty wife. You wear your weakness clearly enough. You think others—including our enemies—won't exploit it?"

Noah pinched the bridge of his nose. Nothing Hower said was truly surprising, but the bluntness of his delivery was. Knight had been dancing around these ideas for the last couple of years.

So what had changed?

The world. The world has changed. A shadow is growing once again.

The answer hummed in his mind before he could even think about it.

Knight—and even Hower—could bloviate about patriotism and need and national pride, but it all belied a deeper concern that anyone with any sense could see. In one short year, changes had been enacted in Germany with breathtaking speed. Alarming ones.

And his own government wasn't content to let him sit this out. They'd made it clear they wouldn't stop coming for him.

For many months now, Noah had only grown in his belief that he only had two choices—cooperate with them now, while they were still willing to make concessions, or be forced to play their game later, when he had no leverage left.

Ginger hadn't seen it that way, though, clinging to her idealism and belief in some sort of innate human goodness because *she* was good.

"And if I don't agree to help?"

"Others have tried to go around us, Benson. It hasn't gone well for them. And surely you have a vested interest in protecting your own family—don't you?"

The words sent an unnerving chill down Noah's spine, but he gave no physical reaction.

If he didn't have command of an excellent memory, he might not have noticed; the words might have rolled right off him without significance. But they stirred a memory instead. Of Jack, sitting across from him at a chessboard, using that *precise* verbiage to imitate Prescott Federline.

Noah didn't believe in coincidences—not in this world.

And not when people's lives were at risk.

Two unconnected men making similar threats?

Impossible.

His throat went impossibly tight as he stared Hower down. Knight might not be connected to Prescott Federline's Blackwell organization, but Hower could be. And if Blackwell had infiltrated MI5, who knew how deeply that went? Noah didn't have time to question whether his contacts or the people he knew in MI5 were trustworthy. Any one of them might be compromised to Blackwell's probing.

Which meant that any help Noah could hope to offer Jack through official channels was dead. One plant in a world like this marked everyone as potentially suspicious. Jack didn't want

Prescott Federline to be able to track his progress in finding Alice and Kit, but Federline's reach was too deep.

Only one way to be sure—and he'd have to be stealthy about it.

They'd made a mistake in not restraining him.

Noah lunged suddenly, barreling into Hower with such unexpected force that he knocked the man clear off his chair and onto the floor. The man shouted with shock. Grabbing Hower by the right arm, Noah forced him onto his stomach and pushed his knee into the man's back, then shoved his neck down with force.

"Roche!" Hower called, his voice a muffled garble.

Footsteps came running.

Noah pushed Hower's bent arm up behind his back, his grip like iron. The position forced the man's sleeve down, enough to expose his wrist, where a wristwatch peeked out.

But there—just barely visible—was the outer edge of a small triskelion tattoo.

I thought so. The discovery brought no satisfaction, though. Just cold, slick dread.

The door opened and shouts sounded. Not just Roche but two French policemen, guns drawn, shouting at Noah.

Noah leaned down menacingly toward Hower. "Call them off," he gritted into the man's ear. "I have no intention of harming you, Hower, and am open to negotiations. But you will not threaten my family again."

He eased off the pressure on the man's back and neck, standing with his hands raised.

Hower scraped himself from the floor, his face red as a beet. "Stand down!" he spat, wiping his mouth with a handkerchief. He glared at the police, then at Roche. "You're dismissed. I have everything in hand."

Roche raised a brow. "Do you?"

Hower adjusted his sleeves then threw a vicious punch at Noah, his fist connecting with painful force that sent Noah reeling backward. He gritted through his teeth, swallowing the pain, then stumbled back into his seat.

He should have expected that.

Noah rubbed his jaw, only vaguely aware of the police and Roche filing back out once again. His mind whizzed with the potential consequences of the situation before him.

Taking his visa was one thing. A minor inconvenience.

What would be next?

If Hower was Federline's man, then Jack was out of options —nothing could be done to recover Alice through official channels or by using known contacts in the intelligence world. The level of infiltration could go deeper than they realized. But Hower couldn't know that Noah knew he was a Blackwell operative. It would be too dangerous. For now, Noah would have to play along.

There were no good choices left. Only worse ones. And if he didn't take control of the leash they were gripping, someone else might. Someone he trusted even less.

Noah wasn't about to sit around and find out. Ginger would come around, he was certain of that. He just prayed this was the best solution.

As the door closed, Hower turned back toward Noah, his eyes lit with fury. "Was that ugly display really necessary, Benson? I assumed you to be a gentleman."

"You assumed wrong." Noah rubbed his jaw. "If I work for you or for Knight or Kell——you will stay away from my family, do you understand? They will never enter the conversation. You will not contact them, and you will withdraw surveillance from my house. I'll give you three months of my time, and then we'll discuss future arrangements from there. My transit visa will be restored, and I'll have the ability to travel as I see fit. *And* you'll instruct Alain Roche to help Jack Darby—and open any other door Jack needs right now."

"Within reason, of course."

"Of course."

"Three months is hardly enough time to train an asset, let alone embed yourself—"

"Take it or leave it. I'm not the one who's desperate, nor do I need training."

Hower's nostrils flared. "Very well. But Knight won't be happy about it."

"That matters little to me." Noah narrowed his eyes. "And, Hower?"

The man tilted his head. "Yes?"

"You do not want to make an enemy of me. I know better than most the fluidity of a government promise. But if my family is harmed in any way, it won't be the government I come after. It'll be you."

Hower chuckled. "Spoken like the man I need for this job."

The skin on the back of Noah's neck prickled, a feeling roiling his gut as though he'd just made a deal with the devil. He pushed the feeling away, determined not to show any signs of insecurity. "Where am I heading?"

CHAPTER ELEVEN

GINGER

"No, I will not calm myself." Victoria's voice rang out across the vastness of the parlor and Ginger stood, setting a steely-eyed gaze on the police inspector. In the posh London home of her Aunt Madeline, Ginger could almost recall a time when both she and Victoria had belonged to the upper-class world—where police inspectors would expect them to show complete decorum even in the midst of despair.

"Constable Jones, you must understand. Our children have been missing for five days. We're well past the point of false alarm." Ginger crossed the room toward where the man stood by an end table near a sofa. Victoria hadn't invited him to sit when he'd come into the room.

"That may be true, madam, but Lady Fisher does not have to shout, either."

If Gran were still alive, she'd have insisted someone get Victoria a cup of tea by now, to stop her pacing.

Ginger swallowed the wave of emotion that always followed with the thought of Gran's death four years earlier, her sadness particularly strong in light of her fears about Alex and Ivy. For three days, they'd scoured the countryside before coming to London. The only tip they'd received was from a porter who *thought* he'd spotted a boy and girl who looked suspiciously like them on a train bound for the city. If he was right, they'd left Somerset hours before Jack and Noah had gone.

After that, the trail went cold.

"Thank you, Constable, that will be all," Ginger's mother said as she rose from her chair. She held her hand out, indicating the door. "Thank you for coming. We continue to appreciate your help and discretion."

"Of course, my lady." The man frowned under a dark handlebar moustache, then nodded. "Good day."

As he left them, Ginger rolled her shoulders, her eyes burning with lack of sleep. Her mother wore deep wrinkles on her forehead, her face a similar mask of worry. Her once-red hair, now more white than red, even looked messy—which was saying a lot for Mama. But Alex and Clara were the center of Lady Elizabeth Braddock's universe.

"I don't see how he can say nothing more can be done at this point," Victoria said, pausing only long enough to glance out the window. She resumed her pacing. "They've barely searched for them."

"What a terrible time for Noah to have decided to take a trip to Egypt," Mama said unhelpfully from the sofa. She shook her head at Ginger. "Still no word from him, darling?"

Ginger shook her head. Not that it was surprising. Travel to Cairo would take several days—and she had no way to be certain that the frantic message she'd sent to Alastair Taylor had even reached him. If anything, Noah's silence seemed to suggest that Alastair hadn't been in touch with Noah or Jack. Noah would have found a way to contact her by now if he'd heard the news.

"I still can't help but feel Alex and Ivy may have tried to

follow Noah and Jack," Ginger said, sitting on the sofa. A headache pulsed at her temples, and she rubbed them gently.

"But—how? They left by sea, didn't they?" Victoria wore her distress in every feature. "Besides, if they left for London beforehand, that doesn't at all suggest they intended to follow them. And why not contact us in the meantime? Surely they must know we're worried sick. They must have been taken."

Cold and clammy fear clamped down on Ginger's gut despite her best efforts to remain hopeful. "If they'd been taken, they wouldn't have been seen traveling alone on a train for London, though. And they aren't small children. They would have known to alert someone if they were under duress."

"Maybe. Maybe not." Victoria set her hands on her hips. "But if this gets back to the Fishers, they'll be infuriated. Every day that passes without me informing them of the situation is already a risk. I can't afford to give them any more ammunition to declare me an unfit mother."

Ginger gave her a measured look. She understood Victoria's fears. The Fishers had never been happy allowing the heir to their family's fortune—Ivy—go without their influence. And though Ivy wasn't actually Stephen's daughter, Lord and Lady Knotley didn't know that. Couldn't know that. Ivy would lose everything. Ginger and Noah were the only people whom Victoria had confirmed that fact to, though she hadn't told either of them who Ivy's real father was.

However underhanded Victoria's reasons for silence were in theory, Ginger couldn't fault Victoria for them. Stephen Fisher had been a monster, and Victoria's father marrying her off to him had been one last, cruel punishment that had nearly ruined Victoria's life. She'd accepted her fate because she'd been secretly pregnant and had passed Ivy off as Stephen's daughter.

Victoria had dealt with enough—in Ginger's mind, Ivy

inheriting Stephen's fortune was just recompense. But it came with the downside of continued contact with the Fishers.

"Perhaps it's best that you return to the country and wait for news," Ginger's mother said softly. "When they turn up, they're most likely to go back home. And the hospital—"

"No," Victoria said, paling further. "I'm not going home without my daughter." She appealed to Ginger with wide eyes. "I know the needs of the hospital, but Dr. Turner said she could handle things without us. Maybe you can have Beatrice and James come out and help too?"

Ginger hesitated. Dr. Patricia Turner—a friend from medical school who'd come to live and work at the hospital a few years earlier—was experienced and competent, but the workload would be too much for her alone. If they remained away from Penmore for too long—Victoria was right—they'd need to call in more help.

Her old nursing friend, Beatrice Thornton, had ended up unexpectedly marrying Dr. James Clark, Ginger's former fiancé, nearly a decade earlier. They'd come to help with the administration of the hospital during the times Ginger traveled with her family to Egypt—but that was always with extended planning in advance.

"I don't think it would be possible for Beatrice and James to uproot their lives so quickly," Ginger said, sinking back against the sofa. "But I agree with Victoria, Mama. We can't simply go back and wait. If Alex and Ivy left of their own accord, I doubt they could have got too far. They don't have any money or travel papers. Or experience. But, more importantly—we don't know where they were going."

"But we do know what may have triggered this entire disaster—and that's Jack's arrival and Alex's suspicions about his parentage. If he's looking for answers, there are only a handful of people he might go to."

"Which is why I think he may have gone after Jack," Ginger said flatly. She folded her hands on her lap, her heart heavy. How could she have known this would happen? Could she have avoided this by telling Alex about the tumultuous years of her life when he'd been born? She had never intended to keep it a secret, but his hurt was understandable. "If he thinks Jack is his father, he might not have given up trying to find out the 'truth' so easily."

"Has he never looked in the mirror? He's identical to his father," Mama muttered.

Despite the weightiness of the conversation, a smile curled at Ginger's lips. *True enough.* "Despite his intelligence, Alex still uses the logic of a child. If one fact about his past was thrown into question, it may put his certainty about anything into chaos. And you know how Alex is when he fixates on a subject. There's no distracting him from getting the answers he's seeking."

"But why on earth would Ivy have gone with him?" Mama asked helplessly. "And if he has gone after Jack, then we should have an answer from Noah soon enough."

Ginger swallowed a breath, her throat thick. Neither Victoria nor Mama seemed to understand that Noah had warned her he might not be able to contact her for some time—and he had no certainty about where he was going. The Middle East wasn't a small geographical area, and Jack barely knew anything about his sister's disappearance.

"I don't know why Ivy would have gone. Maybe she saw it as a romantic adventure, though I hope not. And I'll have to punish Alex thoroughly if he allowed her to accompany him if it's just a whim of iron. But that's neither here nor there at this point." Ginger pushed a stray strand of hair behind her ear and gave her mother a determined look. "Can Clara stay here in London with you, Mama? I think Victoria and I both might feel better if we travel to Egypt ourselves and see if we can find a trail, wouldn't you agree, Victoria?"

Her friend nodded. "It beats sitting here idly and doing nothing."

Mama's eyes flared with alarm. "Go to Egypt? Ginger, you can't possibly think the children have managed to find their way to Cairo—"

"I think five days of silence is alarming enough that we should explore every possible avenue." Despite the space between them, Ginger felt the warmth of Victoria's relieved gaze. "We'll go to the consulate today—make the travel arrangements. And I'll call Beatrice and James. They may not be able to help immediately, but any assistance they can give Dr. Turner would be helpful, and there's no one I trust more." Clara would be upset by everything, but there wasn't any avoiding that, unfortunately. Ginger wouldn't risk whisking her away to Egypt in the midst of something like this.

If Mama had any inclination to argue further with Ginger, she stifled it and nodded stiffly. "I'll send a message to Lucy. See if she can receive you in Cairo."

"Thank you, Mama." Ginger glanced at Victoria. "Why don't you get ready to go and meet me out on the street in five minutes? We can fetch a cab from there."

Ginger left her mother and Victoria, hurrying out of the parlor. She made a quick trip up to the guest room where she'd spent the night, grabbed her handbag, hat, and gloves, then left the house. Thank goodness Madeline had taken Clara out for the morning to visit an art exhibit. She needed to prepare a bit better before she told her daughter about leaving without her. Clara would want to go and that was impossible.

The streets of London were dense with fog, even in the expensive area of town in which Madeline and her husband lived. Coal fires filled the air with the odor of smoke, and the preponderance of motorcars on the streets now made for a smoggy, unpleasant stench in the air. Ginger cleared her throat and fished a handkerchief out of her handbag, then covered her nose and mouth, looking up. A grey sky, thick with clouds, added to the grim mood of the day.

She had always preferred the country, even as a girl, and had disliked coming to her family's London house for the season. But now that she'd lived away from the city for so long, each time she returned here she liked it a little less. Something about the combination of the dense fog, the crowded streets, and the feeling of grime lent an ominous air to everything here.

The glare of yellow headlamps caught her attention, and she stepped closer to the street, preparing to wave down the car if it was a cab. The long black car slowed, and Ginger got a better look at it—not a cab. A Bugatti, if she wasn't mistaken, and one for only the ultra-wealthy.

Her heart skipped a beat as the car stopped a few feet from her.

The door opened, and a man stepped out. Tall and handsome—but considerably older than she—the man had slicked-back white hair and a piercing blue-eyed gaze. He tilted his head, looking at her with an unnerving intensity that made her skin crawl. "Mrs. Virginia Benson?" he said at last.

Ginger felt the blood draining from her face, a terrible, anxious feeling spiraling through her. "Yes?"

The man smiled, pleasantly enough. "You're even more striking than your photograph, Mrs. Benson."

What?

Her breath caught, pulse pounding in her ears as he continued speaking.

"My name is Prescott Federline. I'm looking for Lady Victoria Fisher. I have news. About her daughter."

CHAPTER TWELVE

JACK

The midday sun blazed down on the terrace of Shepheard's Hotel, bleaching the marble columns and glinting off the crystal stemware and teacups on the tables. Waiters in crisp white jackets moved between the tables with silver trays balanced high, the terrace thick with the crowd here for midafternoon tea.

Jack preferred the American bar inside, but it was a cherished location for military officers and diplomats to convene, and here he was less likely to be interrupted. He sat at a corner table, back to the wall, where he had a good view of the entire vicinity. His sleeves were rolled, collar unbuttoned just enough to thumb his nose at the dress code—nicer dress hat replaced instead by the trusty fedora his grandfather had given him so long ago.

Around him, the clientele was a theater of empire: khaki-uniformed officers, American and English tourists, baronesses and countesses gossiping with their ilk. Cigarette smoke hung like a cloud above the whole affair. Cairo's elite and misfits drifted here for respite—or reconnaissance. For Jack, who'd kept a room at Shepheard's for almost fifteen years now, it was the closest thing he had to a home in Egypt.

He recognized plenty of the people around him: Inspector Fouad el-Serafi with the Cairo police—who he'd helped with a smuggling case a few years earlier. A Russian friend of Alastair's named Vladmir Chertoff, an ex-pat and literature professor who'd come to Egypt after the war. German Baroness Helga Koenig, who seemed to be entertaining some Nazi officers.

And others. All part of a world to which he'd once belonged. A world he'd turned his back on years before.

The tablecloth fluttered gently against Jack's trousers, and he flattened his hand on the edges of the notepaper in front of him. Jack's drink sat untouched, beads of condensation rolling down the sides of the glass and soaking into the unfolded telegram that he'd placed under the edge of the glass. He'd scrawled half a dozen lines of cipher decryption on the notepaper in front of him, pausing every so often to glance across the terrace.

The code had been recognizable—Noah's. With a cipher key only the two of them knew. That he'd taken the trouble to send a message in code meant one thing for certain: he wasn't coming.

His message, once decoded, had been even more concerning:

Going to Jerusalem. Don't trust Roche or MI5. Gopher.

He tapped his pencil against the table.

Dammit, Noah.

Always the cryptic one. God forbid he send a normal message like *help*.

Whatever trouble Noah had run into, Jack shouldn't have left him to fight it alone. Things must be bad. And if he said not to trust Roche, Jack wouldn't waste time second-guessing it.

Alice and Kit were still missing. His allies were dwindling. He was running out of options. He'd considered going to Alastair again—but that was a last resort. Every time he reached out, he risked dragging his friend into Prescott's crosshairs. And Alastair didn't deserve that. He had too many people who depended on him—young orphans who *needed* him. Alastair had saved countless lives.

And, truthfully, Jack shouldn't even be in Cairo. He needed to go to Baghdad and look for Gretchen Herbert.

But the path to Baghdad was made even more difficult by that one little word at the end of Noah's message: *gopher.*

They'd been friends long enough that they had their own code words, and *gopher* was one of the ones they'd come up with during the war. It meant go underground, out of sight, without using official channels or checkpoints.

It meant that if he was going to get to Iraq, he'd need to sneak into the country.

Which meant he needed resources. Unscrupulous contacts—ones willing to break the law.

If that wasn't bad enough, Prescott's silence hung over Jack like a lightning storm ready to strike. He wasn't foolish enough to think Prescott had simply slunk off silently and let Jack go his separate way.

Wherever Prescott was, whatever he was planning, he was smarter than anyone Jack had ever met. He may have reached out to Jack in desperation, but he'd done it knowing he could spur Jack into action. If Jack had any hope of finding Alice and Kit and *not* alerting Prescott to his success, he had to be extremely careful about whom he trusted now.

Sighing, Jack pulled his hat down further onto his forehead, shading his eyes with the brim. Wouldn't surprise him if Prescott was the one snipping the strings behind the curtain. Isolating Jack. Starving him of options and pushing him toward the one thing he swore he'd never do—play by Prescott's rules.

"I've always dreamed of seeing Luxor by riverboat." The

familiar female voice drifted to him from below the terrace, in the garden below. Softly Southern.

And then he saw her.

Ruby Wilkerson—if that was her name—in a sky-blue cloche and matching gloves, all sunshine and misdirection and cozied up beside a sweating businessman as they strolled in the gardens below the terrace, near a palm tree. Either she'd dyed her hair black or wore a wig. *Scammer.* The man—American, by the looks of his god-awful seersucker suit—gave her a lusty smile, not even remotely noticing her hand drifting toward his jacket pocket.

Damn, she's good.

Not just a thief but a pickpocket with quick, skilled hands.

She smiled at the man as if they were old friends.

That sort of talent shouldn't be wasted on crime. At least not petty crime. She had the hands of a concert pianist and the morals of a drunk raccoon.

Jack narrowed his eyes.

Of all the places.

Shepheard's wasn't just a hotel. It was *the* hotel. The place diplomats dined, journalists traded lies, and spies passed coded messages to contacts over gin and lime. Its grand façade was a symbol of everything colonial, with bellboys who carried more secrets than luggage.

Her being here was even more bold than grifting at Mena House Hotel.

And, clearly, Ruby and her ilk were still at their little con games.

Jack would have laughed if it weren't for the memory of that gun at his back and the humiliation that had come with it.

He scanned the immediate area, spotting the man she'd called her brother, Theo, a few moments later. He sat on a bench on the sidewalk, reading a newspaper, face partially obscured. The other man—the one who'd pretended to be Roche—was nowhere in sight.

But that didn't matter.

This could be an opportunity he hadn't expected. He needed someone with talent on his side—someone whose help, if not given by mutual trust, could at least be ensured with good old blackmail.

A half-harebrained idea started to form in Jack's mind as he folded the telegram, then placed it and the notepad in his breast pocket.

Jack flicked his gaze toward Inspector Fouad el-Serafi. Holding back a smile, Jack stood and strolled across the terrace to where he sat at a table alone, keeping company with a book.

"Fouad," Jack said with a charming smile as his shadow crossed the table. "I didn't expect to see you here at Shepheard's."

Fouad stood, his thick black eyebrows drawing together as momentary confusion crossed his face. Then his gaze brightened. "Mr. Darby. How delightful." The man stood, holding out his hands warmly.

They exchanged quick greetings and Jack straightened, not wanting to linger here on the terrace for too long. "I have someone I'd like to introduce you to—would you do me the honor?"

"Of course," Fouad said, lifting a silver-handled cane from its resting place against the table. "Any friend of Jack Darby's is a friend of mine."

Jack nearly chuckled, then led Fouad down the main steps from the terrace onto the sidewalk. They went just beyond the terrace, passing Theo along the way. As he passed, Jack smirked at the man.

Theo paled.

Jack continued, then opened the gate to the garden. Ruby

was still there, arm in arm with the American. *She must not be finished robbing him yet.*

"Ruby, darling," Jack said in a voice loud enough that the pretty thief lifted her chin sharply.

Her eyes went wide as they locked with Jack's.

A mischievous thrill energized him.

He breezed up to her with a smile. "There you are. I was beginning to think you had gotten lost in the city." He strode up to her, then set his arm around her waist. Without an ounce of decorum, he leaned down and dropped a quick kiss to that pretty red mouth, nearly laughing as her body went rigid against him.

The American at her side sputtered. "I-I—I say—"

Jack flicked his gaze at the man, then looked back at Ruby, who was quickly going as red as her name. "Friend of yours?"

Ruby's long lashes fluttered as she tried to recover, the wheels of her mind obviously spinning ferociously. Then anger flashed in her eyes. Her gloved hand whipped against Jack's cheek before he could catch it, and a bright burst of pain flashed through his skin.

"You scoundrel!" she gasped. "You think you can come up to me like this after leaving me stranded for months!" She pulled away from the American, crossing her arms. "I've moved on, Jack."

Jack smiled, then set his arm around her shoulder, shaking his head at Fouad. "Women are so difficult to keep happy, aren't they, Inspector? I leave for three months to toil in the Kharga, and this is what I come back to."

He brushed away Ruby's indifference with a grin, then his gaze sobered. "Anyhow, Ruby, this is Inspector Fouad el-Serafi of Cairo's Criminal Investigation Department. Before I left, Ruby and I were ruthlessly robbed by some thugs—a Theo Wilkerson and a couple of others. Ruby hesitated to make a report—she was too embarrassed. But that's just the sort of criminal investigation you handle, isn't it, Fouad?"

Fouad instantly grew more serious. "Yes, of course, mademoiselle. We handle those sorts of cases with the utmost diligence."

Ruby's mouth opened and closed like a fish.

The American businessman shifted, his face written with confusion. "Theo Wilkerson? Didn't you say—"

"Jack Darby, by the way," Jack said, reaching a hand out toward him. "You staying in Shepheard's, Mr.—?"

"Dillard," the man supplied with a deep frown. "Thomas Dillard. Yes, but—"

"I'm sure Ruby and I would love to meet with you later for dinner. I'll have my man send your man a note, yes? Good. Nice to meet you." Jack gave him a curt nod.

The businessman stared at him, dumbfounded. Blinking rapidly, he turned away, muttering to himself as he left the garden.

Ruby shifted under his arm. "Jack—"

"So, what'll it be, Ruby? Do you want to give Inspector El-Serafi your report now? I'm sure he's eager to catch the criminals plaguing the streets of Cairo."

She swallowed hard enough that her throat bobbed. "Actually, Inspector, there's no need. The man who robbed us was caught—I read all about it in the newspaper. Jack must have missed the news, since he was at the Kharga."

"Ah, well, all's well that ends well." Jack's hand squeezed her shoulder. He gave Fouad an apologetic look. "Sorry to drag you away for nothing, Inspector. I just couldn't pass up the opportunity when I saw you both here. But I suppose it's always good to have contacts within the CID."

"It's not a bother." Fouad smiled warmly, then tipped his hat at them. "Always good to see you, Jack. Please—do come find me while you're here in Cairo. It's been too long."

As the inspector left the garden, Ruby yanked herself away from Jack. "Are you crazy?" she hissed through her teeth.

"Maybe," Jack said, snatching her wrist with a firm hand. "But maybe you should have thought about that before you decided to rob me blind. I'm not entirely without connections— and the way I see it, you owe me. Big." He leaned closer to her, eyes narrowing. "Unless you'd like to see what you look like in prison stripes. I hear jail in Egypt isn't the nicest place for women, especially pretty little things like you."

Ruby gulped a breath, paling further. She blinked back tears suddenly, her blue eyes wide. "He made me do it," she stammered, looking in the direction Theo had been. Theo had vanished by now, but Jack didn't doubt he was probably still lurking nearby. "And we've barely enough to eat."

Jack arched a brow. *Impressive.* The waterworks routine, right on cue. If she could bottle that talent, Hollywood would weep at her feet.

"Save it for someone who'll believe your crocodile tears, sweetheart." Jack winked. "Fool me once, you know?" He released her wrist. "I wasn't trying to compliment you anyway. I like redheads. Ones that walk the straight and narrow." He gave her a dismissive look. "And who don't point a gun at me when I'm not looking."

She scowled, the tears disappearing instantly as she set her hands on her hips. "What do you want? I don't have your money. It's long gone."

"Fortunately for you, I have bigger plans for you." Jack nodded toward the hotel. "Care to take a walk, Miss ..."

She stared at him, then crossed her arms. "Wilson. Ruby Wilson."

He chuckled. "Sure."

"And, no. I'm not going anywhere with you."

"Guess maybe I should call the inspector back here, then. Or, better yet, Mr. Thomas Dillard. He'd probably be interested to learn his missing wallet is in your handbag." He counted a few beats, then decided to take a gamble. "Along with the possessions of the other poor suckers you've fleeced today. I've been tracking you, Ruby."

Her gaze grew frosty. "Lead the way."

If nothing else, maybe I can help a man get his stolen wallet back.

Jack smiled, a satisfied feeling settling in his chest. "We're going to be good friends, Ruby. Just wait and see."

She snorted. "You've got a funny way of making friends, Jack Darby. Ever try not being an ass?"

He gave her a chagrinned look. "Once. Didn't take. And I doubt it's going to start with you."

He led her out of the garden toward the entrance to the hotel. "Bit bold of you and your friends—working the nicest establishments in Cairo. Pickpocketing, I can see how maybe you wouldn't get caught. But what you did to me in Mena House? That's a surefire way to end up on a wanted poster."

Ruby's eyes darted around them. "Yeah, well, I'm not in Cairo for long. And you'd be amazed what a change in hair color can do. Keep your voice down, will you?"

"How's your friend's throat?"

"Still recovering from your brutality." She shot him a glare. "Which is a shame—he's a classically trained tenor. Where are you taking me?" A look of hesitation crossed her face as they ventured further into the hotel lobby, passing the massive granite columns.

"To my room." He didn't falter in his step as he led her toward the elevator.

"I'm not that kind of girl." A muscle in her jaw worked. "If you try anything, I have a gun in my bag—"

"Thanks for letting me know. Does it have bullets this time?" He smirked at her. "But you don't have to worry, I'm not going to hurt you. As it turns out, I'm in the market for a thief."

She cringed visibly, glancing at the awaiting elevator operator as they stepped inside it.

He was enjoying this a little too much. Truthfully, he wasn't worried about anything the elevator operator saw or heard—they turned a blind eye to plenty around here, and Jack had paid more than one of them for secrets and silence before. They knew him here well enough.

Anyway, right now he wasn't exactly acting according to any sort of plan.

Involving Ruby might be a massive mistake—he couldn't trust her as far as he could spit. But she did seem scared to get caught. He could use that.

Chances were, if Ruby and her friends had managed to survive in Cairo without winding up in jail, they had connections to the seedy underbelly of the city. And that's exactly who —and what—Jack needed right now.

CHAPTER THIRTEEN

JACK

Jack dumped the contents of Ruby's handbag onto the bed and grimaced. She hadn't been lying about having a gun. But he'd also been right: she had more than one wallet in her purse—along with two pocket watches and a bracelet.

"You've been busy this morning, haven't you?" he asked with raised brows.

Ruby hugged her arms to her chest, leaning back against a wall, her foot tapping. "A girl could do a lot worse than take some cash off men who will never miss it in the first place."

"*Girl* is a generous word." Jack scowled. "You've got to be—what?—at least thirty? A little old for wasting your life on crime."

Sunlight filtered in through the gauzy curtains, throwing warm light into the room, but Ruby hung back in the shadows, her expression unreadable. "Watch it, Darby. I'll only accept so many insults before I bite back."

"You already bit, remember? And not in the buttering up sort of way you were doing with Mr. Dillard. I didn't even get a single fluttering lash." Jack collected the wallets and jewelry, then fished a key out of his pocket and walked to the wardrobe. Upon opening it, he deposited the items in a safe, pulled out a locked ammunition case, then turned back to her. "So let's talk business."

"What sort of business?" Ruby didn't leave her spot by the wall.

Jack slipped out of his jacket and sat in an armchair, facing her. "How long have you been in Cairo, Ruby?"

Her lips twisted, and she looked away from his, staring toward the window sullenly.

He wanted to feel sorry for her. But he also needed to keep in mind whom he was dealing with. This woman had robbed him without a hint of remorse. And she'd been at it ever since. She was a criminal without a conscience, nothing more.

"Ruby?"

Her mouth pressed to a tighter line, then after a moment, she said, "Eight months."

"And before that?"

"What's it to you?" She glared at him. "What are you, a detective?"

"No." He examined her more closely. "I'm not interested in turning you in to them either. That's just a last resort. I'm … a businessman. And considering that you took a sizable amount of my money, we're going to call that my first payment to you for your services—if you can deliver what I need."

Her eyes widened. "I told you, I'm not that kind of—"

"And I'm not that kind of man." Jack rolled his eyes. "You have my word. This is about business, not that. And you have no reason not to trust me."

She shifted with discomfort. "I have every reason to not trust *any* man I meet." But his words hadn't been lost on her either, apparently. "What do you mean *first* payment?"

"I mean if you help me, I'll pay you. Good money too. More than you could get in a week of working your little con. But first I need to know if you have the right contacts for the business proposition I'm making."

That garnered her interest. Some of the tension in her posture dissolved. "How much money?" Then she seemed to catch herself. "But, more importantly, for doing what?"

"Well, it depends on how useful you can be. Let's talk about you, first. I'm sure you've got someone you're selling all the stolen jewelry and travel documents to."

She blanched. "I don't handle that—Theo does."

"Is he actually your brother?"

She didn't answer.

Time to change tactics. She clearly responded to money. Might even be desperate for it.

Jack unlocked the case of ammunition. From inside, he withdrew a tidy stack of cream-colored certificates, each bearing the insignia of the British government. He held them up. "You know what these are?"

She looked from the certificates to his face, her breath catching audibly. "Bearer bonds."

He slipped them back into the case. "Good. Yes. Each of them are worth more money than you've probably ever lifted off anyone. One thousand pounds sterling each. Don't get any ideas. They're not staying here after our little meeting—I don't show thieves my secrets that naïvely. But if you help me, there will be two of these earmarked for you." He gestured toward the other armchair in the room. "Sit."

Ruby stared at him for another minute before she peeled her hat off, then removed a wig from over her hair, returning to the blonde he'd met at Mena House. For whatever reason, that made him smile.

Don't let her hoodwink you, though. He well knew he often let women get the best of him.

"You know, I wasn't always a thief. I have my reasons for what I'm doing." She sank into the chair with a sigh, smoothing the wig with her fingertips.

"I'm sure you do. So tell me—how well connected are you?"

She glanced back toward the case where he'd slipped the bonds. "I've been working here for long enough that I know people. We switch towns every week or so. Usually come back to Cairo once a month, catch some of the new tourists."

"That's not surprising. Smart, even. In fact, I expect you know a lot of people here in Egypt. So you travel often. Maybe even in the Middle East? Do you know people there?"

She shrugged coolly. "I know enough."

"What about Palestine ... or Iraq? Have any contacts there?"

A moment of tense, suspicious silence followed. "Why do you want to know?"

"Just answer the damned question. I'm interested in knowing how wide you've cast your little criminal net. *If* you can be useful to me, then we can move forward with this business arrangement. I need someone who knows fixers and where to get paperwork. Who has contacts in Egypt, sure, but also up through Palestine, Transjordan, Syria, and Iraq. Can you offer me that, Ruby? You have experience with that?"

Her voice was small as she answered. "Yes."

His eyes narrowed at her. "You're not lying, are you? You take on this job for the money but don't know what you're doing and we'll—"

She glared, her tone instantly harder. Flatter. "I'm not lying. I can do all that. I'm good at getting people to help me—for a price." She gave him a sharp look. "Don't judge me. You have no idea what I come from and what I'll do to meet my goals."

The change in her demeanor almost gave him goose bumps.

"I'm not judging you. Just the methods you use to help your-self." He cleared his throat. "Listen. We're not getting anywhere bickering like this. Here's the deal. I need someone who can help me disappear from Egypt for a while. Someone who can get me across the border with Iraq and without alerting anyone. And I'm willing to pay good money for whoever provides and facilitates that service."

Her eyes narrowed. "You mean *smuggling.* You need someone to smuggle you into Iraq."

"Technically I need a guide. But if you want to add *accessory to espionage* to your resume, I won't stop you."

She blinked slowly, as though processing the information. "You mean to tell me that a man with your wealth doesn't have connections?"

"I didn't say I don't. But mine tend to be more savory than yours, I'll bet. And the unsavory ones … I can't trust right now. I need new ones. Ones who don't know who I am and won't recognize me."

"And if I help you, you'll pay me two thousand pounds ster-ling in bearer bonds?" She arched a brow. "How do I know those are real?"

He leaned forward. "We could go to the bank. Find out together when I deposit them. But you're also welcome to examine them."

She raised her chin. "Both."

"I'd expect nothing less."

Ruby twisted in her seat, holding his gaze as she considered his offer. "And I just have to get you through to Iraq?"

"You'd have to come with me."

"Just how long do you plan on staying there? And where in Iraq?" She huffed. "I don't see why I would need to stay with you."

"Baghdad. As long as necessary—but I'll pay you accordingly.

And why you'd have to stay with me?" He leaned toward her and winked. "I need some insurance to make sure I make it back safely. And that you have all the contacts you claim to have in the first place. It's a lot harder to make that promise when your neck is on the line, too, if we get caught."

"You don't trust me?" She crossed her arms.

Jack chuckled. "Would you?"

She looked away, but her lack of protest made it clear she'd conceded the point. "Why do you need to get to Iraq anyway? You running from the law?"

He shook his head. Telling her too much was a risk, but he'd already risked a lot by involving her. "I'm looking for someone in Baghdad."

"Who?"

Jack's breath grew shallower as he stared at her, his palms suddenly clammy. "A woman. One who may know where my sister is."

The air between them crackled, the room feeling warm and stale despite the humming of the ceiling fan above the bed. Jack watched the fan blades spin, feeling the urge to throw up a silent prayer to the heavens. Several weeks had passed at this point since Prescott had found him and told him Alice and Kit were missing.

Every day wasted was a step closer to a grave instead of a sister. To more questions and even more regrets.

The thought was like ice water to his veins, and he stood suddenly, then crossed to the window and opened it. As warm fresh air filtered inside, he turned his gaze back to Ruby, hoping he wouldn't look as desperate as he felt.

If he was right about her, she actually did know people who could help.

Or she was desperate enough for the money that she'd find the right people to help.

Outside, the call to prayer drifted through the window, carried on the dry breeze that smelled faintly of dust and citrus. God help him if this woman couldn't.

She finally frowned and gave him a cold, calculating look. "Half now, half when we return from Baghdad. In sterling, not bonds."

"Half is too much. Besides, like I said, I already made a first payment."

"It's not enough. And you just took everything I earned today."

"Earned is one way to put it." He turned and perched back against the windowsill, then stretched his legs out in front of him. "If I give you half, I have no guarantee you won't disappear before we leave Cairo. I'm not that stupid. And the wallets and jewelry from today are evidence. If you cheat me … let's just say a certain inspector friend might just find himself on the receiving end of a very good tip about a trio of thieves plaguing the wealthy tourists of Cairo. I may not have reported the theft, but others will."

She clasped her hands in her lap. "I can't return today empty-handed."

"Why? Is Theo holding something over your head?"

Ruby flinched, then shook her head slowly. "He's my brother. I wasn't lying about that."

He'd clearly landed a little too close to the truth for her comfort.

"Okay, maybe not Theo. But someone else, right?"

She nodded. "And if we don't pay him what we owe him by the end of the week, he won't be merciful."

Jack caught the flicker of her hand toward her wrist—reflexive, unthinking. He'd seen that kind of fear before.

He was tempted to ask who. *No. I don't want to know. The less I know about her or her business dealings, the better.*

"All right. Then I'll make you a deal. I'll give you enough to make sure you can make your payment this week. Then the rest you'll get when we return."

"It's not just this week, though." The tough veneer faded. "Every Friday we have to make a payment. If I leave for Iraq with you, I'll leave Theo and Felix vulnerable. And Felix is still recovering from your vicious throat punch. I'm the one who's pulling in the most money right now."

Her plight intrigued him, his curiosity burning. Just who in the hell was coercing her and what did they have on her?

But that wasn't as important as solving her problem was.

"How much?"

She frowned. "How much what?"

"How much do you need in order to make the payment to your debtor?"

Ruby twisted a strand of hair on the wig around her fingertip. "A hundred pounds a week."

Jack let out a low whistle. "You must have really racked up the debts. What'd you do, blondie?" Her cheeks went pink and he pressed on. "I have a friend that can disburse the weekly amount you need—directly to Theo—while you're gone."

She looked doubtful. "You can do that?"

"Like I said, I have connections. Just not the ones I need to get into Iraq right now."

A few more beats of silence passed before she nodded. "I need your word that you'll keep me out of prison. You or your inspector friend. And no lies. You lie to me, I walk. I've had enough of men with secrets."

He almost smiled at her negotiations. He liked that about her. She was sharp. Smart.

She'd be useful.

Jack opened his mouth, then shut it. For a second, the fire in her eyes made him forget why he ever preferred quiet women. He nodded gruffly. "Sounds like a deal. Shall we go to the bank?"

Ruby took a deep breath, then pulled out a slip of paper from a hidden pocket in her dress. "Here. As a show of trust."

Jack took the folded paper, brow raising. As he unfolded it, he saw it was the telegram he'd decoded from Noah earlier.

Holy mackerel. When had she swiped it from him?

He pulled a lighter from his pocket, then lit the corner of the paper before returning his gaze to her. "Remind me to never turn my back on you."

"You already did once."

True enough. He'd have to watch himself with this one.

CHAPTER FOURTEEN

ALEX

Alex's stomach rumbled with hunger, and he scratched a rising welt on his temple. Even aboard a cargo ship in the middle of the Mediterranean, mosquitos seemed to find a way to get to their prey. Maybe he should learn a thing or two from them.

The corridor reeked of coal tar, stale seawater, and the metallic, sour tang of condensation leaking from the overhead pipes. Alex crouched low behind a bulkhead where a brass rail ended, pressed flat against the cold steel wall, and listened.

Above him, the deck groaned beneath booted feet. The upper grating flexed as a man passed with slow, heavy strides. Not a sailor—one of the men whom he'd been following since home. Alex knew their rhythm by now. The guards walked like they owned every board in this rust bucket. The real crew moved faster, heads down, and spoke exclusively in Arabic.

Fortunately for him, he'd been speaking the language for years.

That had helped more than he'd realized. Angry as he was with his father for—well, whatever it was they were keeping secret from him—Papa had spent years giving him instruction and knowledge that had served Alex well during this unexpected and sometimes terrifying adventure.

If I ever make it back home again, I might not be so eager to roam.

Fending for himself had meant days of thirst and hunger, brutal elements, and fear.

He counted as the guards passed, holding his breath. *One, two, three ... four.*

The footfalls faded. Silence again.

He moved, fast, taking almost noiseless steps, toe to heel, down the corridor. The overhead light was a weak yellow filament caged in wire and swinging with the ship's motion that highlighted the glistening condensation on the pipes. A loud hiss of steam burst from a junction ahead, and he slammed to a stop, heart hammering.

A steadier breath left him, and he waited for his heart to slow.

He was two decks below the galley, one aft of the engine. This corridor was for storage and cold rooms.

Ivy was in one of them.

There hadn't been time to go for help when he'd seen her get shoved into a motorcar near Penmore. He'd been at the farmhouse, spying on the men who'd been watching the hospital all morning, when he'd seen her walking the familiar path toward him, dinner basket nestled in the crook of her arm.

They'd grabbed her. And he'd taken off running.

He'd barely had time to grab onto the car and hitch a ride on the sideboard as they rode into town and toward the train. They must have threatened her, because she'd walked with them onto the train, and then later boarded her onto this ship, without her saying a word. He'd managed to sneak on after her each time, but it hadn't been easy.

And now they were here, ten days later and in sight of an

Egyptian port. Not Alexandria—he'd docked there enough that he'd recognize it. Most likely Port Said.

Since stowing away on the ship, he'd mapped it one sliver at a time: memorized crew shifts, found crawlspaces, timed patrols to the minute. He'd jimmied open a fuse panel for a tool. Lifted wire scraps from a crate. Borrowed a hinge pin from a lifeboat crank. No one noticed.

Alex reached the service corridor—unlit, narrower, the walls hemmed in by mesh cargo cages and rope coils slung on hooks. He ducked beneath one, careful not to snag his filthy shirt. Then he knelt beside a maintenance hatch half hidden behind a rotting sack of potatoes.

He scraped his fingernail along the top bolt to loosen it. The hatch eased open, and he slipped inside, gulping a breath. He didn't like tight spaces, and the duct was barely eighteen inches wide—just enough for his shoulders. The space inside was freezing, and his breath fogged the space in front of him as he inched forward, ribs brushing the walls as he crawled.

This was not the time to think about getting wedged so tight that he'd starve here slowly, his body recovered only when the stench of his decay got bad enough to attract someone's attention.

He drew a slow breath and counted every bolt. Every rivet. Ten feet.

Twenty.

The smell changed—less grease, more brine—and the temperature dropped too.

He'd reached her compartment.

Alex shifted forward, bent his head, and pressed his face to the slatted grate at the junction.

Ivy sat slumped against the wall of the cold room. The room was lit by a single hanging bulb with a chain switch. A metal bucket sat in one corner, a tin cup beside her. A blanket on the floor served as her bedding. He knew they'd been feeding her, at least. That was something.

He tapped the vent twice with a knuckle, trying to restrain his anger.

She jumped. Then she turned, eyes sharp, scanning until she found the vent.

"Ivy," he whispered.

Her eyes darted nervously toward the door. "Alex?"

"I've got it ready. You need to listen to me carefully. We're almost at the dock and we don't have a lot of time."

Ivy pushed upright and winced. "Are you inside the wall?" The other times they'd spoken, he'd managed to whisper through the door, but he couldn't take that risk now.

He rolled his eyes. *As though it's that hard.*

"Yes. The lock's set. I disabled the tension spring last night and jammed the catch. When you turn the handle, it'll stop at the midpoint. Then push hard—it'll give."

"You rigged the lock?"

"And the whistle," he said. "I'm going to spark the relay and make it look like a pressure blowout. When it sounds twice, you count to six, give the guards time to clear, then open the door. Then we'll find an exit, and either jump into the water or climb onto the dock."

Or so he hoped.

Ivy didn't respond right away. "They said if I try to escape, they'll kill Mama," she whispered, a tremor to her voice. "That they have a man waiting at Penmore to make sure I cooperate."

He couldn't believe that was true. Kill Aunt Victoria? What purpose would it serve?

More than likely, Aunt Victoria was driving herself mad with worry over Ivy, the way she always fussed over everything where Ivy was involved. Somehow the thought of Aunt Victoria's being anxious bothered him more than the thought of what his own family might be thinking and feeling. Mama had a stoicism to her personality that gave Alex every assurance she'd survive his absence with more calm.

"Your mom can take care of herself, Ivy. And as soon as we're free, we can find a way to send her a telegram and warn her," he said. They'd been friends for long enough that she knew his schemes didn't always turn out as planned. And even though he tried to sound confident, he knew she must be terrified. "Besides, I doubt they're serious. What would be the point of killing your mother? They're just trying to scare you."

"Are you sure this will work?"

He couldn't lie. Not to her. She probably was the only person he'd never fibbed to.

"No," he said, setting his forehead down against the cold wall. "But it's the best shot we've got."

Please, Ivy. You've got to try.

She *could* be brave, if she wanted to be. It didn't just come as naturally to her as it did to Clara. Ivy always hesitated a bit more, worried more about getting injured. Sometimes he wondered if it was her mother's influence—his own mother seemed unfazed by their scrapes and bruises, while Lady Victoria frowned at him whenever Ivy showed up with an injury.

But in the last year or two, he'd sensed Ivy was changing too. In ways he couldn't quite understand.

Come on, Ivy. Do be brave.

A faint creak—her weight shifting. "Where do I go once I'm out?"

Relief filled him. *Thank goodness.* "I'll be waiting two doors down, behind the coil racks. Soon as you're out, turn right. Hug the wall. We'll move together from there. Don't stop."

She sighed, a tremble to her breath. "I'm scared, Alex."

"I know." His voice dropped, and a sudden, unexpected

urge to hug her filled his tense muscles. "But you'll be all right. I'm right here. They lose any sort of leverage they think they have by killing you. It's in their best interest to keep you alive."

A few more beats of silence followed before her voice came again, smaller somehow. "Okay."

"I'll be no more ten minutes," he said in a low voice. "I'm going now to do it." Alex backed out of the duct slowly, his elbows scraping against the tight curve of the metal. The walls scraped his chest with every inch he crawled, the cold biting through his shirt like a layer of frost. His shoulder snagged on a bent bolt, and his teeth clenched as he hissed with pain.

Damn. He tested the word on the tip of his tongue, remembering the scolding he'd received from Mama for using a foul word just a few weeks earlier. God, she must be so worried about him. *Furious, too.* That was one of the nicer things about this sudden bout of independence. He doubted he could make her more disappointed now—and that was oddly freeing.

With a sharp exhale, he forced himself forward until his feet hit the rim of the hatch.

One arm, then the other, braced against the sides as he slid down and landed in a crouch beside the sagging sack of potatoes. The stench made him want to vomit and, for the first time in a few days, he was grateful he had little in his stomach to get rid of.

The air outside the shaft was warmer, but not by much. The sourness of the rotten food mixed with rust and the faint acrid scent of fuel oil drifting up from the bilge. He reset the area in front of the hatch quickly. This would be a poor moment to leave behind clues of his presence here.

He needed to move.

Alex straightened and slipped out of the alcove, into the deeper corridor. Here, the lights were further apart, casting long shadows in irregular patches on the floor. Every step he took echoed faintly, a soft padding of worn soles against iron.

He crept past a crate and sidestepped a drip from a pipe overhead, its leak forming a slow steady puddle. A rat bolted across the floor just ahead of him, vanishing under the rim of an open hatch.

He didn't flinch. Rats had been his companions this whole trip.

He reached the panel and studied it.

A rust-flecked rectangle of steel, bolted in with flatheads no longer sat flush. He crouched, wiped the sweat and grease from his fingers, and eased his makeshift screwdriver—a butter knife —into the groove. Each twist made his wrist ache. The third screw stuck. He worked it loose, breathing shallowly through his mouth.

This has to work.

He didn't have a backup plan.

At last, the panel dropped open with a soft *clink*, revealing a nest of tangled wires and oxidized terminals.

He took out the scrap of wire he'd pre-stripped—tucked into his boot, already coiled with a loop on one end. His hands shook as he worked, fingernails blackened from days without washing. He slipped the loop over the main contact stud and braced the copper lead against the outer casing.

The whistle relay sparked once.

Then the ship let out a raw, teeth-rattling scream—a blast that vibrated the air around him, loud enough to make the ceiling rivets shake. It echoed up through the ducts, across the deck, and down again like thunder trapped in a steel drum.

He counted the beats of his pulse.

One. Two. Three.

Then he bridged the terminals again.

Second blast.

This time, the whistle almost howled—a higher-pitched, unsteady screech that frayed at the edges. Alex yanked the wire away, shoved it into his pocket, and slapped the panel back into place. It wouldn't hold, but it didn't matter.

He tore into a sprint as the deck above exploded into noise—clanging boots, shouted orders, the unmistakable panic of men thinking something was about to blow. Thudding steps moved toward the aft ladder well, just as he'd predicted.

He didn't slow. Didn't stop.

Down the corridor, left at the junction. His shirt clung to his back, slick with sweat.

Skidding around a corner, he dropped into a crouch behind coiled ropes just in time to see the door to Ivy's compartment open.

The light behind her cut a wedge into the corridor, spilling yellow across the floor. Her silhouette stood motionless, one hand still gripping the latch. Then she stepped into the dim corridor of the ship.

Alex rose silently and reached for her.

She gasped as he touched her, whirling toward him, her face written with fear. Then she relaxed as her grey eyes met his. A moment later, her arms were tight around his neck, and his heart squeezed so hard he felt it might burst.

Still, he peeled away from her. "We have to go."

A deep echoing clang came from the engine room. A new flurry of boots pounded on metal. No time to waste.

He took her hand and pulled her gently but firmly down the corridor, toward the last turn that would take them to the open hatch at the galley chute.

"Stay low," he murmured. "Keep left and watch for oil slicks."

They moved quickly. Quietly. Just two shadows darting through the underbelly of a groaning steel beast.

He had to hope they'd be close to fully docked by now, otherwise they'd need to swim to shore.

The passage narrowed the closer they got to the aft galley. Here, the floor pitched more steeply with the curve of the hull. Alex guided Ivy with a hand to her back, careful not to rush. Her steps were unsteady. She wasn't limping, but she seemed weak.

The whistle had gone silent now, but the aftermath echoed. Shouts rang out, unintelligible but urgent. They had to move faster—the sabotage might be discovered sooner rather than later.

Alex paused at the final turn, ducking behind a vertical steam pipe, and peeked down the next corridor. The galley refuse hatch, just outside the scullery, taunted them. Only steps away. Alex had spent the last two nights oiling it so it wouldn't groan when opened. There might be someone still in the scullery. Just beside it, a battered canvas sack and a length of mooring rope coiled like a sleeping snake.

No one in sight, thankfully.

He turned toward Ivy. "You'll have to climb through the chute to the outside. It's tight. Hold onto the rope and climb down—if we're lucky, we'll be close to the dock. Otherwise, climb to the end of the rope and jump into the water."

She nodded, her face anxious. Thank goodness she knew how to swim. His father had taught all three of them.

"Try not to fall. It'll be about fifteen to twenty feet to the water."

Her eyes widened with fear. "Fifteen …"

His palms grew clammy with the thought of that sort of fall, but he just nodded grimly instead.

"Will you be right behind me?" she asked.

"Of course."

He crouched, pulled the refuse hatch open in two swift tugs, and warm midday air rushed in. It hit him like a slap, damp with salt, thick with diesel and port grime, but fresh in a way that nothing inside the ship had been—despite the smell of rotten food that clung to the rim of the hatch.

He peered through the hatch, stomach churning.

The ship had docked fully. Aft-facing port. Just above the dock.

Thank goodness.

The timing was better than he could have hoped.

He tossed the mooring rope through the chute and over the side, testing the anchor knot one last time where he'd looped it to a drainage pipe the night before.

It held.

"Go," he said.

Ivy hesitated for a half-second—then dropped to her knees, swung her legs out, and started down the rope. Her knuckles were white as she gripped, clenching with her knees and feet, inching downward. Alex leaned in just enough to track her descent.

Just a few more feet.

Then she slipped out of his view.

He let out a held breath, grabbed the rope, and followed. *If we make it out of this ship, I'm never sailing again.*

Then he was out of the ship, the warm, salty air damp with humidity. Ivy dangled below him. She'd reached the end of the rope and clung to it as though unsure of what to do—it was still several more feet to the dock, and if she misjudged her jump, she'd land in the water.

"Push off the hull and jump onto the pier," he hissed, looking down at her.

Her face was white. "I can't!"

"Dammit, Ivy, this isn't the time for fear!"

She nodded, trembling, then let go with a scream.

Her feet hit the dock. *Thank God.*

His boots scraped the hull, rope swaying as he steadied himself against the ship, the iron warm under his palms from the engine heat. He didn't look down, just kept his eyes on the rope.

Then a shout rang out above—sharp and angry.

Ivy's scream had attracted attention.

A gunshot tore into the air, a bullet whizzing past him.

Alex gasped, looking up to see someone leaning over the rail. They'd been spotted but they weren't shooting at Ivy—they were shooting at *him.*

Alex slid the last few feet, rope burning his palms, then jumped, landing in a crouch. His knees jarred as Ivy reached for him.

"They're coming," she said.

He didn't have time to look—just grabbed her hand and ran.

The dock was cluttered with cargo, wooden crates, canvas bundles, coils of netting, and rust-streaked barrels. Between two stacks of crates, he spotted an opening—a narrow alley between dock warehouses.

If they could get off the quay, they could disappear into the chaos of the port.

They ducked into the shadows and didn't look back.

CHAPTER FIFTEEN

JACK

The station smelled like old stone and soot, cinders drifting in on the inky black smoke from the train Jack should have boarded ten minutes ago. Jack stood near the edge of the platform, shoulder brushing the sun-warmed iron pillar behind him. A distant train hissed, brakes squealing, the sound sharp enough to grate his already frayed nerves.

He checked his watch.

Ruby was late.

He hadn't been entirely idiotic about the whole plan—she wouldn't get the first weekly payment until she met him at the train station with the forged travel documents she had promised she could get for him.

Jack hadn't asked about her contacts—and the truth was, he didn't want to know. Working with the scum of Cairo's criminal underground had never been his preference, even if Noah had resorted to that option frequently during the war. But Noah had always been willing to get his hands dirty in a way that Jack hadn't wanted to. Noah blended with the criminals and the people around him in a way that even impressed Jack.

Like Noah, though, he was able to wear the loose-fitting galabeyah Egyptian tunic well. Together with a headscarf and the scruff he'd been growing the last few days, it did wonders for altering his appearance.

Funny how slipping undercover like this made him feel as though the world was at war once again. His need to be always on alert had never really faded, but since leaving the Kharga he couldn't help but notice everything he'd turned a blind eye to in the fifteen years following the armistice.

Whispers on the streets, men and women who seemed to be sharing more than pleasant conversation. Something stirred restlessly.

Even here at the train station, Jack had spotted more than one character that made his shoulders tense. He kept a close watch on his surroundings, half expecting Prescott's men to be here, following him despite his best efforts. Prescott's silence in the last few weeks was unnerving, but Jack didn't doubt for a second that it was intentional too.

He scanned the crowd on the platform again. Around him, the train workers weaved through clusters of travelers, the wheels of the trolleys clattering over the ground. Jack shifted his weight, taking in every face closest. A woman in a white hat approached. *Not her.*

He wiped his hand across his jaw, trying to loosen the clench of his muscles. If Ruby didn't show, he'd go without her. He'd figure it out, the way he always had. Even if he had to ride across the border of Iraq on camelback through the desert.

Inconvenient, yes. And he'd lose valuable time. God knew he'd already lost enough.

Then he saw her—plain brown travel dress, blond hair hidden under a drab scarf, eyes sharp even at a distance. And at her side ... *Theo.*

His stomach sank.

Ruby's brother could pass for her twin. He wore a trench coat, despite the warm weather, and a flat-topped hat with a wide brim covering his curly blond hair.

A flash of irritation went through Jack and he pushed himself off the pillar, moving toward them. The whistle blew again. "We need to get on the train," he said as a greeting. He didn't bother looking at Theo. "What's he doing here?"

Ruby crossed her arms. "He's coming with us. I'm not comfortable traveling alone with a man I don't know."

"I don't have a ticket for him," Jack snapped. "And this isn't what we agreed to."

The last thing he needed was another variable he couldn't control.

And the less he could control.

"We bought him a ticket to Kantara at the office. You can reimburse me." Ruby shrugged, chin lifted in that defiant way he was beginning to understand came with her stubborn spirit. "Either he goes or I stay. Your choice."

Steam hissed down the length of the train. Jack glanced at the second-class car, then at Theo, who met his stare without blinking. *Dammit.*

Fine. He could manage this.

"Get your things," Jack said, his voice hard and flat. "We're boarding now." He turned toward the train, not bothering to wait for them.

The crowd around them had swollen as they moved down the platform. Jack stayed a step ahead, eyes sweeping the crowd for any hint of Prescott's men. A flick of his gaze back revealed Ruby's exasperated glare on him as she bumped through passersby, struggling to keep up. Jack smirked as he looked away.

Let her be angry—she'd forced his hand, and now Theo was dead weight he'd have to drag along.

Up close, the railcar revealed sun-faded paint flaking at the seams. Jack caught the conductor's eye and handed over their tickets. The man barely glanced at them before punching them, then waved them toward the carriage door.

Inside, the air smelled of old leather and stale sweat. Jack squeezed down the narrow aisle, the wooden floor shuddering under his boots. Compartments were packed—families hauling children and crates, young couples, an old woman fanning herself with a magazine.

He ducked into their assigned compartment, dropping his battered satchel onto the worn seat. Ruby and Theo followed, the tension between them crowding the small space as Theo closed the door to the private space. Ruby slipped off her scarf, hands trembling.

Theo set a protective hand onto her shoulder, squeezing gently, and Ruby gave him a grateful look. He narrowed his eyes at Jack. "Next time," Theo growled, "plan for an extra ticket. She's not your woman to boss around—money or not."

Jack let out a short, humorless laugh. "This should be fun. How about next time you stay out of my way? I haven't forgotten Mena House, *Theo*. And I might be willing to work with you and your sister temporarily, but that doesn't mean I've forgiven what happened there."

Outside, a final whistle split the air. The train lurched forward, wheels clanging over the track. Jack leaned back against the cracked leather seat, eyes on the corridor beyond the glass.

Jack scanned the crowd again, his heart squeezing when he caught sight of a man in a dark suit leaning against a wall, eyes hidden behind wire-rimmed glasses.

He seemed to be staring right at Jack's window.

Jack looked away as the train pulled away.

One of Prescott's men?

Nothing was beyond the realm of possibility. Prescott's silence was always the worst kind of noise.

Tense silence filled the air as they left Cairo. The trip to Kantara offered plenty of time for them to discuss the finer details of the plan, and right now he wasn't in the mood.

He'd hoped to send a telegram to Fahad al-Najjar, his old friend from Jerusalem and someone he could be certain he could trust. But after Noah's cryptic telegram in Cairo, contacting Fahad was too risky. Telegrams were notoriously easy to spy on, and Fahad was a known contact of Jack's. If Jack showed up to Fahad's house in Jerusalem, he may as well throw up a smoke signal to Prescott, announcing his location.

So, instead, he was stuck relying on the transports Ruby had arranged through her fixers in Cairo. And once he got to Baghdad, the real work began—finding a trace of Gretchen Herbert.

Good God, Kit, why'd you have to send me on a wild goose chase?

If only she'd reached out to him. His chest went impossibly tight as he remembered her. It'd been so long since he'd seen her that his memories of her had faded into fragments he rarely allowed himself to revisit.

Prescott had known what he was doing by telling Jack about her. Alice was entirely *too* painful for Jack to think of. He'd loved his little sister and done everything to protect her, but ultimately he'd been forced to accept that she'd grown up and chosen a life that he could never reconcile himself with.

But Kit?

Kit had hated Blackwell as much as he had. Had wanted nothing to do with her father's organization.

If this Gretchen Herbert was *his* Kit—and he was convinced she was—then she'd clearly wanted to get his attention. Why write under that name otherwise? She had to remember she'd told him about the alias.

Maybe she'd been afraid of what he'd think if she sent a

more direct message. If she was really working for Blackwell now, then she'd turned her back on everything that she and Jack had believed in when they were younger.

But then why use the alias at all? What message was she trying to send him?

As the familiar scenes of Cairo gave way to a blur of desert, Jack pushed the troubling thoughts away and leaned down toward his satchel. He'd gone through the *Guardian* papers he'd taken from Penmore while traveling from France to Cairo, clipping any article he'd found written by Gretchen Herbert and pasting them into a notebook.

Then, in Cairo, he'd made an even more startling discovery —articles by Gretchen Herbert in *The Egyptian Gazette*. He'd dug as far back as he could, visiting the Khedival library, and found several articles, starting the previous December. Nothing before then.

Something must have forced her hand around then. Made her desperate enough to reach across the vastness that separated them.

The feeling of someone watching him closely broke Jack's concentration. He frowned, his gaze flicking up to see Theo studying him. Jack frowned and shut the notebook. "What?" he asked in a flat tone.

Theo shrugged. "Just trying to get a better sense of who you are, Jack Darby. You've got money but apparently no friends. You act respectably enough, but then you blackmail an innocent woman into working for you—and want to deny her the comfort of her own brother's presence."

"Innocent?" Jack raised an eyebrow at Ruby, who rolled her eyes, shifting in her seat.

"Knock it off, Theo. He's paying us well enough. We don't have to be friends; we can all just sit here quietly and get this trip over with, and then Jack will let us return to our lives, right?" Ruby gave him a pleading look as though asking him to play nicely.

"It's going to be a long trip if we all sit here without talking." Theo reached into his breast pocket and pulled out a cigarette case. He removed a cigarette and slipped it into his mouth, then took out a lighter. Curling his hand around the cigarette, he lit it, then took a drag. "And I asked around. Everyone said he's just a washed-up old archeologist who only made minor discoveries. A hermit with no friends left in Cairo."

Dammit. Theo had asked about him? What if he'd said something about Ruby smuggling him to Iraq?

"You flatter me," Jack said with a tilt of his head. "*Minor discoveries* sounds pretty successful for the likes of me." His glare deepened. "But asking about me goes precisely against my instructions to your sister. If you told the wrong person—"

"Relax," Theo said, lazily stretching his leg out. "What are you, a spy or something?"

Jack chortled. "A spy wouldn't be stuck on a second-class carriage with you two as dead weight, Theo. Count your blessings. If you said the wrong thing to the wrong person, my patience with you will evaporate immediately."

Theo glared. "I didn't say anything about your demands on my sister. I'm not stupid."

Ruby leaned over and snatched the cigarette from his lips, then extinguished it in an ashtray by the door. "Oh no, you most definitely are." She smacked him against the shoulder with her palm. "I told you not to say anything to anyone."

"For all we know, he's dragging you out to Baghdad to sell you to the highest bidder. I needed to know what type of reputation he has. Don't worry, I was discreet."

"You're doing a remarkable job of making me want to sell *you* to the highest bidder," Jack muttered, palming his face. *Amateurs.* This was what he got for working with people he didn't know and couldn't trust. Only a few miles out of Cairo and he was already beginning to question his life choices.

Jack cleared his throat, then said, "*If* I wanted to sell your sister, Theo, I wouldn't have paid so much money to her in the first place. You may not believe it, but she's not cheap."

Ruby shot him a look sharp enough to cut glass. "Excuse me?"

"Kidding," Jack said with a smirk. "Mostly."

Theo reached for another cigarette but found the pack empty. He frowned at the one Ruby had extinguished, as though considering picking it back up again. "Don't worry, the only reason we're here is because—"

"Because I'm paying you to be." Jack tossed him an irritated look. "If you're going to be coming along, we're going to have to establish some rules. First of all, if I say not to do something, I've got a damned good reason for it. You don't question it. Don't go around me. You do what I say, or you could get yourself or someone else killed—got it?"

Theo gave him a cutting look. "If you say so." He rubbed the whiskers above his upper lip, then snatched the discarded cigarette and lit it once again.

"So. What's your plan when we cross the border? Or are you making this up as you go?"

Given the circumstances of their meeting, Jack had never liked Theo, but now he *really* missed the time when he'd thought of the fellow as quiet. He'd already explained the route to Ruby—that she hadn't shared the details of the itinerary with him was interesting.

Or maybe it meant nothing. Maybe he was just trying to play dumb and be purposely obtuse.

Jack's eyes flicked to the window, then back to Theo. "We'll take the train to Kantara. Take the ferry across the Suez, then take the line straight up the coast of Palestine to Lydda station, then to Haifa. From there we'll go to Damascus, then take Nairn Transport Company's desert bus to Baghdad."

Smoke curled from Theo's lips. "Don't you think that's a bit risky? You want to avoid officials—but you're walking straight into them and going by all the official checkpoints." He leveled a hard gaze at Jack. "It'd be faster and safer for us to go from Jerusalem to Amman by car, *then* take a desert convoy."

Well, at least he knows his geography.

Truth was, Jack couldn't afford to take Ruby or her brother for idiots. They'd survived as thieves in Cairo long enough without being caught. Jack sighed, wishing he could just return to reading the articles from Gretchen in the notebook—but Theo, apparently, didn't want silence.

"This is the route," Jack said in a tone that made it clear he didn't want to be argued with.

Theo snorted. "You're a real mastermind. You realize half that route's crawling with British inspectors? You'll get yourself pinched before you even see Damascus. Ruby knows a man in Jerusalem that could get us to Amman."

Pinching the bridge of his nose, Jack tried to remain calm. Problem was, Theo's worries echoed Jack's own thoughts when he'd been planning the route. Not that he was about to let Theo know that. "Then stay in Kantara for all I care. Go back to Cairo. No one is forcing you to come."

Ruby looked between them, then said in a firm tone, "He's coming. And you'll thank him if you end up needing a backup plan. He's not entirely wrong about Amman. I could—"

"This. Is. The. Route," Jack repeated, punctuating every word through his teeth.

His tone must have startled her, because she seemed to shrink.

"Theo, if this is the route Jack wants to take, I don't think we should question it. We're not paid for our opinion," Ruby said, exchanging a look with her brother. She grimaced at Jack. "Sorry—he's just suspicious, you know?"

"Don't apologize for me," Theo snapped.

Jack caught the quick flicker of hurt in Ruby's eyes. He hated how that did something reckless to his chest. She glanced at him then, and for half a heartbeat, he felt that itch—the one that reminded him how badly he wanted to trust her. *Someone.*

And how dangerous that is.

Then again, Jack hadn't been too polite to her, either.

Ruby stiffened, color creeping up her neck. "I'm not apologizing *for you.* But we all have to get along if we're going to spend the next several weeks together." She bit her lip and appealed to Jack. "Maybe it would help if we knew a bit more about you, Jack. And why you're going to Baghdad."

Jack's eyes snagged on the pale line of her neck where the scarf now rested, the faint glint of a chain resting just under her collarbone. He looked away, jaw flexing. *Some lines aren't worth crossing—especially not with a woman like her.*

Plus, Theo was getting on his nerves—fast.

But Ruby didn't deserve to get rudeness on two sides, no matter how little Jack trusted her. "I'm not sure I'm ready to share too much," Jack said without taking his gaze off Theo. He stared him down hard. "But trust is something you and your brother are going to have to earn."

Theo did his best to stare back defiantly. At last, he shifted, looking away with discomfort. "I'm going to see if I can buy some cigarettes," he announced, then stood. "I'll be back."

Thank goodness for that.

As soon as Theo had left, Ruby shot Jack a sidelong glance, her eyes bright with irritation. "You know, you could at least pretend to back me up if I bother speaking up for you. Especially if he's being impossible."

Jack arched a brow. "You want my help handling your

brother? Thought you were perfectly capable of handling men all by yourself."

Her lips twitched—almost a smile. "Not all men are worth the trouble of handling, you know."

Something in her words made his blood heat and he held her gaze for a beat too long, his heart flickering under his ribs. He shouldn't take the bait, but for some reason he couldn't help it. "You'll have to let me know which category I'm in."

She looked away, but her cheeks flushed pink. "Trust me— I'm still deciding."

Strangely satisfied, Jack crossed his arms and glanced at Ruby. He liked her. Thief or not. She had a way about her that was charming. Maybe it was fake or maybe he just hadn't been around women enough lately, and she seemed like a glass of water after a thirsty ride in the desert.

In a low voice, he told her, "I'm trying to find my sister, by the way. And a friend she was traveling with. I suspect I might be able to find clues about where they were in Baghdad. Is that good enough for now?"

Something in Ruby's gaze shifted. Perhaps sympathy. She nodded, then said softly, "Something serious must be involved if you need to be smuggled into Iraq to find them, otherwise you would have gone to the consulate."

Something serious.

She had no idea. Only the most dangerous man Jack had ever met.

Jack only nodded.

The door to the compartment slid open once again and Theo sauntered back in, a fresh cigarette in his mouth. He said nothing as he sat, the relief over his absence instantly disappearing.

After a moment, Jack looked back at Theo and said grudgingly, "We might go to Jerusalem. But if we do it'll be a brief stop—and I doubt Amman is worth the trouble. That route to Baghdad is filled with desert bandits and risks a much higher chance of dying of thirst if our lorry breaks down."

Theo frowned, several beats of tense silence passing between them. Then, at last, he nodded. "You're the boss."

Jack swallowed hard, the victory in Theo's admission hollow. More importantly, he didn't *feel* in control.

He needed allies. Someone he could trust.

But every mile closer to Baghdad, hope felt thinner than the desert air.

By now, Noah might be in Jerusalem—and Fahad too. Maybe it would be a risk to involve them, but he felt out of his depth and rusty. He was a war veteran returning to a lifestyle he was no longer sure he could survive in.

And that terrified him.

CHAPTER SIXTEEN

GINGER

Ginger paced on the verandah, fanning herself despite the relatively mild heat in Cairo. Being here should have been a relief—she and Victoria had just arrived from Alexandria that afternoon—but coming to her parents' old estate in Anglo Cairo always unsettled her in more ways than one.

This was the last place her family had been a family before her father's and brother's brutal deaths during the war.

She tried to hold on to the good memories. She'd shared laughter and happiness with her parents and siblings here. And other, special moments had happened here too—she'd made love with Noah in her room on their wedding night.

But now, despite her attempts in years past to reclaim the place for her own family when they came to Egypt during the winter season, the ghosts of her past seemed to be lurking in every corner this morning.

With that horrible man making threats against Ivy, and with Alex's whereabouts completely unknown, old fears seemed to crowd Ginger's mind. There hadn't been time to have any of their loyal Egyptian servants prepare the house for Victoria and Ginger's arrival. All the furniture was still shrouded with sheets, a layer of undisturbed dust on all the surfaces inside.

The sound of an approaching motorcar made Ginger pause mid-step, then she turned toward the street.

Alastair and Lucy pulled up to the gate of the house, and Ginger left the verandah and hurried down the short driveway toward it. Alastair had already left the driver's seat, and, despite everything, Ginger's heart warmed when she saw him. However terrible it sounded, she had more affection for her brother-in-law than her sister, even though her relationship with Lucy had become much more pleasant over the past decade.

Alastair met her at the gate, which she hadn't bothered to lock. "Ginger, dearest," he said with a broad smile.

She opened the gate and embraced Alastair tightly, unexpected tears springing to her eyes. His presence was calming—safe—in a way that only Noah and Jack had offered her in the past. "You're a sight for sore eyes," she said, her voice hitching.

Alastair pressed a kiss to her cheek, then held her by the shoulders. "How's my favorite sister? Why didn't you warn us you were coming? We would have met you at the station."

"Oh, you know Ginny," Lucy said from the car with a shake of her head. "She likes to keep those of us who like to plan on our toes."

Ginger pulled away from Alastair and attempted a smile, her eyes brimming with tears. "If you knew what I've been living through, you might forgive me. I'm so glad you're here."

He clucked and gave a slight wink. "I abandoned everything and drove straight here when Victoria called. Is she here?"

"She's inside," Ginger said. She pushed the gate open, stepping to the side as Alastair climbed back into the driver's seat. He drove through the gate and she closed it, the hinges giving an awful squeak.

At least we'll have some forewarning when Mr. Federline's messenger arrives and comes through the gate.

Her heart squeezed at the memory. When Mr. Federline had found them in London, he'd been the picture of a gentleman. It wasn't until later—when he'd told them that he "regretted the inconvenience" but was keeping Ivy "safe" in Cairo—that he'd revealed his true villainy.

Victoria and Ginger had left for Cairo as soon as possible, leaving Clara under Ginger's mother's careful supervision.

Ginger followed at a distance from the car, waiting for the dust kicked up from the tires to settle. Perhaps the only good thing about being here was that the weather in Cairo was so much nicer this time of year. She'd never really realized how much she loved Egyptian weather until she'd left after the war. Yes, the heat was a struggle, but she preferred it to the rain in England.

Alastair parked and went around to the passenger seat, then opened the door for Lucy. Lucy stood, her dark hair coiled elegantly under a rather expensive-looking hat. Alastair spoiled her, and it was just one more thing Ginger had to be grateful to him for. Maybe they weren't a love match, but he treated her well.

"You'll have to tell us what's happened," Lucy said with a wide-eyed look of concern. "You look pale, Ginny. We've been so worried about you since Alastair received that message to have Noah contact you."

Before Ginger could respond, Victoria opened the door to the home and rushed down the front steps. Her face was drawn, and she focused her dark-eyed gaze on Ginger rather than greeting Lucy or Alastair. "I just heard back from Shepheard's," Victoria said, her agitation making Ginger's heart flutter. "Jack checked out this morning. We've just missed him."

Alastair looked from Ginger to Victoria. "Jack was in Cairo?"

Ginger frowned. "You didn't hear from him or Noah?"

Alastair shook his head. "No—which, I'll admit, if they were here, is surprising. I just assumed they skipped Cairo altogether." He took Victoria by the elbow gently. "Why don't we go inside and chat? You can tell me all the details."

Thank goodness for Alastair. Of Noah's friends, there might not be anyone better to go to for help—including Jack. Noah had often relied on Alastair during the war to get him out of serious scrapes. And there was no one Noah trusted more than Alastair, other than Jack.

They went inside to the parlor, the only room where Victoria and Ginger had taken the time to strip the furniture coverings. Victoria settled in a lounge chair beside Alastair, rubbing her knuckles in a nervous gesture that Ginger had become familiar with over the years. In many ways, Victoria had never fully recovered from the traumas she'd experienced during the war at the hands of her father and Stephen Fisher.

Truthfully, Ginger admired Victoria more than anyone else she knew. Seeing her so agitated, so close to breaking, hurt deeply.

Victoria waited until they were all settled before she said, "I won't bore you with the details of what heralded this—I'm sure Jack already involved you to some extent, Alastair—but after Jack visited at Penmore and left with Noah, we noticed that Alex and Ivy had gone missing."

Lucy gasped. "Oh my goodness."

Acknowledging Lucy's response with a nod, Victoria went on, her voice growing more emotional. "We searched for several days without success until we at last went to London. And there —" Victoria's voice broke. She gulped a breath, but then shook her head, pressing her fingertips to her lips with an urgent plea in her eyes for Ginger to continue.

Ginger turned toward Alastair. "A man came to see us. He

made it clear we weren't to repeat his name to anyone but gave it to us saying that Jack would know who he was. And then he informed us that he had taken Ivy for 'safekeeping.' That we were to tell Jack that he was to turn over what he was looking for to him directly, and Ivy would be safely returned. Unharmed."

"So you came to find Jack," Alastair said, a somber expression in his eyes.

Ginger nodded. "Yes—and to receive confirmation that he has Ivy and she's unharmed. He told us he had sent her to Cairo. Victoria paid a fortune to get us here as soon as possible on Imperial Airways."

Alastair frowned, absorbing the information as he sat back in the chair. He said nothing for a few beats, then turned toward his wife. "Lucy, why don't you take the car and go fetch Bahiti? I'm certain Ginger and Victoria could use a servant or two to help them around here with everything they have going on."

Raising a brow, Lucy tilted her head, clearly annoyed at being dismissed. "Well, I will. But, first—what about Alex? You said nothing at all about Alex. I'd like to know what happened to my nephew."

A roiling feeling tumbled in Ginger's gut. "I wish I knew," she said softly. "The man said nothing about Alex, and I didn't dare mention him. But it can't be coincidental. And if the man had taken both Ivy and Alex, I doubt he would have only used Ivy to threaten us with." She gulped a breath. "If I know Alex, though, and he witnessed something happen to Ivy, he would have gone after her."

Either that or he interfered and they've killed him.

She shuddered, unable to voice the horrific thought.

Yet it pressed in on her anyway, with the same cold fear that came every night when the darkness brought nightmarish possibilities.

Lucy paled and she nodded. "I'll go fetch Bahiti," she said. She rose to leave but paused briefly by Ginger. Wordlessly, she gave Ginger a quick, unusually affectionate hug, then hurried out of the parlor.

When she was gone, Alastair gave Victoria and Ginger a close look. "I'll need the name of the brigand who did this to Ivy, but I have a feeling I already know it."

"I don't want to endanger you, Alastair," Ginger said, biting her lip.

He smiled gently. "My dear woman, have I ever run away from danger when it means failing the people I love? Let me venture a guess then. Prescott Federline? The fellow has been a thorn in Jack's side for most of his life. I'll do everything I can to help."

His words stabbed Ginger deeper in the chest. If Alastair knew about Prescott Federline, there wasn't any way that Jack hadn't told Noah about him too. And while she knew Noah kept his secrets when he felt they were too treacherous to share, she wished Noah had shared more about what he and Jack were dealing with when they'd left Penmore.

"Oh, Alastair," Victoria said, dabbing her eyes. "I don't know what we'd do without you."

"I'm not sure what you *can* do, to be honest. He seems to be holding the right cards at the moment. But it would be good if we could talk to Noah and Jack." Even though it wasn't Jack's fault, Ginger couldn't help the irritation brimming within her. Jack had involved Noah in something dangerous, obviously, and brought trouble to their doorstep. And now she couldn't even reach her own husband to let him know their son was missing and unaccounted for.

"I'll do my utmost to find where Jack has gone. Knowing him, he's attempting to be some sort of martyr and not involve me with this whole nasty business with Federline."

"Do you know where they were heading?"

Alastair grimaced. "My guess would be Iraq. But where—I'm not certain. I believe his sister was last seen working at the Royal Tombs of Ur."

"Then maybe we should go there," Victoria said, sitting straighter. "I'm certain I could arrange transportation and—"

"Iraq is a large country, dearest. One that I wouldn't send two well-bred Englishwomen to without important preparations. Jack and Noah could be anywhere."

"My daughter's life is at stake, Alastair. I can't afford to risk a delay in communicating with Jack."

"And we can't afford to risk a delay by not heeding Alastair's advice," Ginger said gently. "Besides which, we don't know when Mr. Federline will contact us with whatever next steps he has."

Victoria shifted with discomfort. "I called the man Federline said to contact here. Told him we'd arrived earlier than expected and to meet us here. He's on his way."

Oh no. Ginger resisted the urge to scold her. She was desperate and had mentioned several times throughout their journey that she hoped the proof Federline would offer of Ivy's well-being would be an opportunity to see her.

But Ginger was hoping they'd have a chance to settle in first. Talk to Alastair, make a plan for what to do next. And she hadn't wanted to invite Federline's messenger directly to her home.

"In that case, we might think of moving that meeting to a room where I can hide my presence." Alastair surveyed the discarded furniture covers. "The fact that the house is still shuttered might help, but your father was a suspicious sort, wasn't he, Ginger? Surely he has a room or office in here that might provide a good covert space to hide."

"Yes, his office has a servants' door that would work." Ginger stood, a nervous feeling rising through her. Her father, God rest his soul, had been the one who'd set her on the path of intrigue and danger—more than once. As a girl, she'd sometimes wished he'd be more exciting. More adventurous.

Now she wished he'd been more boring.

"Try to check your emotions when Federline's messenger arrives," Ginger said with a warning look toward Victoria. "I know it isn't easy—believe me, I'm as desperate to hear *anything* about Alex. But we have to trust that we'll find a way through this and get both our children back whole and safe."

Victoria raised her chin, a fierce look glittering in her eyes. "Whole is a relative term, Ginger. Ivy and Alex may not be harmed physically from this ordeal—and I pray to God they aren't or I will murder the men who did this with my own bare hands—but they *will* be changed by it, I promise you. And you know it. These are the sorts of events that define who we become, like it or not."

Ginger stared at her friend, her stomach dropping.

She's right.

However, Ginger didn't want to think about that yet.

Alex was precocious, but he was still fairly innocent. And Ivy … she was such a young, beautiful girl. She couldn't allow herself to consider the possibilities of what the thugs who had her might have done by now. If anything, having been a physician the last fifteen years, Ginger had witnessed more abuse to women than ever. She didn't have any delusions of what could happen.

"Don't be pessimistic," Alastair said, cutting into her thoughts. He crossed his arms, looking from one woman to the other. "I stand before two of the bravest, most accomplished women I know who *both* dealt with their fair share of treachery. Our scars don't define us, Victoria. They're just window dressing. We all have the choice to be slaves to the dark parts of our souls or not. And both of you are exemplary examples of individuals who have chosen not to be."

The buzzing of the bell at the gate interrupted them and Victoria shot from her seat, lacking any of her familiar poise. "That must be him."

Ginger nodded. "Why don't you go and invite him in? I'll take Alastair to the office and hide him away—and you can bring the man there."

They parted, and Ginger led Alastair quickly through the foyer and into the hall, turning on some lights as she went. Opening the door to the office, she released a held breath and flipped on a light. This place had changed significantly since Noah had converted it to his own office and schoolroom for the children when they wintered here. None of the dark mahogany furniture her father had favored—instead locally crafted furnishings filled the space—along with a few nods to Egyptology and Bedouin wares.

Yet Ginger still wondered if someday she might knock into the wrong wall panel and find yet another of her father's hidden secrets. Noah had cleared the room of smuggled antiquities long ago, but what if he'd missed something?

She shook her head. *I must be letting my worries about Alex and Ivy get the better of me.*

She hurried to the servant's entrance in the back of the room and let Alastair into the dark space there. As she started to close the door, Alastair reached for her hand and gave it a tight squeeze. "All will be well. Keep your wits about you. And I think you were right—it's better not to mention Alex at all. Chances are the lad is trying to be a hero, like his father."

Goodness, I hope so. That was better than any alternative Ginger could think of.

She nodded wordlessly and shut the door. Alastair would have to keep his ear close to the door to hear, but it was better than keeping it open and Federline's man discovering him there listening.

A minute later, the sounds of voices and steps approached, and Victoria opened the door to the office. She seemed to have recovered her sense of control and she walked in slowly, shoulders drawn back.

The man behind her was no messenger, though, but Federline himself.

What in the world? How did he get to Cairo so quickly?

Ginger straightened and smoothed her hands over her skirt, crossing the space toward them. "Mr. Federline," she said. "I wasn't expecting to see you here, given that we parted from you in London so recently."

He took in every inch of the room with sharp precision, his eyes reminding her of a cat's, before his gaze swiveled to hers. "I'm able to fly to where I need quickly these days."

Ah. Then he was enormously wealthy—and had resources at his disposal. Yet another way for him to flex his muscles. Who *was* this man? And why had Noah and Jack not told her anything about him?

"That must be quite a luxury," Victoria snapped, her patience seeming to fray. She positioned herself beside Ginger. "Now where is my daughter?"

Federline frowned, then wandered over toward a wall, where Noah had hung a large map of the world to a corkboard. "This is a nice home," he said, touching the pins Clara had placed on the map the year before with an arrogance that rankled Ginger. He turned toward Ginger and sized her up. "It was your late father's, right? Earl of Braddock. The title seems cursed, though. Your father and brother shot dead. His heir— suicide a few years later?"

Ginger crossed her arms, feeling uneasy and exposed. She didn't like thinking about her father's and brother's deaths, which she'd not only witnessed but caused. And Lucy's first husband, William Thorne, had killed himself shortly after Lucy had abandoned him and he'd gone bankrupt, leaving no heir to the title.

But none of that was as concerning as the fact that Federline had taken the time to learn all of that about her family, digging up old skeletons she'd hoped would stay in the closet.

But why me? It's Victoria's daughter he's holding.

As though he could read Ginger's mind, Federline's catlike eyes focused on Victoria. "Though I guess Lord Reginald Helton's story is more sordid. An English gentleman sires an Egyptian prostitute's whelp—then raises her to be his spy and informant. To seduce men of influence and blackmail them." His lips smirked cruelly. "Though, it looks like he was a lucky man. His daughter had the looks for it. I'm sure you served him well."

A shiver of repulsion went through Ginger, and she narrowed her eyes at him. "Enough. Your point is proven, Mr. Federline. Where's this proof you promised to provide of Ivy's well-being?"

He folded his hands in front of him, squaring his shoulders. "I've changed my mind. You're in no position to negotiate, and I'm not feeling very generous at the moment." He dusted the shoulder of his linen suit. "You just deliver my message to Jack —then we'll talk."

Victoria steadied herself on Ginger's arm, the only tell that the news had hit her like a physical blow.

"We don't know where Jack is," Ginger said in a low, barely restrained voice. She hadn't realized until then how much *she* needed that confirmation of Ivy's well-being. Not only because she loved Ivy like a second daughter but because she was a link to Alex too.

Alex, where are you?

She wished she could transcend the ether, communicate with her son—or, for that matter, his father.

But she couldn't let those fears derail her now.

Mr. Federline gave her a long stare. "I'm certain you'll find a way to get my message to Jack."

"You're not the only one with resources." Ginger steeled herself with resolve. "And without proof that you're holding Ivy unharmed, you're hardly in a position to make demands either."

Mr. Federline took a slow step toward her. "You're clearly an intelligent woman, Dr. Benson. How would I know about Ivy being missing?" His eyes crinkled at the corners. "Or Alex? A mechanical boy. Good with tools—isn't he?"

Ginger's knees almost gave out, and Federline must have seen the alarm in her face.

His look skewered her. "Yes, I know about him. He's with Ivy too. But the boy isn't quite as well behaved as his little friend. Perhaps I should punish him accordingly."

Federline let his words settle into the hush of the room, his eyes glittering with amusement that made Ginger's skin crawl. Slowly, he adjusted the cuff of his immaculate suit as though discussing the brutal fates of children was nothing more than idle conversation.

He stepped closer to Ginger, leaning in just enough that she could feel the menace of his proximity. "Seven days, Dr. Benson," he said, his voice velvet-smooth and merciless. "Tell Jack he has seven days to contact me, or you'll never see either child alive again."

Victoria's hand clamped around Ginger's arm, her nails biting through the thin fabric of Ginger's sleeve. But Ginger held Federline's gaze, forcing her expression into something calm even as her pulse pounded in her throat.

Thank goodness Alastair is nearby. She didn't doubt he would come to their aid if necessary.

"Take me instead," Victoria cried, her desperation at last cracking. "Return Ivy and Alex and hold me ransom if you must."

His eyes flicked toward her, eyebrows furrowing, as though he'd forgotten she was even there. Or didn't care. "You're of no use to me. I need someone Jack cares about much more."

Victoria blanched.

Federline dipped his head in a mock-bow toward them—an obscene parody of gentlemanly civility—then turned and strolled from the office as though he had every right to let himself out. Ginger scrambled to follow him, barely holding on to her wits, but he didn't look back, his footsteps echoing down the corridor as he strode toward the door.

The front door shut with a quiet click, and Ginger's heart stuttered. Swallowing hard, she rushed up behind the door and locked it. *As though that could protect us from this man.*

She set her forehead against the smooth, cool wood of the door, trying to slow her pulse.

He has Alexander.

Alex.

My God, he has Alex. He's alive.

That Alex wasn't dead in a ditch somewhere was the only consolation she could find in all this. She finally knew where her son was.

Tucking a strand of hair behind her ear with a shaky hand, she crossed back toward the office, toward the only person who knew and understood what she was going through. Victoria sagged against a covered armchair, blinking, her face drawn.

With a few quick strides, Ginger moved toward the servants' door and tugged it open. Alastair stood there, half in shadow, his face set in grim lines that made him look older and more dangerous than she'd ever seen him.

He stepped into the light and brushed a film of dust from his sleeves. "Well," he said, his tone deceptively mild, "he's a charming bastard, isn't he?"

Victoria let out a brittle, startled laugh—the sound of someone on the edge of breaking. She pressed a trembling hand to her mouth.

Ginger went over to her and squeezed her shoulder, then sank against the arm of the chair, the fight gone from her legs. "Seven days." Her voice was barely above a whisper. "And we don't even know where Jack is. Or Noah. Or—"

"Ginger." Alastair's voice cut through her rising panic. He frowned, taking a cautious approach toward her. "Listen to me. We are not helpless children. We've all survived worse threats than him."

"Threats to *ourselves*, Alastair—not to our children," Victoria said sharply. "And I don't understand. How does he know so much? How could he possibly know—"

"Information is his currency," Alastair said. "And he's exceptionally good at using it for blackmail, I understand. Which is why he's picked the children as his targets. We can't afford to seem any weaker to him than we are though. All he's asking is for you to deliver a message to Jack—which means Jack must have eluded him at last. For all his poise, I heard a current of anger in his tone. If Federline is angry, it must be because he feels threatened. And that's not a bad thing to exploit. We just may have to find a way to beat him at his own game."

Though it hurt to breathe, Ginger nodded and met Victoria's gaze, an old, unyielding fire lighting through her. "Alastair is right, Victoria. And we've both lived through monsters before. We won't allow this one to break us."

Victoria still didn't look convinced, but Alastair nodded, approving. "Good. Then we must do what we must." His tone was firm and steady. "Federline thinks he's got you cornered. He doesn't. While he's watching you, I can make myself useful and get word to Noah and Jack, through channels Federline won't see coming."

Victoria straightened. "We'll need money. People we can trust."

"Leave that to me," Alastair said. "Fortunately, I have every reason to be here thanks to the family connection. I have no doubt Federline will be looking into me, but I can find a way to use that to our advantage. It's time he learns that the prey can bite."

He moved to a drinks cabinet and tugged the cover to the side, then rummaged until he found a bottle of good whisky. After pouring a stiff measure into two glasses, he handed one to Ginger and to Victoria.

Ginger accepted it, staring at the amber swirl as she lifted it to her lips. The burn of the alcohol stung her nostrils, then her mouth, as she took a slow sip, which steadied her.

Victoria exhaled shakily, but the drink seemed to return some of the color to her cheeks. "And if he's right about Alex? What if they have him too, Ginger?"

Ginger closed her eyes, her throat clenching.

Somehow I hoped he couldn't be caught.

Her darling son. Goodness—he was out there right now, held captive by a horrible beast of a man, and he'd been so heartbroken and betrayed by his parents *before* this. What must he think now?

There had once been a time in her life when Alexander had been the reason her heart kept beating. When the life stirring within her had kept her from collapsing and, after he'd been born, his little cherub face had made her *feel* again.

And she'd hidden everything she'd gone through for him *from* him.

Maybe it was time he knew. Maybe then he would never doubt the depth of her and Noah's love for him.

The warm and reassuring grip of Alastair's hand on her shoulder brought her back to the present. "If Federline has Alex, I'm certain Alex is being a damn nuisance to him. And that's exactly what we'll count on. The boy's a Benson—he'll find a way to survive. So will Ivy. They just need us to find Jack—and fast."

A thin, incredulous laugh slipped from Ginger's throat. "God help me, Alastair, but I want to believe you."

He squeezed her shoulder once more. "Good. Now dry those eyes. We have a snake to corner and a family to get back."

Victoria nodded, reaching for Ginger's hand. She held it tight, her fingers clasping Ginger's.

If Victoria can summon the will to fight through this, so can I. We can do this together.

For the first time since London, Ginger felt the tiniest spark of hope.

Sharp, stubborn, and alive.

CHAPTER SEVENTEEN

NOAH

*D*usk shrouded the hills of Hebron, the sun slipping behind the low limestone ridges and stone houses. Noah—tonight Yusef Karim—slowed with Fahad as they approached the diwan of the sheikhh's house, the stone-walled structure detached from the man's home. Even from here, Noah smelled the earthy coffee poured from the copper dallah into the cups of the men gathered in front of the sheikhh on rugs.

A fly buzzed by through the warm air, the voices of the men still low murmurs. Noah exchanged a look with Fahad, and the older man gave him a patient smile, but Noah saw the tension in the slight pull at the corner of his mouth. Fahad had reassured him that he trusted Noah for this, but once this line was crossed, there was no going back.

Fahad would stake his reputation on Noah. If Noah was discovered, Fahad would bear the shame—or worse.

Noah's stomach roiled at the thought of the price they both might pay.

Hower had explained in crisp detail what the British wanted him to do in Jerusalem—infiltrate the Arab nationalist circles and report back like a good, loyal informant. Specifically, he was to learn of any plans to meet with the Germans.

But these were the people whose plight he sympathized with. And, yet, the loyalty wasn't simple. He was British too. The empire had brought rails, infrastructure, schools, order—but at what cost? He'd seen the ugliness of occupation of these foreign lands with his own eyes, the stolen antiquities funneled out of Egypt, the lies sold to Arab tribes during the war, the Balfour promises that contradicted other promises on paper but bled the same in the dust.

Those lies now stirred unrest and murder. Here in Palestine, especially. The Arabs had believed whole-heartedly that the entirety of the Levant—from Palestine to Transjordan and Syria —would be theirs to rule freely after the war.

The French and the British had denied them that. If those who felt betrayed looked to new allies who would help them achieve the freedom they sought, Noah understood it, even if he couldn't support it. He hoped, instead, the British would do better. Fix this mess with the Arabs before it was too late. But the situation here was a knot of half-truths and betrayal.

And I'm about to pull it tighter.

Acid burned Noah's throat as he followed Fahad into the diwan. The long light-colored linen thobe swished over his sandaled feet. The keffiyeh head covering rested across his shoulders, the black agal biting faintly against his temples. He looked like any man from the plains villages.

But Fahad had warned him not to be fooled by the sheikh's simplicity—he came from a well-respected and influential family who had deep connections throughout the entire region. Most importantly, the sheikh still openly supported dialogue with the British authorities—and often expressed his friendship to those of Western cultures.

Stepping into the diwan felt like stepping out of time—back

to the war, when a borrowed name and a slip of a lie could mean a shallow grave in the sand.

The voices stopped as they entered, the four men in the space looking toward them. A thin, barefooted boy paused by a stone wall covered with rifles, the coffeepot on the brass tray in his hands. The only man who took a chair—Sheikhh Omar— gazed up at Fahad and Noah.

His keffiyeh was draped loose around his shoulders, the edge of it fluttering as he shifted. His eyes, deep and dark under a prominent brow bone, flicked from Fahad to Noah. Weighing, not welcoming yet.

The corners of his lips turned up in a slow bloom of a smile meant for Fahad alone. "*As-salaam alaykum*," the sheikh said as a greeting, then stood and approached Fahad.

"*Wa 'alaykum as-salaam, ya Sheikhh*," Fahad answered. He stepped forward, shoulders squared, and the sheikhh met him halfway. Their hands clasped lightly, and then they leaned in— one kiss on the right cheek, one on the left—an old, familiar ritual that closed the weight of silence.

Fahad turned toward Noah, his hand settling on his shoulder with firm, reassuring pressure. Even without words, Noah could feel the meaning of the gesture. *Hold steady.*

"This is Yusef Karim," Fahad said in Arabic, his voice low. "A man I trust as I trust my own kin."

Noah dipped his head and answered in soft, perfect Arabic, "It is an honor, Sheikhh Omar."

The sheikhh's eyes narrowed by a fraction, his gaze drifting to Fahad's fingers pressing into Noah's shoulder.

The press of Fahad's hand eased, but the hush held on as the men gathered continued to assess him. The sheikhh invited them to sit, then the thin boy moved again, the brass tray balanced with the care of someone taught never to spill. When the boy reached him, Noah lifted his eyes just enough to meet the boy's gaze. In those dark eyes, he read the question they were all too polite to ask aloud—*who are you?*

Noah took the tiny porcelain cup in both hands. Bitter coffee steam touched his nostrils, the warmth of the cup seeping into his palm. Could he really do this again? During the war, it had all felt so different—at least at first. Breaking bread with strangers he planned on betraying was necessary to keep bullets out of his countrymen's bodies.

But now?

Fahad, now settled on a rug at Noah's side, accepted his cup last, and the boy retreated to his place by the wall.

Sheikhh Omar drank from his coffee cup, eyes still focused on Noah, then he set it down on the rug in front of his feet. "What brings you here tonight, Fahad?"

"There are whispers in Jerusalem, Sheikhh. Whispers of new alliances on the horizon. Of new money. Yusef seeks to help where help is needed. He spent four years as a youth in Berlin and can be useful to our cause."

The sheikhh didn't look at Noah. His eyes flicked once to the rifles on the wall, then back to Fahad. "You trust him?"

"Like my own son." Fahad inclined his head without a flicker of doubt. "And much more than any man who sits in Jerusalem's cafés and calls himself a patriot."

That earned a grunt of amusement from the eldest of the watchers, a grey-haired man who shifted his cane across his lap.

The sheikhh's eyes moved to Noah. "And you, Yusef? What is it you want from my house tonight?"

Noah kept his shoulders loose. "I want nothing that is not offered, Sheikhh. I came because I have heard too many promises made behind closed doors that turn to ash and dust. Too many lies that cost us everything. If the Germans oppose the Zionists, I'm interested in hearing what they have to offer our people."

"Did the Germans send you, then?" The sheikhh raised a brow.

There it is. An opening.

"No, I am seeking those who might *introduce* me to our friends who have been speaking to the Germans. Fahad tells me you may be able to arrange this." He waited for a moment, then added, "I hear talk that the Germans send men to promise what the English won't. I want to know if that talk is wind or worth listening to."

The sheikhh said nothing, but his gaze shifted to Fahad again.

Noah kept still, feeling the burn of distrust settling between his ribs. Fahad's word carried weight, but if these men decided Noah was a liar—or a spy—Fahad would lose everything.

The sheikhh leaned back, fingertips drumming against his knee. The silence was only broken by the sound of the boy feeding another pinch of charcoal to the coals in the brazier. An orange glow flared across the rifles on the wall.

"You speak of promises, Yusef Karim," the sheikhh said at last, his tone mild, "but whose promises do you keep? A man can say he hates the English or the Germans and yet line his pockets with their gold all the same."

Noah felt the weight of his words press into his throat. He paused, forming his response carefully. "I have seen the worth of English gold. They give generously, then shoot while our backs are turned and steal it for themselves once again."

The elder with the cane let out a soft huff—whether in approval or doubt, Noah couldn't tell.

"And what would you do," Sheikhh Omar asked, "if you found out the talk was true? That the Germans do whisper?"

Betray whoever allies themselves with the Germans. His instinctive response burned in his throat. That's what Hower and the British wanted him to do, of course. And what he *had* to do.

Find out who might be talking to the Germans and report on them.

He wished, instead, he could attempt to persuade his Arab brethren that alliances with the Germans were madness—and would most likely only end in more betrayal and death. But he said, "I would listen. And carry those words where they might do some good—for us."

Fahad bowed his head. "His tongue is mine. If it runs false, so does mine. He will bring back what he hears."

The Sheikhh's mouth curved at last. "There is a man who speaks of these things—not here, not tonight. But his ears are sharper than mine. His reach wider." He leaned forward, elbows on his knees, and peered closer at Noah. "If you are what you claim to be, he will see it. And if you are not ..."

He didn't have to finish.

Noah kept his gaze steady. "When?"

The sheikhh grunted. "When he wishes it. I will send word through Fahad. Until then"—he flicked his fingers at the boy who was already stepping forward with the tray—"drink more coffee. Sit on my rug. And remember ... the hills hear more than you think."

Threats and progress. At least they were getting somewhere.

Noah drank the second coffee, the bitter flavor biting at his throat. Nothing more to be done about learning about the Germans tonight—that much was clear. The sheikhh wouldn't trust him or set up a meeting yet.

But Fahad had said Sheikhh Omar knew of *all* comings and goings in the area—and even beyond. That might be useful too. If Jack had come through here, the sheikhh might know of it.

"I also seek a man. A man who came through Jerusalem asking about two American women. The women are archeologists—one fair and one dark. The dark one bears a tattoo on her forearm."

The sheikhh made no reaction—but the boy carrying coffee did. The tray tipped suddenly, a jerky motion that sent drips onto the rug below him.

Was that fear?

"Out." The sheikhh gave the boy an annoyed glance, and the boy fled with soft, inaudible steps. He looked back at Noah and frowned. "Two American women? What use do you have for them?"

"I do not seek the women," Noah said, but his heart ticked faster. *Could it be possible that the sheikhh has heard of Alice and Kit?* "But the man who searched for them."

The sheikhh's eyes grew darker. "Why?"

"He owes Yusef a debt," Fahad said quickly, the warning in his face to Noah clear—*back down and let me handle this.* Noah had clearly said something alarming. "He came through our village, asking for information. Promised a reward if Yusef asked after the women. He never paid."

Time stretched as the sheikhh considered Fahad's explanation.

A few tense beats of silence held.

At last, the sheikhh nodded. "That is unfortunate." He gave Noah a warning look. "Be careful whom you agree to help, Yusef. Let it be a lesson to you." But the sheikh's eyes said what he did not—Noah's questions worried him. Made him suspicious.

He did not trust Noah.

He might not ever trust him now.

Noah released a slow breath, cautious not to let the men around him see any hint of nerves as Fahad and Sheikhh Omar moved into a quiet conversation.

His eagerness had almost cost him dearly. He'd hoped maybe the sheikh could lead him to Jack, but hadn't considered the possibility that someone other than Jack might have come asking about Kit and Alice.

Then his gaze traveled to the doorway where the servant boy had fled.

Did the boy fear the man who'd come asking about the women?

It couldn't have been Jack the boy feared—Jack would never do anything to make that boy so afraid.

Then who? Prescott? Or one of his cronies?

Either way, the sheikhh knew more than he'd admit. But Noah may have ruined his chances with him already. And if Noah was to learn anything—about the Germans, Prescott, the women, *or* Jack—he'd have to listen twice as carefully and push half as hard in the future.

One slip and the desert could silence him forever.

CHAPTER EIGHTEEN

JACK

The first, fingerlike streaks of hazy morning sunlight had crept into the sky as Jack stepped down from the train carriage into Lydda junction, a few miles southwest of Tel Aviv. A maze of rail lines and stone buildings planted in the middle of Palestine fields, the hub served as a central location to all the major Middle Eastern rail lines—and here they would face British border control again.

The fact that they'd made it through the border agents at Kantara with no issue had relieved some of Jack's worries about Theo and Ruby the night before. The forged paperwork had held up, and neither of them seemed to blink twice or show a bit of discomfort under the scrutiny of the officers.

Then again, they are criminals. They're good actors.

Gravel crunched against Jack's boots on the packed-earth platform, the station seeming to come to life with the train's arrival. They'd traveled overnight from Kantara—much to Theo's dismay—and Jack hadn't slept well. Maybe if it had just been Ruby there, he would have been all right, but Theo's presence made Jack feel as though he needed to always keep one eye open.

Jack clocked the immigration control office near the exit gate—a whitewashed box with a Union Jack limply hanging in the still air. Britain had taken over administration of the region with the Palestinian Mandate after the war, but Jack had been in the region for so long that he still saw the ghosts of the Ottoman officers who once patrolled here. He half expected to turn a corner and see them there, wearing their fez hats.

Not that he missed the Ottomans. But so much had changed for this region in such a short span of time.

"Nervous?" Ruby asked, stepping beside him. She followed the direction of his gaze toward the border agents.

Somewhere beyond the platform, the train for Jerusalem whistled sharply, announcing an imminent departure. Jack rolled his shoulders back, feeling tension coiling in his gut. If the forgery was discovered, or someone recognized him, everything would fall apart fast.

But, no—he wasn't nervous.

"I'm fine," he said, then gave her a tense smile. "You?"

Ruby adjusted her headscarf and grinned. "Would I sound crazy if I said this is actually fun?"

Fun? That's one way to put it.

"Yes," he said with a chuckle. Her Southern accent had remained during their last few interactions—maybe it was her real accent after all. "But I don't mind crazy from time to time."

Theo came up beside his sister and rolled his eyes. "If you two are done making cow eyes at each other, we should get through immigration."

Jack shot him a glare. "You always this punchable first thing in the morning?"

"Always," Ruby said with a laugh. She linked arms with Jack. "Let's go."

She had a warmth to her that startled Jack, especially for someone that had to be used to seeing the uglier side of humanity. And, amid the mix of scents at the train station, she smelled good too. Like roses or something.

He'd forgotten how appealing that could be. He hadn't enjoyed a woman's company for a long time—maybe a bit of penance from his younger years, when he'd tried to forget his love for Kit and bury the horrors of the war in the arms of women who hadn't meant anything at all. He tried to be careful —didn't want to end up with a war baby or in the ward for venereal diseases like so many poor saps had done—but it hadn't really helped that much, either. Short love affairs left him emptier and lonelier than before.

And after Ginger had chosen her marriage to Noah over the one with him, he'd sworn off women altogether.

They drew closer to the immigration officer's station, and Jack focused on the man's bent head. Beside him, Ruby shifted her weight and released his arm, fanning herself with her hand. The morning was still pretty mild—maybe it was jitters making her sweat.

At last, it was Jack's turn. He turned over the forged paperwork, giving the officer a curt smile. The officer barely glanced at him, thumbing through the paperwork with a grim, bored expression. A rubber stamp moments later completed the process, and the officer waved Jack through with a grunt.

Maybe he isn't fond of mornings, either.

Either way, Jack was through. The tension in his chest unknotted slowly as he stepped through to the other side of the station, leaving Ruby and Theo behind him. He oriented himself as he adjusted the strap of the satchel over his shoulder.

Thank goodness that was easy. He'd expected more of a hiccup, to be honest, and maybe it was just that he felt pessimism creeping in on him more the older he got.

He started in the direction of the ticket office, when a male voice behind him called, "Jack Darby."

Jack paused mid-step, his mind jolting at the sound of his name as his heart kicked in his ribs.

Dammit.

Oh, God. If someone recognized me ...

For a heartbeat, he wondered if he'd misheard. A trick of the crowd, the steam, the bleating train whistle. Maybe if he kept moving—

A hand clamped around his elbow, iron hard, killing that hope.

He swung around, pulse snapping with electricity, already trying to think of an excuse. The man in front of him was a stranger—British uniform, polished boots, pistol already drawn.

The man menaced closer. "All right. You're coming with me."

Jack's mouth went dry. Behind the British officer's shoulder, the station blurred—faces, carts, crates. He searched for Ruby, found her halfway through the immigration checkpoint, her eyes wide with horror, her lips forming a frantic *no.*

Don't do it, sweetheart.

But she took a step toward him anyway, desperation in every line of her body.

She's going to give herself away.

Theo grabbed her from behind, gripping her tight enough to restrain her. His name slipped from her lips, just barely loud enough for him to hear. She struggled against him, but he hissed something in her ear that stopped her cold.

Jack's stomach twisted. He could bolt, but with Ruby trying to come after him, she would pay for it—and that was the goddamn problem.

Think. Breathe.

Jack lifted his hands, dimly aware of the stares of other passengers around him as he mustered a slow, hollow laugh.

"No need for dramatics, mate. I'm not armed." That was a lie, of course, but it might settle the officer for now.

The officer's scowl barely moved. "We'll see about that." His eyes flicked to the satchel, then back to Jack. "Move. This way. Keep your hands in front of you, where I can see you."

Jesus H. Christ. He moved forward through the sea of staring strangers. *What a fool you are, Darby. You knew this was coming.*

Breathing slowly, Jack kept his expression hidden, scanning for any opportunity to bolt and run. This wasn't a great place for it—British military police and local authorities were all posted nearby … and he could get shot. But if he didn't run?

He'd get through this. This wasn't the worst scrape he'd been in. So long as he figured a way out of this before the authorities reported this to anyone and Prescott got word of his location, he'd be able to get back on track.

Of course, once authorities *did* report this, Prescott and his men would know his last known location by hours rather than days.

He kept his gaze down as the officer led him to a squat stone building nearby. Holding the door open, he waved Jack through.

The office—if that's what it was—was a simple, stifling box. A single barred cell stood in the corner, a weathered wooden desk beside it. Two rickety chairs—one in front and one behind the desk—rounded out the décor.

The gate to the cell gave a loud groan as the officer opened it. "Give me your bags and get inside."

Jack restrained a sigh, removed the satchel and his kitbag, then slipped into the cell. The cell door slammed shut behind him, followed by the metallic scrape of the key into the lock. Jack turned and shot the officer a look, but he was already sitting and lighting a cigarette.

A minute later, the door to the building opened and Theo strutted inside, smug as a tomcat who'd found the cream. He stopped, gave Jack a long glance, and the corners of his mouth twitched.

He looks ... pleased.

Jack frowned, looking for Ruby to follow, but ... nothing. She didn't appear.

Is this some sort of ridiculous rescue mission?

Theo closed the door, then latched it shut. He tossed a glare at the officer. "Could you have been any more obvious? You were seen, you know."

"And?" The officer blew out a stream of smoke, bored. "I have every right to arrest him."

The exchange had been too familiar.

A sinking feeling spread through Jack's chest, and his hands shifted to the bars of the cell. That irritating grin of Theo made him grind his teeth, his knuckles feeling an old, familiar itch to punch someone. If he hadn't been locked in the cage, he'd have laid the bastard out cold. He set his forehead against the cold metal. "Friend of yours, Theo?"

"Shut up, Darby." Theo approached him with a cool look. "You see, I'm not the one breaking the law here. I crossed the border with my own passport. Ruby too. So the way I see it, if you want to avoid prison, you'll pay up. Now. Every last cent you promised my sister and more. And then we'll go our separate ways."

Theo smirked, then sauntered over to one of Jack's bags and started rifling through it.

Jack ground his teeth. *Not again. This asshole isn't really trying to rob me again—is he?*

But he'd been foolish. He'd shown the depth of his pockets to two thieves.

Just when he'd started to like Ruby a bit more too.

He could kick himself. Like her for what—smelling nice and having a pretty face? He didn't know anything about her.

God, what did I expect? Loyalty from a street thief?

Jack let out a soft, humorless laugh. "You and your sister really ought to take your grift to Hollywood. They'd eat it up."

Theo sneered. "Save your jokes. I don't have to listen to them anymore."

"And you?" Jack ground out to the officer, who just sat there, smoking without a care in the world. "What do you get out of this?"

"Roger will be compensated. And if you cooperate quickly, he'll even let you through the border so you can find another way to get to Baghdad."

Jack dropped his hands from the bars. He wasn't completely caught yet, then, and maybe he could find a way to spin it to his advantage. He didn't have that amount of money on him right now anyway, so he could always make some excuse about needing to contact the bank or someone to disburse the funds.

"Tell me something," he said, his voice low, almost a growl. "Did you rehearse this? Or is it your natural gift to be an insufferable bastard?"

Theo's grin widened, but his eyes hardened. "You're not half as clever as you think, Darby. Are we done exchanging pleasantries? The money. Now."

"What—do you think I have it on me? I'm not the one with cabbage for brains."

A knock at the door was so soft it nearly got buried under the distant whistle of the departing train. Theo's head snapped toward it, eyes narrowing. He unlatched the door an inch.

"Theo," Ruby's voice came, tight but calm. "Let me in."

Then she is in on it.

An acrid feeling crept through Jack's throat, biting with acidity.

"Stay out of this, Ruby."

"You wouldn't make it two seconds without me. Now open the door. I'm not going to ask again."

A dark look crossed Theo's face, and he scowled. "I told you to stay back."

Ruby pushed her way through, silk-smooth. No fear in her eyes, just that infuriating calm. She didn't glance at Jack but went straight for the officer, and her voice dipped low and sugar-sweet. "Roger. Still crooked as ever, hmm?"

Roger stood, flustered, cigarette dangling between his fingers. "Ruby—this wasn't part of—"

She stepped in close. Too close. A lover's distance. Her arms wound around his neck.

Jack's heart stuttered. *Don't do this, Ruby. Don't tell me you're playing me too.*

"Always a pleasure, Ruby," Roger said, his arms around her waist.

But then her hand slipped free, and Roger went stiff. As she drew back, Jack saw the reason: Ruby had pulled a Derringer out and now held it at his throat, silver glinting in the dim light.

Well, that's interesting.

Theo swore. "What the hell—"

"Not a word, Theo," Ruby snapped. "Or I swear, I'll blow Roger's throat out right here. He's about as loyal as a flea—aren't you, darling?"

Roger choked on a half-formed protest.

"What are you doing?" Theo demanded, taking a step closer.

"Uh-uh," Ruby warned, digging the gun deeper into Roger's skin. "Not a step closer, darling idiot brother. I'm warning you."

"I'm doing this for you," Theo growled, his teeth baring. "For *us.*"

Jack almost barked with laughter, his brain spinning. "You mean she's not taking your orders on this one, Theo? Sounds like poor planning."

"Be quiet, Jack, I'm trying to save you here. Don't make me second-guess my choice."

Jack couldn't stop the low laugh that rasped out of him. He met Ruby's eyes through the bars. Something fierce glinted there—fierce, reckless, and true.

Maybe I've got her wrong. Maybe I haven't. But at least she's aiming the gun at the right bastard.

"Keys and gun," she ordered Roger. He fumbled them free, and Ruby tossed them to Jack.

"Let yourself out."

Jack sorted through the seven keys, trying to guess the right one.

"Hurry up, old man. We don't have time to waste."

Jack's grin felt rusty but good as he tested the jangling keys on the lock. "I'm moving, sweetheart."

Theo still came closer. "Ruby—"

"I will shoot you and Roger if it comes down to it, Theo." Ruby glared at him. "I'm not letting you ruin this for me again. You're threatening the loss of the best-paying job I ever landed. And maybe that means nothing to you, but I haven't forgotten why I'm doing all this—have you?"

Theo stopped short, glowering at her. "No, I haven't forgotten. Why do you think I'm trying to buy us some time? It could be weeks before we get back from Baghdad. Every day we lose, we will never get back."

The right key turned in the lock at last, and Jack pushed the gate open. He moved to retrieve his bags as Ruby nodded toward the cell. "Roger, in the cell."

Roger sputtered as he took slow steps toward it, his face turning a deep shade of red as he went inside. "This isn't what we agreed to, Theo."

"Don't worry. You and Theo will have plenty of time to

discuss what went wrong together," Ruby said, now aiming the handgun at her brother. "You get in that cell too."

Theo blanched.

Jack stood, replacing his bags over his shoulder as he watched the scene unfold. He hadn't been expecting this from her—and now that she was doing it, he wasn't sure what to think. He should have been angry. He *was* angry. But, even more, he felt the bitter taste of relief.

She'd done this—for him? For the money? *Hell if I know.*

But she'd done it.

For the first time in days, he felt that old battlefield clarity slip back in. He met Ruby's eyes. *Don't you dare break my trust now. Just don't.*

"Ruby, don't do this," Theo said, lifting his hands. He didn't move toward the cell but instead went closer to her. "You wouldn't shoot me anyway."

"Will you still pay me if I help you?" Ruby asked, her gaze flicking to Jack.

He nodded. "Every cent."

She lifted the gun higher, aiming for her brother's head. "Then I guess you'll just have to find out if I'll shoot, Theo. Now, in the cell. And not a word to anyone about Jack. Or else I'll make sure you and Roger pay for it."

Theo's glare was filled with resentment and fury, but he did what she'd said.

"Lock them in, Jack," Ruby said, still aiming the gun toward the two men. "Now."

"You don't have to tell me twice, sweetheart. I'm not stupid enough to question a woman with a gun." Jack hurried to the cell.

"You need me, Ruby!" Theo called out. "You always need me."

She laughed, soft and sad. "I used to."

Jack shoved the cell gate shut with a final clang. "You're all heart, Theo. Really." He leaned in, voice dropping to a conspiratorial murmur. "You know what the difference between us is? I'd die for my sister, but you'd sell out yours for pocket change."

Theo lunged for the bars, but Jack had already pocketed the keys.

Without waiting for Ruby, Jack started for the door. She was only steps behind him, already storing her gun in her handbag as they stepped out into the busy sunlight-filled station. It hit Jack like a slap—sharp and blinding after the dim cell.

Ruby grabbed his hand, tugging him into the blinding stream of people.

"Do I want to know if this is your first time holding up a customs officer?"

Her laugh was breathless, wild. "Buy me dinner in Baghdad, and maybe I'll tell you." Then she winked. "You said you like crazy."

A shout from Roger behind them made them exchange a look. "Hurry!" Ruby said. "This way."

Am I making a mistake?

But what choice did he have? She'd saved him from that cell. And left her brother in his place.

He followed Ruby toward the rail line. "I didn't expect you to be my guardian angel today," Jack admitted, taking long strides to match her jogging pace.

"Yeah, well, I made you a promise." Ruby shrugged. "I'm not all bad, you know."

God, how I hope that's true.

She was heading toward the train for Jerusalem. "I grabbed us tickets while Roger locked you up," Ruby said, thrusting one into his hand. "I know it's not what we planned, but you told Theo about Haifa. And this train is leaving now. It will buy us some time."

Jack swallowed hard, still unable to shake the feeling of distrust, despite everything.

But Ruby had brought him this far.

And the screaming whistle of the train told him he didn't have time to make a different choice. Roger and Theo might have already been discovered.

Ruby slipped her arm into his once again. "You owe me a hell of a bonus."

Jack leaned close enough to catch that rose-scented warmth. "I'll consider it. But, next time, don't make me like you if you plan on selling me down the river."

She laughed—a wild, bright sound that cut through the chaos of the station.

Then they ran for the train.

CHAPTER NINETEEN

ALEX

The abandoned train coach sat forgotten at the edge of Kantara's rail yard, its faded green paint peeling like sunburnt skin. Alex squinted as he hurried toward it, keeping a close eye out for watching eyes, even at this early hour.

The savory scent of warm lamb drifted from the *sambouseks* Alex had carefully wrapped in a newspaper after filching them from a sleepy street vendor. Sweat trickled down his neck as he climbed the warped steps of the coach, careful not to let the rusted door squeal.

Inside, the air was cooler. Broken windows let in the grit of the desert wind and the battered seats were splintered and broken.

They'd slipped out of Port Said by the skin of their teeth—catching a midnight train south along the desert line, hidden in the cheap third-class compartment while the men of the ship searched the city behind them. Now, Kantara was just another stopover before Cairo. If they could reach his uncle's house in Old Cairo, they'd be safe. He hoped.

He held his breath as he slipped further inside the coach, half expecting her to be gone. He hadn't wanted to leave Ivy alone, but it was better than taking her with him. Ivy had a way of standing out in a crowd. She didn't know how to sneak around like Alex did, either—which meant that she was more likely to get them caught.

His footsteps echoed softly against the wooden floorboards, then Ivy's head popped up from behind a broken seat in the back. She gave him a relieved smile. "What took so long? You've been gone ages."

"I was trying to find a wineskin so we could have water, but I didn't," Alex said with a rueful look. "There's a spigot close by. We can get some there if we need." He stopped in front of her and knelt, offering the newspaper bundle. "And good news—breakfast. Here, I got us one each."

Ivy pushed her long, dark hair from her shoulders, eyelashes fluttering as she took the food hesitantly. She sank back onto the floor and unwrapped it, then gave a suspicious look at the fried pastry. "What is it?"

"A meat pie." Alex discarded the newspaper from his own, half reading the headlines upside down. He liked the way the neat columns of letters stacked, his brain appreciating the order of letters and numbers. But he was too hungry to think about that and he tore his gaze away, then bit into the pastry. The taste made his stomach growl, and he glanced at Ivy, hoping she hadn't heard. "I *borrowed* them from a street vendor."

Ivy bit her lip, looking guiltily at the stolen food for a moment longer before she took a hesitant bite. The taste must have done away with her worry—another, larger bite followed.

"Don't you feel bad?" Ivy asked a few minutes later. "Stealing things from people?"

"*Borrowing*," Alex corrected. "As soon as I can get my hands on some money—legitimately—I'll find a way to pay the vendor. Even if it takes a while. I never forget a face."

Ivy rolled her eyes. "You're far too optimistic for someone who was just shot at yesterday. I still think we need to turn ourselves over to the police. They'll be able to help us better than anyone and keep us safe from those men. They might still be following us, you know."

"They're not," Alex said confidently. "We lost them in Port Said." That, he was sure of. The men from the ship had given them a good chase at first, but they'd managed to get away and stay out of sight until nightfall.

Alex polished off his pastry and looked regretfully at the discarded newspaper. He should have taken a few more. A fly buzzed near the closest broken window, the air inside thick with the scent of warm, dusty wood and the ghost of old coal smoke. The whole coach smelled like rusted iron and secrets lost to time. "Our safest bet is to go to my Uncle Alastair's house in Old Cairo. My father always taught Clara and me that if anything happened to us while we were in Egypt, we should go to him."

"But this isn't the type of situation your father was referring to," Ivy said, frowning. "Sure, Uncle Alastair might be able to help if you came up against an antiquities smuggler—but not kidnappers. This is serious, Alex. Who better to help us than the police? Or the consulate. They'll protect us. It's their job."

Alex ran his fingertip over a grease smudge on the newspaper. "You really think the same people who waved your kidnappers through customs will keep us safe? Those men who took you didn't look worried about getting caught—they looked connected. Men like that don't get caught. They get paid not to. And then they pay others to keep quiet about it."

Ivy finished her pastry and leaned back on her hands. "I guess you're right."

Frowning, Alex let his eyes drift onto the inked words of the paper—*The Egyptian Gazette*, actually—which meant the words were in familiar English. "I just don't understand why they took you in the first place."

"They didn't mean to take me," Ivy admitted softly. She swallowed hard, her eyes downcast. "They thought I was Clara for a while."

Oh.

That hit Alex hard, like a fist in the stomach. Outside, a train whistle howled—distant, but sharp and haunting.

His little sister.

He frowned. They would have had their hands full if they'd taken Clara. No way Clara would have let them drag her into the car or a train without kicking and screaming the whole time. The men wouldn't have known that, though. They'd probably tried to take Clara because they thought she was easier to kidnap than him.

A sick feeling bit his throat.

Maybe it was better that they'd grabbed Ivy. Who knows what those men might have done to keep Clara quiet. They could have hurt her. Ivy's cooperativeness might have earned her their mercy.

Not that he'd tell Ivy that.

"Well, don't worry, we'll find a way to get back home soon," he said, offering her a reassuring grin. "Once we're in Cairo, we'll be safe. It's only a few hours away from here by train—I'll go out again in another hour. Disguise myself as a local boy and beg for *baksheesh* from tourists. Hopefully I can get enough to get us both tickets by the end of the day."

"I'll disguise myself too. Two of us begging will get us the money faster."

Alex grimaced. "Maybe. It's hard work, Ivy."

"I don't mind hard work." Her brow furrowed and she scanned his face a moment longer. A defeated slump settled on her shoulders. "That's not it. You think I'll give us away—don't you? That I don't have what it takes to survive this world." A grim, determined look flashed in her face and she twisted the hem of her skirt, knuckles white. "I'll have you know, I was thinking of running away."

Alex furrowed his brow. "Running away ... from the men who kidnapped you?"

"No," she said, not meeting his eyes.

He didn't understand. "From me?"

"No, silly. From *home.*" She continued twisting her skirt in her hand. The garment was far dirtier than anything Alex had ever seen her wear. *Which must be killing her. She's always been like a porcelain doll.*

He almost let that last thought distract him enough that he didn't fully comprehend what she'd said. And then ... it hit him. "You were thinking of running away from home?" He gave her an incredulous look.

Never—not once—would he ever have imagined Ivy would consider running away from home.

Clara, sure. She liked her adventures just as much as Alex did.

And Alex regularly hopped on trains and rode his bike past the limits of where his parents had deemed acceptable.

But *Ivy?*

She had a strong stomach, to be sure—she'd been following Mama around in the hospital for years, helping where she could. She had a genuine interest in medicine and science, even though her own mother likely saw it as a passing hobby.

But beyond that?

Ivy was the one whom Clara and Alex always had to prod to accompany them for anything that might earn her a scolding. When she returned from her grandparents' or Aunt Angelica's house, the clothes and things she came back with were so expensive that Alex worried about walking within ten feet of her and getting her dirty.

Alex's startled silence must have bothered her, though. She frowned, meeting his eyes, then said in a rush, "Mama is thinking of sending me to Roedean next term. For the foreseeable future, actually. And—I don't want to go, Alex. I want to stay home. With Clara … and …" A lump moved in her throat as she swallowed, still holding his gaze. She didn't finish the thought.

The news hurt, somewhere deep in his chest, but he gave her a stiff smile. "Roedean's a good school, though, Ivy. It'll open lots of opportunities for you."

She sighed. "Opportunities? For what—a gilded cage?" She shook her head bitterly. "Mama doesn't think I know about it— she hasn't even told me yet. Mama wants me to be some society lady, sit pretty for the family fortune. And the thought of it makes me feel sick."

"There are worse things than being handed a family fortune and an excellent education," Alex said wryly, lifting a brow. "You're luckier than you realize. Papa may have done a good job teaching me all he knows, but I won't get into a good university without a scholarship—"

"Which you'll earn. Easily."

"But that's not the point. The point is that my educational opportunities are limited. Especially right now. Do you know what I wouldn't give to be able to—"

"I should have known you of all people wouldn't understand." Ivy turned her body away from his. "All you ever think about is your books—and how to get your hands on more of them. That's all you care about. Education."

He stared at her, mouth open, trying to understand her.

She's so incomprehensible to me.

She frustrated him in a way he couldn't quite verbalize. Of

course he cared about books. And learning. And why shouldn't he? It had gotten him out of more than one scrape before—including helping free her from the men who'd kidnapped her.

But he sensed he'd hurt her feelings somehow. He didn't know what he'd said that had bothered her so much. Going over it, everything had been perfectly logical. Roedean was a good school. She'd be a fool not to go. "If you think I should have told you that running away is a better option than getting an education, I don't know what to tell you," he said at last. "Besides, you wouldn't last two minutes as a runaway. Though maybe Roedean would be wasted on you."

Ivy's face paled, then outrage flowed into her eyes and she stood, fury in her stance. "Why, because you think you're so much smarter than me? I was doing just fine on my own in that ship before you came along, you know. Maybe they kidnapped me, but I wasn't stupid about it either. I took the opportunity to listen in on their conversations when they thought I was sleeping. And I heard lots that I can use to get them in trouble once we get to the *police*. Which is where we should be going."

"I don't think I'm smarter than you," Alex said lazily. He stretched his legs out, nonplussed by her reaction. "We're equally intelligent. You just don't bother trying to learn more than the necessary about anything. And you don't apply yourself. If you did, you'd *want* to go to Roedean."

"Oh, I don't even know what I was thinking telling you about any of this." Ivy stamped her feet, turning around in the rusty coach as though looking for an exit. A shaft of sunlight spilled through a hole in the far corner of one side, revealing glimmering cobwebs.

Why is this making her so upset?

"What did you expect, Ivy? You're like a sister to me. If you tell me nonsense about preferring to run away over going to school, I'm going to tell you the truth. I'd do the same thing if Clara came whining to me like this."

His words made her stiffen. She turned back to him, slowly, then gave him a long, hard stare as if scrutinizing him for the first time. Her hands flexed into fists at her sides, as though she was contemplating pummeling him, then she relaxed them, a defeated, sad look darkening her eyes.

"Why do I bother with you?" she whispered, then sat once more, further away than before.

"Because we've been friends since birth," he said with a pointed look that he hoped would calm her for once and for all. Then he grinned. "And I can be awfully persuasive. And charming."

Despite her apparent anger, he seemed to break through to her resistance, and a soft smile tugged at the corner of her mouth. "Charming is one word for it." She sighed and scooted closer to him. Her hand brushed against the discarded newspaper on the floor between them, her fingertips traveling over the letters. His mind traced the ragged edges of the words without meaning to, taking in each letter. Little details no one else noticed—that was how his brain worked.

A single beam of sunlight cut through a crack overhead, catching on Ivy's hair and the newsprint in her lap. Dust motes danced in the light, drifting like ash in the stillness.

They sat in silence for a few minutes, then she drew a shallow breath. "Alex … I need to tell you—"

"Wait a second," Alex said, tugging the newspaper from her. His gaze had snagged on the lines right where a sliver of sun hit the ink. His brain caught the hitch before he knew what it was —a hiccup in the neat rows of type, like a wrong note in a melody he'd always known by heart.

She gave him a startled look. "What?"

He brought the paper closer to his face, eyes narrowing.

Letters lined up like obedient soldiers—but every fourth one stood out to him, breaking the formation, deliberate in its defiance.

What on earth?

He counted under his breath, heart pounding now, hot and wild in his chest. He almost thought he'd imagined it. But, no—there it was. Clear as day.

A null cipher, written right into the article. Out in the open where no one would think to look. Patterns were second nature to him. This one wasn't a mistake.

He looked at Ivy—her startled face, the flecks of pastry on her skirt, the longing for a safe world to run back to—then blinked away, back toward the cipher.

He pulled each fourth letter, but he had already figured out the message before he finished spelling it.

His throat went dry.

HELP ME

CHAPTER TWENTY

JACK

The weather-beaten motorcar rumbled down the road from Jericho, rocks kicking up under the tires, a cloud of dust billowing into the midday air behind them, leaving a trail. From the backseat, Jack looked over his shoulder, adjusting the scarf over his mouth to keep himself from inhaling the dust. Ruby had similarly ducked her face behind her scarf when they'd started out, and she kept her head down beside him.

No one appeared to be following them for now.

Good. Jack let out a slow breath, but the tension that had coiled his shoulders since Lydda station stayed locked tight. Ruby seemed convinced Theo would let the matter drop and realize he'd lost, but Jack didn't have that sort of confidence— Theo didn't seem like a man who liked losing face. And even if Theo kept quiet, Roger—the customs officer they'd locked in that cell—would have to tell someone what happened. British authorities didn't shrug off forged papers and smugglers at the edge of Palestine.

Behind them, the motorcar's rattling engine drowned out

the hush of wind in the low hills. The desert heat blurred the horizon ahead, a wavering mirage of freedom that felt miles out of reach.

Everything about this trip feels haphazard. So dangerous.

The incident at Lydda station had solidified one thing—Jack couldn't risk going to Fahad for help. If Roger reported Jack this close to Jerusalem, anyone looking for him would likely approach his known friends and allies first. He'd never wanted to drag Fahad into this in the first place. Now it was impossible.

The motorcar slowed. Ahead of them, pulled to the side of the road, a goods lorry waited, two locals standing beside it. Waiting.

The driver of the motorcar parked behind the lorry and killed the engine. Jack flicked a glance at Ruby, who sat straighter and gave Jack a tense smile. This was all part of the new plan—have smugglers take them across the Allenby Bridge to get through the official checkpoints into Transjordan, then travel with them to Amman, where they could take Bedouin tribal routes to Baghdad.

And it was, quite possibly, the most dangerous route to Baghdad imaginable.

Besides drug smugglers and desert raiders, they'd have to trust their Bedouin guides to get them to Baghdad—and while Jack had spent plenty of time with the Bedouin, he didn't know any of the tribes between here and Baghdad.

This is when Noah would have been worth his weight in gold.

The smugglers opened up the back of the lorry for Ruby and Jack. Wooden crates filled the back, stacked amidst a thick layer of straw that reeked of barnyard animals. One smuggler led them toward the back of the lorry and pointed to a large wooden crate half covered with a grey blanket. He opened the crate. "In," he said gruffly in Arabic.

Ruby paled as Jack translated. "Does he mean both of us?"

Jack grimaced and asked the smuggler, who nodded.

Ruby released a shaky breath. "This might not be the best time to mention it—but I'm a bit claustrophobic."

"It'll only be for a little while," Jack said in a reassuring voice. He offered his hand out to her. "Until we've gone over the bridge and gotten through the checkpoint, I'm sure."

A beat of silence passed, and Ruby stared at his proffered hand warily. At last she took it, then went toward the crate with him. Jack climbed inside, relieved to find it empty and lined with a sheet. The scent of overly dry wood and some sort of fuel tickled his nostrils, and he wrinkled his nose as he tried to settle as comfortably as he could. He was too tall to stretch out —his knees would have to be bent, and that would get painful fast.

God, I hope we're in here only a short time.

Ruby climbed in after him, and she trembled as she lay beside him. He stretched an arm out, letting her curl into the crook of his arm and rest against his shoulder. "Th-this is cozy," she managed, taking short, shallow breaths.

"Eh, we'll be fine." He fought the temptation to feel badly for her. This was part of the job, after all, and she was getting well paid for it.

A pitchfork tossed straw on top of them, and Ruby froze. "Are they going to bury us?" she yelped.

A few bits of straw drifted down his collar as sweat trickled behind Jack's neck. The air grew staler and, somewhere by his ear, a winged insect buzzed. "Cover us, it would seem." Jack's hand tightened around her. "Close your eyes. Try to breathe. Deep breaths."

"If I breathe deeply, I'm going to sneeze," she hissed, her breath growing shallower.

A blanket covered them fully then, blocking most of the light from above them, followed by more straw—and then something with some weight. With each addition, Ruby's breathing became less steady.

When the crate lid closed, she shook, and in the dim light from the gaps between the crate slats, Jack caught sight of her tightly closed eyes.

"You're doing well," he said gently. The gate to the lorry slammed shut.

She gritted her teeth. "The things I do for money," she said with bitter self-deprecation. "My family better appreciate this someday."

Her family?

Despite the fact that they'd been traveling together for a couple of days, he knew so little about her—he wasn't even sure if she'd given him her real name. But this was going to be a long trip through the checkpoint if she didn't calm down some. They might not even make it *through* the checkpoint. The officials were likely to check the cargo, and her panic might give them away.

"Where are you from, Ruby?" he asked in a low voice. The engine of the lorry rumbled.

"Y-you really feel l-like talking now?"

"Could help. Besides, it's better than thinking about how my legs are cramping already."

His words caused her to shift, her knees bumping against his thigh. "T-Texas," she whispered after a moment. "My f-folks had a farm in Bulverde."

Texas.

He'd spent plenty of time there—his grandfather had lived there, near Dallas. And Jack had lived in Arizona for a while, before that. "They still there?"

Ruby shook her head. The crate creaked with the movement of the lorry. As the vehicle dipped, a dull thud from the cargo near them made Ruby flinch. After another few beats of silence, she said, "N-no. My parents died of yellow fever, and we went to live with my grandparents."

"Did they live in Texas too?"

She sniffled, then sneezed. "Sorry—the hay …" She turned her head toward him, eyes open now, but she was close enough that he couldn't really meet her gaze without having to close the eye closest to her.

He squinted at her and offered a smile. "You okay?"

She gulped a breath. "Trying. Keep talking."

"So are your grandparents in Texas?"

She shook her head. "They lived in Germany. Near a village named Oberstdorf." She shifted again, clearly uncomfortable. "My mother was Catholic, father was Jewish. His family is from Munich. My grandparents opposed their marriage, so they ran away to America together. All of the rest of my family is still in Germany."

He did his best not to react physically.

She's German?

He didn't want to make any assumptions of her loyalties—during the war, afterward, or now—but the thought was an unsettling one. He chose a slightly safer question instead. "So are you Catholic or Jewish?"

"Catholic," she said in a quiet voice. Her shaking had settled. "I know what you're thinking—"

"Oh, do you?" He wasn't even sure *he* knew what he was thinking.

She nodded. "You're wondering if I'm a Nazi, aren't you?" She gave him a bitter smile. "Well, I'm not. I'm expat now. Theo, Felix, and I were all part of a traveling theater troupe, and we were out of the country when the Nazis took over after the election last March. Our show was considered too political—they made it clear we couldn't go back."

Whatever relief that brought to him was quickly overshadowed by the unsettling realization that what Ruby had been hiding all along wasn't just a seedy criminal past. *Oh no.*

He remembered her words when they'd escaped Theo in Lydda station, the dots suddenly connecting for him. *"I haven't forgotten why I'm doing all this—have you?"* she'd said.

He cleared his throat. "And your family?"

Ruby sighed, and for a moment only the sound of the rocks tumbling beneath the lorry's tires filled the space. "Visas are hard to get right now. Emigration is getting harder, especially for the Jewish side of my family. They're trying to go to Palestine. There's a man we met—he specializes in smuggling people out, but the cost keeps going up and we have a big family."

As the puzzle pieces fell into place, Jack's throat tightened.

Of course. That's why she's here. Every stolen pound, every lie—all to buy freedom for people waiting on the other side.

Guilt pressed down on his chest, cold and heavy. He'd leaned on that desperation. Driven her to do this. No denying it now.

"I don't want you to feel sorry for me."

"Not sure if I can help that, Ruby."

"I chose this. Maybe there were better ways. Less morally depraved. But money isn't the easiest to come by when people only look at you as a pretty face and your only talent is pretending to be someone you're not."

"I don't know—I hear some of those Hollywood girls do pretty well."

She chuckled bitterly. "They don't have a deadline hanging over their head. I'm terrified something horrible is coming, and I've not only got to get my family out before it's too late, I have to find a way to convince them to leave. All without being able to go back home freely. Why do you think I know smuggling networks so well, Jack? I wasn't just blowing smoke, you know."

His fingertips tightened against her, and he was instantly

more aware of how close they were together in this crate, their bodies stuck so tight that they were sweating. Not romantic in any way. But still—he couldn't help but feel more ... *exposed?* No, that wasn't it.

He wasn't really sure.

But he did know one thing—the thought of her sneaking into Germany didn't settle well with him. "If the Nazis have made it clear you're *persona non grata* and they catch you there, they might ..."

Jack didn't finish. Truth was, everything about what the Nazis were doing with their political prisoners was just rumor. Speculation based off intelligence that no one was talking about and Jack had only heard from the brief conversations he'd had with Noah on the way to France.

"They opened a camp for political prisoners in Dachau last year," Ruby said. "I'd probably end up some place like that. One of my cousins in Munich whom we managed to get out with his wife and son and bring to Palestine—he said they're sending political threats to the camp."

Jack's fingertips brushed against her wrist, searching for her hand. He slipped his hand into hers, words failing him.

He knew what it was like to feel so desperate to help someone he loved that he'd do just about anything. *That's why I'm here.*

And he couldn't judge her for it. The Nazis worried him— and he didn't have family there confronting their erratic behavior. "What did your cousin say about how things have changed there?"

Ruby shuddered. "It's bad, Jack. Especially for the Jews. They've been cut off from the civil service, the law, academia ... and there are nationwide boycotts against Jewish businesses. President Hindenburg is nearly useless in his opposition to the Nazi policies. My Catholic family is faring better, but even some of them are fearful. And my siblings—there are five of us. Three of them are still in Oberstdorf."

"I wish you'd told me this sooner," Jack said as he moved his free hand up to shift some of the straw away from his face. More straw fell to take the place of the piece he'd moved.

The roar of the engine filled the tiny space, the bumping of the road making the crates around them sound like living, breathing things offering squeaks of conversation and complaints about the discomfort of the journey.

"Would it really have made a difference? You're doing this for your sister, right? Besides." She sniffed. "I'm not a charity case. I did my best to try to get help for my family where I could—no one cared. Or they don't believe my family is in danger." She shook her head bitterly. "Not even some of my family believe they're in danger. My uncle joined the Nazi party. Another one told me, right before I left—'*You really think they'll make life worse for us? We fought for Germany. We're brothers.*'"

She released an angry, choked laugh. "Brothers. Until they decide you're not. You can't help me, Jack—only your money can. And, let's face it, you wouldn't have given it to a girl who robbed you at gunpoint, would you?"

He winced. She wasn't wrong. If she'd told him this bleeding-heart story in Cairo, he probably wouldn't have believed her. She was a good actress, after all, and she *was* a thief.

And now?

What reason does she have to lie? He was going to pay her if she got him to Baghdad and back safely. Her motivation to tell him all this was substantially less … complicated now.

Which means she's probably telling the truth.

The lorry dipped over a rut in the road, sending a jolt through them. The squeal of the brakes cut through the stillness.

Her story sounded genuine. A lie of that detail would be hard to keep straight. "So why are you telling me now?"

"Because you asked." She sighed. "Besides, what else are we going to do while stuck in a tomb on a way to a foreign checkpoint where we could be detained and jailed if caught?" She let out a laugh that hinted at her continued lack of calm at their current surroundings.

"That's true." He squeezed her hand, trying to offer her some reassurance.

"Enough about me. Tell me about you. Or your sister. What was she doing in Baghdad?"

He wasn't sure how much he was ready or willing to share with Ruby yet, but she'd revealed some deeply personal details. If he avoided doing the same, she might be hurt by it.

"Truth is, I haven't talked to my sister in twenty years." He scratched at his neck, trying to ignore how badly his legs were starting to cramp. "She and I had a falling out around then, and we haven't talked since. It wasn't until recently that a mutual acquaintance approached me and told me she'd been working at a dig in Ur and gone missing."

"Oh." Disappointment was thick in her voice. "Then you're not close." The fact seemed to bother her. "Why did you fall out?"

Why? Jack didn't want to think about it. He didn't want to remember how he'd pleaded with Alice, begged her to see reason.

"She started working for a man I consider to be my enemy. A real ruthless, amoral son of a bitch. And she knew—she knew—the only reason he wanted her to work for him was to stop me from trying to make sure he met the justice of a firing squad."

"Stop you? How?"

"Because if I ever did anything to him, he'd make sure Alice —that's my sister—paid for it. Whether he was dead or alive. So she was his insurance. And, despite knowing that, she chose to work for him anyway."

Ruby cleared her throat. "It sounds like she was trying to protect you."

What?

He laughed skeptically. "How would that protect me?"

"I don't know. But maybe you're not seeing the full picture. Maybe he was threatening her too. Were you two close?"

The idea that Alice might have ignored everything Jack had told her to protect him wasn't a new one, but he didn't want to think about it either. Alice had a *choice.* Jack would have taken care of them—the same way he always had. He would have taken her to the other side of the earth and gotten as far from Prescott's reach as he could, same way that Kit had.

In the end, Alice's choice had been to ignore Jack's pleas.

He gave a gruff nod. "She was one of the only people I gave a damn about. I would have done just about anything for her."

"Then that's probably what it was. Your enemy, whoever he is, must have used her love for you to convince her to work for him. Listen, I speak from experience here. I'm willing to do just about anything for my family. Lie, cheat, steal. Let myself be plastered to a sweaty man and smuggled into Iraq. Nothing is beneath me if I can save them."

He chuckled, her joke breaking the tension. "Hey, I bathed a couple days ago. You're no less sweaty than I am."

"Yes, but I'm a lot prettier to look at."

"You don't think I'm pretty?" He smiled. "That might be the meanest thing you've said yet, Ruby W—" He paused. "Is Wilson your actual last name?"

"Hmm ... don't you think I've shared enough secrets, Jack Darby?"

"So the answer is no."

The squeak of the brakes cut into their conversation, and

Jack twisted his head, more alert to their surroundings now. They must be approaching the Allenby Bridge. Which meant they were a stone's throw from Transjordan.

One step closer to getting to Baghdad.

Of course, to get there, they still needed to leave the Jordan Valley for Amman, then face the treacherous route through the desert.

Now he knew something that would probably haunt him every mile to Baghdad: this wasn't just his life or Ruby's on the line. Every person counting on her—her siblings, cousins, and more—they were all at risk. And the desert didn't care who needed saving.

CHAPTER TWENTY-ONE

JACK

The crack of gunfire jolted Jack from a hazy dream and he startled, only to find himself unable to move. At his side, Ruby stiffened. "What was that?" she hissed.

She was answered by the hideous screech of the lorry's brakes, followed by a sickening bounce, then a swerve.

Then the lorry stopped. Shouts sounded outside.

Desert bandits—or worse.

"Stay quiet," Jack whispered, the shouts growing closer. "Not a word until I say so."

For the first time since they'd crawled into this infernal crate, the claustrophobia clenched Jack like a vise around his ribs. He could barely reach the pistol at his waist, let alone prepare for whatever was out there. And even if he got out of the crate, he doubted he'd be able to stand—his legs were numb from being bent in one position for so long.

Just how long had it been?

He checked his wristwatch—six hours. The smugglers had stopped in Amman for about a half hour to refuel, and Ruby and Jack had taken a short break to eat some stale bread, sip water, and relieve themselves. But they'd had to hide directly there-after, where they were to remain until Azraq Castle.

They had to be getting closer to the ancient Roman fortress … and dusk.

The splintering crackle of more gunfire drew his focus, closer now, followed by the distinct shattering of glass.

Dammit. We're sitting ducks here.

Then … silence.

Ruby's breath came quickly, her heart pounding so hard that Jack felt it against his shirtfront. He hadn't noticed when she'd curled her body into his, but now her breath was warm against his neck, her hands shaking.

Footsteps crunched against the gravel, drawing closer to the back of the lorry. The engine went dead. A few voices—two, maybe three men? Jack couldn't tell. He'd be deluding himself if he tried to make estimates based on such limited information.

A hinge squeaked—the gate of the lorry being lowered. Then a hard thud of steps as someone jumped into the back.

A nearby male voice—not on the lorry, but not far either—called something indiscernible. Jack knew Arabic, of course, but dialects sometimes stumped him. He was more familiar with the Egyptian Arabic, but here in the Jordanian desert, who knew what they might speak? Once again, he regretted having gone his separate way from his friend. Noah could navigate his way through Arabic, Kurdish, Assyrian Aramaic, and even Turkish with ease, even if he wasn't fluent—but that's what made him so invaluable to British Intelligence.

Jack's heartbeat thudded in his ears as steps drew closer. What had happened to their smugglers? If the bandits were on the lorry, Jack couldn't imagine it had gone well for them. A nauseating acid rose up his throat. They might be criminals—hell, they might have even been on this route smuggling something other than Ruby and him—but if they'd died, their deaths still fell upon his shoulders.

How many people was Jack willing to sacrifice to get Alice and Kit?

And that was *if* this one lead he had to Kit was a good one.

Ruby's words from earlier in this journey rang in his head. *"Nothing is beneath me if I can save them."*

Did he feel the same? Was he willing to do *anything* to get to Kit and Alice?

Beside them, the bandits had started sifting through the cargo. A crate was smashed open, contents spilled out. Jack breathed slowly, considering his options.

If they opened this crate, he'd only have seconds to act.

His fingers curled around the handle of his pistol. From the spaces between the crate, he caught sight of the bandit standing only inches away, his back to the crate.

Did Jack dare risk moving now? If he shot through the crate slats, he could wound the man.

But it also would call the attention of the bandit's accomplices.

Ruby trembled harder, and Jack slid a hand to the nape of her neck, cradling her head gently. He wished he could reassure her. Give her some sense of hope.

I never should have dragged her out here for this.

The bandit turned toward the crate and the top cracked open, as though pried with a crowbar. The blanket above them shifted, just slightly, and Jack held his breath, his fingers steady around the pistol.

A voice came from the side of the lorry again, in a harsh, rapid tone.

The bandit retreated, boots thumping against the bed of the lorry, then dropping as he jumped down.

A moment later, the engine roared to life again. A door

slammed, and the lorry lurched forward. *Dammit. Who's driving? The thieves?*

Jack didn't hesitate—he shoved the covering above them away, straw scratching his face and hands as he sat up in the crate. The outside air rushed in, sweet and fresh, a relief to his senses.

Ruby pushed herself up too. "What happened?" She gasped in fresh air, physically relieved despite the circumstances.

Despite the cramp in his thighs, Jack climbed from the crate and scrambled toward the still-open gate. Even from here he could see the prone bodies of the two smugglers who'd driven them from the Allenby Bridge.

Dead. Left as food for jackals.

"Luck. Or something. We need to get off this lorry," Jack snapped over the sound of the moving vehicle. He moved back to Ruby and held out a hand. "Hurry up."

"Get off?" Ruby shook her head, dragging a piece of straw from her hair. "They'll see us, Jack—they might come back for us and kill us. Besides, how are we supposed to survive in the desert without a truck?"

"We can't be far from Azraq Castle ... maybe there we can find help."

"Help isn't losing our transportation," Ruby said, a stubborn glint in her eyes.

At least she'd gained some of her spirit back now that she wasn't stuck in the close quarters of the crate. He could work with that. Her determination and grit would make all the difference in the world here.

Jack faced the front of the lorry and clenched his jaw. His days of crazy acrobatics seemed so long in the past—yet he'd managed to jump from a train in France.

Maybe it was time to try to regain some of the person he'd been before. Test his own mettle.

He pulled a loaded pistol from his bag and handed it to Ruby.

"Stay here until the lorry stops," he said. "If anyone other than me comes through that back gate, shoot them. Don't hesitate. Shoot to kill, Ruby."

She nodded, taking the gun from him.

He paused a moment longer, searching her bright blue eyes, wishing he could think of something worth saying to this brave woman.

Instead, he winked. "Try not to miss me too much. See you soon, kid."

He didn't wait for a good-bye from her before he moved toward the open gate. The desert was a blur of orange and beige dust in front of him and he inched toward the passenger side of the lorry, gripping the canvas-covered frame that shielded the back from the sun.

Just as he was about to pull himself onto the frame, a hand gripped his.

Jack turned to see Ruby there. She stood on the tips of her toes, then pressed her lips to his, her mouth colliding against his with a surge of warmth and electricity. His breath caught, his eyes locking with hers as the moment held.

He hadn't expected her or this but he returned the kiss, his lips molding against hers gently as heat flooded his skin.

Then she pulled away and smiled. "For luck."

Jack grinned, then pulled himself up, his feet bracing against the side of the bed. He slid one foot over the other until he had climbed around the canvas and was outside, gripping the frame while standing on the side.

Each bump of the tires against the uneven terrain was exaggerated now, the thumps sending his fingers tighter against the frame. He was tall enough that he could hold on to the topmost bar of the frame, but his arms were above his head, and he still had to balance on the metal side of the bed.

And remain unseen.

Fortunately, there wasn't a mirror on this side, which gave him the leeway to creep his way closer to the cabin of the lorry, one foot at a time. From there, he'd need to—

The lorry gave a hard lurch, tires dipping into a deep pothole in the ground and Jack's grip slipped, his feet going flying over the side.

He clung to the frame, trying to find purchase for his feet once more. The toe of his boot smacked into steel, scraping, sliding until—he exhaled—he had a toehold. His hands ached, his arms feeling as though they'd nearly been pulled out of the sockets at his shoulders.

"Dammit," he growled, then threw himself toward the back of the cabin, his fury at the slip turning into adrenaline. He couldn't afford to be careless now, but he hated how easily he'd almost fallen from this damned thing.

He braced his weight against the back of the cabin, careful not to be overly noisy as he set his feet against it and pulled himself up onto the roof. One foot, then the other, and he was on top of the cabin.

From here, he saw the desert stretch out around him. The bandits must have been lying in wait to attack the lorry—the lorry appeared to be alone rather than followed by any other vehicles or even someone on a horse or camelback.

Jack let his breath return to normal, the wind rushing past his face, carrying dust and grit with it. Any unexpected movement from the lorry now could mean he'd go tumbling right off the side—and slam face-first into the dirt. His palms ached with the thought of falling, and he steadied himself on his hands and knees, crouched over as he gathered the nerve to move forward.

As a kid, he'd had no compunction that prevented him from leaping onto the back of a train or hitching a ride on a precarious surface like this.

When had he lost his courage?

That kiss from Ruby—for a moment it had reminded him of the way he'd loved to show off. His overconfidence and arrogance, with too little concern for the consequences.

Or had it always just been bravado?

Had he been playing a role—Jack Darby, American maverick, independently wealthy thanks to a treasure horde he'd found in his youth, answering to no one and free of attachments?

But, then again, he'd made attachments. They'd just detonated and left his heart in pieces too far flung and broken to gather.

The sight of a fortress in the hazy distance made him focus.

The sun hung low in the sky, bleeding gold and rust across the desert. On the horizon, Azraq Castle rose from the earth like a bruise against the pale sandstone—its basalt walls stark and dark, hunched like a waiting predator at the edge of the oasis. Square and low-slung, it looked ancient and immovable, a fortress carved from shadow and stone. Even from atop the lorry's roof, Jack could make out the worn battlements and the empty, watching slits of windows.

Who knew who might await these bandits there? Or—worse still—if they bypassed it, Jack and Ruby would need to find a way back there, or they'd lose the last oasis and opportunity for water before crossing the desert. His dry lips reminded him of just how thirsty he already was.

He moved, creeping toward the passenger-side window. He couldn't know for certain how many men were inside the cabin, but there had to be at least a couple. And the instant he was inside, all bets were off—he might not last two seconds. But he needed to get control of this car unless he wanted to end up at the mercy of desert bandits—and any other friends they might join up with.

He turned, hooking his fingers on the top of the window frame but careful not to reach too far. A gust of wind kicked up the grit around him, stinging his eyes as the lorry jostled beneath his boots. The cabin window loomed below him—his only way in, his only chance. Below, one of the bandits barked something over the engine's growl. Jack didn't wait. He braced himself, muscles coiled, and swung feetfirst into the open window.

His boots crashed down on the bandit in the passenger seat as a shout split the air—*only two men, after all.*

The driver swerved hard, gravel spraying from the tires as the lorry bucked beneath them. Jack barely kept his footing, one hand gripping the door frame to steady himself. The passenger twisted beneath him, shouting in Arabic, reaching for something—maybe a knife. Jack didn't wait to find out. He rammed his elbow backward, felt the sharp crunch of cartilage, and the man let out a strangled grunt, curling sideways in pain.

Jack shifted his weight and dropped fully into the cab, one knee jabbing into the passenger's thigh to pin him. The driver barked a curse and fumbled beneath the steering wheel, his fingers closing around the butt of a pistol wedged between the brake lever and the seat. The gun scraped free, but Jack was already moving.

He slammed his shoulder into the man's arm, knocking it askew just as the weapon cleared the holster. The gun clattered to the floorboards. The lorry jolted again—wheels catching in a rut—and Jack was thrown against the door.

The driver reached again, snarling, but Jack drove a fist into his side—once, twice—then another into his jaw. The man reeled, dazed, one hand slapping blindly at the door handle for leverage, still attempting to drive despite the chaos. Jack grabbed a fistful of his robe and twisted, shoving the door open with his elbow.

Desert wind roared through the cab, hot and sharp with grit. For a breathless moment, the driver clung there, half in, half out —then Jack wrenched him sideways and kicked with all the force he could muster. The man's body tumbled from the cab, bouncing once in the sand before disappearing in the rising plume of dust.

Jack quickly slid into the driver's seat, boots braced, hands tight on the wheel. The windshield was cracked with a spidery web, a bullet hole in the center. The metallic tang of blood hung in the air—maybe from the passenger—but possibly from the smugglers the bandits had killed.

The lorry drifted again—veering toward a shallow ditch that could flip them if he wasn't careful. Jack yanked the wheel hard to the left. The tires skidded, caught, then held. The engine howled in protest.

Beside him, the passenger groaned, one arm dragging across the dash, smearing blood from his nose.

Jack shot a glance his way. *Still breathing. Still dangerous.*

"Don't," Jack warned in Arabic, voice low, flat.

But the man pushed upright anyway, eyes glassy, reaching clumsily toward his belt.

"Damn fool," Jack spat and lashed out again, grabbing the man by the back of the head and slamming it once against the side window. The man slumped with a groan, limbs going limp.

Jack exhaled slowly, just once, then tightened his grip on the wheel and pressed forward. Only then did he notice a three-inch-long piece of glass protruding from his forearm. Blood dripped from the wound down to his elbow, sticky and warm. The pain hadn't caught up with him yet.

His heart rate slowing, Jack eased off the gas and shifted out of gear, then brought the lorry to a crawl. Reaching across the unconscious passenger, Jack pushed open the passenger door, then shoved the man out onto the ground. He'd be bruised and battered, but he'd live.

With a wince, Jack tugged the glass from his forearm, then tossed it out the door before pulling it shut again. The cut on his arm gave another gush of blood, but he didn't have time to deal with it now—better to put some more distance between themselves and the bandits.

He threw the lorry into gear and lurched forward again.

The road ahead was long and empty, the sky streaked violet and bronze as sunset crept over the eastern desert. And in the distance, Azraq Castle loomed—dark and weathered, its stones catching the last light like a fortress carved from obsidian.

The British kept a small presence there—one that Jack would have to avoid—but so did the Bedouin, from whom they could get food before continuing on their way.

Sleep wouldn't be in the cards tonight. Not without the smugglers. The smugglers had planned to let them move freely in the back of the lorry once they'd cleared Azraq. Now Jack would have to drive.

As he drew closer to the town, he slowed, the pain from his encounter with the bandits edging in at last. His wound was still bleeding, and he needed to bandage it with something—and he needed to check on Ruby.

Jack stopped. Leaving the engine idling, he climbed down from the cabin and went around to the back of the lorry.

"Ruby?" he called out, peering into the dark shadows between the crates.

Silence.

He frowned, then furrowed his brows and dragged one leg into the back.

He didn't get far. A soft footstep sounded, then Ruby emerged from the shadows, still clutching the gun he'd given her, stepping toward him.

He gave her a tired smile, then stood straight. "There you are. I was beginning to think—"

The sound of her slap across his cheek jolted him before the actual impact of it. He blinked in surprise, then frowned.

Ruby stepped away, her eyes unusually bright. "Do you have any idea what I've been through back here, Jack? I heard a shot. And then the lorry tossed and turned and stopped. I thought I saw you fall—God, I thought it was you in the sand! And this whole time, you've kept me back here, thinking something had happened to you! How dare you? I had no idea whether I was driving to my death—or worse—and I was—"

This time, he was the one to silence her. His hand tugged at her waist, the relief of her presence and her concern overwhelming him in a way he couldn't verbalize. Pulling her into his arms, he dropped his lips to her mouth, silencing her protests with a fierce kiss.

She stiffened, then sank against him, her arms sliding around his neck as her lips softened and returned his kiss. Her lips tasted of her tears, and her breath collided with his, warm and sweet, thawing something deep inside him that he hadn't known even existed anymore.

Pulling away, Jack set his forehead against hers. "I told you not to miss me."

She closed her eyes, her long lashes rimmed with moisture, then she nodded and stepped back. "Apology not accepted."

"You'd be amazed how often that's the thanks I get for my heroics." He grinned and offered her a hand to dismount from the back. "I wouldn't have it any other way, Ruby Whoever-you-are."

She glared at him, then ignored his hand and hopped off the back gate, alighting with an unexpected grace.

She surprises me.

And that was something he hadn't felt in a long time.

CHAPTER TWENTY-TWO

NOAH

The boy traveled down the road, accompanied by a servant woman—probably his mother—his thin frame barely visible in the dim moonlight. Noah watched them, unmoving from the olive grove where he'd been monitoring the sheikh's house with binoculars since midafternoon. He'd nearly given up, but once the minutes had stretched into hours, it hardly seemed to matter if he continued here longer.

Unfortunately, unlike the previous night when he'd visited with Fahad, Hower had followed him this time.

He'd been stealthy, of course, but … *not enough.* Maybe Hower was careless. Noah doubted that, though. He wouldn't be one of Blackwell's men if he wasn't good at what he did.

No, Hower's presence here was purposeful. He *wanted* Noah to know he was being watched, which was interesting.

A breeze rippled across the plain, carrying the sound of scattering stones and the sting of dust. Noah knelt beside the crumbling edge of an ancient stone wall, squinting against the grit in the air. After it had passed, he straightened and lifted his binoculars back to the road. The boy was nearly out of view.

Time to move.

Noah slunk away from the olive grove, careful to stay off the main road. Hopefully Hower would at least use some measure of caution when following Noah—not give them both away. He hadn't stopped Noah yet.

Keeping to the shadows, Noah followed the boy and his mother at a careful distance.

No matter what Hower claimed, Noah was convinced he'd find no evidence of German spies in Khirbet Qeiyafa, the dig to which he'd been assigned, twenty miles outside of Jerusalem.

Hower had assured Noah *this* was the place to be in order to learn about German spies in the area, but Noah had seen no evidence of the fact during his work in the day. He'd learned more about the whispers of German spies from the brief encounter with Sheikhh Khalil than he had among the archeologists and their hired help.

And something about that bothered him.

He'd spent enough time in the intelligence world to know that it wasn't everything that the public imagined—far less glamour and much more paperwork. But at Khirbet Qeiyafa?

There it felt as though he was wasting his time. For all the talk of German agents moving through Palestine, the dig site felt like a theater set: dust, ruins, and a perfectly arranged absence of clues. Maybe Hower had known something about German activity in the area that he hadn't admitted to. Or maybe Noah had happened upon a time of unusual silence between the Germans and their contacts in the Arab world.

But neither would help Noah get MI5 the information they wanted—and win the freedom to go home. Nor would it help Jack find his sister and Alice.

So he'd returned here, despite the risk he took with Hower following him, to pursue the one lead that seemed promising.

Noah continued along the edge of the road, his sandals

crunching against the dirt and stone. Thankfully, Hower kept his distance. In fact, he seemed to have stopped following when Noah had moved more into the open.

The boy and his mother approached the local village, a ramshackle collection of stone houses that stood in stark contrast to the estate where Noah raised his own family. Not for the first time, guilt pressed hard against his chest. Guilt for the luxuries he so often took for granted.

The edge in his thoughts surprised him. Maybe it was the heat or the dust, or the gnawing ache of too many sleepless nights, but his patience was fraying fast.

He missed Ginger. Missed the quiet of her presence, the grounding weight of her hand in his, the competence of her logic. Even the chaos of the children felt like a different life entirely—soft, warm, real.

Here, everything felt like an illusion. As if he was reenacting the spy games he'd once romanticized through the lens of nostalgia—but, this time, he was simply pretending. Layers of deception went deep here, yet he couldn't find an entry point. It made him feel less like a man and more like a pawn—moved one square at a time toward a goal someone else had decided.

Noah's jaw clenched.

He entered the village, shifting the way he moved. Strangers would be noticed here. Nothing could be done to remedy that, but he'd do better as someone who looked like he was simply passing through rather than pretending to fit into a place where he didn't.

The village was a mixture of scents and quiet sounds—hot food and woodsmoke, barnyard animals and soft conversations—and Noah kept his gaze low as the boy and his mother entered one of the houses right off the road.

It wouldn't do to sit and watch the house from the road, so

he drew nearer, then passed it, heading toward the well pump closer to the village center.

He paused at the well, drawing a few creaking pumps from the handle before letting it fall silent again. Water gurgled, then spurted out from the spigot. He caught it in his hands and splashed his face, then drank deeply. Around him, the village hummed with domestic rhythm, but no one paid him much mind.

Hower didn't show his face either.

Noah didn't like the possibility that Hower might see who he'd been waiting to speak to—it brought back memories of a distant time, when he'd often employed the help of young orphaned boys in espionage—and one of them, whom he'd loved like a member of his own family, had paid the cruel price of Stephen Fisher's vengeance and lost his hand. After that, Noah had entrusted Khalib to Alastair's care.

Alastair had done a better job than Noah ever could have in raising Khalib—but Noah had never forgiven himself.

Still, he waited. Watched. Counted windows, tracked movement, studied shadows.

This boy was the best prospect he had to make any of the time he'd spent away from his family count for anything.

Eventually, the boy slipped out again. Alone this time. No sign of the mother. He headed toward a goat pen at the edge of his house, a small pail swinging in one hand.

Noah let him get a little distance, then peeled away from the well and followed.

The pen backed up against a broken stone wall, the kind that didn't bother to divide much anymore—just a relic of something older, crumbled by time. Noah waited until the boy set the pail down and began scooping feed, his narrow shoulders rising and falling with the effort.

Then he stepped forward.

"*Marhaba*," Noah said softly.

The boy flinched and turned. His eyes went wide.

Noah raised his hands, palms open. "I'm not here to hurt you," he said in Arabic.

Silence.

"I saw you at the sheikhh's house. Yesterday. When I mentioned the American women."

The boy didn't speak. Didn't run either. Just stared.

"You know them." Noah stepped closer to him, then squatted in front of him, closer to his eye level. "Or of the man who came looking for them."

Still nothing. But there was the shift in the boy's stance—the slight tilt of his head, the tension in his arms. Recognition. Fear.

Noah reached into his pocket and tugged free a Palestinian one-pound note. More than this child could possibly hope to earn in weeks of work. "The women are my friends. Maybe in trouble. I need to find them. They were here, weren't they?"

The boy's gaze fixed on the money in Noah's hand, and Noah felt the soft tug of guilt. The loyalty of a child was remarkably easy to buy, sadly—especially one that might be poor and hungry.

"I don't know anything," the boy said at last. His voice trembled.

"That's not true." Noah pulled out another note.

The boy's eyes darted toward the house behind him.

Noah dropped his voice. "I'm not going to tell anyone what you tell me. This will be our secret. Either you know about the women themselves—or someone else who came looking for them. Which is it?"

"The sheikh told me not to talk to you," the boy whispered. "He doesn't trust you."

That didn't surprise Noah. "And he shouldn't. Too many

men offer ready promises and are quick to break them. Your sheikh is a wise man. He doesn't know me."

If he pushed too hard, the child would be more likely to give him bad information in exchange for the money. He stood slowly and bowed his head. *"Ma'a is-salame."* He turned and started away.

He'd nearly reached the edge of the pen when the boy called softly, "Wait."

Noah's pulse quickened, and he looked over his shoulder. "Yes?"

The boy flinched again and took a hesitant step forward. "You won't hurt them?"

Them.

The women?

He raised a brow. "The women are sisters to me," he said, setting a hand over his heart. *"Wallah."* I swear it.

The bleat of the goats cut the silence between them, with one of the smallest goats nudging the boy's pail. The boy kept his head low, not meeting Noah's eyes. "The sheikh hid them. When he came looking. But I don't know where they went after that."

Did that mean Prescott had been here?

But also—if the sheikh had protected them, then not only did that mean that Alice and Kit had been here but that the sheikh himself might know why they'd gone missing. But getting the sheikh to tell him anything would likely be a dead end.

Noah had to be cautious. A wrong word might shut down the boy's reluctant help. And neither could he accept the information at face value. "And how do I know you're telling me the truth?"

The goat nudged the boy's pail again. "The fair one helped my sister when the fever came. She gave her medicine."

"And the man that came looking for them?" It *had* to have been Prescott.

The pail shook in his hand.

Noah knelt in front of the boy once again. This time he took out five bills. "I will pay you for the truth. And I promise you my silence. But I can't help them unless you tell me what you know."

The boy hesitated, then set the pail down and wiped his hands on his cloak. "Sharif al-Rashid." A whisper, like a secret barely allowed out.

Noah inhaled sharply.

Not Prescott.

"When?"

"After Eid il-Burbara."

In December then. Three, almost four, months ago.

Noah pressed the money into the boy's sweaty palm, then stood and patted his head. "You must trust your sheikh. Do not speak to anyone else."

The boy looked away, face filled with shame.

Noah left him there and headed back out onto the road with urgency heating his blood.

Kit and Alice had been here. And Prescott didn't know. If he had, Prescott would have come looking.

Then who?

Who was Sharif al-Rashid? Could he possibly belong to Prescott too? Somehow Noah doubted Prescott kept highborn Islamic nobles in his pocket.

And if the sheikh had hidden Alice and Kit from the sharif, then it also meant al-Rashid had been a threat to them. No friend of Prescott's, by extension.

He'd barely left the village when the loud roar of a motorcar's engine caught his attention. The driver was a lower ranked military fellow from Khirbet Qeiyafa that Noah recognized. And the passenger … *Hower.*

The motorcar pulled off to the side of the road just behind him. "Benson?" Hower called, without any regard for who might be watching or hear.

Either he was reckless about Noah maintaining his alias or he simply didn't care.

Noah restrained a sigh and went over to the car.

"Get in." Hower held the door open.

Arguing would be pointless and attract more attention. He did as Hower said instead and settled into the warm backseat, which smelled of baked leather and motor oil. The driver started back up again, and Hower set an arm around the seat back, turning to face Noah.

"Enjoy your afternoon of leave?" he asked with a raised brow.

"I didn't take leave." Noah rested against the seat, stretching his legs out. "I was following a lead."

"A lead about what?"

He didn't dare mention Kit and Alice to Hower. "The Germans in the area."

Hower frowned, his voice carrying loudly over the noise from the motorcar and the rush of the wind from the open windows. "That's what you're supposed to be doing at the dig site."

"I found a lead elsewhere," Noah replied coolly. "It will all be in my report."

"Perhaps you've been out of the service for too long, Benson, but that's not how we handle our affairs here. You *ask* permission to investigate—not tell me after the fact. I'm your superior officer, not a colleague waiting to collaborate with you."

Noah gave him a long stare without answering. He hadn't been able to make sense of Hower's role in all this. He worked for MI5 under Knight, but why did Prescott Federline want him here?

"Why were you watching the sheikh's house? And following that boy?" Hower pressed.

He offered only the information that Hower could find out easily on his own. "The sheikh is a local pro-Arab nationalist. A man of influence who is known to be connected to other Arab nationalists. Surely, he would be a good place to start looking for whispers of the Germans."

"And a good way to expose your work here," Hower countered with annoyance.

When it came to people he didn't trust, he'd always found that a mix of minor lies with major truths served him the best in dealing with them. "The sheikh has been quietly purchasing arms," Noah said with a bored glance. Fahad had told Noah that, but Noah didn't need to tell Hower where he'd gained that piece for information. "That was easy enough for me to learn without giving myself away, Hower. And the boy is a good target to use as an informant. I made more progress trying to investigate this sheikh than I made at the dig site the last week."

Hower's eyes narrowed. "That's impressive. You certainly are everything they promise, aren't you, Benson? Resourceful. Arrogant. Entirely no regard for authority. Tomorrow I'll be sending you to Port Said to board a ship for England. You've compromised our mission here—I intend to tell Knight to dismiss you directly."

Noah shifted his weight on the seat, trying to make sense of Hower's line of reasoning. It still felt odd, returning to a hierarchy that required him to ask for leave and inform of his whereabouts. As if he'd gone back to his military days, before he'd risen in rank enough to have more freedom on his operations.

But, also, if Noah didn't know any better, it felt as though he was being kept distracted here.

Hower could pretend that he wanted to offer Noah assistance, but Noah's record and past work spoke for itself. He could understand that Hower might not trust him, but Knight had been chasing him for years. Would Knight really dismiss Noah for so little cause, based on Hower's recommendation? And why bring him out here in the first place?

Hower had been wasting Noah's time on so-called espionage work that was far beneath Noah's skill. And to threaten to dismiss him now for doing the job he'd been hired for? Either Hower was bluffing …

Or Hower doesn't want me to actually find the Germans.

Maybe that's the point.

Hower was a Blackwell operative. Planted by Prescott—ultimately more loyal to Blackwell than to the British. Could Hower have been directed by Prescott to ensure Noah found nothing of use? Something wasn't adding up about Prescott's efforts here—both to keep Noah from helping Jack and having Hower in control of Noah's actions.

Noah couldn't afford to go to Knight with what he'd learned of Hower's loyalties, though … the rot could go much further up the chain of command than Noah believed. Noah had stupidly played into Hower's hands back in France, and he was no closer to escaping from the web Hower had woven to entrap him.

Maybe it wasn't about what he was supposed to find. Maybe it was about what he wasn't supposed to help Jack uncover. Every hour he spent here, playing pretend in someone else's game, widened the distance between him and the people he loved. And Hower knew that.

Noah cleared his throat. "Let me see if I have this correct. I tell you that I've made progress on the objective given to me—

find out about German spies and assets in the region—and you threaten to dismiss me?"

"The manner of your work concerns me, Benson. I can't have someone under my authority who has no regard for the rules."

"Did you expect me to simply wait for a German spy to pop up his head at the dig site? The place is as bereft of interest to humanity as it was thousands of years ago. The archeologists there are too busy grasping at straws for biblical connections that may not exist—not waiting to make covert government deals under the desert sun. I heard of a lead and I moved on it, simple as that."

Hower removed a handkerchief from his pocket, then mopped the sweat on his brow. "Yes, of course. Best to chase a lead before it goes cold, hmm? But you mustn't forget protocol either." He nodded at the driver.

The driver took a sharp U-turn, which threw Noah against the window in the backseat. Dust kicked up from the tires as they spun, then the driver floored the engine, barreling back toward the village Noah had left moments before. The reckless pace didn't stop until the driver slammed to a stop in front of the boy's house in the village.

Noah locked eyes with Hower, his heart racing.

No.

But Hower had already opened the door to the motorcar. Already started toward the boy's house. A glance at the driver revealed the man held a pistol in his lap already. Noah didn't doubt the man's loyalty to Hower—or that the bullets in that gun would be meant for Noah if he stepped out of line.

To Noah's horror, the boy opened the door to Hower's knocking. His eyes went wide as Hower grabbed him by the collar and dragged him out toward the motorcar. From inside the house came a scream, then the boy's terrified mother appeared at the doorway, clutching a young girl at her side.

Hower shoved the boy against the motorcar's bonnet and pressed a gun to the back of his neck. "Tell me what you told him," Hower gritted in Arabic through clenched teeth.

Noah tore out of the seat, hands extended up. "Don't do this," he said, keeping whatever calm he could muster. He walked slowly toward Hower. "The boy is innocent." He swallowed, his chest tight.

By now, several of the villagers had exited their homes or stared from windows. Noah's fingertips brushed up against the holster at his waist, but he didn't dare draw his weapon yet. If he managed a shot at Hower, the driver's response would follow, without question.

Hower leaned closer to the boy's face. "Tell me what you told him." His Arabic was heavy accented but clear enough that the boy understood.

Noah's gaze locked with the boy's, who appealed to him with wide, tearful eyes. Then he looked back at Hower, his tone changing. "If you hurt him, I will kill you, Hower. Maybe Knight didn't explain to you who I was or the reason he wanted me— but make no mistake: I don't flee from my enemies. I bury them." Then, more loudly, he added, "Even the ones that work for Prescott Federline."

Hower whirled his head toward Noah, eyes furious. "You think you're so intelligent, don't you, Benson? That you can beat us at this? You haven't begun to understand how many steps ahead of you we are. You think Jack can find Alice and Kit without us? The people loyal to us are everywhere. We made contingency plans long before he even left Kharga Oasis. Now tell me what this brat told you."

What does that mean?

Was Jack being watched?

Or—*worse still*—had they planted someone with Jack, even despite Noah's warnings to him? Maybe Jack hadn't listened and gone to Roche or someone like him.

He had to find Jack and help him.

Noah's heart rate slowed, his senses heightening as he locked in on Hower. The villagers would all memorize Noah's face, unmask him to the sheikh or anyone else of importance in the area. The driver—loyal to Hower without question—had lifted his pistol, his hand curling around the handle.

And the boy, with tears falling down his cheeks and sizzling against the hot metal of the motorcar's bonnet, who was *begging* for Noah to save him.

This is why children didn't belong in a world of espionage and secrets. Why it was so dangerous to involve them in any way.

Noah should have known better.

And he wasn't about to repeat any of the mistakes of his past. Allowing someone like Hower to come back and haunt him later would end badly. He'd learned that much with Stephen Fisher. He should have killed that son of a bitch long before he finally had.

When he spoke, his voice was calm. "If you're so brilliantly ahead of the game, then why do you need the boy? Clearly you don't know everything."

"Enough of your games, Benson." He straightened and hauled the boy up. "I'm going to question you both. Separately. And if your answers don't line up—I'll shoot the boy." He started toward the house, the boy firmly in his grip.

A mistake.

Hower had turned his back on him, relying on the driver to threaten Noah.

"Like hell you will," Noah snapped, drawing his gun at last. He fired a shot toward the driver first, then turned it toward

Hower. He fired ruthlessly, carefully aiming to avoid the whimpering boy.

The boy's mother screamed, diving out of the way, her arms going around her daughter.

Hower was dead before he hit the ground, a bloody heap of flesh and brain matter splattering against the dirt and walls to the house.

The boy was unharmed—though a distinctive patch on the ground below his feet made it clear that he'd wet himself with fear.

Noah said nothing to him, going instead toward the motorcar. He went to the driver's side and grabbed the driver by the throat, then hauled him out of the car. The driver trembled, blood covering both hands from a wound in his chest, though he continued to weakly grip the barrel of his gun.

After tossing the man onto the ground, Noah kicked the gun from his hand and then knelt in front of him, setting his knee on the man's chest.

The man rasped, blood seeping out of the corner of his mouth and from the bullet wound in his chest—he didn't have long to live.

"Does the name Sharif al-Rashid mean anything to Blackwell?" Noah demanded in English, his chest heaving with the exertion of his movements. Sweat trickled down his brow.

The driver shook his head, the veins in his temples and forehead bulging. "P-please ..."

"Tell me what you know." Noah eased the weight of his knee against the man's chest. The release of pressure allowed the man a strangled gasp, and Noah reached for his right arm. He pushed the man's sleeve back, just enough to reveal the small triskelion Blackwell tattoo he'd been expecting.

The man's eyes widened at Noah.

"You think your loyalties will save you? They won't. I'm not the only one who knows all about Prescott Federline. Who do you think sent me to make certain Hower was doing his job?"

Noah drew back his own sleeve, his eyes narrowing at the dying man. Then Noah exposed the triskelion tattoo he'd asked Nasira to ink into his skin when he'd first arrived in Jerusalem. Fahad's wife was a Bedouin and skilled in the art form. "Now tell me about al-Rashid."

The man hesitated a moment longer, then whispered. "Al-Rashid … h-he wanted t-the throne … of I-iraq."

The throne?

Noah furrowed his brow.

The man smiled, his gaze going hazy. His teeth were coated in his own blood. "Y-y-you've killed me …"

Noah returned the weight of his knee to the man's chest. His eyes bulged, his face turning purple, lips blue.

Once the life had faded from his eyes, Noah stood and wiped his hands against his thobe, leaving bright streaks of blood. He flicked a gaze up, where a crowd had gathered, watching him.

"Burn the bodies," he said in a flat voice, in Arabic. "Don't leave a trace of them."

Then he climbed into the motorcar and drove out of the village, the engine's growl the only sound in his ears as a plume of dust swallowed the road behind him.

CHAPTER TWENTY-THREE

JACK

The engine sputtered.

Jack leaned forward in the driver's seat, clutching the steering wheel as a rumble shook the lorry from front to back.

Not good.

Another jerk of the engine, tossing them forward. Ruby grasped the dash, her eyes wide as a metallic groan sounded, a choking, dying sound.

Then everything went quiet, the lorry still.

Jack's stomach dropped and he sat there, blinking at the expanse of dark desert beyond the windshield, listening to the creaking *click*s of a cooling engine.

"Well," Ruby said, straightening as she pushed her headscarf back, "that's not good."

Jack exhaled through his nose and reached for the door handle. "Yeah."

Outside, the desert night pressed in—a black bowl of sky pricked with stars. A dry wind moved across the sand, heavy with the smell of oil and something burnt. In the distance, there was nothing—no castle, no road, just an endless stretch of rock and bone-dry emptiness that he hoped would take him to Baghdad.

He dropped into the sand, boots kicking up dust as he rounded the front of the lorry and crouched low, pulling a small flashlight from his satchel. The beam caught on something slick beneath the chassis. He reached out, rubbed two fingers along the undercarriage, then held them up to the light.

Black. Oily. Still warm.

No.

"Damn," he muttered.

Ruby's door creaked open, her boots crunching over gravel. "What is it?"

He didn't answer right away. Just stood, wiping his hand on a rag, and glanced behind them. In the beam of the flashlight, the trail stretched out behind the lorry like a ribbon of shadow in the sand—thin, dark, and nearly unbroken. Probably miles of it.

"Tell me this is fixable." Ruby came closer.

He didn't look up. "Depends how you define 'fixable.'"

"Well, don't hold out on me, Darby. What the hell is it?"

"They hit the oil line," he said finally. He turned the flashlight off and stuffed it back in his bag. "Back when they fired on us. We've been leaking since dusk. We were lucky to make it this far."

"Lucky," Ruby muttered, glancing up at the star-studded sky. "Sure. Let's go with that." She stood with her arms crossed tight over her chest, her jaw clenched. Then she stalked back toward the lorry, to the driver's side this time.

"What are you doing?" Jack asked as she slid into the seat.

"Not giving up, for starters. Even if we can go back a few miles and get closer to Azraq, we'll be better off than stuck out here." She turned the ignition.

Jack held a hand out. "I don't think that's such a good—"

Too late.

The engine gave a pitiful cry, then sparks erupted from the ignition. Another spark leapt—

Jack's stomach twisted. "Ruby, get out of the—"

The spark hit the hot engine, the leaking oil, and burst into flame.

"Goddamn it," Jack growled, dashing toward the driver's side. He helped Ruby out, then grabbed their bags from the floor of the cabin.

Landing back on the ground, he grabbed Ruby's hand. "Hurry—we have to grab that barrel of water we got in Azraq."

The flames were already higher now, quickly spreading up the engine block and licking their way up the windshield.

"Water? B-but—"

"Dammit, Ruby, don't you remember? The smugglers had extra barrels of fuel to take into the desert. As soon as that fire hits the cargo—"

Her eyes widened. "Oh my God." She bolted for the back.

Together they lowered the gate, then climbed on. The water barrel was close to the back and Jack moved behind it, shoving with all his might. Ruby joined him and they pushed, barely budging it.

The barrel moved by an inch.

"It's too heavy," Jack said, stepping back.

"We can't leave it," Ruby cried, shaking her head. A fiercely determined look settled in her brow. "We won't survive in the desert without water."

The fire had already engulfed the cabin, the heat and sting of it uncomfortably hot.

"Ruby, leave it! We have to go." The fuel barrels wouldn't just ignite—they would explode.

"But, Jack!"

"Leave it!" Jack wrapped his arms around her, then hauled her off the back. They grabbed their bags, then dashed into the desert, running at top speed as the burning lorry was engulfed in flames behind them, casting a scorching red glow into the darkness.

Boom.

Jack dove, tackling Ruby in his arms to cover her as a shower of dirt, sand, and debris rained down on them. The scent of burning fuel and oil filled the air, the crackle of fire a haunting contrast to the barren, chilly desert around them.

He waited a few heartbeats, then rolled away from her. "You okay?" he asked, climbing onto his hands and knees. He'd scraped his hands and face, but the pain was insignificant.

"I think so," Ruby managed, scrambling up as she looked back. She groaned, her brows furrowing in consternation and dismay. "There goes our shelter for the night. And our water."

"I have my canteen." But she wasn't wrong. That little water wouldn't be nearly enough.

"How far back to Azraq?" she asked after a moment.

"About fifteen miles. Too far to walk before morning." He sighed, letting the full weight of the situation settle in before he stood and helped her up. "But we'll have to cover part of it at least. It's cold, but we'll be warmer moving, and it's better than doing it once the sun comes out."

She let out a slow breath. "Fantastic. Just what I was hoping to hear."

Icy night wind stirred again, carrying ash and smoke and tugging at his sleeves, evoking a shiver.

Jack turned toward the horizon. No lights. No structures. Just miles of scrub and basalt and sand stretching out into nothing. Somewhere in the dark, a jackal screeched—a distant reminder that the desert was never truly silent, never truly empty.

He could feel Ruby's eyes on him. Waiting for a plan. Maybe hoping for a miracle.

He didn't have either.

What in the hell are we going to do?

"We need to keep moving before the temperature drops too far," he said. "We're gonna freeze if we sit here."

Ruby gave a dry, humorless laugh. "Great. Bandits by day, hypothermia by night. Really loving this trip so far."

His anger flared.

As though he was to blame. Like he wasn't *furious* that they'd lost the help of the smugglers, been shot at, and now lost their vehicle. Baghdad felt further out of reach than ever.

"Technically, you're the one who blew up our transportation." The tone he used was dry—less biting and irritated than he felt—but he was too tired to care. "And now I've lost even more precious time. Time that could mean the difference between life and death for my sister."

She scowled. "I was trying to help. You know, I'm not a professional smuggler—you're the one who came to me. Blackmailed me. I barely know what the hell I'm even doing out here."

Those stolen kisses after the bandit attack had clearly made him forget all those troublesome details to their dynamic. In Azraq, they'd managed companionable banter and silence, prepared for the night drive with a warm meal from the Bedouins.

He'd even caught himself watching her … thinking about how damned pretty she was.

He narrowed his eyes at her. "You forgot I *paid you*."

"Yes, I forgot. *If* I survive the arrests, breaking you out of jail, shooting bandits, and the desert—none of which you mentioned when you gave me the choice between helping you or turning me in to the Cairo police."

"Don't blame me. I'm not the one who decided to rob me." He collected his bags and turned toward the nearest ridge—low, jagged rock maybe a quarter-mile off, where the rocks would shelter them from the wind as they walked—then started walking without waiting for her.

"Not to worry," she said, hurrying to keep up with him. "I regret the moment Theo laid eyes on you and suggested it. How's it make you feel that he thought you looked like an easy target, Jack? A miserable, friendless loner. Everyone else walking into Mena House that night seemed to know other people there."

Jack didn't rise to the bait, though her words cut him through. *Miserable. Friendless.*

Why does it matter what she thinks?

And why should I care if it's practically true?

He'd been living the life of a hermit for years now on purpose.

Once he'd been well connected in Anglo Cairo society. Invited to everything. Sure, many of those folks had left the city after the war. Even more had moved out of Cairo after Egypt had gained its independence in 1922 and nationalists made it clear that the continued British presence was less than welcome.

But now? "You know nothing about me, sweetheart."

"Don't call me that," she snapped, stamping her foot. "You hired me. That's all."

He stopped and spun toward her. "You go around kissing everyone you work for? Because I'm not the one that muddied the waters."

"I—" She stared up at him, blue eyes shining in the moonlight. A few beats of breathless silence passed, and he searched her gaze, looking for the woman he'd encountered while traveling in that damned crate. Maybe she didn't wear bravado and sass—which he couldn't deny he liked—but *that* woman had been real.

Ruby opened her mouth, as though considering her words, then closed it again. Swallowing a breath, she sighed and shook her head, continuing walking. "I'm an actress, remember? I'll kiss anyone depending on the part they're expecting me to play."

So that's how it's going to be.

Fine.

He said nothing more, letting the sound of their footsteps fill the silence. A glance over his shoulder revealed the lorry still burning, a plume of thick smoke rising into the sky like a signal. If anyone had wanted to follow them, they practically had a sign pointing right to them.

But, right now, being followed wasn't the problem. Surviving the night and the trek back to Azraq would be. Thank goodness March in the Jordanian desert wasn't as harsh as other times during the year—but the nighttime temperatures could get close to freezing. The days were milder but would feel hot compared to the night. And they didn't have water. Or a source for it.

Out here a person could make peace with their Maker—fast. No wonder the desert showed up as a theme so often in the Bible.

But Jack had grown up around arid deserts like this in Phoenix. He was comfortable in them. His family had moved there because of Alice, when the doctors out East had recommended the climate there for her asthma. Unlike his mother, Jack had grown to love it, and his father had found work as an archeologist—but he'd also found the saloons and poker tables. The final nail in the coffin of Frank Darby's crumbling career.

Mom had fled back East before Dad's death, abandoning Alice to Jack's care.

But for a long time before that, it had always been Alice and Jack, a little family all on their own, against the world.

Against his better judgment, he snuck a glance at Ruby, the anger from the lorry explosion beginning to thaw. They were alike in many ways.

Stubborn.

Willing to do the unthinkable for their siblings.

Grudgingly, he offered, "I know you were trying to help back there. And I'm sorry I was so harsh."

Her lips pursed, but her shoulders relaxed some. A few more footsteps passed before she said, "It's my fault. I shouldn't have tried to start the truck."

He sighed. "Fact of the matter is, without a mechanic out here to fix the damned thing, it was already useless. I just took my anger out on you."

She nodded but didn't respond.

Great. Guilt was the last thing he needed right now.

"Ruby, I'm sorry," he said again. "You don't need to feel responsible for this on top of everything."

She scowled. "Why do you care what I feel?"

"I don't know. But I do. Call me a sucker for pretty blondes carrying the weight of the world on their shoulders."

"Is that all you see me as? Someone vulnerable to take advantage of?"

"No, Ruby, no, I—"

"I didn't tell you about my life so you could reduce me to a caricature."

"Stop." Jack pinched the bridge of his nose and then reached for her, catching her hand in his before she could move out of his grasp again.

The feeling of her fingertips brushing against his made goose bumps rise on his arms.

She stopped walking, though. Didn't let go of his hand.

God, he *wanted* to believe she wasn't just doing this for the money. That somewhere back in Lydda station, she'd decided to help him because of *this*. This connection between them that he'd felt growing since the moment he'd met her.

But that wasn't true.

She's only here for the money.

And he needed to make his peace with that.

Maybe in another time, another life, another world, they would have had a shot at ... *something*. Something that wasn't based in shallow motivations and necessity.

But, then again, he didn't need her to be good.

Didn't need this attraction to amount to anything. Fact was, he had nothing left to offer her. What little had remained of his heart after Kit had gone to Ginger.

And part of the reason I'm here is because of Kit.

The idea of Kit being alive was something he couldn't quite wrap his head around, and yet it was powerful enough of a motivator that here he was, in the middle of the desert, chasing clues that he was sure she'd left in a newspaper just for him.

Prescott had known that Jack could never stop loving Kit—which was why he'd held her out as bait to look for Alice. He'd started this whole thing off thinking about Kit. Driven to find her because he'd never forgotten her.

So why am I letting Ruby get to me so much?

Why did I kiss Ruby?

Somehow, she'd found a crack in his armor. Gotten in, even though he didn't want her there.

And the worst part was—she didn't want to be there either.

As though she sensed the war going on inside him, Ruby interlaced her fingers with his and stepped closer. "Don't feel bad. Considering that I robbed you and you blackmailed me, we probably have too much to overcome to be friends, anyway, Jack."

Jack stared at her, tempted to kiss her again. Her lips had been so soft. So pliant.

Seductive.

Lust curled through his veins, with a force he hadn't expected, and he let himself bathe in it for a moment. She wouldn't be good for him, but why should it matter? He'd had brief love affairs before—none of them wise—but with minimal damage.

He closed his eyes.

Kit.

He could barely remember her face.

The memories were there, but the sound of her voice—gone.

And if she'd lied to him, faked her own death, gone to work for Blackwell … did he really owe her any loyalty now that he'd found she'd lived after all?

The buzzing sound of an airplane cut into his thoughts.

Jack startled, dropping Ruby's hand as he looked up into the sky, searching for a sign of the plane.

His pulse quickened.

Of course.

"What is it?" Ruby asked, scanning the sky with him.

"A plane. There's an old RAF airstrip at Azraq. Desert patrol might still use it." Then, excitement cut through him. "I have an idea. But we have to hurry. Get back to Azraq before the plane heading there leaves again."

She gave him a bewildered look. "Weren't we heading for Azraq anyway?"

"Yes, but this time we might have a quick way out of there. To Baghdad. If we can reach Azraq in time, I might be able to get us a ride. I know someone at the airfield in Rutbah—he still owes me."

"And you're just remembering this useful friend now?" Ruby arched a brow.

Jack smirked. "I wouldn't entirely put it like that. It's just more that up until now I didn't want to go anywhere close to British officials if I could avoid it. Now I'm running out of options. And sanity."

He started forward once again, adrenaline quickening his pace.

"So much for sleeping," Ruby muttered with a shake of her head.

"We can sleep in Baghdad. Let's go."

CHAPTER TWENTY-FOUR

JACK

"*I* don't think I can manage another step without some rest," Ruby said, slowing to a stop.

Jack checked his watch. Nearly midnight.

They'd been walking for three hours. Azraq hadn't appeared in view yet, but Jack hoped they were only a couple of hours away by this point. Close enough that, were he alone, he'd likely push through the exhaustion and aching muscles and feet and just keep going.

But I can't ask that of Ruby.

He nodded toward a ridgeline of rock. "Why don't we stop over there? It'll shelter us from the wind."

They trudged toward it, Jack feeling the sting of the biting wind against his cheeks despite the warm flow of blood through his body. Once they settled in, it would get cold, fast.

They found a small cove amidst the rocks and Jack pulled out his flashlight, checking for scorpions or snakes before they set their bags down. The desert didn't have any good options for firewood and, once he sat, he realized he didn't have the energy left to build a fire anyway.

After a few sips of precious water, Jack cleared an area on the ground as best he could, moving pebbles and rocks to the side.

"Here," Jack said, pulling out an old army blanket. He laid it out on the ground, then set his bags on one end as a lumpy pillow. "If you don't mind sharing, we can wrap ourselves in this. Keep some of the cold away."

Ruby nodded. "I don't mind."

They lay down on the blanket—a poor option for a bed, considering the ground was hard and rocky. Even in Kharga Oasis, Jack had lived like a king compared to this. *But, better than nothing.*

The makeshift bed was cozy, the warmth of Ruby's body radiating against him. Her shoulder bumped his and didn't move away. The brush of her sleeve against his arm was barely there, but it grounded him in a way nothing else had in days.

In that one small way, this was better than Kharga. For the first time in ages, he wasn't alone.

"My feet are throbbing," Ruby said with a moan. "I'm tempted to take off my shoes, but I don't think I can move."

He groaned in response. "Now that we've stopped, starting the trek is going to be so much harder." His shoulder brushed against hers. They'd be more comfortable if she was lying against him, but given what had happened after they'd spent that time in the crate, Jack didn't suggest it.

The last thing he needed was to complicate this any further.

"Who's in Rutbah?" Her voice was thick with sleep.

"A friend. Ned Harris with the RAF. We go way back from the war. Whoever flew into Azraq will know him—everyone even remotely connected with the RAF in this area does. I'm hoping I can leverage that into getting a ride to Rutbah. From there, Ned will take us to Baghdad—no question."

"I thought you wanted to stay away from British officials and keep out of sight."

"I do. But I can trust Ned. He's one of the few people in this area I *would* trust blindly, actually. He won't give us away. He's the kind of man who'd lie to his own CO if it meant saving a friend. And since we've had terrible luck with the smugglers and criminals, it might be time for a new strategy. One that doesn't involve nearly getting us both killed."

"Hmm …" She was quiet for several beats, as though struggling to stay awake, her eyes closing. The sound of crickets—somehow still singing despite the cold—filled the air, a nighttime insect chorus that Jack took comfort in. "You know, for someone who's been estranged from his sister for so long, you're sure going to a lot of trouble to find out what happened to her."

He shifted, a rock under his thigh digging in painfully, and blinked up at the myriad of stars above them. "I've always missed her," he admitted quietly. It shouldn't be hard to admit that fact—but he'd never given it a voice.

Noah had told him once—after his own brother had been killed in Gallipoli during the war—that he was a fool for pushing Alice away.

But, even then, Jack hadn't been able to admit how much the rift between Alice and him hurt. He used to tell himself the distance between them had been her choice. That she'd walked away. That it wasn't his fault. But, deep down, he'd known better. He was the one who stopped fighting harder to get her away from Prescott. Who didn't push harder.

And when she disappeared?

Even then—he hadn't acted because of Alice. Not right away. Because in those first few days, all he could think about was Kit. Kit, with her stubborn fire and impossible promises. Kit, who he'd thought had vanished for good long ago.

But something had shifted since Ruby showed up. Since they'd been thrown together in that godforsaken crate and nearly blown up by bandits. Since he'd seen her refuse to give up—on her family, on herself—even on helping him.

He hadn't even mentioned Kit to Ruby. Not once. And somehow it hadn't felt like a betrayal.

Maybe it was because he was starting to feel the same fear for Ruby's fate that had once lived in him for Kit. The same gnawing protectiveness. But it felt different this time.

Kit had never needed anything from him.

But Ruby ... she did.

Enough.

He couldn't let himself get carried away by the notion that someone who needed him for his money might ever need him for anything else.

"What happens if you don't find her, Jack? If you fail?" Ruby's eyes were open now and she turned toward him, a crease of worry between her brows. "That's the thought that keeps me awake. Night after night. If I fail helping my family, what will happen to them? Felix thinks they'll be all right. That I'm making too much of a fuss of it all. And who knows—maybe he's right. But if he's wrong? How do I live with myself if I could have helped and didn't?"

In the dark, her pupils were large, her eyes expressive. He let the moment hold, unsure of what to say to comfort her—and himself. Because ... what if he failed? *Could I live with myself?* Was that last argument with Alice the last time he'd ever talk to her?

The stars were so vivid they seemed to pulse in the sky. Alice used to trace constellations for him when they were children, naming them after imaginary heroes. He tried to find the Archer now—but the sky blurred. Maybe it was the wind, or maybe it was the weight of too many memories.

The desert was too quiet. Every thought echoed louder in the silence.

"We're not going to fail," he said, at last, with a conviction he didn't feel. "Neither of us." He went on gently, "But it's also not entirely up to us. There's only so much either of us can control. And if I learned anything during the war, it's that we can put our heart and soul into something, and the damnedest, most unexpected things can take it all away. And there's nothing you or I can do to change that."

She released a slow, sad sigh, then leaned back again. "That sounds a lot like resigning yourself to the inevitability of fate. *Like as the waves make towards the pebbled shore, so do our minutes hasten to their end; each changing place with that which goes before, in sequent toil all forwards do contend* ... right?"

He smiled. The way she'd recited the sonnet had a transcendent, spellbinding quality. "Shakespeare?"

"Mhmm."

He hadn't heard someone quote Shakespeare in years—let alone in the middle of a treacherous wasteland. Not like that. Not like it meant something.

Her voice had carried the cadence of something deeper than performance. There was a rhythm in it that tugged at some forgotten part of him, like music half remembered from another life. It didn't sound rehearsed. It sounded lived-in.

She hadn't just spoken lines. She'd summoned them—as if they'd been sitting inside her, waiting for a moment when the silence got too loud.

He'd seen plenty of women who could charm a crowd, but very few who could quiet the desert.

"You really are an actress," he said again, softer this time. As if he were speaking to the version of her that existed before all of this—the one who might've stood in the light, not the shadows.

She yawned. "I used to be. Now I'm nothing but a common thief."

He pursed his lips, the desperation that had driven her to that choice unsettling him—more than it had before. Rather than continue to force her to discuss it, he asked, "So how *does* Felix play into all this? I understand you and Theo. But Felix? Why's he wrapped up in your life of crime? Or is he trying to save his family too?"

Her breath caught softly. "No, he's English."

"Then what's his motivation? What's his role in all this—other than taking punches from men like me?" Despite his best efforts, Jack hadn't found it in him to feel remorse for punching Felix in the throat that first night he'd met Ruby. Felix had held him at gunpoint. He deserved the punch.

Ruby cringed at his joke, though. "He's in love with me," she said, her voice thinning like a thread pulled too tight. "He's the one who found us the contacts in the Middle East, who knows the people who will help my family—for a price, anyway. I think Felix is hoping I'll marry him if he helps me."

Jack turned at the hesitation in her voice. She was looking away, but the way her fingers twisted the edge of the blanket betrayed more than her words.

"Ah ..." The unsaid was clear. *She doesn't feel the same way about him. But ...*

The next thought made his gut clench.

"Does he think you'll marry him because you've got some sort of understanding?"

A sharp gust of wind howled around them, and she shivered.

"I haven't told him I'll marry him, if that's what you're implying."

She was quiet for a moment, the wind tugging a strand of hair across her face. Jack watched as she tucked it behind her ear with slow, deliberate fingers—as if the act of moving gave her something to hold on to.

"I've tried," she said at last, voice low. "To love him, I mean. It would make everything simpler. Safer. Felix is kind. Steady. He sees me as someone worth saving." She let out a bitter breath. "But it's hard to love someone who's in love with a version of you that doesn't exist anymore."

Jack didn't speak. He knew what it meant to feel like a ghost in your own life.

"Sometimes I think he's in love with the idea of being a hero. He wants to swoop in, fix everything. Save the girl." Her voice caught on the last word. "But I'm not that girl. I never was. And I'm tired of pretending I might be, just to make him feel like the world still makes sense."

Jack didn't know what unsettled him more—how much of himself he heard in her words, or the quiet ache in her voice when she said she was tired of pretending.

He understood that kind of exhaustion. The kind that didn't come from running or fighting but from trying to live up to who people needed you to be—even after you stopped believing you could be that person.

His jaw clenched. She hadn't completely denied that she'd been stringing Felix along either.

"So does Felix know he's on a fool's errand?"

Then she moistened her lips, almost nervously. "I've told him I don't love him. But that hasn't stopped him from holding on to hope."

"And … he's useful to you right now, so maybe it's convenient to let him go on hoping?" He winced at his own words but didn't take them back.

She turned her face toward the sky, scooting away from him some. "You really do think the worst of me, don't you, Jack Darby?"

He gave a dry chuckle. "Don't take it personally. I think the worst of everyone."

"Why?" The corners of her eyes crinkled. "Who hurt you so badly? Clearly something drove you to be a cynic and lose your faith in people. Your sister?"

Jack felt his chest tighten.

Alice? Yes. She'd hurt him.

And so had Kit. Kit's words came back to him—quiet, sharp, final. *"The timing between us is never right. Maybe it's the universe trying to tell us we're not right for each other, Jack."*

He'd tried to forget the way Kit looked at him that day. Not sad. Just ... so certain.

And Ginger and Noah—hearing them whisper behind closed doors, knowing he'd already been replaced. Of all of them, Noah came the closest to being blameless. Noah had loved his wife. Wanted her back. Jack couldn't fault his friend for that. But ... that hadn't made it any easier. Their friendship had been tested by fire and barely survived.

Prescott's hand on his shoulder. A smile like a razor.

"You're smarter than your father ever was. Maybe you'll survive."

Jack had been seventeen. Naïve. And Prescott had used him like a pawn before he ever knew the rules.

A better question would be: Who hadn't found him wanting?

The names didn't matter anymore. What mattered was that every time Jack had reached out, someone had pulled away.

That's why he didn't reach out anymore.

And if Ruby thought she could fix that, well ... she was more naïve than he realized.

He bristled, the weight of his thoughts making him feel as though his skin were crawling. "I thought you were tired," he said, his voice more strained than he'd anticipated. "You should sleep while you can, Ruby. We can't afford to rest for too long— and not just because I'm hoping we can find a way to Rutbah.

Once that sun is climbing in the sky, we'll be in a race against the clock for water."

Jack shifted slightly, and Ruby's knee brushed his. She didn't move away.

"Sorry," she murmured.

"You warm?" he asked.

"Getting there."

"You're not as bony as I expected."

Ruby let out a quiet laugh, and as she tilted her head, her temple brushed his.

She didn't move. Neither did he.

The warmth of her skin lingered like the last ember of a dying fire—too subtle to ignite, too stubborn to fade.

"You want to know what I think?" she said.

"I'm sure you're going to tell me—whether or not I actually want to know."

The corners of her mouth twitched in a smile. "I think somewhere, deep down, you're just a hopeless romantic who's a lot nicer than he's been pretending to be. You wouldn't be doing all this for your sister if you weren't."

Jack smirked. "Sounds like another way of saying I need to keep practicing my poker face." He leaned closer, his tired eyes burning now. "Maybe you should give me some acting lessons."

Ruby tilted her head against his, the contact surprisingly comfortable. "You don't need acting lessons. At least, not from me. You're a good man, Jack Darby. Maybe someday you'll remember that again."

She reached out, eyes closed, almost absently, and rested her hand on his arm. Within a few moments, her breathing deepened. Sleep had gripped her at last.

He released a tight breath, then relaxed, but just slightly. He didn't know what surprised him more: how comfortable he was with her touch or the fact that he didn't want to pull away. He told himself it was exhaustion. That tomorrow, in the light of day, he'd remember why he didn't get close to people anymore.

But tonight he let it be what it was: warmth.

A gust of wind scattered sand across the blanket, gritty and unwelcome. Jack brushed it off.

Just like we keep brushing off the truth. But the wind always comes back.

The stars were brilliant tonight—too brilliant, as if they were shining too much light on everything he wanted to keep hidden.

The last decade had taught him one thing: it was easier not to be seen. Easier to pretend the world wasn't still turning while everything inside him had stopped.

CHAPTER TWENTY-FIVE

GINGER

"Well … I have good news and bad news," Alastair said as he came into the dining room of Ginger's home in Cairo for dinner.

Ginger looked up expectantly, then exchanged a glance with Victoria. "Go on, then. Holding either of us in suspense right now is just cruel."

Alastair smiled. "I've found Noah." He sat in the chair across from Ginger, then removed his napkin from beside his plate. "He's outside of Jerusalem."

A servant hurried toward him with the soup that Victoria and Ginger had already eaten.

Pausing mid-cut into a piece braised chicken, a hopeful look came into Victoria's eyes. "With Fahad?"

"No. Not with Fahad. He's been working at a dig at Khirbet Qeiyafa. But it's Fahad who confirmed his location. They've seen each other. But what he's doing there … it's hard to say."

Oh, thank God. Noah.

The news that Alastair had found him—and that he was alive and well—brought more relief to Ginger than she'd expected.

She had no real reason to be worried about Noah's safety, but after everything they'd been through during the war, a part of her always remained fearful every time he left home. She'd made herself a promise to never let him go away without kissing him and telling him how much she loved him—but that did nothing to make her feel better.

"And Jack?" Victoria asked.

"He has no idea where Jack is." Alastair grimaced. "Apparently, they aren't traveling together. However—I did just pick up some chatter about a fugitive from British authorities, who had escaped from Lydda station in Gaza. One Jack Darby, traveling under forged papers—just this morning." Alastair's eyes twinkled as he reached for his soup spoon.

Before Alastair could get a bite in, Victoria stood, nearly knocking her chair down in the process. "Then we're going to Jerusalem. Fahad must be mistaken—Noah *has* to know where Jack is. And if we can find Noah, we can find Jack."

Ginger frowned at her, then gave Alastair a cautious look, unease simmering in her gut. "Why would Noah be in Jerusalem and not send word to me? I sent a telegram to Fahad that I needed to speak to Noah urgently."

"Well, you're here of course. He probably has sent word—to Penmore. He can't know what's happened with Ivy and Alex."

Victoria set both hands on the table and leaned toward Alastair with a determined look on her face. "Send word to Fahad. Tell Noah that we're coming and he's to meet us in Jerusalem. We can't afford to waste a moment."

In moments like this, Ginger was reminded of the way Victoria's father, Lord Helton, had taught her to take command of every situation. Of the socialite who had wrapped all of Anglo Cairo around her finger during the war. All those qualities had made her a formidable ally in running the hospital the last decade—and a calculating foe when the two women had been antagonists before they'd become friends.

Alastair leaned back in his chair, his expression growing darker. Yet his gaze remained sympathetic. "We risk leading Prescott to Jack if we're not careful, Victoria. And since—for now—that seems to be what Prescott wants most, not only could we lose our leverage by acting rashly, we could do more harm than good. Delivering a message to Jack from Prescott is one thing. But only Jack can decide what to do with that information. He has good reasons to want to avoid Prescott's surveillance."

"And I have even better reasons to see Prescott's demands satisfied," Victoria gritted through her teeth. "All he's asking is that Jack *contact* him, after all. But we're running out of time for Jack to do that. It's already been a full day. By the time we get to Jerusalem and find Noah, it could be another two more—and that's *if* Noah can contact Jack immediately. I'm not waiting until the last moment to do whatever is possible to save my daughter." She leveled a fierce look at Ginger. "Frankly, I'm appalled you don't agree."

The stillness that followed Victoria's outburst wasn't silent. Ginger steadied her breathing, her gaze flicking to the blank expression of the servant who'd been serving their dinner—the stiff demeanor, the bowed head that expressed embarrassment. Ginger gave him a smile and dismissed him, then set down her fork, her appetite gone.

"I know you're scared," she said gently, glancing from Victoria to Alastair. "We all are. But rushing into Jerusalem without a plan isn't brave. It's reckless. And we've all lived through enough war to know what that leads to."

Victoria opened her mouth to argue, but Ginger raised a hand. "Let me speak." Her words weren't sharp but formed with the quiet firmness that had calmed wounded men in field hospitals and stubborn patients in sick wards.

A chastened expression crossed Victoria's face. *Thank goodness for that.* When Victoria felt strongly enough about something she didn't back down easily.

"I'm not saying we wait around and do nothing," Ginger went on. "But we must proceed with caution. Go carefully. We can't allow ourselves to be driven by fear. We have to be smarter than Prescott believes we are."

Alastair folded his arms. "I'm intrigued. What are you suggesting?"

"How many times did I travel in disguise—and in plain sight—as a nurse during the war, Alastair? If we can get the proper documents, we can get past inspection quietly enough. Say we're traveling to Jerusalem on a humanitarian mission for the Red Cross or something of that sort. Surely, you've got a friend or two that can help you obtain what we need for the paperwork."

A corner of Alastair's mouth lifted. "I can work on the travel papers tonight." He paused, then added, "But that still leaves Prescott."

"We can't let him follow us," Ginger said flatly. "Not if it leads him to Jack. Alastair is right, Victoria—we don't know the lengths Jack has gone to remain invisible to Prescott. What sort of allies would we be if we exposed him?"

"Then we don't let him follow," Victoria said, her eyes narrowing. She tilted her head at Alastair. "Is there any way to draw him off? *And* make him believe that Ginger and I are still here in Cairo? Just to give us a head start?"

Alastair considered, drumming his fingers against his upper arm. "If I plant a few misleading pieces of information—drop hints that Jack's heading toward Alexandria, maybe boarding a ship—Prescott might bite. I'd need to move fast. I'll think of something to convince him you've stayed put. Maybe Lucy could help with that."

Ginger swallowed, a wave of emotion washing over her. Lucy *wanted* to help, but thus far they'd mostly kept her in the dark—for her own safety. But, yes, Lucy might be useful here. She was known in Anglo Cairo society. She might be able to make a show of some sort of decoy.

She nodded tightly at Alastair. "Then let's do it. If we can buy even a day or two, it could make the difference."

The ticking clock from the end of the dining room marked the seconds too loudly. Ginger reached for her water glass. The condensation had left a ring on the table and she dabbed at it with her napkin, her hands steady despite the tension humming beneath her skin.

This was not the life she had chosen. She had left the war behind, or tried to. She was a wife. A mother. A physician and hospital director. But none of that mattered if she couldn't help save her son.

And Ivy.

The thought of the two of them, so young and so helpless, stung in a way she hadn't expected.

Victoria stared down at her plate, untouched since Alastair had entered the room. She sank slowly into her chair, her fingers gripping the arms as if she needed to anchor herself to something solid.

"It still won't be enough," she murmured. "I don't know much about him, but I know enough. Prescott is perceptive in a way that takes my breath away. I've gone up against men like him a few times. He terrifies me."

Ginger exchanged a glance with Alastair. *What is she getting at?*

Victoria's voice was softer now, but no less desperate. "Even if we make it to Jerusalem, even if we find Noah—what then?

We'll need help. Jack will need help if he wants to survive Prescott's game. Someone with authority. Connections we don't have—maybe once I knew men with that sort of power ... but not anymore."

Ginger hesitated for a few moments, Victoria's words sparking an idea.

A mad one.

And Victoria might hate me for suggesting it.

Victoria had once told her that she didn't dare tell Ivy's biological father about her—not just because Ivy could lose her inheritance from the Fishers—but because the repercussions would shatter that man's life.

But Victoria had been become pregnant while her father had still controlled her work—sending her to seduce powerful men in Anglo Cairo society. If Ivy's father was one of those men, and the information could be used to sway him, *maybe ...*

"There's someone else we could reach out to," Ginger said quietly.

Victoria lifted her brow. "Who?"

"You've never said who Ivy's father is," Ginger said, not unkindly. "But if he's someone powerful, someone in Anglo Cairo with influence ... he might have a reason to care about what happens to her. Or we could induce him to help, if it comes down to it. And that could be a kind of leverage we haven't tried."

Victoria gripped the arms of her chair more tightly.

Alastair didn't speak, but he leaned forward, his eyes bright with interest.

"I'm not saying we involve him directly," Ginger added. "But if he has resources—friends, political favors, money—maybe it's time to ask."

A long pause. "We can't," Victoria whispered.

"I know it's a frightening prospect, but—"

"You don't understand. It won't help. He's the reason Ivy's in this mess in the first place. I don't know how Prescott knew—I didn't think it was so obvious, but he knew." Victoria's hand trembled and she lifted her glass, then set it down again without drinking.

What on earth? "I don't understand," Ginger said, her unease growing. She shifted, a startling idea, one maybe that she'd been too blind to see, starting to bloom before her eyes.

Victoria's eyes were bright with tears. "Ivy *has* someone," she said in an emotional voice. "Someone who would burn the world down to keep her safe. But he doesn't know—I never knew how to tell him. And now it's too late … I'm certain Prescott kidnapped Ivy to destroy him."

Ginger's breath caught, the pulse in her ears growing loud.

Alastair's spoon stilled halfway to his mouth.

Victoria didn't look at them. Her eyes were fixed on some distant memory, something too old and too tender to speak of easily. She looked at Ginger then, the truth stark in her expression.

"Ivy's father," she said, "is Jack."

CHAPTER TWENTY-SIX

ALEX

Alex shifted in his seat, watching the fan make circles on the ceiling above the wide oak desk. A glance out of the corner of his eye revealed Ivy trying to hide the nervous bounce in her knee. He fought the urge to reach over and set his hand on her knee, help her feel more settled.

She'd smiled when they'd seen the Union Jack in the front of the consulate. The first time she'd truly smiled since Penmore. Seeing her relieved like that had settled some of his misgivings about coming here.

After what Alex had discovered in the newspaper, though, Ivy had convinced him they needed to go to the British consulate once they arrived in Cairo. Not to turn themselves over—in fact, Alex had given his name to the consular official as Alexander Darby and told them his father was Jack—but to take the evidence he'd found in the newspaper that the foreign correspondent, Gretchen Herbert, was in trouble and needed aid.

Trouble was, Alex only had the one newspaper clipping to back up his claims. And the word of a fifteen-year-old didn't hold much weight. Also problematic was the fact that Alex had no idea when the paper had even been published. For all he knew, whatever help Gretchen Herbert had needed was no longer relevant.

The consular official had taken notes while Alex had explained the situation, saying little and betraying even less with his expression. Whether or not he believed Alex—he couldn't quite say.

But the official had left Ivy and Alex sitting here for over forty-five minutes now, and he hadn't reappeared.

"I think we should go," Alex said, shifting in his seat. "Something doesn't feel right."

"I've never taken you for such a nervous ninny," Ivy said with a teasing smile. "What do you think is going to happen here at the consulate of all places—I'll be kidnapped again?"

"No, that's not it." Alex bristled, then loosened his collar. "I can't really even explain it, but being here just doesn't feel right. I would feel a whole lot better if we'd been able to talk to Uncle Alastair first."

They'd attempted that—gone straight to Aunt Lucy and Uncle Alastair's house in Anglo Cairo after arriving at the train station. Neither of them had been there, and the servants hadn't shared any information on when they might return. Bahiti, Aunt Lucy's long-time servant and the only one Alex knew, hadn't been there either, so they'd left a note and gone again.

Now Alex felt more certain than ever that they should have stayed, even if the servants hadn't gone out of their way to make them feel welcome. They were both disheveled and dirty—the servants probably hadn't believed they were family. Right now they looked more like beggars from the streets—stained clothes, grime mucking their skin. Covered in cinders and ash from the trainyard.

Maybe that's why the consular official had left them here

too. Though he couldn't have denied their perfect English, he probably doubted their story.

"I don't think he believed us," Alex said, giving voice to that worrying thought. "Maybe he's even trying to contact Uncle Jack—tell him we've turned up here."

Ivy frowned, her dark gaze scanning his. She bit her lip, hesitating, clearly uncertain if she should speak at all, then managed, "Alex … is there any way that those letters could just be a coincidence? I don't claim to know anything about ciphers, but are you *absolutely certain—*"

"I'm certain. It's a cipher. The mathematical probability of it being anything else is astronomical. Besides," he added with a calculated shrug that he hoped made him look easy and confident—he didn't like the fact that she didn't seem to have complete faith in what he'd discovered— "Besides, this isn't the first time I've spotted a cipher in a newspaper. They do it in plain sight like this all the time. I first started checking after I read a story—maybe with Sexton Blake, I can't remember—years ago."

"But why on earth would someone leave that message? Especially with a cipher? It seems like it could have been easily missed. And if this journalist really needed help, why put it in the paper at all? Why not go to someone who could help her, like the police?"

He restrained an annoyed look. "You really put too much faith in the police, Ivy. There's a reason even novels like the Sherlock Holmes stories don't paint them in the best light."

"And there's a reason those are *novels,* Alex." She rolled her eyes. "You have the soul of a cynical old man sometimes, you know that?"

He flattened his palms on his knees, feeling strangely unnerved by her criticism. "And you're too naïve." Maybe even too good for them all. She spent her day like some sort of peni-

tential saint, following Mum around and tending to the sick—
what did she know anyway?

No wonder Mum loves her better than me.

That thought came out of nowhere, unbidden and sinister in
the sick curl of jealousy that spread through him. Or maybe he
was just hungry, irritable, and tired.

She didn't answer, her eyelashes lowering as she stared at
her lap.

Guilt followed. "I didn't—"

"It's fine," she answered. She offered a sweet smile, full of
forgiveness and warmth. "We've both had a long couple of
weeks. And how could I be mad at you, anyway? You saved my
life."

And there it is—that saintly piety.

Just once, he'd like to see her get angry and stay angry. In
fact, that moment in the abandoned coach when she'd told him
about Roedean might have been the most frustrated she'd been
with him for ages, which seemed a silly thing for her to get
upset about.

The distant clack of typewriter keys filled the silence that
settled between them. Occasionally, Dad spoke of his days in the
war, working for the Arab Bureau, and Alex imagined him
sitting in an office like this, filing paperwork in the dusty heat
of Cairo while soldiers lost their lives and suffered in the
trenches of France.

That reality didn't give Alex a lot to be proud of—but he
didn't dare ever say that to his parents. *Both* of his parents, actually, had missed all the action and important battles of the war
and served instead in the obscurity of the Middle East and
Egypt. Some of his friends from the village had real heroes for
fathers. Ones with medals and injuries that proved the hard-
ships they'd faced.

A thud of approaching footsteps jerked Alex from the

unpleasant thoughts, and he lifted his head as the consular official—a Mr. Jones—opened the door. He gave Alex a nod, then opened the door more widely for another man, an older, well-dressed gentleman with white hair and piercing blue eyes.

"Here they are," Mr. Jones said to the gentleman, relief in his expression. A mottled, red flush had risen from his neck onto his jawline. "Just where I told you they were."

"Excellent." The gentleman entered, his movements brisk as he went around to the opposite side of the desk. He unbuttoned his jacket, revealing a matching suit vest below it, then flicked his gaze at Mr. Jones. "You can leave us. Thank you."

Mr. Jones seemed only too happy to comply. He backed out quietly, closing the door behind him with a *click*.

Ivy shifted beside him, her gaze remaining on the door, then leaned toward Alex.

"Did you see that?" she whispered, her voice barely audible to him. "He looked afraid."

Alex glanced over, frowning. He hadn't noticed. "Afraid of what?"

"I don't know. But Mr. Jones looked pale."

As though he could hear her, the gentleman's eyes moved to Ivy, the scrutiny of his gaze seeming to unnerve her. She sat straighter, smoothing her hands over her dirty skirt. No doubt she hated her appearance right now. If she had any flaw, it would be a smidge of vanity.

Then the man looked at Alex. His lips twitched, the corners of his eyes narrowing as his stare hardened. He looked back at Ivy for just a moment, as though comparing them side by side. If Ivy was dirty, Alex was filthy. He'd spent days crawling around in shafts in the ship. The man's white brow raised.

"Alexander Darby, yes?"

Alex nodded.

"And you are?" he asked Ivy.

"Ivy … Darby."

Come on, Ivy. She didn't sound comfortable enough with the lie.

"Then you're siblings?" the man asked.

"Twins, actually," Alex said, clearing his throat. "Listen, Mr. —?"

"Either way, you're quite young for having found such an *interesting* cipher."

The man reached for the scrap of newspaper that Mr. Jones had left on his desk and took out a pair of spectacles. He set the spectacles on the bridge of his nose and lifted the newspaper. "What type of cipher?"

"A null cipher," Alex said, sitting straighter. For the briefest moment, a flicker of insecurity went through him, as though he wanted—needed—to prove himself to this man. He saw intelligence in the gentleman's gaze. A perceptiveness that gave Alex the impression that he was staring at someone intellectually equal to himself.

The gentleman didn't respond right away. He lifted the scrap again, angling it toward the light. "And the key?"

"Fourth letter of every fourth word in the fourth paragraph," Alex said. "I recognized the structure. It's subtle but familiar."

"Familiar to whom?"

"To someone who enjoys patterns. Cryptography. Numbers." He shrugged. "It's the kind of thing you'd use if you wanted to warn someone without drawing attention."

The man gave a quiet hum of approval. Beside Alex, Ivy shifted. Not the restless kind of movement—more like the wary sort, the kind she made when her mum was about to ask a question she didn't want to answer. Her spine was straighter now, her hands perfectly still in her lap. That usually meant she was on alert.

Interesting. Maybe she was more cautious since her kidnapping.

"And your sister?" The gentleman glanced at her, watching her closely. "Did she notice it too?"

"No," Alex said quickly. "I saw it." He hesitated. He didn't want to make Ivy seem useless—or have the man question why she'd come. "First, anyway. But she's just as good as I am at this."

She flinched.

The man gave a slow nod, still watching Ivy for a second too long, and her jaw tightened further. She didn't like this. Of course she didn't. *She probably wants to throttle me for lying.*

"You understand," the gentleman said finally, returning his gaze to Alex, "that spotting such a cipher isn't something most adults could do—let alone a fifteen-year-old."

Alex felt heat crawl up his neck. "It wasn't that hard."

"You remind me of someone I once knew. Sharp mind. Eager to prove himself. Good with numbers." The gentleman's smile was small, assessing. "But he made the mistake of under-estimating the weight of the work."

"What work?" Alex asked.

"Let's not get ahead of ourselves." He folded the paper with quiet precision. "Tell me—do you speak any other languages?"

"French and Arabic. I'm pretty good at German too."

"Ah." He tapped the edge of the folded paper. "And your father taught you?"

"Mostly. He's strict about languages." *About school, really.* It was the one area where his father always demanded excellence.

"And you enjoy this? Breaking things apart, finding patterns?"

"I do."

Another pause. Ivy's fingers had curled slightly into the fabric of her skirt. She barely seemed to be breathing—still and focused like she got when she sensed something wasn't quite right but didn't yet know what.

"Then I'd like to make you an offer," the gentleman said at last, and his tone shifted to something cautious. "But …"

An offer? Alex tried to restrain himself from leaning forward eagerly. If he didn't know better, it sounded as though the man wanted to employ him. He exchanged a glance with Ivy. "But what?"

"But, on the other hand, you're runaways, aren't you? It would be highly irresponsible for me not to turn you over to the police."

"We're not runaways," Ivy cut in quickly. Her eyes were wide, her face white.

The gentleman frowned. "Am I to assume that you don't want me to turn you in to the police for a *different* reason? Nothing nefarious, I hope."

"No—nothing like that," Alex said. He reached over and set his hand on Ivy's, hoping to keep her from speaking. She wouldn't do a good job concealing the truth. "I know our appearance isn't the best, but it's just that our father is an archeologist. We were at a dig when I came across this cipher. Thought it would be important to turn it in immediately."

"Ah, that makes sense." The gentleman's face brightened. "Excellent. That was quite sensible of you." He sat back in his chair. "If that's the case, then I'd love to make a proposal to you, though I may need to speak to your father about it."

Alex hesitated. This lie was quickly spinning out of his control. If the man insisted on talking to Uncle Jack, this could all get out of hand. "What's the offer? Our father won't mind. He's not in Cairo right now—went to Luxor for a few days. He was needed to … consult at a dig."

"Of course. A famed archeologist like your father is likely to be in demand." The gentleman cleared his throat. "It's a modest offer, of course. But, you see, I have several other newspaper articles written by this 'Gretchen Herbert' I'd like you to review." He gave Ivy a taut smile. "Both of you, of course. I'll need you to search for hidden messages, perhaps even a pattern. Come stay with me for a few days. Room, board, and something in your pocket for your time."

Ivy's hand closed tightly around his. Alex felt it before he saw the expression on her face—a barely veiled alarm in her eyes, the tension creeping into her posture. She didn't trust this man. Not even a little.

"Why?" Alex asked, ignoring the way Ivy's fingers were practically drilling into his skin.

"Because sometimes the world needs people like you." The gentleman's gaze was steady. "Quiet minds with sharp edges."

Ivy's thumb tapped once against his wrist—a signal. A warning.

"And I always make a point to invest in potential before someone else does."

An offer to work as a cryptographer? *For money?* And from a British government official, no less. A shiver of excitement went through Alex. No one had ever offered to pay him for something like this before.

Ivy cleared her throat, drawing Alex's attention to her for a moment. She shook her head in warning, more forcefully this time, then leaned toward him and hissed in his ear, "We don't even know who he is."

The man smiled. "How silly of me. Did I forget to introduce myself? My name is Prescott Federline. It's a pleasure to make your acquaintance."

CHAPTER TWENTY-SEVEN

NOAH

Fahad's home had transformed from the warm, welcoming sanctuary where Noah had always sought refuge while in Jerusalem to a darkened, desolate place. Bereft of laughter and the scents of Nasira's cooking, the main room felt hollow. Noah sat with his back to the wall, guilt pressing down like a boulder.

Usually filled with the clatter of dishes and children's laughter, the house now sat cloaked in silence. The rugs still smelled faintly of saffron and woodsmoke, but the hearth was cold and the cushions stacked instead of scattered. Even the walls, normally softened by the glow of extinguished brass lamps, seemed sharper in the daylight. A home stripped of life—because of him.

He'd been reckless by involving Fahad in this once he'd found out about Hower's connection to Blackwell, but Fahad was one of the few people in Jerusalem whom he trusted absolutely. Returning here last night, after he'd stripped Hower's car of any recognizable markings and burned it out to a hollow shell, Noah couldn't help feeling as though he'd betrayed Fahad.

After Noah had explained the situation—his killing of Hower and his driver, the fact that the entire village had witnessed his actions and him speaking in English—Fahad had sent his family to stay with a relative of Nasira's.

Then Noah and Fahad had set to putting a plan in motion.

Because that's the type of friend Fahad is. Faithful to the end, even when I've abused his trust and hospitality.

Noah's gaze moved to Fahad, who stood waiting by the door, stroking his salt-and-pepper beard, his brows set in grim determination.

The sheikh's men had been watching the house since before dawn, when Fahad had sent a servant boy to relay an invitation to the sheikh himself. Whether the sheikh would accept Fahad's invitation wasn't clear. He'd already been suspicious of Noah. Now he might think the setup was a trap.

And it was—in a way.

Just not for the sheikh.

Noah couldn't stay hidden for long. When Hower didn't turn up, British officials were likely to come looking. Absent of the evidence that Hower had been Blackwell and with little certainty about how far up the chain of command the rot went, Noah had decided to take his chances spending what little time he might still have as a free man finding a way to expose the corruption—or getting the British government the intelligence Hower had claimed Knight wanted him here for.

If Knight himself was a Blackwell operative, then maybe that evidence would be enough for Noah to save his family, if not himself.

The low growl of an engine broke the silence, distant at first, then growing louder, steadier, and deliberate. Noah moved to the edge of the curtain, heart thudding once before he tamped it down. The tires ground against the dirt road. Whoever it was, they weren't trying to hide.

Noah squinted toward the window. He stood in the shadows of the room, golden midday sunlight slanting across the floor beside him. The driver pulled off to the side of the dirt road in front of Fahad's house.

"Sheikh Khalil?" Fahad hissed with a questioning look.

"Alain Roche," Noah answered in a low voice as the man opened the door and stood. Roche seemed out of place here in his fancy French clothes, and he shaded his eyes against the glare of the sun. He sized up the house for a few moments, his expression entirely neutral.

Since he'd left France, Noah had wondered about the Frenchman—how trustworthy he was, what he might know. Alastair had sent Jack to him because of his expertise in the region's politics. The fact that Roche had immediately turned around and delivered Jack to Knight either spoke of shrewdness in keeping his well-placed contacts like Knight happy ... or perhaps something more nefarious.

Perhaps, even, a connection to Blackwell.

Roche approached with his usual smug confidence—just the sort of arrogance Fahad despised. The French, in his eyes, had carved up the Middle East like meat on a butcher's slab and tossed the Arab leader, Faisal Hussein, from Syria after all he'd done for the Arab revolt.

Noah remembered the first time he saw Faisal—robes of white, eyes that missed nothing. There'd been a gravity to the man, a quiet certainty that peace was possible. That idealism had felt contagious once. Now it was just another casualty of the unending war Britain could never hope to control.

Faisal had been used poorly. Together with his father, the emir of Mecca, and his brother Abdullah who now ruled the Transjordan, Faisal's dreams had been to join the Arab world under a pan-Arab government, where Moslems—both Sunni and Shia—Arab Christians, and Jews could all live in peace. The land mandates after the war had robbed him of his "kingdom of Syria" and pushed him into becoming king of Iraq, a land where he was unknown and had been met with a hostile, unwelcome response.

And now he was dead.

Only twelve years after being installed as king of Iraq, Faisal had apparently died of a heart attack the previous September. A heart attack striking a man who was only forty-eight.

Quiet, convenient.

Though Noah had heard whispers of poison and hadn't trusted the official account then, he trusted it even less now after what Hower's driver had said about Sharif al-Rashid.

The knock on the door jarred him from his thoughts and he stiffened, his hand tighter against the handle of his gun.

Fahad opened the door. "Mr. Roche," he said in accented English. "Welcome. Please come in."

A footstep shuffled as Roche stepped into the dark. He blinked, eyes clearly adjusting. "If it's all the same to you, I would prefer to remain outside. The air is rather oppressive indoors and—"

Click.

Noah stepped out of the shadows, gun already well aimed. "Hello, Roche."

"*Mon dieu.* You've taken to theatrics now?" Roche's eyes locked on Noah, his hands lifting in surrender. Fahad stepped in behind him and pressed his own gun to Roche's neck, then shut the door with his foot.

Once, Noah might've welcomed Roche with a brandy and a conversation about Arab unity. Now, he watched the man as if he were a cornered jackal—because that's what this war of shadows made of them all.

"You give an odd meaning to the word *welcome*," Roche said, tilting his head back, just a fraction, toward Fahad.

"My apologies." Noah came closer, his menacing stance unwavering. "Fahad is acting at my insistence."

"The invitation was yours, then. Of course."

"Indeed," Noah said with a taut smile. He nodded toward Fahad. "Check him for weapons."

"You'll find only a penknife. For utility, not protection. I don't carry firearms—*c'est un peu vulgaire*, don't you think?" Roche said, bristling as Fahad ran his hands over his white linen trousers. "I prefer civility among gentlemen."

"That's your mistake, I suppose," Noah said with a smirk. "You should never make any assumptions about my civility."

Roche's eyes darkened. "No, I'm well aware of that, Benson. I tried to tell Captain Knight that your sympathies in the Arab world aren't as ambiguous as he seemed to think. I'm not naïve enough to believe you fight for king and empire. Your reputation suggests otherwise."

Noah didn't bother with an answer at first. Roche wasn't wrong about his loyalty to the pan-Arab nationalist cause—not because of his mother's Egyptian heritage, though, but because it was the only way he saw a path of peace forward for the warring tribes that had lived with centuries of conflict in this region of the world.

And yet ...

"I'm here on behalf of Britain, aren't I?" Noah asked, raising a brow.

For Jack. And to try to buy some security for my family from Knight.

But Roche didn't need to know or believe that.

Fahad removed a fountain pen from the breast pocket of Roche's jacket, along with the pocketknife, and handed them to Noah.

Noah waited until Fahad had resumed his place behind Roche with the gun, then slipped his own back into the holster.

He examined both the pocketknife and the pen—the latter revealing a screw top hiding a small pill. Noah lifted it between his thumb and forefinger, and Roche shrugged. "A precaution, nothing more. You can't blame me for not wanting to suffer needlessly, if it comes to it."

Likely cyanide, then.

Roche said, "Forgive me, but I prefer to know why I've been detained. Or is ambiguity part of the performance?"

Noah frowned, then came even closer. "Your arms, please."

Roche did as instructed, and Noah checked him for the distinctive Blackwell tattoo.

Nothing.

As he lifted his gaze to meet Roche's, the man furrowed his brow. "What were you expecting to find?"

"What do you know of Blackwell, Roche?"

Roche froze. Then blanched.

For the first time since Noah had met him, the smugness was gone from his face, fear flickering in his eyes instead. "N-not a thing," Roche stammered.

"A wise response." Noah stepped back slowly. "Then I take it you didn't know Hower was a Blackwell operative?"

"H-Hower?" Roche sputtered.

Interesting. His surprise seemed genuine. Still, Noah couldn't let his guard down so easily. "Who ordered you and Hower to apprehend Jack and me in France?"

"Captain Knight—I believe. He ordered me to apprehend you, anyway. If you turned up in France. Then Hower found me, said Knight had sent him. That you'd been spotted."

So it was possible that Hower hadn't been sent directly by Knight, then. *Or perhaps not an MI5 agent at all.* "And you verified that Hower worked for MI5?"

Roche stiffened further, if it was possible. "He ... knew all about Knight's orders. I had no reason to question him."

Noah nodded toward Fahad, who led Roche toward a low, comfortable divan covered with red and gold cushions. Roche sat, beads of sweat now lining his forehead. Clearly he knew enough about Blackwell to understand the seriousness of Noah's implications.

Pinching the bridge of his nose, Noah tried to piece together what he could, his mind racing. If Prescott Federline had sent Hower to intercept Jack and Noah in France and Hower had simply pretended to be MI5 the entire time, it might mean that Knight wasn't part of all this. He'd wanted Noah for the job when they'd met in England, yes, but Noah hadn't spoken to him directly since then—all his communications had been with Hower.

Had Hower's real job been to distract him? Or monitor him, waiting to see if he reconnected with Jack?

If Knight was part of it, even tangentially, Noah had to move with speed.

Fahad had already told him since he'd arrived last night that Ginger had gone to Cairo and sent an urgent message for him to contact her. Desperate as he was to do so, he needed to exercise caution. Another wrong move could threaten his family—and he'd already killed Hower and the other Blackwell operative.

Rather than risk contacting Ginger, Noah had sent a cable to Alastair, asking him to take Ginger to a safe house. He'd join her there as soon as possible.

Even more motivation to find out just what Roche might know that would be of use.

Noah pulled a wooden chair from a table, then carried it over toward Roche. As he did, Fahad moved away, stepping into the shadows Noah had occupied before, which gave him a view of the road. His gun remained in his hands, though, but no longer aimed at Roche.

Setting the chair a few feet from Roche, Noah straddled it, bracing his forearms against the wooden frame of the back. "Tell me what you know of Sharif Kamal al-Rashid."

Roche gave him a curious look. "Al-Rashid? I fail to see how he is relevant."

Noah's expression didn't change, and Roche shifted. "No matter." He cleared his throat. "Al-Rashid is a Hashemite. I'm not clear on his relation to Hussein bin Ali, the former emir of Mecca, but I believe he's a distant relative."

That much Fahad had already told him.

"What does he want with the Iraqi throne?" Noah asked tersely.

Roche leaned back against the pillows on the divan, wiping his palms against his trousers. "Officially—nothing. You won't find a word about him in the newspapers or official reports."

"I'm more interested in the unofficial accounts."

Roche smiled pleasantly enough. "Off the record then, al-Rashid has been stirring up support among the Shia Moslem majority in Iraq for the last few years, using their conflict with the Sunni to sow discontent with Faisal and now his son, Ghazi. He believes Faisal was too soft in his response to the British and French—little more than a puppet. And he's loudly anti-Zionist."

Noah tensed, watching Roche's face closely. "In other words, he'd be the perfect candidate to seek alliances in exchange for support for his own causes from other countries that might view Britain as an enemy. Like the Germans."

Roche nodded, looking around the room with less caution, and Noah followed his gaze as it trailed along the thick adobe walls of the sitting room, cool despite the sun. Most of the shutters were drawn, slats leaking bars of light onto the tiled floor. Roche's polished shoes looked absurd against the worn rug.

"And he likely would have wanted Faisal dead," Noah mused, rubbing his chin. Fahad's gaze was on him now, alert.

"You aren't the first to theorize that, though, Benson." Roche crossed one knee over the other. "For an expert in the region, you're woefully uninformed and out of touch with the current state of things. But there's no evidence Faisal was murdered. Or that al-Rashid had anything to do with it." Some of his confidence appeared to have returned.

No evidence ... that Roche knew of.

But what if someone else had found it? Someone who'd been in Iraq. Who'd disappeared under mysterious circumstances. Who Sharif al-Rashid had come looking for.

The idea sank through Noah's stomach like a stone.

If Alice and Kit had found proof—real, damning evidence—that tied Sharif al-Rashid not only to the Germans but to the death of Faisal himself ...

Then they wouldn't have just uncovered corruption. They would have upended a would-be kingmaker's entire plan.

And now they were gone. Not disappeared—taken.

They might also no longer be alive.

Noah breathed slowly. But Alice and Kit were smart. They'd been working in the espionage world for long enough to know that their best hope of survival would be leaving the evidence they'd found somewhere that someone else might find it—and a trail. With that threat lingering, al-Rashid would have less reason to simply kill them if he captured them.

And the fact that they hadn't resurfaced strongly suggested that they'd been captured.

The air felt thinner suddenly. If they'd been taken—if the wrong people had found what they uncovered—then they were either bargaining with death ... *or already gone.* And Jack didn't even know.

But it was a lead, nonetheless.

Noah stood slowly, his gaze now fixed on Fahad. The sheikh still hadn't come, and it was well past the time Fahad had invited him for.

He's not coming. He doesn't trust either of us now.

And without his help, Noah's last link to Kit and Alice might be lost.

But the boy had said the sheikh had hidden the women from al-Rashid, which meant he couldn't be one of al-Rashid's allies. It also meant the sheikh might be able to help Noah trace their movements before and after they'd been taken, if they'd been captured.

Noah turned toward Roche. "Thank you. You'll be working for me for a few days, Roche. In exchange, I promise no harm will come to you and we'll part this as friends and allies."

Roche chuckled. "And if I don't?"

"Then I'll sell you out to Blackwell. Hower is dead. They'll be looking for whoever killed him and I'll be more than happy to supply your name."

Roche went white once more. "What do you want from me?" he whispered.

"We'll start by using that infamous well-connected network to help me find out where Jack Darby was last seen. And then you'll help me follow the trail his sister took before she disappeared. We have no time to waste."

CHAPTER TWENTY-EIGHT

JACK

The plane dipped low over the plains as the sun broke free from some clouds across Mesopotamia, a pale gold light beaming down in rays onto the buildings. Jack pressed his palm to the cold frame of the biplane, the roar of the engine and strong rush of the wind still overtaking most of his senses, and watched the city take shape below.

Baghdad didn't announce itself like Cairo or Rome or London. It revealed itself in whispers—mudbrick and palm, smoke and shadow. From above, it looked ancient and incomplete, as if time itself had abandoned the job halfway through. Here, where so many believed humanity had dawned and civilization had taken shape, he could see what had spawned the idea of curses from a wrathful God.

The Tigris shimmered beneath them, sluggish and brown, cutting the city in two like a scar. On either side of it sprawled clusters of flat-roofed houses and winding streets stitched together by centuries of conquest, collapse, and rebirth. He could just make out the domes of mosques, the squat Ottoman-era barracks, and, somewhere beyond that, he imagined the bones of Babylon still sleeping beneath the earth.

The engine whined as they drew closer to the earth. Ruby, seated beside him, had gone still and quiet. Her eyes were closed, but she didn't look afraid. Just peaceful. As though she was enjoying the wind and sun on her face, despite the tight squeeze of the cockpit, which forced her body to press against his. Not that he minded the contact.

She hadn't said much since they'd left Azraq. They hadn't had much time there anyway. The RAF pilot they'd found there hadn't seemed to care too much for explanations or the reason they needed to fly to Rutbah and find Sgt. Maj. Ned Harris—that Jack knew him appeared to be enough of an explanation.

And once they'd gotten to Rutbah, their path to Baghdad had been even easier. Ned agreed to take them without hesitation. They'd left within the hour of arriving at Rutbah, which meant it was late afternoon now, though Jack had lost his sense of time.

For once, luck seemed on their side.

But he still had to face Baghdad itself, an enormous city that was rife with tension and where he had little idea of where to start looking for Kit.

The last time he'd set foot in Baghdad, the war had only just ended. Ottoman boots still echoed in alleyways, and the British flag flew without apology. Now it was March 1934, and the kingdom of Iraq was trying to stand on its own feet. But the lines of the mandate still ran deep. Jack could feel them—under the sand and the skin of the city.

The death of King Faisal had been a blow to the alliance with the British Empire here. Faisal had been a steady hand, if not always a clean one. He'd kept the tribes in line, soothed British egos, and promised just enough reform to keep the revolutionaries at bay. Now, with his son Ghazi on the throne—barely a man and already in the pockets of Arab nationalists—Baghdad felt like a powder keg with the fuse lit. The British embassy might still swagger through their corridors and bark orders at ministers, but Jack knew better. The city was restless. Watching. Waiting.

The tires hit dirt, and the jolt rippled through his spine. The aircraft lurched forward with a screech and rattle, kicking up a storm of dust that blurred the horizon.

Jack exhaled, slow and tight.

They taxied to a halt near a makeshift hangar—corrugated metal, half-sagged canvas roofs, and sandbags piled like afterthoughts. A line of date palms leaned wearily along the edge of the field. An RAF officer stood waiting under the shade, uniform starched and eyes hidden behind mirrored spectacles. *Best to stay away from him, if possible.* Jack had his forged paperwork, but he didn't want to test it after the incident with Theo at Lydda.

Heat rose from the runway as Ned brought the biplane to a stop. Jack snuck a glance at Ruby, who'd donned an aviator cap before leaving Rutbah. She looked adorable, frankly—not that he'd tell her that.

As Ned killed the engine, she lifted the goggles from her eyes and grinned. "That was incredible," she said, leaning toward Ned. She squeezed his shoulder. "I'm jealous that you get to do this every day."

Her smile was genuine, her exhilaration palpable. For the first time since he'd met her, Jack had a feeling he'd finally gotten a glimpse of the *real* Ruby. Maybe the one that had existed before she'd been ejected from Germany and become a criminal … the side she now kept tightly under lock and key.

What had she been like before this? Before fear and desperation had robbed her of everything? Innocence was the furthest thing Jack would associate now with a woman like Ruby, but he could almost picture her on a stage, a picture of grace and beauty, a woman that men would daydream over.

A hot flush went through him, burning like acid up his throat. He smiled, then stood and offered her a hand. "Shall we?"

Ned helped them both down from the plane, and as Jack set foot on the dusty runway, he frowned at the proximity of the nearby hangars. Ned had brought them to the airfield where the RAF was stationed, of course, and even though he'd logged them under aliases when leaving Rutbah, Jack couldn't help but worry that someone here might recognize him.

He took his bags from the cargo hatch, then held a hand out to Ned to shake it. "I think I'll leave you here. Only want to get so close to the others here."

"Understandably." Ned shook his hand. "Listen, I'll be here in Baghdad until about noon tomorrow—if you need to catch me for a flight back. If you're not here, I'll assume you don't need me and just leave without you."

Jack nodded. "I don't know how long this will take. I doubt it'll only be a twenty-four-hour trip, but you never know. Thanks for everything."

Before Ned could respond, Ruby looped her arms around his neck and kissed his cheek. "Glad to have met you, Sarge."

Ned's gaze warmed, and he flicked a glance at Jack.

Jack hadn't explained who Ruby was, and Ned hadn't asked. But Ned smiled. "Sounds like a keeper," he said with a crooked smile to Jack, then gave a mock-salute. "Do try to not get shot. Especially if you're flying back with me. Nothing more difficult to get out of the leather than a bloodstain."

"I'll do what I can." With a smirk, Jack waved and headed away from Ned, slinging his bag over his shoulder.

Ruby was steps behind him. "I didn't know getting shot in Baghdad was a possibility," she said, her voice wary.

He gave her a smile over his shoulder. "It's always a possibility, sweetheart. Haven't you learned that by now?"

She rolled her eyes. "You know, I think you failed to fully inform me what I was taking on when I signed up to help you." She frowned, scanning the airfield. "Where are we heading now?"

"Not really sure." Jack's grip tightened on the strap of his bag. This was the part of this journey he'd been dreading—which seemed ironic now, given what they'd had to go through to get here. They were in need of a bath, a bed, a decent meal, and a good night's rest, and all of that seemed more appealing right now than attempting to comb through the city with only a name to go on.

But it wasn't just any name. It was the name Kit had said she'd use someday.

I have to keep going.

"There's a journalist who was with my sister," he managed in a strained voice, "named Gretchen Herbert. I'm hoping if I find her, I'll be able to find Alice. So I'm thinking we start with the local telegraph office. She would have needed to send cables through there, I'm sure."

Ruby raised a brow. "A female correspondent? Sounds like my type of girl. So is she here in Baghdad?"

"I think so. From the articles I found, she was a freelancer." Jack unbuckled his satchel and dug in his bag for the notebook in which he'd pasted Gretchen's articles. He fumbled around for it, then paused, his brows furrowing.

Where is it?

He'd put it back in his satchel—hadn't he?

Ruby stopped walking, watching him intently. "What is it?"

"A notebook. I'm sure I put it in here." He knelt, setting his bag on the ground. A more thorough search turned up nothing.

What the hell?

He pulled his other bag around his torso—the one he'd used for clothes and survival supplies. As he sorted through it, Ruby bent beside him. "When did you last see it?"

"I don't know …" He set a rolled pair of pants on top of a folded shirt. "I had it on the train from Cairo, for sure. I've had my satchel on me or in my sight the whole time."

That had been the last time he remembered holding the notebook. He'd intended to try to take it out, read through the articles again, but after Lydda station …

Jack gave Ruby a sharp look, his jaw clenching.

Goddamn Theo.

"You know the only time anyone else touched my satchel? Theo. At Lydda station."

A divot formed between Ruby's eyebrows, and she paled. "You don't think Theo—"

"I absolutely think Theo." He shoved his belongings back into the bag and stood. He didn't wait for her, stalking away. He shouldn't be angry with her, after all. She couldn't control what her brother did any more than he could control what Alice did.

"Why would he take it? What motive could he possibly have had?"

"He's a thief, isn't he? Thieves like to steal things without any regard or remorse for what they might be taking." His tone was more cutting than he wanted it to be, but maybe it was better that he get this out in the open. He had allowed the last couple of days to lull him into a sense of confidence with Ruby that he really shouldn't have.

Then he noticed Ruby wasn't walking beside him. He turned, frustration rankling him, and found her still where he'd left her—crouched, eyes downcast into the dirt. His boots kicked up small clouds of dust as he stepped back toward her. "What?"

"I know you're right," she whispered softly. "The first time I ever stole anything from anyone my hands shook so badly afterward—they didn't stop shaking for hours. It was a locket. A locket that I noticed a woman had hanging out of her pocketbook. I found out after I took it that the clasp was broken. And inside ..." Ruby hung her head for several moments, and when she lifted it her eyelashes were wet with tears. "Inside was a picture of a baby boy. A ringlet of hair was on the other side. And I just kept thinking, kept wondering, what if that locket was all she had left of him? What if I'd stolen her only memory?"

A tear worked its way down her cheek, and she stood wiping it away with her fingertips. Jack didn't move to comfort her, much as it was his instinct. Because ... *what can I say?*

Maybe she even deserved her guilt.

But, at the same time, he'd peeled back the layers behind that persona enough to understand that she wasn't just some unfeeling, cold criminal without a heart.

"Someone I once knew used to tell me, 'Tomorrow is an opportunity. A new chance to mend what we've broken and to move forward. Let's not waste our todays mourning our yesterdays when we've been given the gift of tomorrows.'"

"That's a mouthful," she said with a dry, tearful laugh. She sniffed. "And I'm not sure I can fix what I've broken. I can't replace everything I've stolen, Jack."

He sighed, then pulled her into his arms. Maybe against his better judgment. But her tears had already soothed his irritation at her. Theo might be a damned irredeemable bastard, but that didn't mean Ruby was. "The fact that you can shed tears about it is proof enough that you're not a bad person, Ruby. You have a conscience, and that's a good thing. It'd all be a whole lot worse if you didn't give a damn who you hurt."

When she pulled away, her tears had slowed, but the brightness that had crept into her pretty face during the flight had all but withered. They started walking again, in silence this time—as though neither of them knew quite what to say.

They exited the field through a side gate without incident, bypassing a British officer there who paid them no notice. A few piastres to a local boy with a cart got them a ride to the city proper. Jack kept his head low, his collar turned up.

The cart dropped them just past the old Ottoman barracks, near where the river curved through the eastern side of the city. From there, Jack and Ruby walked, careful in their steps along the uneven flagstones.

Baghdad, for all its heat and haze, was a city trying to stand taller. There were signs of ambition everywhere: freshly plastered walls, scaffolded façades, new telephone wires stretched above the narrow lanes like string over a chessboard. But beneath the veneer it still felt like a city caught between worlds—straining toward modernity while its bones remained ancient, stubborn, and unpredictable.

They passed the king's administrative district, a series of squat buildings trimmed with both Hashemite emblems and lingering British signage. It was quieter here. The scent of diesel faded into the faint perfume of jasmine from a garden wall. Uniformed guards leaned in shaded doorways, their rifles slung casually but their eyes sharp.

Jack paused at the corner of a pale stone building near Hindenburg Street—a place that might once have been a merchant's house, now converted with modernity in mind. A rusted brass plate affixed beside the arched doorway read "Post and Telegraph Office."

The Union Jack fluttered limply above the entrance, its colors dulled by the sun.

Jack hesitated. The weight of being here pressed in, making

him ever more aware of the heat, the fatigue, and the uncertainty. The fear that he'd made a mistake coming here. That he wouldn't find Kit at all. That he'd only unearth more ghosts.

"Something wrong?" Ruby asked, glancing at the entrance.

Jack gave a small nod.

"So much for independence, right?" Ruby tilted her head toward the flag. "If Iraq joined the League of Nations a couple years ago, you'd think the British would be a little less obvious."

"The empire doesn't leave that quietly." He gave one last glance toward the street behind them, then moved through the door.

The moment Jack pushed open the iron-framed glass door, a wave of thick, dusty warmth wrapped around him like a wool blanket soaked in ink and sweat. The scent of paper and hot metal was unmistakable—cut through faintly by the tang of old citrus polish clinging to the wooden counters and desks.

The room was narrow and high-ceilinged, its plaster walls once whitewashed but now faded to the color of old parchment. Rows of battered stools lined the front wall beneath arched windows, their slatted shutters cracked open to let in ribbons of sunlight and noise from Hindenburg Street.

To their left, a door stood slightly ajar, revealing the rhythmic *click-tap-click* of a Morse key from the telegraph room beyond. Somewhere inside, a telegraphist was tapping out someone's news to another corner of the empire.

Against the opposite wall stood the long service counter, a waist-high barrier of dark-stained wood topped with brass grilles. Behind a desk sat a pale middle-aged man with a pinched mouth sporting a pair of wire spectacles perched halfway down his nose, a pencil behind one ear. The clerk didn't look up until they were at the counter. "For domestic or international?"

"Neither." He looked past the counter to the open ledger.

Names, destinations, and reference numbers marched across the page in tight, hurried script.

Then his heart thumped. He had no doubt Gretchen had been here. Somewhere, her words had passed through this desk, these cables, this room.

The clerk frowned at him, as though annoyed by his answer. "How can I help you, then?"

Jack smiled as pleasantly as he could. "Connor Smith. I'm hoping to inquire about an American journalist I've been sent to find—Gretchen Herbert. She was working in Baghdad over the past few months."

The clerk's eyes flicked between him and Ruby. "Then why haven't you gone to the American Legation?"

"I have. They sent me here. Said you might have more information to offer me."

The clerk frowned. "We're not in the business of providing information on foreign nationals." Then curiosity seemed to get the best of him. "Is she in trouble?"

"No. Not unless you count being overdue on a deadline." Jack offered the smallest, most harmless chuckle he could manage. "I'm from the *New York Times*. She was freelancing under our masthead and then stopped all contact. We're concerned. Do you remember when you last saw her?"

The clerk stared another moment, his face giving nothing away.

Ruby exchanged a look with him, then asked in a sweet and polished English tone, "Do you remember her at all, sir? We've come all this way."

Her feminine charm seemed to work, as his expression softened—slightly. "Yes, I remember her. Bit of a firebrand, if you ask me. Rude."

Jack kept his face blank. That sounded like Kit.

The bell at the door jingled as another customer came into the building, stepping in line behind Jack and Ruby.

"Do you know if she listed an address in her cables?" Jack asked, forcing a polite tone.

"I can't tell you about a home address. The logbooks aren't accessible to the public, no matter your press credentials. If you'll excuse me." The clerk waved the customer behind them forward, clearly dismissing them.

Logbooks. *Yes, those would be key.* The telegraph offices were required to keep a copy of all messages sent, including the recipient's and sender's information.

His heart rate kicked up a notch as he and Ruby stepped away from the counter.

"What do we do?" Ruby asked in a whisper, searching his gaze.

"I don't know, but we need those logbooks," he answered, his voice so low he could barely hear himself.

She nodded. "Where do they keep them?"

"Under lock and key in a file cabinet. Probably in a back office. The clerk will probably have the key, though."

Ruby's eyes glinted, then she tipped her mouth in a smile. "Follow my lead."

She marched back up to the counter, pushing past the customer. "Excuse me, sir, but we simply must have a bit more information. Anything you could tell us about Miss Herbert would be invaluable. *Please.*"

The man pushed his spectacles up, annoyance flickering clearly through his expression. Then he gave a long, exaggerated sigh. "She spent an awful lot of time with that German journalist, Rudolf Meyer, at Café Shahbandar. Down on Hindenburg Street. He was her fiancé, if I'm not mistaken. Now, if you'll excuse me ..."

Jack sucked a breath in through his teeth, the only outward sign of the punch to his gut.

Fiancé?

German fiancé?

His mouth went dry, and for the next several moments he heard nothing the man continued to say.

Gretchen—Kit—was engaged?

The news shouldn't have come as a surprise. She'd been married once before, after all. Her husband had been killed though.

What did he think—that she'd spent all this time waiting for him?

So why did it feel as if he were losing her all over again?

He couldn't let himself get sidetracked. There wasn't time to overthink this.

He swallowed hard and joined Ruby back over by the counter. "Is Meyer still in the country?" he demanded. The other customer, an older English gentleman, shook his head and muttered something under his breath.

The clerk's face pinched, his eyes flashing. "Do I look like an address book, sir? Now if you have no legitimate business here, please step aside."

"There's no need for such a tone—" Ruby gasped, then set her hands to her stomach. "Oh!" She stumbled, folding over.

The three men all watched her with caution.

Jack was at her side a moment later, taking her by the elbow. "What's wrong?"

"I-I don't know." Ruby released another gasp. "Darling, I think it might be the baby. All this discord a-and the heat ..."

The baby?

Jack fought the urge to raise a brow. But, truth was, her acting was clever enough that she had fooled him at first. Jack took her by the arms, then shot a look at the clerk. "A chair, man! Get my wife a chair."

A red flush crept into the clerk's face, and he spun on his heel, then came out from behind the counter and dragged a chair toward them.

The other customer stiffened. "I'll return in another hour," he said, then fled from the front office.

As the clerk set the chair beside Ruby and she released Jack, she gave another cry, stumbling once more—this time, directly into the clerk's chest. He barely caught her, then helped her into the seat.

"Water," Ruby rasped. "A sip of water."

The clerk nodded, then hurried away, back behind the counter.

Ruby held a hand out toward Jack, her eyes pained, and he came closer. "Are you all right?" he asked, still keeping up the ruse.

Her chest heaved with deep breaths. "Better."

Then he felt her hand slip into his pocket—and a sudden weight settle there.

Something heavy. Metal.

What on earth?

It wasn't until several minutes later—once Ruby had sipped on her water, and then recovered enough to excuse them both— that Jack dared to reach into his pocket.

As they stepped onto Hindenburg Street, he pulled a key ring out.

Jack quirked a brow at Ruby and she smiled, all traces of the ailing patient left behind. "You said you needed the man's keys—I got you his keys." She looped her arm through his. "You didn't hire a thief for nothing. I figured it's about time I put those skills to good use. We can come back later and break in. Get the logbooks."

He fought the urge to kiss her.

He looked down at Ruby, warm and alive beside him—and in his mind, Kit flickered beside him on a moonlit street in Malta, her arm looped through his, her laughter echoing against stone.

But that was years ago. And she hadn't come looking for him. Maybe it was time he stopped holding on to something that had already died.

CHAPTER TWENTY-NINE

GINGER

Thick with the scent of dust and motor oil, the air in Cairo stifled—as if the city itself had begun to sweat beneath the sun's relentless gaze.

In the shaded rear courtyard of Dr. Jane Radford's clinic, the heat clung to everything—skin, linen, breath. Even here, surrounded by whitewashed walls and the clipped hush of palm trees rustling in the breeze, Ginger felt the weight of her restless thoughts pressing on her chest.

She tied off the last bundle of gauze with a sharp tug, her fingers deft despite the low buzzing tension in her shoulders. The borrowed nurse's uniform stuck to her back, damp from Cairo's early spring heat. It was a strange comfort—how quickly old habits returned. She hadn't worn a nurse's uniform since the war, but her body remembered the habit of adjusting her cap, of smoothing her hands against the white linen apron tied around the blue dress.

This place, too, was familiar. Jane Radford's small clinic sat nestled in a quieter corner of Cairo, not far from the Nile. A few modest rooms, clean tile floors, cabinets of supplies shipped in from England. Patients came out to the courtyard to convalesce or when their level of contagion required them to be outdoors, which meant that even the walls here had shelves of medical equipment—every inch of the space was well utilized.

Ginger had volunteered here during the winters when Noah brought the children to dig around on archeological expeditions —as much as she loved to join her family, she felt useless on those digs. Here, at least, she could help Egyptian women and children in the way she knew best.

But now she wasn't a help to anyone—not her own patients at home nor to Jane and her patients, whom Ginger felt badly for. Jane had not only inspired her to be a doctor in the first place but had provided the reference to Dr. Louisa Garrett Anderson, who had helped Ginger into medical school. Jane had also forgiven her for lying to her during the war. She'd become a close friend to Ginger over the years, and now she was helping her—once again—by providing her with a nurse's uniform and papers.

In a few hours, she and Victoria would be on a train heading for Jerusalem, posing as nurses with forged papers and borrowed names. A week ago, Ginger might have found the whole idea reckless. Now, it felt inevitable. Ivy and Alex were still missing. Jack had vanished into the desert. And Noah— God, Noah—given the level of silence from him, he was either in danger or walking into something far darker than either of them had been prepared for.

He'd never been one to stay out of touch for this long, not even when it was tough to communicate with her. Not after his disappearance during the war—he was too cognizant of how that experience had nearly broken them both. There was always a letter, a coded message, a whisper of reassurance in the shadows. But now, nothing. Had he gone too deep? Was he trapped?

The thought of Ivy was somehow *more* troubling.

Even now, the sound of Ivy's name stirred the shock of that evening like a reopened wound. *Ivy's father is Jack.* Victoria had said it in the quiet after dinner, her voice low but certain, and the words had landed like a confession no one in the room was ready to hold.

Ginger had stared at her for a long beat, waiting for some sign that it was a mistake. When it didn't come, the questions had spilled—how had it happened, why hadn't she told Jack, what did she think keeping it secret had protected? Victoria's answers were clipped at first, her fingers tightening around the stem of her glass: an affair born in the brittle loneliness when both had been captured together, a fear of ruining Jack's life, a belief that her silence was a kind of shield from the wrath and vengeance of Stephen Fisher.

There'd been a tremor in her hands, though, and when her eyes went glassy, Ginger had stopped pressing. She'd respected the silence since, but her own mind hadn't stopped circling the truth.

Most of Victoria's inner circle had known Stephen wasn't likely to be Ivy's father—and Victoria had confirmed it to Ginger before this.

But this?

What would it mean for Jack if they found Ivy now? What would it mean if they didn't? She'd seen the way he carried his ghosts—this one buried deeper than most—and it terrified her to think what Prescott could do with the knowledge if he really had figured out the truth, as Victoria suspected.

But how would Prescott know, when Victoria had never told a soul? Or were Victoria's fears of someone learning the truth informing her suspicions about Prescott?

And, beneath it all, a quieter fear: If the moment came and

Victoria still could not speak, would it fall to Ginger to tell Jack? And if it did, would he ever forgive either of them?

Her hands were steady as she shut the gauze tin, but her heart thudded unevenly, the weight of her worries making each movement feel mechanical. She'd come out here to pack a few basic supplies to make the ruse look believable. But the quiet pulse of the clinic only deepened the ache in her chest. Was Noah in danger? What if they never found Ivy and Alex?

"Ginger," Jane said, her voice low from behind her, "your sister is here."

Ginger frowned and straightened, glancing to see Jane standing under the archway to the courtyard, stethoscope draped over her neck, face written with concern. *What on earth is Lucy doing here?* "My sister?"

Jane nodded. "Should I let her through?"

Ginger's stomach sank. Lucy didn't come here. Not unless something was wrong. "Yes, please. And fetch Victoria. I think she was changing in the exam room."

Biting her lower lip, Jane slipped back through the doorway into the heart of the clinic.

Moments later, footsteps clattered across the tiles in the hallway. Lucy appeared in the doorway, breathless and eyes wide with panic. A shawl hung loosely around her shoulders, forgotten gloves dangling from one hand. Her hair, always so precisely arranged, clung about her face in disarray, strands sticking to her forehead as though she'd just sprinted through the streets.

Ginger's stomach lurched—this wasn't Lucy's usual composed demeanor.

"They were at my house," Lucy said, not even offering a greeting.

Ginger blinked. "What?"

"Alex. And Ivy. They were at my house yesterday. I've been

searching for you everywhere—went to Alastair's house, and he was gone too. I've been half mad with worry. I know you all aren't telling me everything, but—"

"Ivy and Alex?" Ginger felt the world narrow around her as she rushed toward Lucy. She gripped her by her forearms. "They came to you? Are they with you now?"

How had they gotten there? When? Was it possible?

Lucy shook her head rapidly and pulled one arm away, reaching for her handbag. She removed a crumpled scrap of paper. "No. I wasn't home. I'd gone to Shepheard's for lunch. When I came back late last night, my housekeeper told me a boy and girl had come to the side entrance—said they were asking for me. They looked like street kids, she said. Dirty. Sunburned. She turned them away. Thought they were begging. Bahiti wasn't home or she would have recognized them."

Ginger took the note from her trembling hands and opened it.

The paper was stiff with dust and creased from too much folding. But the handwriting—

She recognized it immediately. The sharp angles, the careless loops—so similar to Noah's.

Alex.

Her throat closed.

Aunt Lucy—Went to the British Consulate. If you get this and we haven't returned, please meet us there. Can't stay long—it's not safe. We'll try to come back.

"Ginger?" Victoria's voice wavered as she stepped through the door.

Ginger turned to see Victoria already dressed in the nurse's uniform she'd planned to travel in. Her veil hung loose around her neck. One glance at Lucy's face stopped her short.

"What is it?" she asked. "What's happened?"

"They were in Cairo," Ginger said quietly, holding the note out toward her. "Ivy and Alex went to Lucy's house. Yesterday."

Victoria's expression faltered. "They were here? In the city?"

"I wasn't home," Lucy said again, anguished. "They left this but never returned."

Victoria stepped closer and took the note, her face paling as she read it. "The consulate? Has anyone from the consulate called you since then to come collect them?" she asked Lucy.

Lucy shook her head. "Not that I'm aware of. I spent most of the night out searching for you, but I did go back home three times to see if there had been any word from them—including this morning. I've heard nothing."

Ginger folded the paper, slow and deliberate, as if handling something fragile. "The consulate is a safe place to go." She cleared her throat, trying to be optimistic. "And if they went straight there, someone should have seen them. Or maybe they're still there. We should go."

"But what if they didn't make it?" Victoria's voice trembled at the edges. "What if something happened along the way? The consulate would have contacted Lucy immediately, wouldn't they? She's the next of kin closest to them here. And Federline also could be watching Lucy's house, for all we know."

"I didn't know," Lucy whispered, her eyes wide with anguish. "I didn't know they would come to me. I'm so sorry. I should have been there."

Ginger gave her sister's arm a comforting squeeze. "How could you have known, Lucy? It isn't your fault." She stepped toward the door, moving past Victoria. "We'll go to the consulate and find out what's happened to them. Right now. There has to be *some* trace of them there, at least." *If they made it there.*

She didn't wait for Victoria and Lucy to follow, knowing full well they'd be only steps behind her. Close to the main lobby of the clinic, she ran nearly headlong into Jane, who was bent before an Egyptian toddler clutching the hand of her mother.

Jane straightened when she saw Ginger. Her gaze traveled back to Victoria and Lucy, then she frowned back at Ginger. "Is something the matter?"

"I'm not certain." Ginger gave her a tight-lipped smile. "But, thank you, as always, for your help. Hopefully I'll see you again before we leave Cairo."

They left the clinic, with Lucy leading the way out toward the street. "We can take my car. It'll be the fastest way of getting there," she said, a determined look in her face.

Ginger felt a tug of unexpected warmth toward her sister. The years had changed Lucy—even though she was still a socialite, she wasn't afraid of a challenge. Or of doing what was necessary to help the people she loved.

The car smelled of sun-warmed leather and gasoline as they crawled into it, and its engine growled as it wove through Cairo's congested streets. Horns blared, barely cutting through the thickness of the silence between the three tense women. Victoria sat stiff-backed beside Ginger, eyes fixed on the window, hands curled into fists in her lap. Lucy sat in the front, silent, her posture brittle.

Ginger fixed her gaze on the street ahead of them, willing the driver to move faster through the traffic. What if Alex and Ivy had been seen? What if someone else had intercepted them?

She couldn't afford to think like that. Chances were if Alex and Ivy had made it to the consulate, they were perfectly safe and being well cared for.

Victoria finally spoke, her voice barely audible. "They came to us. And we weren't there."

"They're smart," Ginger said. "They went to the consulate. That was the right move."

"But—"

"But we'll find them." She reached for Victoria's hand, silencing her worries with a squeeze. "If they're not at the consulate, we'll trace where they went next."

Victoria glanced at her sharply. "But the consulate should have contacted Lucy by now. Do you think they've been taken?"

"I think," Ginger said, "we should stop guessing and start asking questions."

The rest of the ride passed in silence, save for the rattle of traffic and the hiss of tires across stone and dusty roads.

The consulate loomed pale and rectangular on the corner of a wide boulevard. Here in the heart of Anglo Cairo, the buildings and streets were European in architecture—built to be "Paris on the Nile" during the rule of the Khedive. Since Egypt had gained independence, the British had stepped back in administration, but their presence was still quite clear here—a fact that rankled the nationalists in Egypt who wanted Egypt to stand with its own sovereign dignity rather than be the empire's puppet.

Ginger knew Noah was among those who favored full Egyptian independence. But, like her husband, she also understood the importance of the Suez Canal to her own countrymen and allies. She might not feel as torn about the matter as Noah did—she was far more English than he was—but she did sympathize with both sides.

Inside the consulate, the women rushed into a small tiled waiting room where a well-dressed young man looked up from a counter. His eyes widened slightly at the sight of the three women as they hurried inside, but he stood and gave a polite nod.

"May I help you?"

Ginger stepped forward, setting her hands on the counter. "We're looking for two children. A boy and girl. Teenagers.

English. They may have come here yesterday—possibly today. Alexander Benson and Ivy Fisher."

The clerk opened the logbook on the counter and ran his finger down the columns. "I'm afraid I don't see any record of them. No names fitting that description. No unaccompanied minors logged."

Victoria leaned forward, trying to see the entries. "Could they have come through another entrance? Not been written down?"

The clerk hesitated. "It's possible, I suppose. But unlikely. We log all visitors at the main gate, even unofficial ones."

Lucy pressed her hand to her mouth. "Can we look through the logbook?"

The man's mouth opened, as if to protest—but then he stopped, perhaps due to seeing the desperation on their faces. "Here you go," he said, turning the book toward them.

Lucy and Victoria crowded around Ginger as they scanned the list of names.

Nothing.

Then Ginger's eyes narrowed at the times listed of entry. *Howard Shipley ... 2:45 in the afternoon ... Cassandra Laverton 7:22 in the evening ...*

Her brow furrowed and she gave a sharp glance at the clerk. "Is it normal for there to be such a long gap between visitors?"

He gave her a quizzical glance. "What's that?"

"Here—" Ginger started to turn the book toward him and paused.

She gripped the edge of the counter, suddenly aware of the tension in the air. The clerk's voice was a soft hum in the background as her heart picked up pace.

In the very bottommost corner, between the two pages of the book, a tiny scrap of paper. The remains of a torn piece.

She jerked her head to the side, narrowing her eyes at the clerk.

"Who's taken a page of the logbook?" Ginger demanded coldly, anger surging through her.

The clerk's face reddened. "I-I—well, there's no need for such an unruly display. And to suggest that someone has taken a page from the logbook is rather uncalled for."

Ginger's pulse slowed. This man wasn't likely to be helpful—but she also doubted he knew anything.

And if a page was missing … it meant someone was hiding something. Someone with the authority and means to cover up the presence of two teenagers the day before.

"Thank you," she said, her voice flat. "That's all." She glanced over at Victoria's and Lucy's curious expressions. "Let's go."

Thankfully, neither of them protested. They seemed to know, as well as Ginger, this was a dead end, after all.

The three women stepped outside into the blinding sun. For a long moment, no one spoke.

Then Victoria exhaled shakily. "They didn't make it."

"Or they did and someone betrayed them here." The nurse's uniform felt suddenly hot, the veil sweltering.

Lucy turned to Ginger, eyes wide with fear. "What does that mean?"

Ginger's mind spun. "It means someone has a much further reach than we imagined. That Alex and Ivy may have walked right into a trap once again."

Victoria's hands curled into fists at her sides. "You think it was him?"

"I think if I were Prescott Federline and I knew two children might expose what I'd done … I wouldn't let them walk into the British Consulate. Or I'd make certain I could stop them while there. Either way, he must have them again."

The city pulsed around them—horns, wind, the faint echo of a call to prayer.

Victoria's dark eyes flashed with agonized worry. "What do we do?"

Ginger swallowed hard, staring at her apron.

If they could find out where Prescott Federline was lodging, they might be able to turn the tables. Corner him. Make their own demands. "I think it's time we stop waiting for him to make the next move. Go see what—or hopefully even who—he's hiding here in Cairo."

CHAPTER THIRTY

JACK

The rooftop terrace of the Tigris Palace Hotel glowed with lamplight and river reflections, its white-linen tables scattered beneath a striped awning that flapped gently in the warm night breeze. A gramophone played faint waltz music from a corner near the bar, half drowned by the hum of conversation and the clink of silver on china.

Jack sat with his back to the balustrade, instinctively watching the terrace entrance. His jacket was slung over the back of his chair, sleeves rolled to the forearm, exposing the poorly stitched wound on his arm from his scuffle with the lorry bandits. A medic in Azraq had stitched and bandaged it, but after his bath this evening, Jack had removed the dressing.

Across from him, Ruby looked like she hadn't just crawled out of the desert this morning—golden hair pinned up, a deep green dress that made her look more like a visiting socialite than a grifter.

Checking into the hotel hadn't been in Jack's plans, but following Kit's trail had led them here. At Café Shahbandar, a waiter had told them Gretchen kept a room at the hotel, so they'd headed here. Renting rooms had been the easiest way to not only check the register and find Gretchen Herbert's room—but to also give them the ability to slip into the room in the privacy of night.

He could almost picture Kit here, sitting in a corner table, sipping on a glass of cognac, book in one hand. Maybe she'd come here with that fiancé of hers—the waiter had confirmed his existence, too, though he hadn't seen the man in months—and shared dinner, smiles …

Ruby stabbed a fork through a piece of lamb and said, "Don't look so happy, Jack. We made good progress today, didn't we?"

He snapped out of the dark thought and lifted his glass of wine. "To progress."

Ruby frowned, then dabbed her lips with a cloth napkin. "I don't understand. Didn't you say finding this woman would help you find your sister? And yet you seem completely dispirited."

He didn't answer. She couldn't possibly understand what he was going through. Not with Kit. Not with Alice.

She toyed with her fork, eyes briefly dropping to her plate. "You know, when we first had to leave home, getting news from my family was difficult. I thought the not-knowing would eat me alive. I'd have done anything for a scrap of news—good or bad. But more than anything, I was angry with myself. I lost so much time with them while I was off pursuing the limelight and cheering audiences. Time I know I'll never get back because of the choices I made. They built a life without me while I was gone."

He knew that kind of regret. The wasted time. Alice's face in his memory growing older without him there to see it.

Jack raked his fingers through his hair and sighed. He needed to do a better job of hiding his emotions—Ruby was reading him a little too clearly for comfort. "Sorry. I'm just tired." He forced a smile. "You're right. We're closer to finding Alice than we were yesterday. And that's all that matters."

She gave a dry laugh. "You sure about that?"

"Well—the hard part isn't over yet. We still have to break into Gretchen's room, not to mention the telegraph office. And if we find anything useful then, we'll just be back to following the trail of clues, hoping they don't lead to a dead sister. So yeah, I'm not sure. I'm not sure about a goddamned thing anymore."

Ruby flinched.

He tossed his napkin down on his plate, rubbing the back of his neck. "Sorry. I think I just need to sleep for a few hours. And my appetite is gone."

Reaching for her wineglass, Ruby stared at him with narrowed eyes, scrutinizing him. "You know, if I didn't know any better, I'd say something else is bothering you. Something you're not telling me."

"I didn't realize we were sharing all our deepest, darkest secrets now," he said flatly. "One cozy night in the Jordan desert doesn't make us friends or you any more trustworthy."

A look of hurt crossed Ruby's face. She picked up her wine, but didn't drink. "You know, for a man who says he doesn't trust me, you've let me watch you when you think no one's looking." Her tone wasn't teasing—it was almost gentle. "That's how I know something's eating you."

Her lips pursed, she took a long drink from her wineglass, and then she set it back down and stood. "Thanks for dinner. Wake me up when you're ready to leave."

Regret curled through him, roiling his gut.

"Ruby, wait—"

She didn't though. She turned and hurried from the space, her svelte figure swaying with every step.

Dammit, Darby.

You're a fool.

Ruby was a deeply flawed woman, but she was here—wasn't she? Had saved him from her idiot brother, faced gunfire, freezing temperatures, and explosions too. Without her, he wouldn't have gotten nearly as far as he had today. Sure, she was getting paid a pretty penny, but she could have taken the sleazy route Theo had. Made a mockery of him.

Maybe there was honor among thieves or maybe she just wasn't as rotten as he'd expected her to be, but either way, she didn't deserve his unkindness now.

He sighed and called for the waiter, then paid for their meals and left the restaurant. Maybe he should have anticipated that staying here would put him in a foul mood—he'd even considered booking a room at the Maude Hotel, further down the riverbank. The place had risen in reputation among the Britons in Baghdad.

And it had the benefit of not being so filled with the ghost of the woman he'd once loved more than life itself.

Somehow, he needed to make his peace with the loss of her.

Finding Kit was a necessary evil now—one that might lead him to Alice. His sister deserved twice the effort he'd given to finding her, and yet she'd been less than half of his motivation.

He hurried toward his room, the heady buzz of a few glasses of wine numbing his senses—not enough to do any real harm, but maybe to help him fall asleep more easily.

Good. He wanted to be numb.

He wanted to forget.

To sleep.

As he stopped at his door, he paused, hand on the knob. His gaze fell on the door beside his—Ruby's room.

A slow, exhaled breath puffed from his cheeks.

Ruby.

Ruby Whoever-you-are.

Thief. Actress. Heroine.

Against his better judgment, he tapped on the door.

No noise stirred from further inside and he rested his forehead against the door, his palm flattening against the cool wood.

He should just go to bed.

As he resolved to do just that, a soft click told him the lock was sliding from its place. He stepped away just as the door opened a crack.

Ruby stood there, long hair already unpinned from the carefully arranged curls she'd worn at dinner.

Tears streaked her cheeks, marred her rouge.

"What do you want?" she asked, her tone defensive as she hugged her arms to her chest.

He could barely draw a breath, his chest had tightened so hard. His gaze traveled from her tear-fringed lashes to the red, full lips—lips that knew how to dazzle with a brilliant smile. A smile he hadn't seen often enough since meeting her.

Then his eyes dared further down the soft curve of her neck, tanned and freckled from days in the Egyptian sun, to her chest, where the soft mounds of her breasts peeked daringly from the neckline of her dress—now exaggerated by the way her arms pressed against her bodice.

You, Ruby. I want you.

But I don't know what I'm thinking.

As a younger man, he would have pressed his luck. But what type of idiot would it make him if he forgot everything he'd learned the hard way thanks to a few glasses of wine, unsatisfied lust, and a pretty face?

Not to mention that he couldn't—wouldn't—offer her anything beyond the companionship of one night. And Ruby didn't deserve that.

He searched her face a moment longer, then said, "To apologize."

Her throat bobbed as she swallowed, her eyes hesitant. "Apology accepted," she said in a soft tone. She nudged the door open a bit further, then stepped onto her toes and kissed his cheek. "Too bad we didn't meet in some other time, Jack Darby." She stepped back from him, one hand on the door. "Goodnight."

Still fighting the urge to pull her into his arms and kiss her thoroughly, he nodded instead and stepped back. "Goodnight, Ruby."

The door started to shut, then she paused. "Weber. Ruby Weber."

He tilted his head. *Is she telling the truth?*

Yet, she didn't say it with an ounce of guile. The corners of her lips curved in a small smile, then she started to shut the door.

Why had she chosen to tell him tonight?

He wasn't sure why it landed heavier than it should have—a name was nothing, and yet coming from her, it felt like the slow turning of a lock. People like Ruby didn't hand over pieces of themselves unless they wanted you to keep them.

Before he could stop himself, Jack wedged his foot in the door frame, his body blocking the hall light. Ruby's eyes flicked to the obstruction, then back up to him—surprise flashing before it settled into something more cautious.

He stepped inside, shutting the door behind him. She didn't move away, but the faint scent of her—powder, warm skin, a trace of whatever floral water she'd dabbed at her throat— reached him before her hands did.

When he kissed her, it wasn't the bruising hunger he'd expected from himself. It was tentative, almost a question. Her answer came in the way her arms went around his neck, pulling him in as though she'd been holding her breath all night. Her mouth was warm, the faint taste of wine and salt from her tears clinging to her lips.

Jack felt the slight tremor in her shoulders, the tension in her spine—not resistance, but the kind of guardedness that came from too many years of being careful. A guardedness he recognized in himself. He smoothed a palm over her back, tracing the curve of her waist with his thumb, trying to ease her closer.

She pulled back just enough for her breath to ghost against his cheek. "If you're going to leave," she murmured, voice low, "make it quick. I'd rather know now."

She said the words lightly, almost with a wry lift at the corner of her mouth, but her eyes betrayed her—that flicker of old hurt surfacing before she could shut it away.

"What makes you think I will?"

Her gaze moved over him as if measuring the truth of him in the lines around his eyes, in the way his jaw tightened. "Because people always do."

The air between them grew heavier, the waltz from the restaurant seeping faintly through the window glass, too slow for his heartbeat.

She unfastened one button of his shirt, then paused, her fingers lingering against his skin. "You want the truth?" Ruby whispered. "I've been alone for so long I can't remember what it's like to trust a man not to take more than I'm willing to give. I've survived by keeping the doors locked and the lights on— and I don't know what to do with someone who isn't asking for anything."

Jack covered her hand with his, feeling the slight tremor there. "I'm not asking for anything."

She gave a faint, humorless smile. "Not yet."

Her gaze held his for a long moment, weighing something unspoken between them. Then she exhaled, slow and deliberate.

"Then maybe," Ruby said, her voice gaining an edge of daring, "I'll be the one doing the asking tonight."

The change was immediate—in her tone, in the set of her shoulders, in the glint in her eyes. She stepped back only far enough to reach to her side, tugging the zipper of her dress downward with a purposeful slowness, her eyes never leaving his.

Then he pulled her into his arms.

His mouth descended on hers with unrestrained passion as her arms slipped around his neck, her body pressing against him. The spark that had been there for days now burst into a sizzling flame, sweeping through his arms and tingling into his hands as they roved down her backside, curling around the softness of her body. Pushing her against the thick hardness of his length, he groaned as her sweet mouth parted for him, her tongue flicking against his.

When he kissed her, she answered with sudden fierceness, her fingers locking behind his neck as if she were afraid he might pull away. Her body pressed to his with a desperation that wasn't just about desire—he could feel it in the way her breath hitched against his cheek, in the tremor that ran through her shoulders. Jack slid one hand to her lower back, the other cupping the side of her face, wanting to steady her and terrified of breaking whatever fragile thread had drawn them to this point.

She was delicious.

In every way a mesmerizing, breathtakingly gorgeous woman.

Maybe they didn't have what they needed to have in common.

Maybe it didn't matter.

He'd spent years running from anything that made him feel anything and, in a few short days, this woman had turned him on his head. Made his heart feel like *life* could pump through his veins again.

Like maybe, just maybe, he didn't have to be alone.

"Ruby," he managed, pulling away just enough to whisper her name. "God, Ruby—"

She smiled, taking his lower lip gently between her teeth. A soft nibble elicited a moan from his breathless lips. "Don't make me regret you, Jack."

"How do you know it won't be the other way around, sweetheart?"

Somehow, as though he'd passed some test he hadn't known he'd been taking, his words made her smile. A real smile.

The type he'd seen on that airplane.

He groaned again as her hands slipped from the back of his neck, then made their way to his shirtfront. Her mouth traced his jawline, then slipped onto the skin of his neck, tracing down his throat.

Her fingers undid the buttons of his shirt, trailing down one by one, her lips following the path she made to his bare chest underneath.

She stopped at his waistband, untucking the rest of his shirt, then knelt in front of him.

Jack drew in a shallow breath as she reached for his belt buckle.

This wasn't love. He wasn't dumb enough to believe that.

But comfort?

Yes.

Necessary?

God, yes.

He hadn't allowed anyone this close in years. And for the first time in ages, he couldn't remember why. She was sweet and kind in her own sort of way—and maybe, just maybe, she needed this as much as he did.

The belt loosened, followed by the button of his trousers.

How in the world could she look so innocent and so seductive at the same time, staring up at him with those big blue eyes and wet, parted red lips.

Ruby stood. When she stepped back, it was only to shimmy out of her dress. The fabric whispered down her body, pooling at her feet. The lamplight caught the pale sweep of her shoulders, the delicate line of her collarbone, and he couldn't look away.

She's so damned beautiful.

Jack's pulse throbbed in his throat, mesmerized by her as she unlatched her bra and revealed full, spectacular breasts with large pink nipples, now hardened by arousal. He brushed the back of his knuckles along her hip. Her skin was warm, almost fevered, and she shivered under his touch. She pushed his shirt from his shoulders, her nails grazing his chest. The rhythm of it —touch, glance—felt as intimate as their kisses had been.

Somewhere, a sliver of conscience tugged through the lust heating his body. He should walk away. Even still. Even after her mouth had consumed him the way it had.

But he wasn't that strong.

And more than that—he wanted her. Wanted *this.*

The clothes came away in slow increments, each piece a small surrender. The soft rasp of linen as he undressed, the muted thud of a shoe on the floor, the faint shift of the mattress when she sat down and drew him with her.

When he finally lay beside her, she curled against him with the instinct of someone who'd forgotten how to do it but found it again in muscle memory. And for the first time in years, Jack didn't fight the feeling that maybe—just maybe—he didn't have to be alone.

His arm came around her waist, fingers brushing lightly over her skin, tracing lazy circles along the curve of her hip.

"I thought for sure," she murmured, "that in that hallway you'd just...walk away."

He turned his head, pressing a kiss to her hairline. "Are you nuts? I couldn't in a million years."

Her gaze lifted to meet his, and something earnest flickered there—not the guarded wit he was used to, but something unarmored. She held him there for a long beat, as though deciding whether to let him see more.

"Yes," she said at last, her voice almost trembling. "I'm nuts about you, Jack Darby. I didn't expect you. I never thought you'd be the sort of man you are." She swallowed hard, her fingers tightening on his chest as if needing to feel the steady beat beneath. "I've been alone for so long … fending for myself, trusting no one."

He didn't speak—just let her words hang there, watching her search his face.

"But tonight…" She gave the smallest, almost shy smile, her voice steadying. "I don't want to be alone."

The decision was in her eyes when she leaned in, her lips finding his. This wasn't the heated kiss in the doorway—this one was deliberate, lingering. Jack returned it, cupping her cheek, his thumb brushing over warm skin. A sense of relief, unexpected and deep, washed through him.

Ruby didn't reveal who she was easily, but there were tiny moments—snippets, really—when she offered something deeper. Let him in.

And tonight they were two lonely souls who'd somehow found each other amid the madness.

The kiss deepened gradually. Her hand slid from his chest to the back of his neck, fingertips curling in his hair. His mouth traced the curve of her jaw, the delicate hollow just below her ear. She tilted her head back with a soft sigh, her breath warm against his cheek.

He paused and she slipped her hands onto his chest, her palms warm against his bare skin.

"Please," Ruby whispered.

It was all the invitation he needed.

The kiss deepened and Jack took his time, despite the urging of every fiber of his body. He wanted to taste those rosy nipples, devour the sweetness of her tender flesh, let the moment linger.

But when he slid inside her and she cried out with pleasure, his last sense of possible restraint vanished. He pushed deeper, harder, giving her body all the satisfaction he'd denied himself with a woman for years, until her cries were muffled into her pillow, her body throbbing around him.

He pulled himself out and let his own climax pour out onto the bedsheet then collapsed against her, chest heaving, his forehead pressed to the warm hollow of her shoulder. Her fingers were still laced with his, not just holding but anchoring him there. His awareness of the tiny movements grew—the slow flex of her fingertips, the soft brush of her thigh against his.

For a while, neither of them spoke. The world outside the shuttered window could have been a thousand miles away...the room filled with the sounds of their breathing, the faint ticking of the bedside clock, the slow settling of the bed beneath their weight.

He shifted onto his side, propping himself up on an elbow to see her face. Strands of hair clung damply to her temple. In the dim lamplight, her skin glowed, and the sight made something twist in his chest—something he didn't have a name for.

She's everything I didn't expect.

"You all right?" he murmured, thumb brushing a faint trail along her cheekbone.

Ruby gave a breathy laugh, a curl of sound that was part satisfaction, part wariness. "That depends." Her gaze flicked to him, eyes glistening in the low light. "You going to disappear on me, Jack Darby?"

He frowned, not expecting the question. "What makes you think I—"

"It's just how it is for me." She turned her face toward the wall, as if that might hide her emotions. "Men take what they want, then they're gone. So I learned to make sure I leave first."

Jack's chest tightened. He'd seen Ruby bluff, tease, and lie without missing a beat—but this wasn't that. The words were too bare, too stripped of the usual glitter she wrapped herself in.

It hit him harder than he wanted to admit, stirring a protective anger that surprised him.

He reached for her hand again, sliding his fingers over the delicate bones of her wrist, feeling the faint pulse there. "I'm not planning on leaving."

Ruby's lips curved, but the expression never reached her eyes. "We'll see." She rolled toward him and tucked herself against his chest. The faint scent of her hair filled his lungs.

Jack let his chin rest on the top of her head, one arm curved protectively around her back. Her heart still beat against his ribs, quick at first, then slowing as her breathing evened out.

He stayed awake a little longer, tracing the shape of her shoulder beneath the sheet, listening to the silence settle between them. And he wondered, not for the first time, which part of what she'd just told him was the truth—and which was just another way of keeping him at arm's length.

CHAPTER THIRTY-ONE

JACK

*L*ong after Ruby had fallen into a deep sleep, Jack slipped into the hallway.

Despite his exhaustion, despite everything, sleep hadn't come for him.

Only more worry.

Becoming physically intimate with Ruby had been sexually satisfying—but something in her words had worried him too. What if he *did* hurt her? With everything between them—the way their relationship had started, the promise of money and a payday—how could they ever overcome those things and move forward?

He wanted to forget his worries.

He'd even considered the opposite solution—nudging her awake—losing himself in her arms once again.

But rather than wake Ruby and depriving them both of needed rest, he started down the hall, heading for the stairwell. If he wasn't going to sleep, he should go to Kit's room and look around.

He found the room he'd seen listed in the registry as

Gretchen Herbert's and paused beside it. The hallways were fairly empty—not as ideal a time to break in as later in the night would be.

He'd have to work fast.

Removing a small tool kit from his breast pocket, he sidled up to the door frame. From the case he pulled free a small pick which he slipped into the lock. Kit had taught him how to pick a lock when he was still a teenager.

Funny how things came full circle sometimes.

The pin slid into place with a satisfying *click*, and he was in.

Jack slipped into the dark room, then stealthily shut the door behind him. He squinted in the dark, feeling the wall for a light switch. When he failed to find one, he crossed the space, his feet bumping against objects on the floor, arms in front of him, toward the sliver of light peeking out from the curtains.

Then he paused.

Maybe turning a light on wasn't such a good idea after all. He had no idea who'd been looking for Kit or what trouble she'd run into, but he couldn't eliminate the possibility that someone had been watching her. And if they'd been watching her, they might be watching the room. Especially after he and Ruby had been asking questions about Gretchen Herbert that day.

He took out a flashlight. The moment the light spilled from it, his heart stuttered.

The light revealed a room in disarray.

Either Kit had left here in a hurry—or someone else had been here.

Papers were scattered over the floor, books spilled from stacks on the desk and bed tables. So many books.

So like Kit.

No matter where she went or lived, she seemed to surround herself with books. Like Noah, in some ways. The two most bookish people he'd ever met—and somehow the two most lethal as well. Maybe all that knowledge made for dangerous individuals.

He couldn't begin to know where to look or what to look for. If someone had beaten him here, they might have already found whatever was useful. How long had it been since she'd been here? Was there really even a way to tell?

The desk was the most obvious place to look, but Kit wasn't an obvious sort of person. Like him, she loved codes and puzzles. Kept her own journal and notes in code, in fact.

Maybe a journal would be a good place to start, but he doubted she would have left without it.

Setting a hand on the bed, he knelt beside the spilled books on the rug. A quick perusal of them revealed titles on the spines —not one journal—but that didn't mean the books couldn't be useful either. Yet if Kit had purposely left a trail, she wouldn't have used something as long and complicated as a book for him to find. Her messages would have been short, most likely in code.

He searched under the mattress and pillows, then under the bed itself, looking for a loose floorboard or anything that might be easy to conceal something in like a journal or even a document.

When he found nothing, he moved to the desk.

Papers were scattered on the chair beside it, and he rifled through them. Most of them were typewritten, a newspaper column, but a few words and letters had been crossed out by hand.

His chest squeezed as he saw the writing—an elegant script that he recognized in an instant.

Kit's.

If he'd ever doubted Gretchen Herbert was Kit, here was the confirmation to the contrary.

The papers crumpled in his fist.

What were you thinking, Kit?

Had she faked her own death or just somehow survived?

Was it possible that she thought maybe he'd given up on *her?*

And why—after all this time—had she reached out through space and time to communicate with him? What was the difference now?

Alice.

He had his answer before he could even dwell on the question too long. The difference must have been Alice. Kit knew how much he'd loved Alice. How he would have given anything to save her from Blackwell.

If something had happened to Alice and he would have wanted to know about it or could help her, that might have been enough for Kit to reach out.

Releasing a breath, Jack uncurled his fist, then smoothed out the wrinkled paper on the desktop. He shone the flashlight at it to get a better view, reading the column—an article about the new Turkish government's plan to resettle the people they called the Mountain Turks—the Kurds.

The topic didn't surprise Jack—Kit had always rooted for the underdogs and the oppressed—but the writing did.

Something was odd about the words she'd crossed out.

His brows furrowed, and he peered more closely at it.

If he didn't know any better, she was writing a code into the article.

The realization hit him like a hammer to the face and he nearly dropped the paper, his heart racing.

A code into the article.

Of course.

The absurdity of it—the brilliance—stole his breath away.

Had he not been in Kharga, cut off from the world, he would have been reading the newspaper. He would have seen her name in the column, sooner or later—as he had done. And he would have done exactly what he did … gone to the library and found every archived article he could … looked for something to hold on to in those words. He would have found the code eventually —he was certain of it.

Goddamned Theo.

He almost threw the papers as fury tore through him.

If Kit had sent him a coded message in the newspaper articles, Theo had just set back his ability to find the message by days, if not more. He'd have to go back to a major city to find an archive of recent newspaper articles written by Gretchen Herbert—and who knew what he'd manage to find, if anything.

Dammit, dammit, dammit.

Grinding his teeth, Jack set the paper down, then sank into the desk chair and aimed the flashlight at the workspace. He'd start with this article. This last one.

It doesn't look like she even had a chance to publish it.

He pulled a notepad and pencil from his pocket, then tapped the pencil point on the paper.

A code in a newspaper article would require care and stealth if both parties hadn't already agreed upon a key. Something recognizable to codebreakers like himself—but that would go unnoticed by the average individual, or even someone skilled but not readily looking for a code—he'd missed it when he'd read through her articles before, after all.

But thanks to the help of the notes she'd made on her unfinished article, within a few minutes, he'd found the pattern and started scribbling letters on his notepad.

T-Y-P-E-W-R-I …

… and that's it.

The code finished there.

Typewritten?

Doubtful.

Typewriter, though …

Jack jerked his chin up, his gaze falling on the typewriter pushed further back on the desk. Was it possible Kit had hidden something there?

He rose slowly, every movement deliberate, as if a wrong step might shatter the thought. The desk creaked beneath his hands as he reached across it and dragged the typewriter closer.

An Underwood. Heavy. Sturdy as hell. Just the sort of tool Kit liked.

The room was silent, save for the distant hum of Baghdad night traffic. Somehow that only made his heart pound harder.

His fingers hovered for a moment before he flipped open the ribbon cover.

The spools looked ordinary. No scratches. No forced edges. He probed beneath them anyway, lifting one clear of the post, checking underneath with a fingertip, then the other. Dust. Ink stains. Nothing else.

He swore softly under his breath and grabbed the flashlight from where he'd set it down. The beam swept the desk in a narrow arc, casting the shadows long across the walls. He crouched in front of the typewriter, aiming the light beneath the carriage, angling it low.

The machine was too heavy to lift and search with the same hand, and he was forced to set the flashlight down again, aiming the light toward it as he lifted it. *A damned light would be helpful.* His other hand trailed over the machine's underside, tracing the smooth edges of the base.

Still nothing.

Then his finger caught on something—a lip of metal recessed beneath the keyboard.

Jack set the flashlight between his teeth and leaned in. The baseplate wasn't flush. He pressed gently at the edge and felt it shift. A hidden latch, maybe—no, just an old screw that had loosened over time. He worked it back with care until the panel gave, just enough to slide aside.

The beam of the flashlight caught it: a slim cylinder wedged into the frame, nearly invisible behind the tangle of connecting rods.

His pulse ticked faster.

He reached in, carefully freeing the object from its makeshift bracket. It was no longer than his pinky, sealed tight. His thumb brushed over a faint grease pencil mark scrawled across the casing: *AD*

Alice Darby.

He stood slowly, staring down at the thing in his hand. Microfilm—had to be. A courier's tool. A spy's burden.

And Kit had left it here. Left it for someone to find.

For him?

Suddenly the code made sense. The message might not have needed to be read in full—just enough to bring him here. To get him to look. She'd known he'd see it. She'd counted on it.

Jack turned the cylinder in his fingers, heart thudding harder than he wanted to admit. Whatever she'd uncovered—whatever she was risking—this was only the beginning.

And now it was in his hands.

He drew a deep breath, his heart pounding so loudly in his ears that it blocked the sound of anything else.

That's when he heard it.

The creak of a floorboard. Behind him.

He whirled to face whoever was there, but they were faster.

A jolt of pain crashed against Jack's skull, sharp and powerful.

He crumpled to the floor, the world going black around him.

CHAPTER THIRTY-TWO

IVY

If she ever saw Alexander Benson again, Ivy was determined to strangle him.

She'd seen that glint in his eyes back at the consulate—and she wanted to kick herself for suggesting the visit in the first place—that smug, obstinate look he got when he was especially proud of his own cleverness.

Normally, she didn't care that he thought of himself as being so much more intelligent than she was. He was. They both knew it.

She wouldn't have survived one minute without him in Port Said. Or gotten away from her captors and off the boat at all.

But all that intelligence meant nothing when his pride got in the way of logic. She'd spent a lifetime learning that it was the most infuriating thing about him. Alex's face had practically been beaming with pride when Mr. Federline had handed him that notebook of newspaper articles while they were still in the consulate.

And when Mr. Federline had praised him after Alex had

found a code in a second article—*JERUSALEM*—Ivy wasn't certain if she'd ever seen him more pleased with himself. It had only made her want to slap him for ignoring the warning looks she'd given him.

Now, shivering on the streets of Cairo, well past the middle of the night and getting closer to dawn, none of that fury was doing her any good though. Alex was gone—carted off into a large, luxurious estate home by the Prescott Federline fellow, probably still under some delusion that the man wasn't a villain.

Had Alex even noticed she was missing yet?

She'd only narrowly escaped.

Hands trembling, Ivy rested against the wall of a building in an alleyway, tugging the scarf she'd stolen more tightly around her head. She still felt guilty for swiping the scarf, but she'd been terrified and alone and in need of *something* to better conceal her identity. Even if Alex didn't know she was gone, Mr. Federline and his men would know by now.

She'd been separated from Alex as soon as she'd arrived at the mansion—taken to a spectacularly beautiful bedroom. A bath had been drawn for her. And while she'd been in the midst of disrobing, she'd glanced out the window.

In that second, she'd *known*. Known that she shouldn't have ignored her gut feeling about Mr. Federline. That she'd been foolish to suggest the consulate. That he'd been right all along— the men who had taken her were powerful and well connected.

Because there, walking on the lawn of the house in Cairo, was one of the men who'd kidnapped her in England.

So she'd slipped out of the room and tried to find Alex. But when she'd heard someone coming, she'd taken off. Managed to get outside unnoticed. Then run like the little coward she was.

A fresh wave of tears threatened her, but she fought it back.

Alex had risked everything to save her and she'd left without him. Without even *warning* him. Now she was hopelessly lost, afraid, hungry, tired, and an utter mess.

Alex never would have left her there.

Never.

And as angry as she was with him for letting Mr. Federline's praise stroke his pride, she wasn't certain she could ever look Alex in the eye again knowing she'd simply abandoned him.

Ivy sighed, setting her head back and closing her eyes. And to think that she'd ever considered running away from home.

The shifting noise of something stirring near a stack of crates several feet away forced her to lower her chin.

What was that?

She watched the stack, warily, her heart pounding.

It's probably nothing more than a little mouse. Nothing to be afraid of.

Still, she tucked her feet closer to her body.

The sound came again, then a large creature emerged from behind the crate—a cat?

The glowing eyes, tail, and pointed snout told her differently.

A rat.

A scream erupted from her and she bolted to her feet, then was off down the alleyway.

She ran blindly, heart thundering, breath tearing from her lungs in ragged gasps. The alley narrowed around her like a noose. Stone walls loomed high and featureless, the uneven cobbles slick beneath her shoes. Somewhere behind her, a shout echoed—a drunkard? A guard? A shadow?

She didn't wait to find out.

You're fine. You're fine. Just breathe.

Turning sharply, she darted through another passageway, this one littered with fish bones and broken crates. The stench was choking—urine, garbage, something dead. She gagged but kept going, ducking under a low-hung clothesline and nearly tripping over a cat that yowled and scattered.

She was no longer in a part of Cairo she recognized.

The buildings here pressed in close, narrow-shouldered and soot-streaked, their upper balconies drooping like tired eyelids. Wooden shutters creaked in the wind. Somewhere overhead, laundry flapped—abandoned or forgotten. A lightbulb dangled on a wire, swinging above a doorway but never catching.

She passed a row of cracked stone archways and a broken drainpipe dripping onto the street. A broken wagon wheel leaned against one wall, moss growing from its edge. Her steps echoed louder than she liked, too easy to follow.

Would Federline's men be looking for her still?

Don't think about it. Just keep moving.

She turned another corner and found herself in a slightly wider alley, a crooked lane of sleeping shops. Painted signs in Arabic and French hung crooked above their doors. A few wooden carts had been left out for the night, but otherwise the street was deserted.

She slowed. Her heart thundered, but even that felt distant now.

Cairo was so *big*. And she was so small.

A foreigner. A girl. A stranger in someone else's night.

Had she really thought she could just find her way to Lucy's house?

A lump formed in her throat. *Alex would have known what to do.* Alex always knew.

Her feet dragged, one heel now soaked through. The city stretched like a labyrinth—no landmarks, no lights, just the tangled, silent bones of a place that had nothing to offer her. Not tonight.

Please, God. I don't know what I'm doing.

She stumbled to a halt beside a shuttered storefront, pressing a hand to her ribs where the muscles had begun to stab. A line of Arabic scrawled in chalk above the window caught her eye, but she couldn't read it. She didn't even know if she was heading north or south anymore.

She turned in a slow circle. Every direction looked the same.

She started walking again—though it felt more like drifting—passing rows of locked shops and broken stairwells. A child's doll lay in the gutter, one glass eye missing. Ivy stepped over it.

Her blistered heel screamed with each step. Her ankle throbbed. Dust clung to her skirt. Her scarf had nearly fallen off, but she didn't dare stop to fix it. She felt like a ghost slipping between the cracks of a city that didn't want to see her.

A figure moved in the shadows up ahead.

She froze. Her breath caught in her throat.

But it was only a boy, maybe ten, sleeping on a bundle of cloth near a door. His arms wrapped around his knees. A small empty tin cup beside him.

She moved on, shame catching in her chest.

The narrow alley finally emptied onto a wider street. A battered lorry rumbled past, its headlights off, tires whispering over the compacted dust. The shrill bell of a tram sounded in the distance. A single minaret pierced the horizon, silhouetted against the navy wash of the sky.

She kept moving, limping now, arms wrapped tightly around herself. The air had turned damp with cold. Her fingers were numb. She tried to breathe through her nose to steady herself, but the smell—smoke, petrol, sewage—made her eyes sting.

She passed a shuttered cinema, its art deco marquee boasting some French film she couldn't pronounce. The poster girl on the wall was glamorous and confident, mid-spin in a sequined dress, her arms raised in laughter. Ivy looked away.

A flickering streetlamp threw light across a row of peeling advertisements. All meaningless. They blurred together.

Her stomach growled. Her vision tilted. She'd thought Cairo was magical once—bright and alive, full of color and rhythm and history. A city of domes and minarets and palm trees, of horse-drawn carriages and brilliant lanterns. She'd been jealous each time Clara and Alex got to go and she was left behind.

Mama didn't like to come to Cairo too often. As a result, Ivy spoke some Arabic, thanks to Uncle Noah, but not the way Alex and Clara did.

Tonight, the city was like an ancient tomb.

A maze of locked doors. A terrifying monster sleeping with one eye open. A place too big, too hungry, too hollow to care about a lost girl in worn shoes and a torn dress.

She slowed, dragging her feet, gritting her teeth.

God, just help me. Help me. And if you do ... I promise I'll go to school without protest. I'll be good, I promise.

Another alley. Another turn.

Then ... light.

She blinked, staggering into a proper thoroughfare that was wide and elegant, flanked by handsome buildings of limestone and stucco. Ornate wrought-iron balconies curled over the street. The pavement shone with last night's rain. Electric streetlamps glowed warm and steady, casting soft halos on the sidewalk.

The difference was like waking up.

She heard music—a slow, grainy waltz or ballad crackling from an open window. The scent of coffee drifted on the air, rich and bitter, laced with spice. Somewhere close, the warmth of bread teased her starving senses.

Then she saw it.

Set back beneath a stone archway was Café Riche.

The sign gleamed softly in the lamp glow, and golden light

spilled through the tall paned windows. Lace curtains. Polished wood. A waiter sweeping the last crumbs from the floor. A phonograph turning lazily in the corner.

She'd heard of it—Alex had mentioned it. A favorite of revolutionaries and artists, he'd said, a place where professors and politicians plotted over thick coffee and French pastries.

Two men smoked on the steps outside, heads bent in tired conversation.

The whole place looked like it belonged to another Cairo entirely.

Ivy's steps faltered. Her legs trembled.

She stopped at the edge of the light, almost afraid to step into it, afraid it might vanish if she moved too quickly.

She didn't even care if they mistook her for a beggar. She didn't care that her dress was filthy or that her hair had fallen loose from its pins. In that moment, she would have given anything just to sit, to rest, to be seen.

To not be alone.

Her eyes filled with tears. Her throat ached. She needed help but she was afraid to ask. Who knew what they might do to her.

A young man emerged from the café, descending the steps with quiet ease. His dark hair was neatly combed, his jacket buttoned despite the hour. He moved like someone sure of his place in the world.

And his left hand—

A flash of metal. A familiar prosthesis.

She blinked, stunned.

Her eyes widened. *I know him.*

He was friends with Uncle Noah—she'd seen him with Alastair Taylor before.

She bypassed the food, then rushed over to the Egyptian man. She grabbed his good arm, and he whirled to face her, his brow furrowing.

"K-Khalib?" she sputtered, hoping he'd see beyond her disheveled appearance.

Khalib's expression softened with pity. "No *baksheesh*."

"I'm not a beggar. I'm Ivy Fisher. I met you through Noah Benson, don't you remember? And I'm lost and I—"

Khalib's eyes widened, then his hand clamped over her arm as he gave her a look to silence her. "Ivy?"

She nodded breathlessly.

He looked around the square as though expecting to see someone else with her. His face registered shock as he took in her appearance, then tugged her away from the front of the café, hurrying down the pavement.

"What are you doing here?" he asked, his tone as brisk as his movements.

"I-I told you. I'm lost. I was with Alex—Alex Benson—I was taken from England and Alex helped find me and ... well it's a very long story, but I need help. I have to get to Alex's Aunt Lucy's house. Alex is in danger. Can you help me?"

Khalib's brows furrowed with concern, but he nodded. "You should not be alone out here, Ivy. It's dangerous. I'll get you anywhere you need to go safely."

Safely.

The word was like a breath of fresh air she hadn't realized she'd been starved of. She hadn't felt safe at all in weeks.

She'd also never really noticed how handsome the young man was until that moment, and her heart squeezed. "Oh, thank you," she managed, tears prickling her eyes as he ushered her toward a parked car.

Safe. And on her own.

She'd found her way to someone safe without anyone guiding her. Guilt bit her. Well, maybe Providence had helped. But, still.

You see, Alex? I can be useful without your help.

Khalib opened the door of the motorcar and helped her inside. As Ivy sank against the warm leather, her body relaxed. The car smelled like Khalib, actually.

She closed her eyes for just a second, letting herself be lulled by the scent.

Safe, for now.

CHAPTER THIRTY-THREE

JACK

*P*ain throbbed in Jack's head, cutting through the sound of a familiar voice saying his name, the feeling of weight on his shoulder.

"Jack."

He couldn't quite think straight enough to recognize the male voice.

His torso shifted and he was set gently on his back. Blinking one eye open, Jack peered through his lashes—*maybe they were stuck together with sleep, come to think of it*—and saw Noah leaning over him, concern written in his eyes, his jaw clenched.

Noah exhaled sharply. "I thought you were dead for a minute there."

"Dead?" Jack's voice came out as a rough rasp. Then he winced, his fingers traveling to his lashes. He tugged at the substance caking them.

Not sleep.

Dried blood.

Oh shit.

He tried to sit up, and Noah came to his aid. He glanced around the unfamiliar room, his eyes bleary as his memories of the night before returned.

Dinner with Ruby. Coming to Kit's room in the night.

The microfilm.

His head gave a sharp turn toward the typewriter, but it was gone.

And he didn't see the microfilm anywhere, either.

Dammit, dammit.

A whole slew of curses bubbled inside him as he peered toward the open curtains. Just after dawn, most likely.

How had Noah found him? "How the hell did you get here?" Jack asked with a wince, skimming his fingertips over the side of his temple. They found a gash there—where he'd been hit, and by someone who knew what they were doing.

"Alain Roche—mostly. He got me as far as Baghdad anyway. A friend of his spotted you in Café Shahbandar yesterday, and we flew in from Jerusalem right away. Then, to my surprise ... who should I find at the airfield but Ned. Roche is still there with him." Noah sat back on his heels. "I went to the café, traced you to the hotel, and the rest was just some light detective work."

Light detective work?

Jack ground his teeth.

If Noah had been able to find him so easily, then so could someone else.

Like Prescott.

Which could explain the missing microfilm. The attack.

It also might mean Ruby's in danger.

He bent one knee and stood slowly, head pounding, and Noah held a hand out to steady him. "You may need to take it easy—"

"You don't understand. There's someone here with me—a woman that's been helping me. Her name is—"

"Ruby Weber?" Noah's gaze darkened, and he stepped closer. "Yes, I know. Roche's contact mentioned her too. Why do you think I came right away, Jack? She's a known con artist."

"She's not, though." Jack blinked hard to clear his gaze. "I-I mean, she is. Her name is Ruby Weber. She's a thief, but she's got a good heart. She's trying to save her family—help get them out of Germany."

Noah frowned, his lips pursing as he searched Jack's gaze. "I don't know about that. But Roche did find her brother, Theodore, in Cairo. He was seen with someone there." Noah released a slow breath. "I don't know how else to say it, Jack, but he was with Prescott Federline in Old Cairo. And Ruby and her brother are known in the Cairo underground as the Weber twins."

Twins?

As the weight of Noah's words settled into Jack's mind, his stomach went sour, his throat constricting.

Seen with Prescott Federline?

"Are—are you saying they're Blackwell?" Jack's throat felt unrelentingly dry.

Noah's chin jutted up. "What do you think?"

That was definitely a *yes.*

Blackwell.

Ruby?

Jack sucked in a breath through his teeth, and he allowed the pain from his head to get to him for a few moments. "But ... I hired her." His fingers curled at his sides, his brain feeling strangely numb. She hadn't had the triskelion tattoo either— he'd seen every inch of her. Unless Prescott would have known not to give her one.

Hired her, yes. But she's the one who found me at Mena House Hotel. Hell, she may have even put herself in my path that day at Shepheard's. He'd been sitting out on the terrace, after all—Ruby could have easily spotted him first, then stood where he'd be certain to see her.

Ruby.

The thought of her being Blackwell was like ice to his veins, and his entire body seemed to break out in a shiver of fury and disappointment.

God, no.

She'd played him like a violin. And if she'd been lying the whole time … sneaking around …

Jack's hand went to his temple again. She might have been the one who'd attacked him last night and taken the microfilm.

"Goddamn," Jack growled, stalking toward the door.

Noah followed him as Jack let himself out of Kit's room and headed down the hallway. He found his way to Ruby's door, growing more ill by the second.

How could he have been so blind? So trusting?

So stupid?

He knocked on the door. "Ruby?"

Only silence greeted him.

Jack knocked again, his foolish heart still refusing the reality that Noah had presented him with. He couldn't have done this again, could he? Made such a careless mistake?

Been so inane?

How in the hell did he always end up here?

If Theo had been seen with Prescott … that was strong evidence against *both* Theo and Ruby.

He wanted to kick himself. She'd given him a heart-wrenching sob story about saving her family, and he'd fallen for it like the fool he was.

A pretty face and eyes glistening with tears would be the death of him someday.

"Jack?" Noah's voice came softly from behind him.

Jack didn't answer as he found the tool kit he had in his trousers. He'd left his own room key in the pocket of his jacket —in Ruby's bedroom. So, either way, he needed to get into the room.

He picked the lock quickly, then stepped inside, hoping against hope that he'd find her where he'd left her.

But the bed was empty.

So was the rest of the room.

Had she been the one who'd clubbed him over the head and then taken off running?

The floor seemed to give out from under him, and Jack sank to his knees, his chest squeezing tight.

All his life, he'd been struggling.

From the moment his drunk bastard of a father had gambled their life into ruin and his bitch of a mother had left him and Alice like orphans—without a glance back.

And then … Prescott Federline had come in, like the villain he was, and had taken Alice. Split him from Kit.

Like a coward, he'd fled. He hadn't fought back, just taken it. Crossed the goddamned Atlantic Ocean, thrown himself into the heat of the desert and the study of lives and civilizations that were as forgotten as he wanted to be.

And when he'd loved again, he'd been the fool who had fallen in love with the one woman who should have been off limits. The wife of his closest friend.

And, God, though he'd loved Ginger, that love when weighed next to the loyalty he owed Noah Benson was nothing.

So he'd wound up alone.

He'd made his peace with it—he thought.

Until Ruby.

Only to have Prescott come back and do *this* to him after all these years?

Jack's hands curled into fists and he sank back onto his heels, exhaustion pouring through him. Then tears, hot and unmerciful, pricked his eyes as he covered his face. But they still didn't come, a flood held back by walls he'd put around his heart so long ago.

But ... why?

"God, why?" he growled through gritted teeth.

Noah sat beside him on the floorboards without ceremony, his boots creaking as he lowered himself down. He didn't speak straightaway, just rested his elbows on his knees, the two of them breathing in the quiet. The faint ticking of the clock marked the silence between them.

Jack kept his gaze fixed on the empty bed, as if he stared long enough she might be there, after all. But the impression of her—her laugh, her perfume, the ghost of her warmth in those sheets—only sharpened the ache in his chest. He felt hollowed out, the way ruins looked after a fire—nothing left standing but the jagged edges.

Prescott had taken enough from him already. And yet here he was again, stripped bare.

The weight of Noah's shoulder against his own was the only solid thing in the room.

Jack didn't look at him, but he felt the other man's eyes. Patient. Steady. And in the back of his mind, a truth surfaced. Noah Benson was the only man alive who'd seen him at his lowest and never once turned away. Not for blood, not for money, not for anything. If that didn't make them brothers, Jack didn't know what did.

At last, Noah said, in that even, unhurried voice of his, "You're not the first man to put his faith in the wrong person.

And you won't be the last." He sighed. "The difference is, most men have to climb out of that hole on their own. You don't."

Jack's throat worked. He wanted to say something reasonable, but the words caught behind the ache in his chest.

Noah went on, quieter now. "You remember Cairo, after you and Ginger came back for me when you found out I was still alive? I'd written myself off entirely. You should have written me off too, if I'm honest. She loved you by then. You'd become a family. And you—damn fool that you are—came charging back for me. Told me I wasn't finished yet. Stuck by me when I had nothing to give you in return. You took care of the people I loved when I couldn't and gave me my life back even when I didn't deserve it anymore. That's not something I'll ever forget."

Jack closed his eyes.

They never talked about it like this. That time in their life when the things and the woman they wanted had been the same —and only one of them could have it. *Could have her.*

"She loved you more." Jack's voice scraped through his throat at last. "She was always yours first. And you deserved your family back. You always did. You fought like hell for them."

"Maybe. But she loved you too. She still does. I don't torture myself by thinking about it, but, believe me, I'm aware of what you gave up for me. And it's why I'm here, Jack. It's why when you showed up in Penmore weeks ago, I knew I'd go with you before you ever asked. You're my brother."

Noah raked his hands through his hair and released a slow puff of air through his lips. "I'm not letting you fall to pieces here. Not over Prescott, and not over a woman, however fine she might be. I don't care how far gone you think you are— you're not alone in this."

A long breath eased out of Jack, ragged at the edges. He'd been holding himself tight since the moment he woke with blood in his eyes, but something in him loosened under those words.

He scrubbed a hand over his face. "Christ, Benson … what did I do to deserve you?"

Noah gave a small huff of amusement. "Saved my life. More than once. And bought me a pint or two over the years." His tone shifted, brisker now, practical. "Now, let me see to that gash before you keel over. I'd rather not carry you out of here. It's hell on the back. But we have to hurry. Ned is waiting for us at the airfield, and we need to hurry to Jerusalem."

The corner of Jack's mouth twitched, almost a smile. Not quite. But close enough to feel like the first step back from the edge.

He drew a shaky breath and stood, then walked over to the chair where he'd left his dinner jacket the night before. Searching in the pocket for his room key, his fingers brushed against the metal—and something else.

A scrap of paper.

He frowned and pulled it out. The paper was folded … and stabbed through with the keys Ruby had stolen from the telegraph office the day before.

He unfolded the paper.

Wish you'd stayed—R

The words punched through him, equal parts knife and lifeline. She'd gone on purpose, then. Walked away without looking back. But why leave the keys? A taunt? A farewell? Or the barest thread of trust she thought he might follow?

He turned the note over in his fingers as if it might tell him which. It didn't.

Jack crushed the paper in his fist. The last thing he wanted to do was to waste time figuring out which part of her had been playing him and which—if any—had been real. Whatever fragile trust had been built between them was gone now anyway.

For good.

But he wasn't about to leave this stone unturned. Not after everything he'd gone through to get here—and losing the microfilm.

Jack turned toward Noah, squinting. "My head can wait. There's something we need to do first." He dangled the keys. "How do you feel about breaking and entering this morning?"

CHAPTER THIRTY-FOUR

GINGER

Lucy's parlor resembled a military office now—with tables covered by maps of Cairo and piles of papers everywhere. On the telephone at a small end table, Lucy was chatting in low tones with one of her friends, her body half-draped with exhaustion across the arm of the sofa.

Alastair had returned from Alexandria just hours earlier—having barely gotten there and turned around after Lucy's message to come back to Cairo. He'd taken the last train out of Alexandria the evening before, arriving before the break of dawn. And though Ginger doubted Alastair had slept, he'd buzzed in and out of the room, sending servants out with telegrams or notes to contacts around the city.

Victoria, too, seemed to have cast off her state of worry, now emboldened with the idea that Ivy might still be in Cairo. She'd pulled out her own list of former allies and even less-than-savory underground connections from years ago and started sending messages. Unfortunately, many on Victoria's list were no longer as relevant as she'd hoped.

They just needed to find Prescott. No matter how manipulative the slippery villain was, he wasn't transparent. *Someone* had to know something about his movements in Cairo. He had to have been seen. Someone had to know who he was.

And once they found him …

Ginger had a plan. She'd worked on it all night with Jane Radford, who'd come to meet Ginger at Lucy's house late last night and stayed until she'd left for her clinic after dawn.

As a clinician and a medical officer for the military in Cairo since the war, Jane had quite a bit of sway. Enough to be able to order a house be entered and search a home where there were reasonable grounds to believe it was the source of a notifiable disease, like tuberculosis. Jane was willing to claim she had grounds to help Ginger—they just needed an address.

But now, since Jane had gone back to the clinic, Ginger paced in the parlor, feeling idle. She sank into a chair, trying to calm herself.

The idea that Alex had been so close to freedom—so close to *her*, not even knowing that she'd come all the way to Cairo for him—was maddening. She wanted, more than anything, to hug her son. To kick herself for every time she'd ever scolded him for something as silly as taking equipment from her office. He was smart and curious. She should have always encouraged that curiosity rather than let her trivial worries about the cost of supplies put unnecessary stress on her relationship with him.

Noah had always found a way to avoid letting that precocious side of Alex bother him. *Why can't I?*

For far too long she'd allowed the stress of running the hospital seep into the way she handled her children. While Noah spent so much time with Clara and Alex, Ginger often stayed behind.

She loved her work.

Loved being a physician and running a hospital.

But she loved her family more.

She *had* to find a better balance. Alex and Clara were practically grown.

If she ever got Alex back again—she was determined to change.

The butler entered the room just then and Ginger looked up sharply, hope flaring into her chest and cutting through her thoughts of regret. "My lady," he said, looking toward Lucy. "Khalib is here. He has—"

The butler didn't finish. Khalib opened the door behind him, pushing through. And, at his heels—

Ivy.

Ginger gasped, her chair scraping against the tile as she rose. Victoria's gaze snapped to the doorway and, with a sound that was half a sob, half a shout, she dropped the book in her hands. It thudded to a rug, forgotten, as she rushed forward.

Ginger hurried behind Victoria. If Ivy was here—*what about Alex?*

For a heartbeat, Ginger could only see the tangle of their arms, the press of faces—but the sound of Ivy's voice reached her, small and raw, and it struck her harder than the sight itself. It was the sound of a girl who had run out of fear, run out of tears, and only just remembered she could stop.

"Ivy! Oh, thank God!" Victoria cried.

"Mama," Ivy managed weakly. Tears flowed freely from her eyes, staining the dirt on her cheeks. Her thin arms clung to Victoria's neck, and Ginger couldn't help but notice the state of her clothes and shoes—the same dress she'd been wearing when she'd vanished from home, now limp and dark with dirt and stains.

Her throat thickened with tears. Ginger had known Ivy since infancy—Ivy had spent her whole life with them at Penmore, like a sister to Ginger's own children.

But, until that moment, she'd never truly realized why

Victoria had come to live there while having the money to live elsewhere. Because, despite having spent a lifetime around Ivy, it wasn't until this second that she saw Jack so clearly in Ivy's face.

Her eyes were Jack's. Exactly.

How had I never seen it?

Ivy's shoulders trembled under Victoria's hands. Her gaze darted around the room—the gilt-framed mirror, the polished tea set gleaming on the sideboard—as if reacquainting herself with a world that felt both familiar and impossibly far away.

Ginger let her have those few seconds. Then she tore her gaze from the girl's dirt-smudged cheek to look anxiously at Khalib, then to the hallway behind him. "Alex? What about Alex?" she asked Khalib.

His brow furrowed, his expression blank. "Alex?"

Ivy sniffled, pulling back from her mother. "I escaped on my own," she managed in a choked voice. "Right after a man—Mr. Federline—took us to his house."

No! God, no! Then Alex really was in Prescott's hands.

"I-I saw him talking to someone outside his house. One of the men who kidnapped me. And I ran. Alex is still there."

Despite her best efforts to remain stalwart, Ginger reached a hand toward Khalib, steadying herself on his forearm.

Somehow, she hadn't wanted to believe it. Even after the disappearance. And the note he'd left Lucy. She'd known he was *missing*, but part of her had hoped he was still safe despite that.

But he wasn't safe. "Then Prescott wasn't lying. He's had Alex this whole time," Ginger said dully, still gripping Khalib. She searched Ivy's face. "How did you manage to escape and come here a couple of days ago?" And how was it possible that they couldn't seem to find Prescott's house—surely someone else might know about it.

Or Prescott has ways of keeping people silent that I don't want to consider.

Victoria wrapped a protective arm around Ivy's shoulder. "Why don't you sit, darling? I'm sure Lucy can have a servant draw a bath, too, and get you something to eat."

"Of course," Lucy said, her footsteps echoing behind Ginger.

Ginger turned to see both Lucy and Alastair there, their expressions grim but sympathetic. They'd quietly left their conversations and tasks after Khalib and Ivy's arrival, but Ginger had been so focused on Ivy that she hadn't noticed.

Alastair held an arm out for Ginger, then squeezed Khalib's shoulder. "Well done, son."

Khalib nodded, then gave Ivy a friendly smile. "She found me. I was at Café Riche. I took her back home to Old Cairo first, waited for you to send word from Alexandria. Then Ammon showed up and said you were here."

Café Riche?

If Ivy had found Khalib there—if she'd walked there from wherever Federline had taken her—then Federline couldn't be too far from here.

Ginger said nothing though, allowing Alastair to lead her toward the sofa. They sat directly across from Victoria and Ivy, who'd already taken a seat.

Lucy hurried over with a blanket and tucked it around Ivy's shoulders, then started to clear the coffee table between the sofas. "I've asked the housekeeper to get you tea, milk, and toast with jam. I'll have Cook make porridge too. What else do you want? You must be exhausted."

"I am," Ivy admitted, staring down at her hands, which hadn't stopped trembling.

"It's all right," Victoria said in a firm, motherly tone. She set her hand over the top of Ivy's. "You're safe now. And we'll get you fed and taken care of."

"It would be helpful," Alastair said gently, "if you could give us an idea of where Prescott Federline is hiding Alex, Ivy. We have a plan ready to help extricate him, but we're not certain where to look."

Ivy's eyes were red-rimmed, and she nodded. "I got lost. I walked for ages. But I-I'll try. I'm so sorry," she said to Ginger more directly. "It's all my fault."

"No, darling." Victoria's arm went tightly around her shoulder, and she hugged Ivy to her chest. "No, my love. No. You're no more to blame than Alex is for any of this. Neither of you asked to be kidnapped from home."

"You don't understand, Mama," Ivy said, pulling herself from her. She looked back at Ginger. "Alex saved me. He wasn't kidnapped—I was. He followed me all the way to Southampton somehow … then stowed away on the cargo ship they took me on. Crawled through the vents and found me. He even created an elaborate diversion to free me from the ship and we escaped into Port Said."

Ginger's eyes widened, and she exchanged a look with Lucy, who had stiffened.

Alex … did what?

She didn't know if she should be proud of him or throttle him for it.

Why hadn't he even *attempted* to come and get her or Noah?

Then Alastair chuckled. "Sounds like he's a chip off the old block."

The words hung there, too close to the truth for Ginger's comfort. She thought of Noah when they'd met—all reckless charm and unshakable certainty that he could outwit the world. Alex had that same spark, the same stubborn refusal to stay out of trouble when someone he loved needed him.

It should have made her proud. Instead, it made her want to

shake him until his teeth rattled. She glared at Alastair. "It's not funny."

"I didn't say it was, old girl—no need to get your feathers ruffled," Alastair said with a smile. When Ginger's glare only deepened, he laughed again. "Oh, all right. It's a little funny at least. But, admit it—Noah would have done the same thing. The boy is just like his father. You can't fault him for being brave and selfless."

Ginger frowned. She didn't *want* to admit it. But, then again, it was precisely those qualities about Noah that had stolen her heart so many years ago.

"But I don't understand. You escaped into Port Said, then came to Cairo—only to be captured again?" Lucy asked. She sat beside Alastair and gave his knee a gentle, discreet squeeze, as though to tell him to stop bothering Ginger.

Ivy rubbed her eyes, the exhaustion in her pretty face showing more clearly. Her eyes were puffy, swollen underneath. "Alex didn't want to go to the consulate—I talked him into it, you see. He stumbled across a code in the newspaper we came across in Kantara. A journalist left a message—*help me*—in code, and he was worried. And once we went to the consulate, Mr. Federline came and took us from there. He said he had a notebook with articles from that journalist that he wanted Alex to decode. Alex never knew Mr. Federline had any connection to the kidnapper—I didn't have a chance to tell him before I ran."

No wonder the page had been missing from the logbook.

That was it, then. The whole story. Federline had never intended to kidnap Alex—but Alex had wound up in Federline's hands all the same.

And now they had to get him back.

Ginger leaned forward. "If you look at a map, do you think you can find the area you were in?"

"Wait—what's this about a newspaper code?" Alastair stood, his expression curious. "What code? What journalist?"

Ivy looked increasingly more upset. "I—"

"Alastair, I hardly think that's relevant," Ginger snapped, her patience beginning to thin.

"Well, we don't know that. If Federline is using Alex to decode articles, it very well may be relevant."

"But not nearly as important as getting Alex back immediately." Ginger stood and lifted one of the maps Lucy had cleared from the coffee table. "Ivy, if you'll take a look at this—"

"Enough," Victoria said coldly. She gave both Ginger and Alastair a withering stare. "I know you're scared, Ginger, but Ivy's been through a horrible ordeal. The last thing she needs is to be pressed into service before she's even had a chance to catch her breath or have a sip of water. You're a mother, yes, and I understand that, but you're also a physician. We have no idea what she's been through in the hands of strange men."

Ginger's heart stumbled, a wave of shame cutting through her as she caught the full meaning of Victoria's implication. *Of course.*

And, yet, her desperation continued to pulse at the ragged edges of her mind, flaying through her skin like a knife.

But, my son.

Still, Ginger drew a deep breath and nodded. "I understand."

Ivy sat straighter, pushing the blanket away. "No—it's all right, Mama. I want to help both Aunt Ginger and Alastair. I want to help Alex. He'd do the same for me." A look of determination crossed her face, then she turned and gripped Victoria's hands. "I'm all right. Hungry and tired. But I'm safe. And I'm not a child. I can help."

Her words seemed to have a strange effect on Victoria, who blinked at her with surprise. Ginger had known Victoria long enough to know that it was nearly impossible to change her mind once she decided upon something—but Ivy seemed to know how to defuse her mother.

Before Victoria could answer, Ivy turned toward Ginger. "I don't know that I can find it on a map, but if you put me in a car and drive me, I can find my way there from the consulate."

"Thank you," Ginger said, relief breaking through the wall of pressure constricting her heart.

"Maybe you should rest some first," Victoria suggested.

"No, Mama. It's fine. Toast and tea would be nice, but I can manage."

Victoria nodded. Then her gaze lifted, meeting Ginger's. A sadness lit her eyes—one Ginger understood better than ever, now knowing that Alex had taken off to save Ivy.

Somewhere along the way their children had grown and didn't need them quite so much. As each subsequent year passed, they'd need them less.

And I spent the last few years so overwhelmed that I barely noticed.

Ginger swallowed a lump in her throat. "I'd be grateful for your help, Ivy."

She wouldn't think about the years she'd spent missing family outings for hospital meetings, or the dinners Noah had eaten alone with the children while she stayed late on the ward. That could wait. Regret could wait.

Right now there was only one thing worth her time, her breath, her blood if necessary. She was going to get Alex back—and God help anyone who stood in her way.

CHAPTER THIRTY-FIVE

GINGER

The estate rising before Ginger had the quiet, menacing elegance of a royal retreat—conspicuously grand, impossibly isolated, and yet somehow aware of those who approached. How Ivy had managed to escape—Ginger shuddered at the thought of her climbing over the gates, which she must have done—she wasn't quite certain.

It wasn't the sheer size that unsettled Ginger, though the brownstone walls stretched away in a crescent and seemed to belong more to a fortress than a private home. It was the way the place seemed to stand apart from the city, as if it had pulled back from Cairo itself to brood beside the river.

Tall copper domes caught the afternoon sun, throwing hard light down into the forecourt where clipped palms and tiled fountains flanked a narrow canal that drew its water straight from the Nile. The scent of damp stone and magnolia blossoms drifted faintly on the air, cloyingly sweet against the heat.

Behind the gates, marble loggias rose in three tiers, their arched windows veiled with elaborate mashrabiya screens—like a hundred unblinking eyes watching the Nile. One entire wing faced the river, its stained-glass panels promising views of the sunset through fractured color, a touch that felt almost theatrical.

She could imagine Prescott Federline standing there, drink in hand, surveying the water as though he owned the whole of Egypt. The thought made her throat tighten. A man like that wouldn't hesitate to keep Alex as long as it suited him. And, yet, here she was—standing on his threshold beside Alastair and some of his most trusted Egyptian friends, including Khalib.

Though Alastair had suggested Ginger stay at home, she'd insisted on coming. Victoria and Ivy were now safely in one of Alastair's safe houses, along with Lucy, who Alastair had insisted accompany them. Moments like that reminded her of how much she loved the man—he was as protective of her family as Noah and Jack were.

Her pulse quickened at the thought of danger to any of her loved ones, but she forced her shoulders back. She'd been here before, in other ways. War hospitals. Desperately attempting to save broken men while under fire. This was just another front line.

The guards stepped forward before they even reached the gates, rifles angled just enough to make the point. The taller one planted himself in the middle, his white galabeyah bright against the shadowed forecourt.

"You have business here?" His Arabic accent curled the English into something sharper. His eyes flicked over Ginger, then back to Alastair, scrutinizing them. Ginger fought the temptation to shield her face. Alastair—master of disguise—had given her a prosthetic nose and wig to disguise her somewhat. But she had no doubt Prescott Federline would recognize her if he was here and looked closely enough.

Alastair withdrew a folded paper from his breast pocket with the deliberate care of a man handling something unpleasant. "A member of this household has been linked to a case admitted to hospital two nights ago. Tuberculosis."

The guard's jaw tightened, and his gaze slid sideways toward the other man, as if the syllables themselves could carry infection.

"Who?" the guard demanded.

"A porter whose sister works here. He is in isolation now. We are required to inspect the premises where he has lodged or visited in the last month. He listed this as one of them." Alastair's tone was flat, almost bored, as if the outcome were inevitable. The papers in Alastair's pocket were official and explicit—entry to any dwelling, inspection of any chamber, seizure of articles suspected of harboring infection. Jane Radford had seen to that, thank goodness.

The guard's eyes narrowed, his hand shifting on the rifle stock. "No one is sick here."

"That's fortunate," Alastair said, stepping just close enough that the man had to tilt his head back to meet his eyes. "Let's make sure it stays that way." He tapped the folded paper with one finger, letting the wax seal catch the light. "If we find nothing, you can tell your master you kept his household safe."

From the corner of her eye, Ginger saw the other guard take a half-step back, the way men did when the idea of contagion brushed against them. She'd spent years observing similar behavior from family members of patients in hospital. The taller one hesitated, then signaled to the gatekeeper. Metal scraped, hinges groaned, and the gates swung inward on a breath of cool, damp air.

Inside the gates, the light shifted, the glare of the Nile replaced by the cool gloom of shaded courtyards. A steward in a pale turban hurried toward them, his sandals whispering against the marble. He stopped short when Alastair introduced himself and gave the reason for their visit. The man's eyes darted to the paper, then to the guards, then back to Alastair.

"You will not disturb the master," the steward said, the Arabic clipped. At times like these, Ginger had Noah to thank for her own proficiency in the language. He'd insisted on continuing to teach her long after they'd moved to England.

"That's not my intention," Alastair replied smoothly, switching languages with ease. "We'll start with the servants' quarters. Any who have coughed, fevered, or lost weight recently must be brought forward."

The steward's throat worked. "Wait there. I'll take your papers to my master and return shortly." He gestured them down a colonnade lined with carved cedar doors. Servants peered from shadowed alcoves, their gazes quick and wary.

As the steward disappeared further into the house again, Alastair gave Ginger a subtle nod. Her heart pounded in response.

This was it. She and Khalib would separate themselves from the group, slip away before Federline could bar further entry. If Federline cooperated, then Alastair and his men would help in the search. If he didn't, she and Khalib were on their own.

She held her breath as they moved toward the foyer beyond the colonnade, no doubt the servants' quarters. With so many people watching, she'd be sure to be seen—wouldn't she?

Then, a cough in the distance caught her attention. She lifted her chin sharply. That might be enough for now. "We should investigate," she told Alastair.

He nodded sternly. Then gestured to Khalib and said in clear, loud Arabic, "Escort Nurse Hardwick to see about that coughing. If tuberculosis is here, we must find it."

If the servants watching thought to protest, they said nothing. In fact, the mention of the disease was enough that most of them shrank away as though Ginger and Khalib had brought it with them.

Ginger hid a smile.

Fear and self-preservation were powerful weapons. She'd learned that all too well over the years.

Khalib and Ginger hurried down the colonnade, then slipped into the foyer. No one stopped them, thankfully. Either their fear of the disease or the unknown restrained them.

Ginger kept her pace even, alert for any sign of Alex. She tried to imagine him here, in this strange blend of opulence and domesticity beyond the polished cedar doors, the faint smell of spices from a kitchen somewhere deep in the estate, the oppressive hush that made every footstep sound like an intrusion.

They passed a latticework screen that led further into the house, and Ginger caught sight of a narrow stairwell leading downward, its steps worn in the center from years of use. She filed it away in her mind. If they needed to get out quickly, such stairs often led to servants' entrances.

Would they be keeping Alex here, near the servants? Ivy had said Alex didn't know Federline was associated with the men who'd kidnapped her and that they'd taken them to luxurious guest rooms—but that was hours ago. By now Alex must have noticed Ivy's absence. It would have made him suspicious.

For all she knew, by now Federline had unmasked himself to Alex.

Breathing out, she tried to think. She needed to be logical. If Federline really did need something from Alex—decoding whatever was in that journal—then he wouldn't show himself to be the villain yet.

Which means he's most likely still in the guest rooms.

Ginger adjusted her grip on the strap of the leather medical kit slung across her shoulder, feeling the hard edge of the stethoscope inside among other medical supplies. It was both prop and tool—she would use it to listen for coughs if she had to, but its presence was also her shield, the thing that let her walk freely as though she belonged. The familiarity of it, too, was a comfort.

Her eyes darted around the hallway. "I think this way," she whispered to Khalib, tilting her head to the right. "The left leads closer to the periphery of the home. Ivy said the rooms were upstairs."

He nodded and allowed her to lead the way. Funny how his presence now was meant to act as a form of protection. When she'd met Khalib, he'd been a slip of a boy. Now he was just a few years older than Noah had been when she'd met him—a man, well trained by Alastair, and handsome.

His age made her feel practically matronly, really. Another reminder of how quickly the time had passed. For all she knew, Khalib had someone he cared for by now and would start his own family soon. Or already had.

Her guess about the house's layout proved to be right—just past the hallway was a large door leading to an enormous, opulent foyer. The grand staircase in the heart of the home most likely led to the bedrooms.

Ginger scanned the hallway, looking for watchful eyes.

No one.

Ivy escaped. I can do this.

They had to move fast.

Heart pounding, Ginger tore away from the safety of the doorway and practically sprinted up the stairs, Khalib just steps behind her. She waited for a shout, a voice—any sign that someone would stop her—but none came.

Breathlessly, she reached the top level. Now she had no instinct to guide her. The hallways looked equally splendid, leading to what she imagined would be beautiful rooms. She hurried up to the first door she found and tried it.

Locked.

Whirling toward Khalib, she said, "Try all the doors. Hurry."

They raced down the hallway, trying each doorway as they went.

Every single one of the doors they tried was locked.

The thought made goose bumps rise on Ginger's arms.

A house full of locked doors was somehow more terrifying than she'd imagined.

Desperation seeped in. How in the world could she find her son amidst the dizzying maze of doors and locks? She gritted her teeth, sagging against one door, her heart still thundering so loudly in her chest that she feared she wouldn't hear someone coming down the hallway at all. Then her voice dropped to a whisper as she tapped on the door with a fingernail. "Alex?"

His name vanished into the heavy air, swallowed by the pristine, cold tile and shuttered doors.

No answer.

Khalib moved ahead of her, testing another handle—locked. The click of brass against wood sounded loud in the hush.

She moved to another door. "Alex," she tried again, a fraction louder this time. Her pulse throbbed in her temples.

They split without speaking—she to the left, Khalib to the right —tapping softly on the ornate doors. She pressed her ear against the grain of the wood, straining for any hint of movement within.

Each silence stretched longer than the last, until her chest ached from holding her breath.

Another door. Another locked handle.

Her knuckles brushed the carved wood before she remembered to knock. "It's Mama—Alex?"

Nothing.

Where could he be?

She moved faster now, urgency gnawing at the edges of her caution. If someone intercepted them, the pretense of a tuberculosis inspection wouldn't save her. She barely held on by a thread, her desperation growing by the minute. All this effort. This silly ruse.

Her sense that she was just as far from Alex as ever.

Two more doors. No reply.

As she reached the end of the hallway, her hope faded. Her chest burned with frustration, with fear. There were other hallways, other bedrooms, of course, but they'd been fortunate not to be spotted yet. How long before their luck ran out?

She tapped on the last door, praying for an answer.

God, please. Help me. Help me find my son.

Her knock was answered by the faint scrape of a chair leg on tile.

She froze, hand still on the panel.

Khalib glanced over, his expression sharpening.

A shadow shifted beneath the thin line of light at the door's threshold, and Ginger felt dizzy with hope.

"Who's there?" a voice came softly.

Not Alex's.

A woman's.

Whoever was on the other side of this door might not only be Federline's ally but also someone with the means to report Ginger to him immediately.

As disappointment washed over her, Ginger found her voice answering in the clipped, practiced official tone she used in the hospital when necessary. "Nurse Hardwick, here under order of inspection," she said, pitching the words just loud enough to carry through the wood. "We've had reports of illness in the household."

"Help me. Please."

What on earth?

Every muscle in Ginger's body seemed to tighten. She stepped closer, pressing her palm to the warm polished wood. "Who are you?"

Another pause. "I can't—" The woman's voice broke. "He'll hear me. Please, you have to get me out of here."

Khalib was beside her now, his hand hovering near the hilt of the knife at his belt, eyes sweeping the hall. Every second they lingered here, the danger climbed.

Ginger kept her voice low but firm. "Is there a boy here?"

Before a reply came, another sound made the hair on the back of her neck rise. Footsteps. Faint at first, then unmistakable. Heavy and growing louder down the hall.

Khalib's gaze snapped to hers, caution pooling in those dark depths. They had only seconds to decide—walk away and risk leaving another innocent person to suffer or open the door and risk everything.

Khalib grabbed her by the elbow. "We must go," he hissed in an urgent tone.

"Please. Please. I'm desperate. He's been keeping me here for months."

Something in her words stopped Ginger's heart cold. She exchanged a wary look with Khalib. "Can you pick the lock?" she asked him.

"That won't help—I can do that much myself," the woman said. "There's an iron latch at the top of the door. It's stopping me from opening the door. All I need is for you to flip it open."

"Someone is coming," Ginger whispered.

"Please—I'm begging you. Just flip the latch."

Ginger lifted her gaze, scanning the door. Sure enough, the woman was right. A hinged latch, screwed into the door frame, held the door into place. While most doors opened into rooms, these appeared to swing the opposite way—into the hallway—which was what kept the door sealed shut.

A shiver ran up Ginger's spine. What sort of lunatic designed his home in such a way?

She raised her hand, reaching for the latch. It hovered inches out of her grasp. She appealed to Khalib, who stepped closer, then flipped it.

The footsteps were closer now. Ginger turned to glance, her fingers trembling. They were at the end of the hall, and all other doors were locked—nowhere for them to go. "We're trapped," Ginger said to Khalib. "They'll see us."

A metallic scrape clicked from the door, then the handle turned. "Hurry, in here," the woman's voice said. The door opened. With nowhere else to go and no other chance of escape, Ginger darted inside, pulling Khalib with her.

They shut the door and Ginger turned, breathless, to see the woman who'd opened the door.

She froze, her heart slamming into her ribs as the memory broke over her like a wave—the blinding Maltese sun, the cry of a bird above the cliff, her friend's pale hands slick with blood, the way her blue eyes had searched Ginger's just before she fell backward into nothing. The salt sting, the sickening drop.

Sixteen years, and the scene was as sharp as glass in her mind.

Though the years had passed, the long golden-blond braid was the same. A hint of age—and many more freckles—showed on her pretty face. She was impossibly thin but looked clean and well cared-for otherwise. Ginger took in the cream-colored linen blouse, olive-green trousers, and sandals. In terms of looks, nearly unchanged in sixteen years.

Sarah Anderson Hanover.

Ginger sprang back, knocking into Khalib, who steadied her. "You died," she whispered to Sarah, her voice trembling. The words felt foreign on her tongue, as if saying them here, now, unmade all the years she had carried that grief. Her mind rejected the sight before her even as her body believed it, the same way a wound sometimes refused to hurt until the patient saw the blood.

Sarah's brow furrowed, her eyes wary. Then she came closer, touched the veil beside Ginger's cheek, pushing the wig back and exposing a hint of red.

Her blue-eyed gaze snapped to Ginger's. "Ginger?"

Ginger nodded, her eyes filling with tears.

How could this possibly be?

I saw her die.

She fell off a cliff.

"Sarah …" Ginger's voice was rough and filled with emotion.

For years, Ginger had relived that cliff—the impossible arc of Sarah's fall, the hollow splash, the circling black bird in the perfect blue sky—a loop that had played in her dreams and in the quietest moments of her waking life. She had mourned Sarah like a sister. Now here she was, whole and breathing.

The world tilted beneath Ginger's feet.

Sarah stepped back, sadness in her expression. "I'm not Sarah. I never was. And you're right—Sarah Anderson died that day in Malta, Ginger. My name is Kit. Kit Federline."

Ginger's eyes widened. *Federline?*

Then, the door opened behind Ginger, and a distinctive male voice came before she could turn. "Dr. Benson. I see you've met my daughter."

Khalib stepped in front of Ginger protectively.

"You bastard," Ginger managed, setting a hand on Khalib's prosthetic hand, to hold him back. "How *dare* you? Give me my son."

"Did you honestly think this little health inspection would fool me?" Prescott gave her an amused smile. "I knew right away you must be here. Though I'll admit I didn't expect you *here*." He took a menacing step closer.

Khalib's knife came free from his waist in a flash. He lunged for Prescott, but startlingly, Prescott slipped his own knife from the sleeve of his shirt. He slashed at Khalib, striking him near the neck with a quick, blunt blow.

Ginger screamed.

CHAPTER THIRTY-SIX

ALEX

Rubbing his eyes, Alex sank back into the chair behind the desk, exhaustion aching deeply through his muscles.

His mother had never let him stay up all night like he had the previous night, no matter how often he'd begged her when he was caught in the middle of a particularly intriguing book or puzzle. And look—he was just fine. Tired, yes, but also invigorated.

And maybe a bit hungry.

He'd been so consumed by his work that he'd barely noticed his hunger, though, or the way time had slipped away. A few servants had come and gone, brought him tea, water, and sandwiches that mostly remained untouched on the floor beside him. They'd been in his way on the desk.

But it had been hours since he'd seen anyone, and now the house had gone strangely quiet.

He listened for a few beats then looked back at his work and grinned, setting his pencil down. Leaning over, he scooped up one of the sandwiches that looked the least wilted and sat straight, taking a bite.

I did it.

He'd solved the damned puzzle. The code.

Probably in record time.

That would be sure to impress Mr. Federline.

Not all of the articles had been coded—and that was part of the problem. He'd been forced to triple-check those. Make certain he wasn't missing something. None of it made sense, really, but he was sure of his decoding.

Bits of phrases. Words. Some strange, others clearer:

DON'T BELIEVE FATHER

That one stood out above the others. Bothered him in a way he couldn't quite verbalize.

I HAVE HER

That one frightened him.

Her? Who was she? Why was Gretchen Herbert sending these codes? And to whom?

It didn't matter. It wasn't his job to understand what the data meant—just deliver it to the people who could do something about it. And, maybe, if he proved himself useful, the British government might find a place for him eventually. Or maybe he could even have Mr. Federline write him a good letter of reference for a university, like Oxford, where his father had gone.

Mama had said Oxford might be out of reach for Alex. That with the economic downturn, she wasn't certain what they'd be able to afford. Alex was confident in his ability to get a scholarship, but Papa's lack of achievements didn't help his case much.

And a few weeks ago—learning what he'd learned about Uncle Jack and Mama's divorce and his own questionable legitimacy—the dream of Oxford had dimmed.

But maybe he didn't need Mama and Papa. Maybe his legitimacy didn't matter.

Maybe all he needed was the brain God had given him and his own grit and determination to succeed.

Alex took a bite from the sandwich, relaxing back into his chair. He should really leave the room and go find Ivy. She was likely to be furious with him for abandoning her all evening and morning. But it was so beautiful here, and the servants had told him she'd gone to bed early. She probably needed to sleep for a long time, after what they'd been through.

The sandwich wasn't bad either, given the fact it'd been sitting there for a while.

The legs of the chair scraped back against the tiles as Alex stood, stretching his legs.

A scream pierced the silence.

Alex stood straighter, more alert now, his body tensing.

Something familiar about that scream ...

If he didn't know any better, it had come from a woman.

Ivy?

He cleared his throat, turning in the direction the sound had come from—outside, down the hall. "Hello?" he called out. The door to his room was shut, though.

Alex strode across the room toward the door, his fingers finding the cool brass of the handle. He turned, then stopped short.

The door was locked.

Why on earth would the door be locked?

The hair on his arms rose as his skin pebbled.

He knocked on the door firmly. Loudly. "Hello? Anyone there?"

Silence greeted him, making his stomach roil. He knocked again. "Hello there?"

This time, footsteps approached the door. He stepped back, his fists curling instinctively, and the door opened to reveal Mr. Federline.

"Why was my door locked?" Alex demanded, aware of the hostility in his voice despite his best efforts.

Mr. Federline gave an apologetic smile. "I'm sorry—this door gets stuck."

Stuck? But it hadn't felt stuck. The latch hadn't moved. Alex peered beyond him, into the darkened hallway. "I thought I heard a scream."

As though to offer reassurance, Mr. Federline opened the door more widely and stepped further inside. "You did. One of my servants just found out that her brother has died of tuberculosis, you see. She's understandably devastated. In fact, we've had a visit from the health office this morning to inspect the premises, but you have nothing to fear."

Alex was certain the scream had been one of terror not sadness. "Where's my sister?" he asked, keeping his voice steady

"Your sister?" Mr. Federline raised a brow.

"Yes, my sister, Ivy. I haven't seen her since yesterday." Alex cleared his throat, trying to keep his tone polite while alarm sneaked up his core and flushed his skin. He tried to take a step past Mr. Federline, who blocked him from going out the doorway with a gentle hand to his shoulder.

"Your sister is not here, son. The housekeeper took her into the city for some new clothes. I didn't really have anything suitable for her here."

Something was off. He couldn't put his finger on it, but he had the sense that Mr. Federline wasn't being completely honest. Still, he knew better than to ask him outright. "But Ivy hates shopping," Alex said instead. "I'm surprised she went at all."

"Yes," Mr. Federline said with a chuckle. "She did make that quite clear, but it was much easier to have her go and pick her wardrobe along with the housekeeper."

Alex felt his pulse quicken, a rush of blood pounding

through his ears. *He's lying. He's lying, and I know it. Ivy would never turn down a trip to go shopping.*

Alex gave him a wary smile. "Well, if you could please let me know as soon as she returns, I would appreciate it. I'm sure she's not happy with me for missing breakfast this morning. She's always complaining that I sleep too late."

Mr. Federline nodded, then his gaze went to the desk. "The servants informed me that you weren't sleeping at all though, were you? They said you were up all night working on that code."

Alex nodded faintly. He had to own that much. "I was."

Leaving the door open to the hallway, Mr. Federline crossed the room toward the desk and lifted the journal Alex had been working from. Then his cool blue-eyed gaze snapped toward the paper that Alex had used to work out the code. "May I?" he asked, lifting one of the papers.

Alex nodded.

If Mr. Federline was lying about Ivy, what else was he lying about? Alex knew to be more cautious, but he didn't have enough information to make a true judgment. They'd met him at the consulate, which meant at the very least he was a well-connected man. Someone even potentially dangerous. A high-level spy for the government perhaps?

As Mr. Federline scanned the paper, Alex felt suddenly naked. Ashamed. As though his efforts had laid bare something Alex should have kept hidden.

"Did you complete the assignment?"

Alex felt the urge to blurt the truth, to demand where Ivy was, but he shoved it down. Words were currency here, and he didn't yet know their value.

He had to be careful. He had a feeling decoding those articles would keep him safe for now—and gave him something to negotiate with if Mr. Federline was more than just a liar.

"No," he said smoothly, his throat dry. "There are still more to do. That's all I've managed to decode so far."

"And can you make sense of any of it?"

He chose his words carefully. He didn't want to sound incompetent. "With the right context I could."

Rubbing his temples with his fingertips, Mr. Federline sighed and leaned against the desk. "Have you ever been on an airplane, Alex? There's something I'd love to get your opinion on. I think you could be of great assistance to me."

An airplane?

Despite his wariness, Alex felt a nervous thrill of excitement. He'd dreamed of flying before but hadn't ever experienced it. He didn't want to seem too eager, though. "To where?"

"Not far. Into the desert." The distant soft sound of voices and steps carried down the hallway, and Alex turned to glance in that direction. They seemed to come from another wing of the house.

But what about Ivy? Where was she? "Would Ivy be coming with us?"

"It'd be preferrable to leave sooner rather than later. But we won't be long. And if you'd like, we can take her along the next time." Mr. Federline smiled gently, the sort of look on his face that Alex imagined a doting grandfather might give. He wouldn't know for certain—both his grandfathers had died before he'd been born.

When Mr. Federline rubbed his temple again, though, Alex's gaze narrowed in on a streak of crimson on the cuff of his shirtsleeve.

Blood.

Fresh blood, for that matter.

He'd seen enough of it at the hospital to recognize the look of it on clothing.

The world at the periphery of his vision seemed to swim.

Ivy. God, Ivy.

What had Mr. Federline done to her? The chilling scream he'd heard gnawed his memory, stirring up his deepest fears.

What have I done? What was I thinking? I was so enraptured with the idea of winning this man's praise that I forgot myself. Forgot Ivy. His eyes burned at the thought.

He had to be rational. The man wasn't likely to be a murderer—he had to be at least a respectable member of society to move around so freely and be so wealthy. But he certainly wasn't honest. And if that was the case, both he and Ivy could be in terrible danger.

For now, he had to play along. Find out who this man was, if he could, and where Ivy was.

When he realized he'd barely breathed for a while, Alex managed a shaky smile. "An airplane ride sounds fantastic."

CHAPTER THIRTY-SEVEN

NOAH

*N*oah's hands were shaking.

It wasn't the first time it had happened. Not by a long shot.

He'd first noticed it a few years earlier, one time that he'd been invited by an old army friend out for a hunt in York. He hadn't wanted to go, but Ginger had encouraged him to take the time for himself—keep the acquaintance of men he'd served with during the war, when he'd been little more than a green infantryman.

After the hunt, he'd gone to an inn for the night, and that was when he'd noticed it: his hands, trembling uncontrollably as though something ailed them. The shaking had vanished overnight that time, but occasionally it returned—when he least expected it.

Like right now—seated on the divan of Fahad's house while sipping coffee, while Jack worked on decoding the telegraphs by Gretchen Herbert they'd stolen from the office in Baghdad that morning. Noah's hands hadn't been shaking on the airplane trip back to Jerusalem. Or even after they'd arrived at Fahad's.

He set his coffee cup on the saucer, then smoothed his palms over the rough fabric of his robe, over his thighs. Maybe killing Hower and his assistant had affected him more than he'd realized.

Or maybe it had been the sight of Jack face-down on the floor, a pool of blood beside his head.

I thought he was dead.

The sight had struck him like a bolt of lightning. And then Jack's distress.

God, that had cleaved his heart.

Jack was the most loyal man Noah had ever met. Inexplicably so, given what Jack had been through.

On the other hand, maybe Noah's shaking wasn't about that at all. Maybe it was just time for him to admit the truth—that he wasn't the same man he'd been almost twenty years ago, when he'd been recruited to spy and lie, kill and hurt.

He'd gone soft.

Love had softened him. The love of his wife. The love of his children. The love of his friends. Hell, even the love for people and causes he followed less blindly and more from true conviction.

He wasn't sufficiently stoic for the sort of emotionless detachment that this job required anymore. And being talented at killing and deception held little luster for him.

"God save the king," Jack muttered, slipping his pencil behind his ear.

Noah lifted his head sharply. "What's that?"

Jack released a guttural sigh and shook his head. Then he gestured toward the logbook they'd stolen from the telegraph office. "If she was trying to take it easy on me, she failed. Most of this is absolute nonsense."

"You decoded *JERUSALEM*, though—that's got to mean something."

"I've decoded all of them," Jack replied tersely, then pinched the bridge of his nose. "At least I think I have. None of it makes sense." He shoved the sheet across the table toward Noah. "Like this. *GOD SAVE THE KING*. What in the hell does that mean?"

"Maybe you did it wrong," Fahad said from the end of the table. He took a long drag from a pipe. "You don't always do it right."

Jack jerked his head with a scowl, then grimaced as though the quick movement had pained him. He wore a bandage on the side of his head—one Noah was certain Ginger would say she was proud of him for doing, then promptly redo herself.

Grasping the paper with his thumb and forefinger, Noah turned it toward him, careful not to allow Jack to see the trembling in his hand.

I HAVE HER
JERUSALEM
GOD SAVE THE KING
WAKE UP
DON'T BELIEVE FATHER
HELP ME

Words. Phrases that seemed like gibberish.

"Did she use the same type of cipher each time?" Noah asked, glancing at Jack over the top of the paper.

Drooping against the table, Jack cradled his forehead in his palm. "No. Some were more complicated than others. The one that said *wake up* was a beast to work out."

"Then maybe it's the most important one."

"Wake up." Fahad chuckled, his dark eyes twinkling. "Maybe she knew you'd be falling asleep in the middle of decoding her messages."

"She always did like to keep you on your toes," Noah said with a smirk. He set the paper down on the table and leaned back. He didn't dare take another sip of coffee under Fahad's watchful and eagle-eyed gaze. His shrewd friend wouldn't miss the tremor in his hands. "You should have seen them together in Malta, Fahad. The woman had Jack so tightly wound around her finger that we spent half the time there carrying parcels out of the merchant shops—and emptying Jack's pocketbook."

Jack grunted. "Don't remind me. Lot of good it did me too. I'm never buying another woman anything again in my life."

Noah didn't respond. The humor hid a deeper hurt, thinly veiled as it might be right now. Since Jack had confirmed on that train from France that Kit and Sarah had been the same person, Jack's actions after Malta had been something Noah hadn't wanted to think about.

No wonder his friend had been so devastated when he thought Sarah had died.

Jack had needed just as much consolation from Ginger when he'd married her as Ginger had needed protection from Jack. Noah had just never realized it until now.

And neither did he want to imagine just what form of consolation that meant.

Noah's jaw clenched, and he pushed the thought into a deep, dark place in his mind, where he could keep it locked away and tightly sealed. He turned to the task at hand instead. "Wake up," he said in a low voice, letting his gaze drift over the walls of Fahad's home.

"It could mean something else," Fahad offered helpfully.

Obviously. Noah didn't let the snarky comment pass his lips, though.

"God save the king could be about King George," Fahad suggested again. "Maybe someone is planning an assassination."

Noah pursed his lips. "Much as that would be intriguing, I'd hope Kit would have better sense than to send a message about something like *that* to Jack in code through a newspaper and simply hope he didn't miss it. He very nearly missed *this.*"

"But I didn't," Jack said wearily.

"But only because you went to her hotel room in Baghdad."

"Because I was being distracted by a *woman*, apparently, who wanted to keep me distracted," Jack said bitterly. "If I'd had the chance to spend some more time looking at those newspaper clippings she stole from me, I'm sure I would have found it sooner."

Noah frowned and clasped his hands together. "Then why would she leave you the key to the telegraph office? She had to know you'd go there and get the logbook."

"Why do women do anything the way they do, Noah? If you can solve that mystery, you'll be the best goddamned code-breaker in the universe."

A plume of smoke came from Fahad's lips. "That's true. Ask any man on the streets of Jerusalem. Women are the most mysterious of all of Allah's creatures."

Noah smiled then paused, his gaze darting toward the words Jack had uncoded.

Streets of Jerusalem.

Noah's eyes drifted to the paper again, the phrases stacking in his head. *God Save the King. Jerusalem.* His mind jumped, stitched the two together, and a spark lit through his brain.

He slapped his palm flat on the table, the sound cracking through the room. "That's it."

Both Fahad and Jack jumped, giving him startled looks.

"What's it?" Jack asked, squinting as he raised his head.

Noah leaned forward, an eager feeling energizing him. "The Streets of Jerusalem. King George. King George Street in Jerusalem."

"Is there a King George Street in Jerusalem?" Jack asked, sitting straighter as he looked at Fahad.

"You've been away too long," Fahad said with a shake of his head. He nodded. "For a decade now. By Jaffa."

Jack locked eyes with Noah. "You're a genius, you know that?"

Noah shrugged. "I didn't decode those messages."

"Don't get carried away. I didn't say you were the *only* genius here," Jack said with the faintest glimmer of his normal humor. "What's on King George Street?" he asked Fahad.

"Many new buildings. Merchant shops. The Talitha Komi orphanage for girls."

Of course.

Noah cocked his head. "Talitha Komi?" The barest hint of a smile showed on his lips.

Jack rolled his eyes. "What now?"

"Talitha Komi. In Syrian Aramaic it means *wake up, girl.*"

"Of course it does," Jack muttered, then gripped onto the edge of the table and stood. "Something I never could have known, since I don't know Syrian Aramaic. You sure Kit wasn't leaving this message for you instead of me?"

Noah held his gaze. "I'm sure that Kit assumed you'd turn to your closest friend for help, yes."

He hated to see Jack so bitter. So wounded by this Ruby woman—whoever she was. Jack didn't open up to anyone easily. If she'd managed to have that sort of effect on him, he must have really liked her.

Silence hung between them and Jack drew a slow breath, his shoulders rising with the effort. Then he nodded. "You're right." His eyes sparked. "An orphanage, huh? Who runs the place?"

"German nuns. Christians," Fahad said. He set his pipe down then also stood, rolling his shoulders.

Nuns.

An orphanage of girls.

A *safe* institution of veiled women.

"It's a perfect place for them to hide," Jack said, echoing Noah's thoughts.

"The sisters aren't likely to allow you in, though. Especially if they're hiding Kit and Alice. It'll take someone they trust to do that," Fahad said.

Jack crossed his arms. "Like whom?"

Fahad gave Noah a grave look. "Someone like Sheikh Omar. He is a friend to many—both Christians and Moslem Arabs seek his counsel. He will know either someone within the community at the orphanage or have a friend who can open the doors for you. If he'll talk to you again. Only one man was watching the house this morning. He may be losing interest in you, Yusef."

"Sheikh?" Jack asked, giving Noah a wary glance.

Noah sighed, then rubbed his eyes. He hadn't had the chance to fill Jack in too well with what he'd learned—or what had happened with Hower. Cracking his knuckles, he gestured for Jack to sit once again.

Jack did, giving him a pointed look to get on with it.

"After we parted in France, I was approached by Alain Roche and a man named Clive Hower. Hower claimed to be working for Knight, but I quickly realized he was a Blackwell operative."

"Quickly?" Jack raised a brow. "That's impressive. They don't usually give themselves away so easily." His eyes narrowed, as though he'd suddenly remembered Ruby. "Trust me, I know."

"For the sake of brevity, let's simply say it was an educated guess that I confirmed by locating this on his wrist." Noah flashed the Blackwell tattoo Fahad's wife Nasira had given him.

Jack tilted his head, his eyes sparking with anger. "I didn't tell you about that so you'd go and mark yourself, Noah. You have no idea what trouble that symbol could cause you."

Noah shrugged, unfazed. "I'll tattoo over it soon enough. Regardless, Hower made me an offer—come to Palestine, work for Knight and MI5 to pinpoint any German overtures being made to Arab nationalists, and my family would be safe from threats. He also promised to give you what Knight had promised back in England—the ability for you to move freely in the Middle East and official aid in finding Alice and Kit."

Stretching his legs in front of him, Jack said, "At which point, you promptly sent me a message not to trust anyone because, since Hower was compromised, you didn't know who else might be?"

"Precisely." Noah sank slowly back into his seat. "And, once here, I noticed that the evidence of German-Arab nationalist connections was less apparent than Hower had claimed. As though he was keeping me occupied. I took my job seriously enough—Fahad helped introduce me to a well-connected local sheikh. And, while there, I had the brilliant idea to ask after Kit and Alice—to see if he'd heard of any rumors of American women who'd come through the area."

"It wasn't a bad idea," Fahad admitted with a rueful smile. "The sheikh hears more than most. He's an important man from an important family."

"But it made him wary of you?" Jack asked.

Noah nodded. "Because he *had* heard of two American women. Only, he said nothing. His servant boy, however, reacted in a way that made me suspicious. So I followed the boy and questioned him—and the boy let slip that I wasn't the only one who'd come asking. I thought it might have been Federline, but it wasn't. It was a man named Sharif Kamal al-Rashid. A man who, it turns out—according to Roche—just may have had reason to see King Faisal Hussein meet an early death."

Now Jack's eyes shot to Noah's. "Holy shit," he breathed.

Indeed.

The implication was enormous. King Faisal was dead, after all.

"You think this Sharif al-Rashid murdered King Faisal?"

Noah nodded.

Jack raked his fingers through his hair. "But why would he be looking for Alice and Kit …" Jack shot to his feet once again, then steadied himself as though the movement had made him woozy. "That's what you think Alice and Kit found, don't you? They found evidence of it!"

Then Jack covered his face with his hands. "The goddamned microfilm."

"Microfilm?" Noah asked, keeping his tone even.

Jack's gaze slid away, his fingers curling against the table's edge. "Last night—just before she attacked me—I found something. Microfilm. Inside a typewriter, of all places."

Noah felt the words like a blade sliding under his ribs.

"When I woke this morning, it was gone," Jack finished, his voice flat. "She took it."

The realization made Noah's close his eyes, his hands fisting.

If that was true and Ruby was Blackwell … then they'd just let vital intelligence—intelligence that was potentially explosive—slip into the hands of Prescott Federline.

Noah released a breath, then shook out his fists. He had no time for shaking hands. No time for softness. Not now. "Then let's go. Let's go talk to the sheikh. Let's get back Alice and Kit."

CHAPTER THIRTY-EIGHT

GINGER

Snipping the end of the suture thread, Ginger examined the stitches she'd made on Khalib's collarbone. Prescott Federline had been only centimeters away from slicing into Khalib's carotid artery. If he'd succeeded, all the medical training on earth would have been useless—Khalib would have died.

But he didn't. He's alive.

Releasing a shaky breath, Ginger let her gaze travel to Khalib's face. "You're all stitched up," Ginger said, squeezing the forearm above his good hand.

He grimaced with pain but smiled. "Thank you."

Ginger swallowed hard. Sarah … Kit … whatever her name was—she'd helped Ginger lead Khalib over to the bed in the room. After Federline had struck, he'd left, latching all three of them in the room with a snarled warning that any further screams would lead to Alex's immediate death.

That had been enough to silence Ginger. She hadn't meant to scream in the first place—but due to the location of Federline's strike, she'd feared the worst.

Now that she knew Khalib would survive the cut, bigger, more immediate concerns pressed in on her. She'd been silent while stitching but she looked up to see Kit standing by a barred window, watching her with an unnerving intensity. "You always were good at these things," Kit offered, her tone a mixture of reservation and hesitancy.

Ginger sighed and removed the prosthetic nose, then pushed back the nurse's cap and wig. She sat beside Khalib, feeling the urge to remain within reach of him—not only for her own protection but for his. "I'm a doctor now," she said, meeting Kit's gaze.

Kit. Not Sarah.

The reality was hard to accept.

Almost as hard as the fact that Sarah had been such a liar.

"I know," Kit said quietly. "I kept up over the years."

"But you didn't." Ginger's voice grew colder and she straightened, disappointment, anger, and hurt all welling inside her. "You didn't keep up. You allowed us all to think that you were dead." Tears gathered in her eyes and she blinked them away, her throat feeling thicker now. "Do you have any idea what I went through that day in Malta? What *Jack* went through?"

A dull clang echoed somewhere in the house. Khalib's gaze flicked to the door. The sound faded, replaced by the faint shuffle of boots.

Kit hugged her arms to her chest. "I did what I had to do to help us all. I had no intention of staying away permanently. But then—"

Ginger raised a brow. "But what?"

"Well, Jack moved on, didn't he? *You* moved on. The next time I saw you both, it was in London, after the war. And there you were—the three of you. You, Jack, and your son, walking down the sidewalk. Happy. A family. And when I saw the way Jack looked at you … I knew I could never come back."

There wasn't any accusation in Kit's words. Just fact—as complicated and messy as it had been. Devoid of context, it sounded horrible.

Still, it must have hurt Kit, if she'd really come back looking. Jack had described her to Ginger as the great love of his life the one and only time he'd ever spoken of her.

And then a new, fresh hurt sprouted through Ginger. Jack had never told her that Kit and Sarah had been one and the same. Why hadn't he just admitted it? He'd only said he'd lost her, and Ginger had assumed that meant she'd chosen another man.

Then again, Sarah had been recently widowed to a man named Paul Hanover when Ginger had met her.

Yet another puzzle. Another thing that didn't make sense.

Nothing about this woman made sense.

And right now, Ginger was almost too spent to care.

Khalib had been injured, Prescott Federline had locked them in this room, God knew what had happened to Alastair by now, and *Alex* …

"Where's my son?" Ginger demanded, rising to her feet. If Kit was Prescott Federline's daughter, surely she must know something about what happened in his house. "His name is Alexander, by the way, and he's not Jack's son. He's Noah's. Jack only married me because Noah and I had never gone to the consulate after our church wedding—our marriage was never validated. And then Noah went missing, and we thought he was dead. Jack, being the *loyal* friend that he is"—she didn't care that her words made Kit flinch—"married me to save me from being ruined. To give Alex a last name. Now where is he? Your father kidnapped and brought him here."

Kit paled, then shook her head. "I-I don't know."

Ginger crossed the room toward her, taking slow, deliberate steps. "You expect me to believe *anything* you say? Everything you ever told me was a lie. Where is my son, Kit? What has your father done with him?"

"I don't know!" Kit's voice came out with more strength—and more desperation too. She sank against the wall, settling with her legs drawn up in front of her, then set her forearms on her knees and cradled her face. "I don't know anything. My father and I aren't on speaking terms, Ginger. He's keeping me here against my will too. I *loathe* him." When she looked up at Ginger, her eyes were filled with sadness. "I've always loathed him. I've spent my whole life trying to get away from him."

She looked so broken. So unlike the fiery woman Ginger had met in front of the pyramids at Giza, running her own archeological dig, demanding the respect of anyone who came near.

Ginger wanted to feel sorry for her—and also didn't.

She didn't know what to trust. What to believe.

At the very least, she'd learned some bedside manners over the years—even when dealing with difficult and obstinate patients. She could use that here. "Then why are you here?" Ginger asked more gently at last.

Kit lifted her head wearily. "I'm here because Alice Darby—who works for my father—was working in Iraq, posing as an archeologist with the Woolley expedition at Ur, but in reality doing what my father's operatives really do—digging up information and secrets to sell to the highest bidder. Have you ever heard of Blackwell?"

Ginger shook her head.

"Good. Then Jack's smarter than I believed." Kit rested against the wall, stretching her legs out. "Blackwell is my father's company. He and his workers—elite operatives, hand-picked by him—steal government and personal secrets about high-level individuals globally. They're mercenaries. They turn around and sell those secrets to anyone who is willing to pay for them. And then those secrets are used as blackmail, or burned, or lost permanently … whatever the buyer wants done with them. My father makes quiet millions a year, all unreported."

Outside, something heavy scraped across the floorboards—close, maybe in the corridor beyond the door. Ginger froze, her gaze darting to the handle. The sound stopped. Silence swelled between heartbeats, so loud she could hear Khalib's breathing from the bed.

Kit didn't pause. Her voice dropped lower, as if she was used to people listening from the shadows. "And I'm his chosen heiress—except I don't want it. I never wanted it. I've told my father in every way possible that I don't want anything to do with his blood money. But he won't accept it. He thinks someday I'll change my mind, and so he won't do *anything* to ever hurt me." She gave a bitter smile. "Physically, anyway."

Chills went up Ginger's spine as she stared at Kit.

If she was being honest, Prescott Federline was more of a villain than Ginger had ever imagined him to be.

And Alex was in terrible danger.

"What does this have to do with Alice Darby?"

Kit sighed. "I was quietly minding my own business working as a journalist in Baghdad when I went up to Ur for an article. And who should I run into but Alice—whom I've known since she was a girl. My father recruited her to get back at Jack—he wanted Jack. Jack is brilliant. But Jack wouldn't work for him, and my father knew I'd kill myself if he ever hurt Jack, so he hired Alice to keep Jack in line. Jack and Alice fought over it and lost contact."

As Kit spoke, the muted odor of cigarette smoke drifted under the door, curling into the room like a warning. Ginger exchanged a glance with Khalib. If one of Federline's men was standing guard, their time was shrinking fast.

If Kit noticed it too, she didn't say.

Clearing her throat, Kit went on. "When Alice and I ran into each other, I thought little of it. My father has always known how to find me and where I am. But then Alice came to me, a month later, in the middle of the night. Begged me to help her. She'd discovered something, and what she found scared her. Scared her enough that she didn't want the evidence to be sold as my father planned to do."

Ginger came closer. Out of the corner of her eye, she saw Khalib sit up on the bed, his gaze wary and curious. No doubt he wanted to keep her safe—but he was also intrigued by Kit's words.

"What did Alice find?" Ginger asked, tilting her head.

Kit laughed bitterly. "I'm not dumb enough to tell you—not because I don't trust you, Ginger; I do. You're one of the only people on this earth I've ever trusted. But because when information like this is currency, it's also life-threatening. People *kill* for this information."

Ginger cringed, then exchanged a glance with Khalib. He nodded, ever so slightly, as though to say, *She's right. Don't press for more.*

Kit let out a slow exhale, her shoulders falling with defeat. "So I agreed to help Alice hide the information from my father. And hide her. But my father came looking faster than I expected. I had to go on the run. I started hiding clues about what was happening to me in codes for the column I wrote— hoping Jack would see them and help me. My fiancé posted the articles on my behalf, but my father caught him." Her voice broke. "K-killed him. And then I surrendered to my father, hoping I could convince him to stop hunting for Alice. I haven't been out of this room since that day. It's been months."

Months.

What kind of a monster would hold his own daughter captive for months?

The sort of father who would murder his daughter's fiancé. "You were engaged?" Ginger asked softly.

Kit's eyes were red-rimmed as she lifted them to Ginger's. "His name was Rudolf. He was a good man. A kind one. He fled Germany a few years ago after threats from the Brownshirts, and he wanted to see a peaceful world once again." She swallowed hard, her throat moving with the effort. "And I loved him."

For whatever reason, Ginger believed her. *Wanted* to trust her.

Her story made sense.

Either that or she's the best liar I've ever met.

Ginger signaled back to Khalib that she'd be all right, then moved closer to Kit. She sat across from her, inches away. "If that's all true, your father got Jack involved somehow. Jack came looking for Noah, then your father kidnapped ..." *Jack's daughter.* She couldn't say that, though. Couldn't tell Kit without Victoria's permission and Jack knowing first.

Ginger leveled her chin. "My son. And now he's here. I need to find him. That's why I came today."

Kit nodded vaguely, but a tired expression crossed her face. She glanced at the door. "There's no way out of this room, Ginger. Believe me, I've tried. I spent a whole week pounding on the door. The servants won't help us. They're all afraid of my father. I went hoarse from screaming with the effort. And when my father comes back, he won't have any mercy on you or your friend." Her gaze flicked to Khalib. "Like I said—he won't kill me or torture me. He won't kill Jack because of me. But, other than that, no one is safe from him. The man has no soul."

"Alastair Taylor is here with me. He and some of his men are still out there. They'll help us," Ginger said, standing. "We just have to scream loud enough."

"My father said he'd kill Alex if you screamed again," Kit said with mournful eyes. "I don't think he's lying about that."

Ginger tugged at the hair by the top of her forehead, trying to think.

Ivy had said Federline was using Alex to decode articles.

And Alex—*oh, Alex*—had discovered a message that said *Help me.*

She drew in a gasp. He must have discovered the code Kit had left in her columns.

Brilliant boy.

Dammit. Of course. Alex was so good at those things. He'd seen the code, and that was why Federline had stolen him from the consulate.

Ginger's gaze snapped to Kit's. "He won't kill Alex. He needs him right now. Somehow your father got hold of those articles, and he's using Alex to decode them."

That was enough to force Kit to her feet. She gasped. "Oh no." The color drained from her face. "That will lead him right to Alice."

Despite Ginger's reassurance to Khalib, he moved to Ginger now, his body tense.

"Where is she?" Ginger demanded. "Where is Alice?"

Kit shook her head. "I don't trust these walls enough to say it here. If we get out of here, I'll take you to her, I promise."

"Then let's get out of here." Ginger started toward the door.

Kit followed, just steps behind. "Are you sure? I'm telling you, my father doesn't make empty threats, Ginger."

Ginger turned and held Kit's gaze. "If he's going to kill Khalib and me anyway when he returns, and if he needs Alex, this is the best and only shot we have at getting out of here alive. Alastair is here somewhere. He has more men on standby to radio in if things go badly. We have to take the chance and get Alex back while we still have help."

Kit's eyes were wide. "I hope you know what you're doing."

Ginger held her breath.

Please, God, don't let Federline kill Alex.

Please.

"I hope I do too." Then Ginger pounded on the door.

CHAPTER THIRTY-NINE

JACK

The sheikh clearly didn't trust Noah and Fahad—that much was clear. The last one hundred yards of road to his home was lined with men faithful to him, all holding rifles. They must have assembled the moment they'd realized Noah was on his way. A tethered goat bleated from the shade of a low mud wall, the rope tugging taut as if it too wanted distance from the line of rifles, unwilling to be caught between the sheikh's men and their targets.

Still, Noah and Jack walked with heads held high, side by side, this time in their Western clothes. Noah had insisted Fahad stay home, for his own safety. He'd already risked enough.

The air shimmered in the sunset, and a thin haze of dust kicked up with each of their steps. Eerie silence echoed beyond the mud-brick walls, as if the nearby village held its breath, watching their approach.

One of the sheikh's men stepped forward as the dusty road opened toward the diwan, shifting the weight of his rifle so the barrel angled not quite at them but close enough for Jack to notice how easily a twitch could change that.

The man stopped them, palm out, his gaze unfriendly. "Your names?" he snapped in Arabic.

"Noah Benson and Jack Darby," Noah replied, his eyes fixed on the barrel of a rifle of the sheikh's man nearest to them. He hadn't aimed it—yet. Didn't mean he wouldn't.

"Sheikh Omar says you are not welcome here," the man responded in a gruff voice.

"Ask him to reconsider. Tell him I'm the brother of one of the American women he hid here a few months ago," Jack said in a low voice. Noah had told him about the help the sheikh had given to Alice and Kit. Maybe that would be a start.

The man nodded, then left, striding across the dusty court-yard toward the diwan. A chicken clucked and scampered out of his way as he walked. Then two of the other men stepped in front of him and Noah, blocking their view of the diwan and the sheikh watching from the shadows.

"Just what the hell did you do to make him hate you so much?" Jack muttered to Noah.

Noah grimaced. "In addition to lying to him, I also killed Clive Hower and another Blackwell operative when they caught me questioning the sheikh's servant boy. I left the bodies for the villagers to deal with, and I think somehow they didn't appre-ciate that."

"Were they British?"

Noah nodded.

Ooof. No, the sheikh wouldn't have liked that at all. It made the villagers complicit in hiding the murder of two British citi-zens. Who knew what the consequences of that could be if the British authorities found out.

"You could have mentioned that sooner, you know."

"I had to deal with the damned car. Bodies are much easier to burn by comparison."

"You're a real hero." Jack sighed. "Whatever happened to letting our enemies live another day? Being the better person?"

"I did. We both did. And we only lived to regret it. Those days are over. Someone threatens my family now and they won't be long for this earth."

The fading light of the day gave an ominous timbre to Noah's words. But Jack couldn't say he blamed Noah either. How many times while dealing with Stephen Fisher had they told each other that they wished they'd killed him when they had the chance?

For that matter, how many times had Jack wished he'd done the same with Prescott Federline? Maybe it was how society defined them as good men—not striking preemptively—but knowing what he knew now, knowing how many lives Prescott had damaged, including Jack's own life … was it really wrong to wish he'd been wise enough to eliminate the threat before it realized?

Jack didn't have an answer for that. But he didn't judge Noah for killing Hower, either.

The crunch of footsteps alerted him to the approach of the sheikh's man. Jack looked up as the men blocking his view stepped to the side, revealing not the man but the sheikh himself. He scrutinized Noah, not bothering to glance at Jack. "Noah Benson," he said, continuing in Arabic, "not Yusef Karim? Or a British officer?"

Noah shook his head. "I'm not here on behalf of the British," he said, bowing his head. "And I've given my apology. But you should not hold Fahad to blame for my actions. He and his family are innocent."

"We shall see. I do not easily forgive those who come to drink my coffee and accept my hospitality, all while lying to my face." Sheikh Omar's eyes flicked to Jack. "And you? You are this man's friend?"

"Yes. And the brother of one of the American women you helped."

"If you are this man's friend, you are no friend of mine," the sheikh said flatly, his gaze hard.

"I am this man's friend," Jack replied in Arabic. "He is my brother. But he is also a brother and friend to your people. He fought alongside them during the war, helping Faisal Hussein and aligning himself with the cause of a free land for all Arabs."

The sheikh spat on the ground in front of Jack's feet. "He is British!" His eyes narrowed, and he peered closer at Jack. "Many men make promises. Lie to us. The mayor of Jerusalem, Musa Kazim, lies dying in a bed, beaten by the clubs of British officers for daring to lead our people against the immigrants who would see us driven from our homes. Thirty people died the day Kazim fell. The blood of countless more ran through the streets."

Jack caught the meaning clearly enough. *The British nearly killed our leader for speaking out. You expect me to trust you now?*

The sheikh's words were impassioned, filled with the desperation of a man betrayed. Jack had never envied the role the British had to play here as the authorities presiding over the Palestinian mandate, but he had to believe peace was possible. That a solution might exist for all these warring factions to coexist. A people who lost hope for peace lost their humanity.

This man didn't appear to be one without hope—not yet.

Jack had to use that to his advantage.

"I can't pretend to understand what your people have been through, Sheikh, but I know you are not an extremist. If you were, you would not have hidden my sister. You would have allowed Sharif al-Rashid to find her."

The sheikh flinched, his mouth opening and closing. His eyes narrowed, from Jack to Noah, then he gave a gruff nod to his men, gesturing for them to follow him to the diwan.

Noah exchanged a look with Jack. The guns hadn't lowered yet, and they weren't nearly out of danger or any closer to getting to Alice and Kit, but being invited to the threshold was an enormous step.

Once inside the diwan, the sheikh took his seat while Noah and Jack settled on pillows across from him. Only two of his men remained in the diwan with him—arms still at the ready—but the rest stayed outside.

"Tell me what you know of al-Rashid," the sheikh demanded from Jack and Noah. No politeness here. No ceremonial coffee or greetings. All of that had been dispensed with.

Noah cleared his throat. "I believe al-Rashid may have made arrangements to see King Faisal meet his end, sooner than expected."

The sheikh's lips pursed. A few long, heavy moments passed, the air growing heavier with every heartbeat. Then the sheikh said, "Al-Rashid came to me, over a year ago. He wanted my support. The Germans had promised him arms—arms we desperately need to defend ourselves." He leaned toward Noah. "Tell me, Yusef. Why should we not accept the arms of the men who promise to help us fight against the Zionists?"

Noah held his gaze, unblinking. "Because they hate you just as much as they hate the Zionists. They would see you kill each other and rid themselves of the trouble of having to do so."

Jack couldn't help himself. "And while you're busy fighting, they'll make their way into Iraq and steal Arab oil—which they need."

The sheikh leaned back, looking from one man to the other. Then he smiled. "Perhaps you are not so stupid as I believe." He nodded. "It was for this reason I rejected al-Rashid's proposal. For this reason that I helped your sister," he said to Jack. "But not because I believe in the promises of Western men."

"You have every reason to distrust us, Sheikh. We wouldn't trust you either, if we were in your position." Jack gave him a pleading look, watching the shadows deepen on the sheikh's face as the sun dipped beyond the horizon. "But all I want is to get my sister and the woman I love back and keep them safe. All I need is for you to tell the sisters at Talitha Komi to entrust them to me."

The heavy sound of the sheikh's breathing filled the space. He rubbed his hands together, skin meeting skin in a soft, rhythmic pattern. In the distance, an owl hooted, a reminder of wilderness amid civilization. "Call Salim," the sheikh said to the man on his right.

The man left the diwan, his rifle creaking against his side as he walked. A few moments later, the man returned, a young boy trailing behind him.

"Salim, come here," the sheikh said to the boy.

The boy hurried over, his bare feet whispering against the rug. He was small, with dust caked on his knees and a half-healed scrape along his cheek. His gaze stayed pinned to the floor, but Jack caught the flicker upward toward Noah, one filled with equal parts hope and fear.

Slowly, the sheikh stood, then set his hands on the boy's shoulders. He looked straight at Noah. "You saved his life. By more than one witness's account. For that reason, I will spare you and Fahad. But you will owe me a debt, Yusef."

Relief flooded Jack, but he kept still, not daring to show it.

"So be it," Noah said, offering the sheikh his hand.

The sheikh grasped him by the forearm and nodded. Then he flicked a gaze at Jack. "Meet us at the Talitha Komi orphanage, two hours past midnight. I will help you, Jack Darby."

The sheikh's men escorted them out, as quickly as they'd come.

The words should have felt like a victory, but as they stepped back into the cooling night, Jack couldn't shake the feeling that "help" from the sheikh might cost more than he could pay. Rifles still tracked their movements until the gate shut behind them.

CHAPTER FORTY

ALEX

Midnight was approaching by the time Mr. Federline's car stopped in the barren hills just beyond Jerusalem, where the last pinpricks of the city's lights flickered faintly on the horizon.

Any thrill Alex might have expected from taking an airplane had drained away the moment they'd left the ground—replaced by the hollow awareness that they were traveling faster and further from Cairo than anyone could follow. By the time the flight ended on a dusty strip outside of Lydda, the dull throb of inevitable doom had taken root in his chest.

A motorcar had been waiting at the airfield. He'd smiled for Prescott's benefit, even managed to draw on the encyclopedic trivia lodged in his mind about desert landscapes—little conversational diversions to make himself seem relaxed, casual, the way he imagined a man with nothing to fear might speak.

But with every passing mile, the effort had weighed heavier. Eventually, he'd slumped into the corner of the backseat, letting his eyelids droop in a show of exhaustion until the act blurred into reality.

The slam of the driver's door jolted him.

Through a narrow slit between his lashes, he saw Mr. Federline step away from the car. *Thank God.* Alex worked his jaw, trying to wake up his brain.

He was really, truly alone.

No one could help him. And he couldn't be of help to anyone.

Somewhere along this journey from home he'd miscalculated. Made a terrible mistake.

Now God knew where Ivy was.

If he was going to survive whatever he'd gotten involved in, he'd need to be smart. Smarter than Mr. Federline. He probably thought Alex was still sleeping. Alex needed to use that to his advantage.

A low hum approached from the east, growing into the steady growl of another engine. Alex shifted in his seat, not wanting to call too much attention to himself or let Mr. Federline know he was awake yet. His hand moved toward the handle of the door, and his fingertips met cool metal. Opening the door would be too loud, so he waited, ready for when the next car was close enough that he wouldn't be heard.

He leaned forward, watching the long, crisp shadows thrown by the headlights of the other car as it approached. The light illuminated the scrub and stone of the Judean hills beyond Alex's window, beautiful and pale in the silvery moonlight.

A flash of purple stood out as the light shifted and the motorcar parked.

Alex frowned, his eyes locking on the plant he'd seen in the headlights just off the road.

There. A pale, spindly plant just beyond the edge of the headlight beam. Thick, inflated pods swayed on fragile-looking stems. *Calotropis procera.* Sodom's apple or *ashkhar*—common along the sunbaked roads between the Dead Sea and Jerusalem.

A memory of one of his mother's field guides surfaced, a page warning of the milky sap that could blister skin, blind, even kill if swallowed. The Bedouin used it for its medicinal properties, but Mama had also warned him that they believed any part of the plant could blind.

His heartbeat thudded harder.

If he could slip outside, grab a pod—or even a leaf—he could have *something* to use as a weapon.

He risked a glance out the windshield as the other car rolled to a stop in front of them. The headlights and engine remained on, the roar of it enough to drown out other noises—for now. Alex waited until he spotted the driver's side door of the other car opening, then he popped the latch, and opened the door beside him.

When the driver of the other car moved toward Mr. Federline, Alex pushed the door open just enough to slip out, crouching low onto the desert sand. He crept toward the back of the car, then flattened himself to the ground. The metallic tick of the engine cooling filled his ears as he pushed himself partially under the back wheel.

"Prescott. Right on time." A man's voice broke through the silence. *An American.* Stone crunched, shifting to a stop as the man came to a standstill in front of Mr. Federline.

"You, on the other hand, are late," Mr. Federline snapped. "I'm not amused with your little game, Ruby. You deviated completely from my orders from the moment you left Cairo."

A woman's shadow draped across the desert, softer footsteps accompanying it. "I knew what I was doing," the woman snapped. "I got you your precious microfilm, didn't I?"

A slap sounded through the crisp night, followed by a soft cry. "Yes, by playing a slut, I hear. You know the rules. They exist for a reason, and you blatantly disobeyed me. Now, where is the package?"

Alex held his breath. He had to focus.

The undercarriage was still warm, the smell of hot oil clinging to the air. He ran his fingers along the chassis until he found the copper fuel line and followed it up to the joint where it became a rubber tube disappearing under the frame.

"Where's the sharif?" the man asked Mr. Federline.

A shard of flint lay nearby. Alex took it and began scraping in small, deliberate strokes. Tiny curls of rubber lifted under the pressure. Not enough to sever it—that would be obvious—but enough to weaken the wall, so that heat, vibration, and time would finish the job.

Hopefully buy him time to run too.

"The sharif is meeting us elsewhere. He wants both. The package and Alice. He's not willing to take any chances."

"That's not what we agreed to," Ruby said, her voice stiff. "We don't know where she is."

"Luckily for you—I found someone else who could do the job you couldn't." Mr. Federline clucked his tongue. "I've found out where she is. Only a handful of miles from here. At a girls' orphanage on King George's Street. And I'll need your help to retrieve her, Ruby."

Alex's pulse pounded. *Concentrate.* He had to work faster. If Mr. Federline found him under the car like this, who knew what he might do?

When the cut on the fuel line was no deeper than the thickness of a fingernail, Alex tossed the flint away and brushed the dust from his hands.

Bootsteps scraped against gravel, close enough that he could feel the vibration against his knees. The man answered something Mr. Federline had said, no more than a few feet away on the far side of the bonnet. Alex pressed himself against the car's flank, willing himself invisible.

Then he bolted. Certain he'd attract too much attention, he

pushed himself out from under the car, then pushed the door to the backseat open widely. He popped up, doing his best to look like someone who'd just woken up. "Mr. Federline?" He squinted toward the three figures.

All three of them turned to look at him. "Ah, Alex." Mr. Federline gave him a pleasant smile. "I'll just be a moment."

"I have to … relieve myself," Alex said with a grimace. He wasn't completely lying. It'd been a while since he'd had the chance.

"Of course," Mr. Federline said, gesturing toward the desert.

Alex stepped away from the car, heading in the direction he'd seen the ashkhar, until he was practically standing over it. Turning his back to them, he unzipped his trousers, slipping one hand into his pocket for a handkerchief.

They weren't watching him, thankfully. He finished, waited a beat, then reached down and snapped up a leaf from the plant into the waiting handkerchief—careful not to get any of the poisonous sap on his skin.

He made a quick show of wiping his shoes in case any one of them had noticed him bend down, then folded the handkerchief and slipped it into his pocket. Walking slowly back to the car, he let his heart rate slow, then slipped back into the rear seat, shutting the door with slow, even pressure until the latch clicked into place.

Outside, the conversation resumed, too low for him to make out the words. It didn't matter. The damage was done, and the seed was planted.

A crippled car. A hidden weapon.

When the moment came, he would be ready. Or, at least, he'd have a chance.

Before he could get too confident in his plan, though, the back door opened and the woman, Ruby, climbed into the seat beside him. "Is this really necessary?" she called out the door before it slammed shut.

"Goddammit," she said under her breath, then turned and shot a glance at Alex. "Sorry."

"For?" Alex raised a brow.

"For swearing. You're just a kid. Though I guess if you're one of Prescott's protégés, you're probably used to swearing." Ruby pulled pristine white gloves off, and Alex caught the slight tremble of her fingertips as she tucked a stray strand of hair under her hat.

Her cheek was still red from Mr. Federline's slap, visible even under the dim light.

Something about that made Alex feel like they might have something in common. "I'm not," he said in a quiet but dismissive voice, squaring his shoulders. "I don't really know him."

"Yeah. Sure." Ruby rolled her eyes, fanning her face—not because of the trapped heat in the car, though it was arguably warm, but no doubt because her cheek stung.

"I don't." Alex shrugged. "I just happened to find a code in a newspaper article. So he hired me to decode others."

Ruby smirked. "So, you're just a really smart kid?" She didn't look impressed—or like she believed him. "What's your name?"

He hesitated. He couldn't trust this woman, no matter how much he wanted to believe she didn't like Mr. Federline either. He'd have to give her the name he'd given at the consulate. Stick with the same story. "Alexander Darby."

Her sharp intake of breath made him stiffen. "Darby?" she repeated. She glanced out the window. "As in Jack Darby?"

"He's my father," Alex forced out.

"He has a son?" Ruby's eyes went wide, her brows lifting. Then something else sparkled in her eyes—maybe anger. "What about your mom? Where's she?"

Oh no. Alex opened his mouth, unsure of what to say. He

hadn't gotten that far in planning this lie. Hadn't thought about how to answer that. The lights and engine to the other car cut out, throwing them into sudden darkness.

"You know what?" Ruby scowled. "I don't want to know. Jesus," she breathed, drooping back against the seat. "Forget I asked." Then agitated, she scowled at him. "Your old man know you're out here helping Prescott? No, probably not. Let me guess—he forced you into this?"

The driver's door opened once again, and Mr. Federline climbed inside. Then the passenger door opened, and the man who'd come with Ruby sat, slamming the door behind him.

"What about our car?" Ruby asked him.

"We do what Prescott wants. End of story."

Alex held his breath. So much for his plan. He didn't think he'd have a problem outrunning Mr. Federline—but the other man was another matter. And with two other adults in the motorcar, he was sadly outnumbered.

"Sure thing, Theo." Ruby crossed her arms, giving Mr. Federline a hard stare through the rearview mirror as he started the car. "So you've got Jack's kid here, eh, Prescott?"

Mr. Federline knows Jack?

He hadn't intimated that much at the consulate.

Then again, he hadn't made many things clear at the consulate.

Just who was he?

Mr. Federline glared at Ruby. "Don't you think you've said and done enough, Ruby?"

"I'm just curious. I didn't know Jack had a kid. Does he have a *wife* too?"

Who was *she*, for that matter?

"Why? Does it interest you that much?" Mr. Federline smiled.

Theo stiffened. "Knock it off, Ruby." He pulled out a pack of matches and a cigarette case, then took out a cigarette.

"It just would have been nice to know beforehand."

Before what? Alex peered at her. "You know him?"

"If you had simply listened to my rules, you wouldn't be feeling any guilt at all, Ruby. Instead, you resorted to your own methods." Mr. Federline gave a pleasant smile, one Alex was increasingly starting to recognize as insincere. Snakelike, even.

"My methods get results." Ruby crossed her arms, staring out the window.

"Then why did I have to send Theo to fetch you? He's the only reason you're still here. The only reason our deal is still on. I was about to give the order to get rid of you when he turned up in Cairo with that notebook."

Theo said nothing, lighting his cigarette. He tossed the matches onto the dash, as if he owned the car.

"You were only able to send Theo to fetch me because I checked in, Prescott. Don't forget that minor detail when you call my loyalties into question." The leather vibrated as Ruby lifted her head, then let it drop back again against the seat with a frustrated *thud*.

Alex stared at her, worry gnawing at his chest more deeply.

Get rid of her?

Whatever game Mr. Federline was playing, he seemed increasingly less concerned about taking off his mask and showing Alex his true nature.

Or he already guessed that I don't trust him.

Alex swallowed hard, the leaf in his pocket feeling like a child's attempt at a man's game.

Then the car sputtered to a stop.

CHAPTER FORTY-ONE

JACK

The familiar tang of mineral oil stung Jack's nostrils as he finished assembling the rifle on the table in front of him. Fahad's entire kitchen was littered with weapons—the ones Jack and Noah had brought with them, as well as a great deal more that Fahad had dug up from his cellar outside.

This wasn't the first time since Prescott Federline had found him in the Kharga that Jack had the feeling he'd slipped back in time. He, Fahad, and Noah had all gathered here during the war—just like this—usually going off in different directions. And while Jack had faced his fair share of danger back then, most of the time it had been Noah putting it all on the line, sneaking into enemy territory with little but his training and skills to get him out of whatever scrapes he got himself into.

But this *was* different.

This time, Noah and Fahad weren't here because the government or an army had sent them.

This time they were here for him. *Because of him.*

If something went wrong—with the sheikh's men or otherwise—it would be on Jack.

The air in the small kitchen quarters—normally filled with the scent of Nasira's cooking or fragrant spices like cardamom or cinnamon—bristled with tension and heaviness. Fahad had lit a few oil lamps, their flames casting a soft amber glow that flickered across the tiled walls.

Jack caught Noah's gaze just behind the sight line of a pistol and smirked. "Having fun yet?"

"If I ever grumble again about long days teaching arithmetic and Latin to my children, you have my permission to come clobber me over the head," Noah deadpanned dryly.

"Do you really think we'll need all of this?" Fahad asked, hoisting a rifle onto his shoulder. "The sheikh has given you his word, hasn't he?"

"I trust that sheikh only marginally more than Prescott." Jack rolled his shoulders back. "Besides, most of this is staying in the car. I'm not as worried about the sheikh's men as I am at the thought of transporting Alice and Kit after we retrieve them. Who knows where Ruby slipped off to too. I'm not going to let my guard down until I get them to safety."

"Can't say that I blame you," Noah said. He bent down and placed the pistol in a satchel.

Brakes shrieked on the road outside, a harsh, unwelcome sound that sliced through the stillness.

Jack jerked his head, looking over his shoulder toward the only window in the kitchen—a small one over the sink—which had little visibility.

He shoulders tensed. *Who could be here this late?*

Behind him, chairs scraped. Metal clinked.

Instinct took over. He was moving before the others had fully risen, reaching for the gun holstered at his hip.

"It came from the front," Fahad said decisively.

If the sheikh had changed his mind—or something worse— they wouldn't have much time to prepare for an assault.

He sidled up to the front door as Noah crept toward the window. Moonlight glinted off the edge of Noah's profile, giving his features a hard edge. In the darkness, Noah intimidated, radiating how confident he was. Lethal.

"See anything?" Jack muttered.

Noah leaned closer … then went rigid.

"Bloody hell—" He pushed away from the wall.

"What is it?" Jack exchanged a look with Fahad, who gave a bewildered shrug.

Noah didn't wait for answers. He crossed the room in three strides, yanked open the door, and disappeared into the darkness with a shout, "What the hell are you doing here?"

Jack moved to the doorway.

Cold air rushed in through the open door, sweeping away the stale air. Outside, the car's engine coughed once, then fell silent. The headlights bathed Noah in stark white as he stepped forward, then scooped an awaiting Ginger into his arms.

What on earth? Ginger … here?

Even if he was angry with his wife, Noah's irritation seemed to melt away as their mouths met in a kiss. The sight of it made Jack smile. Noah and Ginger had always been expressive of their adoration for each other in a way he couldn't help but envy.

On the other hand, what *was* she doing here?

Noah pulled back slightly, his hands still cupping her face. His voice cracked on the first word.

"Ginger—when? How—how long have you been here? Where's Clara? Where's Alex?" His eyes scanned her face as if he could extract the answers from her expression. "You were supposed to be in Penmore. You're not safe here—"

"I know," she said gently, her hand pressing against his chest. "You have no idea what I've gone through to get to you. There's something I need to tell you."

Noah's posture went rigid. "My God. What's happened?"

Before she could answer, the headlights on the car behind them clicked off, and the driver's door opened. Alastair.

Then the back door opened, and the entire world around Jack shifted.

Kit Federline.

His heart gave a violent lurch, a blow that almost knocked the air out of his lungs. His hand flew to his chest, but it wasn't pain—it was the disorienting thud of memory, grief, and something that might've been joy all colliding at once.

Kit.

Flesh and blood. Standing in the silver spill of the moonlight. After all these years—after everything.

She was alive.

And yet he couldn't quite breathe.

But … *what about Alice?*

Jack took one stumbled step toward her. "You're—" was all he managed.

The sky was a rush of blurred stars and gleaming moonlight, his eyes filling with tears he hadn't dared to spill since Prescott had dared to give him hope she might be alive.

Kit paused by the car. "Hi, Jack Darby."

It was the kind of greeting one might give at a café in London. Not after years of betrayal, not after heartbreak.

But maybe that was who Kit was—a storm that could pass through, then pretend nothing had been uprooted.

His voice was a rough scrape as he took slow steps toward her. "Hi, Kit."

God, had it been fifteen years since he'd last seen her?

How could it possibly have been so long?

She was close enough that he could reach out and touch her. *Real. Whole.*

His hand twitched—reflexive, as if reaching for a ghost.

He took a step forward, then halted, breath snagging somewhere between his chest and throat. Not only because something strong and unexplainable stopped him but for a moment, when he'd looked at her, he'd seen a flash of Ruby's face.

The memory of Ruby was too close to his skin. Too heavy on his heart.

He blinked, and she was Kit again.

But the ache she left behind stayed rooted in his chest, stealing his breath, reminding him of betrayal—both Ruby's and Kit's—all over again.

For her part, Kit made no effort to move closer and bridge that gap between them.

Just as she hadn't done the last fifteen years.

"What are you doing here?" Jack managed to ask, then swiveled a glance at Alastair, then Ginger.

"It's a long story," Alastair said with a grimace. "One including daring escapes, stabbings, kidnappings, a nauseating airplane ride, and me having to come to the rescue, of course—but what else could one expect when Noah Benson and Jack Darby are involved?"

Ginger pulled away from Noah and set her hands on her hips. "Alastair may be making light of it all, but it's all much more serious than that. Prescott has Alex." Her voice cracked slightly. "Noah—he took him. From Cairo. A plane. Today—yesterday. God, I don't even know anymore." She rubbed her forehead, her composure slipping.

"Alex?" Noah gawked. "As in our son, Alexander?"

Ginger's eyes were dark with worry. "Yes. He and Ivy were missing for weeks—I sent telegrams, trying to find you. Fahad only answered one of them and said little, but that was how we knew you were here, at least."

Alex and Ivy ...

The words barely registered at first. Jack's mind snagged on them like barbed wire.

Missing.

Weeks.

Something cold slipped down his spine. He gripped the strap of his rifle.

How many people had he already failed?

Fahad came to the doorway. "Telegrams aren't always reliable here," he said with a frown. "I'm sorry."

"Wait—what happened to Ivy and Alex?" Jack asked, furrowing his brow.

"My father kidnapped them, apparently," Kit said, coming closer to Jack. "And now Alex has cracked a code I left in newspaper articles for you, and he's found out where I've hidden Alice." She cleared her throat. "There's a lot to tell you about— I'm sorry. I came up with a ludicrous plan to send you a message about Alice using the pen name Gretchen Herbert. I thought if you'd see it, you'd know it was me. It was silly, I know."

Jack held her gaze. "I did see it—and we're on our way to the orphanage right now. I went to Baghdad too. Found the microfilm. Only …"

He exchanged a look with Noah.

Kit reached out unexpectedly, gripping his forearm. "Only what?"

"Only, your father sent someone to take it from me," Jack admitted, tapping the bandage on his temple with his fingertips.

Kit's expression wavered, filling with horror.

Noah looked ready to rip something apart limb by limb. "And you're saying your father has Alex and is on his way here?"

Kit nodded, taking a faltering step back.

Jack looked at Kit—at the panic flashing beneath her composed expression.

He glanced at Noah, whose hand gripped Ginger's like a lifeline.

Alastair and Fahad, who'd always been stoic, wore worry in their brows and eyes.

And in his mind, he saw Alex.

Alone. Terrified.

"Then let's move," Jack said, reaching for the rifle. "This ends tonight."

CHAPTER FORTY-TWO

ALEX

"What the devil?" Mr. Federline slammed his fist into the steering wheel as he attempted to start the engine once again.

From outside the motorcar, Theo lifted his head from the open bonnet and tilted his torch toward the windshield. "I don't see anything—but I don't know what to look for, either."

Mr. Federline threw the door open and stepped out to join Theo.

From his seat, Alex noticed Ruby shift, her eyes darting toward the keys.

She caught his stare, then frowned. "What are you doing here, kid?" she hissed under her breath. "You have no idea what you're involved in, do you?"

Her words struck him with equal parts misery and worry. "No," he admitted at last. "I don't. Mr. Federline dragged me here."

Ruby gave him a long, hard look, then pinched the bridge of her nose. "You didn't by any chance have something to do with the car stalling, did you?"

Alex swallowed hard. "N-no."

"You're going to have to learn to lie better than that." Ruby *tsked* and shook her head. "What'd you do?"

Something about the way she was talking to him made him want to tell her. To trust her. Mr. Federline didn't entirely seem to hold her in his favor, either.

When he didn't answer, her lips curled into a smile. "You're a smart kid, clearly. But you're in over your head."

Ruby looked away for a moment, jaw working. When she turned back, her voice had softened, but her eyes were hard. "If you get the chance, you need to run. Run and don't look back, understand? Get to Jerusalem and find a café Abu Kadesh—there's a man named Felix Carrington waiting there who can help you."

Alex's brow furrowed, his fingers curling tighter around the edge of the seat. *Why is she telling me this?* "And you think I'll get far if I run?"

"I'll do my best to help make sure you escape. Go straight into Jerusalem. We're only a couple of miles outside of the Old City."

He ventured cautiously. "Who are you?"

The bonnet slammed shut.

"A friend of your father's," she whispered, tearing her gaze from him. "Please. Listen to me. If Prescott finds out you sabotaged his car, he might kill you."

Could he trust her? She seemed to be working for Mr. Federline.

The door swung open once again, and Prescott sank into the driver's seat.

Ruby perked up. "Where's Theo?" she asked, glancing outside.

"He's going back for your car," Prescott said, glowering at her through the rearview mirror.

"What are we doing here?" Alex asked, slipping his hand into his pocket. His fingertips brushed against the handkerchief, which offered a fleeting comfort. "Ivy's going to be—"

"Enough noise," Mr. Federline said sharply. "I need to think."

Alex's jaw clenched with satisfaction. *He's rattled. Good.* He needed to try to push carefully—get this man to reveal himself enough. *That'll help me know where I stand.* Still, he didn't want Mr. Federline to think he was suspicious of him. "Do you want me to look at the engine? I know a little about mechanics."

"I'm sure you do, you ..."

Mr. Federline froze.

Ruby stiffened, and Alex's breath slowed. *Dammit. I shouldn't have said anything.*

Mr. Federline turned, slowly, then reached out into his breast pocket. He withdrew a pistol and aimed it at Alex, his eyes narrowing. "You do know quite a bit about mechanics, don't you, Alex? You convinced my men in Port Said that a boiler had exploded on that cargo ship." His lips curled with a cruel smile. "You think they didn't find your little sabotage?"

The ship?

Alex's fingers dug more tightly against the handkerchief.

No.

No, no, no.

Mr. Federline was involved with Ivy's kidnapping? And not just involved—he seemed to have ordered it. Alex's throat dried as he stared at him, understanding dawning on him with a dull snap.

"Prescott, relax—"

"Keep out of this, Ruby," Mr. Federline spat. His cold blue gaze moved back to Alex. "You've been causing nothing but problems for me since the moment you left England. Now what the hell did you do to my car?"

"Problems?" Alex smirked, despite the fear sliding down his core. "I solved your damned puzzle, didn't I?"

"You did. That's why you're alive." Mr. Federline cocked his head to the side. "It's a shame, really. You're clearly talented. If I were a younger man, I would have recruited you to work for me. Made you wealthy beyond your imagination. But I've learned my lesson on trusting anyone named Darby."

From the corner of his eye, Alex saw Ruby's hand moving slowly toward her pocket. Maybe she had a gun too.

Maybe, just maybe, she might help him after all.

He raised his chin. "If you shoot me, you won't get the last of that code. I didn't give it all to you."

"You gave me enough. Talitha Komi in Jerusalem—it's where your Aunt Alice is hiding. But don't worry, after I turn her over to Sharif al-Rashid, I'm sure he'll make quick work of getting rid of her. He's paying a high price for her. And then I'll take care of your father. Eliminate all the Darbys once and for all." He aimed the gun at Alex's chest. "One last time. What did you do to my car?"

Alex's fingertips reached the ashkhar leaf and tugged it from the handkerchief. He snapped the leaf between his thumb and forefinger, smearing the latex on his skin. "Cut the fuel line," he said with a shrug. "You won't be going anywhere in this car."

"Such a shame." Mr. Federline cocked the hammer of the pistol.

Ruby withdrew a tiny Derringer no bigger than her palm. The metal caught a sliver of moonlight as she lifted it.

Alex blinked. *Was she—*

"Alex, run!" she cried.

Crack. Crack.

Two gunshots split the night open, the sound piercing Alex's eardrum.

Mr. Federline flinched, his arm jerking away from the wheel

as one bullet struck his forearm, slicing through flesh. The pistol he'd aimed at Alex veered sideways. The other bullet hit the motorcar's side window, shattering the glass behind him. A howl ripped from Mr. Federline's throat, sharp and animal-like in quality as the window glass fractured outward in a spider-web. It collapsed with a crystalline crash.

Alex's ears rang.

Time lurched.

His body moved before his thoughts could catch up.

Alex lunged over the seat, hitting against the gearstick, and slammed into Federline. His elbow knocked against the dashboard as he clawed for the man's face.

"You little—"

A second shot—louder, closer—fired so near to Alex's ear it left nothing but a high, buzzing void behind it.

He couldn't hear. The ringing in his ears made it barely possible to think. *Who had fired the gun? Where had the bullet struck?*

Then his fingers found their mark—Mr. Federline's eyes. He jabbed hard with his thumb.

Federline screamed, the sound dulled and underwater in Alex's ears. The man thrashed, swatting at air, at pain, at anything that moved. His pistol slipped from his grasp, landing with a thud near the pedals, out of Alex's reach unless he dared to dive that close to Mr. Federline's legs and risk being kicked.

Alex gasped for breath, tasting gunpowder in his mouth. He scrambled over the front seat and reached across the leather of the dash—Theo's matchbook. Still there.

He snatched it. If the car was still leaking fuel, he might be able to use this.

Federline was wailing behind him now, cupping his face. "My eyes! What the hell did you do?"

Alex kept moving, pushing against the passenger side door.

He shoved it open, letting in a rush of cold desert air. The wind bit at his cheeks. Dust scraped across the road outside in whispering spirals.

He turned. *Ruby.*

She was still in the backseat, slumped awkwardly against the door, one leg twisted beneath her. Blood ran in a sluggish stream from her thigh, soaking through her trousers and pooling under her hand. That's where that third shot had gone. The gun in Mr. Federline's hand must have discharged while Alex had fought him.

Her breaths were shallow. "Go," she whispered. "Don't be stupid, Alex. Run. I'm out of ammo."

Alex didn't know if he could get far with her—but he was several inches taller than her, even at his age.

"Get out of here!" she gasped.

His legs twitched.

His heart screamed at him to obey.

Run.

Run!

Instead, he climbed into the backseat, hooked one arm under her shoulders, and hoisted her upward. She gasped in pain, nearly doubling over.

"Dammit, kid," she groaned. "You're going to get us both killed."

"Better than leaving you behind."

They tumbled out of the car together. Ruby staggered as her injured leg buckled, and Alex threw his arm around her waist to keep her upright.

The chill cut through his shirt, biting deeper now that adrenaline thinned his blood.

He turned back toward the car, eyes searching. There. Just beneath the rear wheel—a dark puddle, glinting faintly in the moonlight.

Fuel.

His hands shook as he fumbled the matchbook open.

One strike. Two. The third caught—a thin flame blooming from the tip.

He hesitated for half a breath.

Then threw it.

The flame tumbled end over end—then vanished into the fuel.

Whoosh.

The flames bloomed like a living thing, a brilliant ball of fire and force that consumed the motorcar with ravenous hunger. The heat hit them seconds later, an invisible fist slamming against their backs with a boom.

Alex covered Ruby as best he could with his body, shielding her from flying debris.

Then—silence, except for the crackle of burning metal and the stutter of flames licking through rubber and leather.

He looked back. Against the blaze, he thought he saw a figure moving.

Federline couldn't have survived … could he?

Alex didn't wait to find out.

He crouched, threw Ruby across his back, and stumbled away from the wreckage.

Her breath was hot and uneven against his neck. "God," she rasped, "you really are Jack's son, aren't you?"

Alex's steps faltered, his heart lurching hard.

The name cut like ice.

Jack's son.

Whose son?

He didn't know anymore. And he no longer cared, either.

He just wanted to survive.

I just want to go home.

CHAPTER FORTY-THREE

JACK

The narrow road twisted upward through the sleeping city, winding past shuttered stone houses and dark, silent gardens. Tires crunched over loose gravel, loud in the stillness, as if even the car knew they had no business being here this late. Or this early. Jack wasn't sure which.

No other sound. No other signs of life.

Jerusalem at one in the morning felt like it belonged to ghosts.

The orphanage came into view slowly, like something conjured. It rose from behind a crumbling wall—a long weatherworn building made of pale limestone, shadowed by moonlight. When Jack had lived in Jerusalem during the war, this area had barely been dust and scrubby terrain. Now it appeared that new buildings were being erected quickly—a sign not only of the new wealth entering Palestine but the burgeoning population.

He eased his foot off the accelerator, the car slowing to a crawl, headlights brushing across the entrance. The building didn't appear fortified, but it looked closed off. Like a convent might be. A pressure at the base of his skull that hadn't let up in miles built more strongly, the wound at his temple throbbing.

What if Alice wasn't inside?

What if this was another false turn—another promise that ended in a body?

... or worse?

His gaze flicked to the backseat, where Ginger, Kit, and Noah had crowded in with Alastair—Ginger practically on Noah's lap. Fahad sat in the passenger seat. Everyone wore the same somber expression. The same guarded wariness.

This had been bad enough when Jack had worried that the sheikh might somehow double-cross them. But now, with Alex's life at stake and Prescott Federline hot on their heels, a more urgent sense of responsibility thrummed in Jack's veins.

"Tell me again how your fifteen-year-old managed to crack Kit's code," Jack grumbled, needing to thaw the crackling current of tension in the car.

"According to Ivy, it was a thing of wonder, but Ivy has always looked at Alex that way," Ginger said, her voice soft in a way that couldn't fool Jack. Out of the corner of his eye, he saw Noah's arm tighten around Ginger's shoulder.

"No, it's pretty impressive," Kit said dryly. "I didn't design the codes to be easy. Maybe Jack has finally met his match."

Jack's hand tightened around the shifter.

"Best not to let a man think he's unnecessary before he goes into battle, my dear," Alastair said with a frown.

Choosing not to respond to either of them, Jack parked beside the orphanage, engine humming beneath his feet, then turned the key. The car shuddered once and died.

The silence closed in around them again.

He opened the door, the metal groaning too loud in the hush, and stepped out onto the packed earth. He straightened slowly, hand braced against the door frame, and looked up at the orphanage again.

No lights in the windows. No movement in the shadows. Just the building—long and solid and watching.

He slung the rifle over his shoulder, adjusted the strap, and exhaled through his nose. He was exhausted but not tired. His body buzzed with tension, every part of him wired for threat.

Fahad stepped out of the passenger side and came around the front of the car. Behind them, the back doors opened—Ginger, Kit, Noah, and Alastair all unfolding into the night in varying degrees of silence.

He didn't like being still. Visible.

They felt too exposed here, pulled right up to the front of the building like this without easy cover and no idea who was inside or who else might be watching.

He didn't say it aloud. Knowing Noah and Alastair as he did, he knew they felt it too. Hopefully, the sheikh hadn't decided to come early, like they had.

He glanced back over his shoulder at the others, who were now all standing in a loose semicircle behind the car. Kit looked pale. Ginger had her hand on her arm. Alastair hovered at the fringe, unreadable as ever.

Fahad met Jack's eyes briefly and gave a barely perceptible nod. A signal. Then he and Noah dropped back, away from the group, moving toward posts across the street with their rifles.

Well past the time the sheikh understands two can play at this game.

Jack waited until Fahad and Noah had disappeared completely from view, then he went forward toward the main door. With Kit here now, they didn't need the sheikh. Neither could they afford to wait—who knew when Prescott might arrive? Hopefully, if all went according to plan, by the time the sheikh arrived, they'd already be long gone, with Alice in tow.

Kit knocked on the door, then turned toward Alastair and Jack with somber eyes. "The nuns may not allow you inside. Especially not at this hour. But we'll see. If the sheikh has already made arrangements with them, I'll smooth it over. They trust me."

"Do whatever you need to do," Jack said, his voice gruffer than he expected. He didn't mean to sound so unfriendly toward her.

She was *his* Kit.

Except she wasn't. She hadn't been for a long time.

And maybe she never was.

And yet … Kit had saved Alice for him, hadn't she? She'd explained in the brief moments before they'd left Fahad's house what had happened with Alice, why she'd hidden her.

The door to the orphanage opened, and a tall, narrow-faced nun appeared in the archway. Her dark habit seemed to absorb the moonlight, making her look like part of the stone. Her eyes, sharp and unsentimental, moved over them all with the steady patience of someone who had seen far worse than armed men and sleepless women on her doorstep in the middle of the night.

She probably has seen worse, for that matter.

She didn't speak.

Kit stepped forward. "Sister Agnes. It's me."

The nun inclined her head slightly. "I see that."

"We're here for Alice."

A beat passed and Jack held his breath.

Sister Agnes looked past Kit to Jack and Alastair, then beyond them into the darkness, as if she could sense the two hidden figures across the street.

"I was told to expect Sheikh Omar," she said simply.

"He may still arrive," Kit said. "But we can't wait for him."

Another beat. Then Sister Agnes stepped aside. "Quickly. Before someone sees."

Kit moved first and Ginger followed. Jack touched Alastair's arm lightly, signaling him to keep close, then entered last, pausing briefly in the doorway to scan the shadowed corridor beyond.

Cool stone walls. The faint scent of candle wax and incense. And silence. Dense silence.

The door closed behind him with a weighty click.

He didn't particularly like orphanages, even though he sympathized with their mission. But they made him uncomfortable. Made him think of too many broken hearts and devastated dreams that would never be repaired, no matter how many years passed. Wounds like that went too deep.

Sister Agnes walked ahead of Kit, guiding them deeper into the building. A second nun passed them in the corridor without a word. No one looked surprised to see them. No one asked questions.

That made him feel worse. Would the sheikh be angry that they hadn't waited for him—or feel deceived? Maybe he hadn't considered enough what that might mean for Fahad and his family. His selfishness had already cost too many people too much.

The hallway turned, revealing an alcove lit by a single oil lamp. Its flame flickered against a crucifix on the wall. Before it stood another nun—older, round-faced, her expression hard to read. But she stepped aside as Kit approached and opened a door without a word.

Ginger and Alastair hung back, letting Jack past them.

Inside, the room was dim. Sparse. A cot in the corner. A pitcher and basin. A single window, shuttered, slatted shadows from it spreading across a wall only decorated with a cross, illuminated by a lit candle on the table beside the bed.

And in the chair near the window, dressed as a nun and seated as if she'd been waiting hours—*Alice.*

She stood slowly, and the light caught her face.

Jack's chest seized.

It was her.

Older. Thinner. Her hair longer and darker than he remembered—it had been practically golden when they were children, but now it was as dark as his own.

But her eyes … those were the same.

"God … Alice," the name left his lips with an agonizing gasp.

Alice's eyes filled with tears, her brows coming together with a pained expression. Then she rushed toward him. "Jack," she cried, tears streaming down her face. She threw her arms around his neck, sobs racking her thin frame as she clung to him. "You're here. You came."

Jack stiffened, a memory playing at the back of his head of his sister as a little girl, barely able to breathe from asthma, looking up at him with wide, desperate eyes as she clung to his hand.

Or waking from a nightmare in the middle of the night.

Laughing, on his shoulders, as he carried her across the yard at his family's home, with chickens squawking around them. Jumping into the creek, patiently teaching her to bait a hook, and showing her how to read.

Then, all those tears he'd been holding back—for *years*—flowed freely down his cheeks as his arms wrapped tightly around his sister. Jack's throat locked up, his arms rigid around her as if were he to let go now she'd vanish again.

She sobbed into his collar, trembling. "Oh, Jack … Jack, Jack," whispering his name like a prayer.

Something inside him split open.

He hadn't even let himself hope.

He'd followed the signs, tracked the codes, crossed cities and deserts and oceans—but always with that cold sliver in the back of his mind that told him that the girl he'd known and loved was gone. That he was too late. That this, like everything else he'd touched, would end in ruin.

But she was here. Real. Alive. Fragile in his arms.

The realness of her broke him.

His knees buckled, and he sank to the stone floor, pulling her with him, cradling her like a child. Her weight barely registered, but the pain and hurt of years of unspent tears lanced up through his chest and throat and into his skull like fire. He pressed his face into her hair, and the sobs came without warning. Raw, choking, gasping sobs he couldn't stop if he tried.

"I thought I'd never see you again," he managed. "I thought—I left, and I never—God, Alice, I never even looked for you."

"It's my fault," she said, still holding him. "Jack. I should have listened to you. Believed you. You didn't know I changed my mind. I didn't know who Prescott was until it was too late and then I was alone and I didn't know how to get out."

"I was too afraid of what he'd do to you to punish me." His voice cracked. "That's the truth. I was too scared to find out. I just … ran. I've been running ever since."

He shook his head, gripping the back of her head as if it could anchor him to the present. "I should've found you. I should've—" His voice dissolved into another sob. "I'm sorry. I'm so sorry."

Alice pulled back just enough to look at him, her hands framing his face. Her eyes were red, her cheeks wet. "You're here now. You came back."

"I don't deserve that," he whispered.

"Maybe neither of us deserved what happened. But I'm still glad you came back."

She leaned in again, resting her forehead to his. For a long moment, they just breathed.

The weight of nearly twenty years of silence burned into his soul, his hands shaking with the emotion. The grief. The ache of every version of himself he'd had to become just to survive it.

The room was quiet around them. Jack lifted his gaze, his eyes locking with Kit's for just a moment. Kit stood near the door, her arms crossed tightly against her chest. Ginger's hand covered her mouth. Alastair looked away, giving Jack the dignity of privacy.

The only three people in the world he didn't give a damn saw him like this.

"Thank you," he mouthed to Kit, and she gave him a sad smile, tears in her eyes.

The candle flickered on the bedside table, casting its light over the cross on the wall.

Jack didn't pray. He hadn't in years.

But in that moment, holding his sister like a man pulled from a wreck, he wanted to believe that something—*Someone*—had kept her safe long enough for him to finally catch up.

Then one of the nuns approached. She went directly to Kit and whispered something low and undecipherable in her ear. Kit stiffened.

"We have to go," she said softly, her voice barely carrying in the room. "A car has just pulled up in front of the orphanage—and it's not the sheikh."

Prescott.

Jack nodded. They couldn't linger here, no matter how much he might want to. Not if Prescott was here. The moment Alice found out, she'd be terrified.

But it wasn't as though they could simply avoid Prescott, either. They needed to get Alex back too.

Jack released Alice, who gathered a bag in the corner of the room, then they hurried out, following Ginger and Kit down the hallway. Alastair remained behind them, taking up his position as a sentinel without being asked.

Their footsteps sounded harsh and loud in the stone corridor, every step reminding Jack of everything they'd had to face to get here—and what they still needed to overcome. "Prescott is here," he told Alice in a low tone, grasping her hand. "And he's gotten hold of the microfilm."

Alice flinched.

For now, she doesn't need to know that's my fault.

"He's taken someone close to me. We have to get him back."

Alice's head tilted. "Are you suggesting you're going to use me as bait?"

Jack didn't have the chance to answer before Alice nodded, then said, "I think you should. I've caused too much trouble already."

"We'll see about that."

They neared the main door, and Jack glanced at Alastair, then Ginger. He released Alice's hand and reached over, squeezing her shoulder. "We're going to get him back, Red."

Only the quick rise and fall of Ginger's breathing gave away the panic in her body. She only nodded.

Alastair and Kit pulled guns from their holsters, readying them.

Jack pushed open the door to the orphanage and stepped into the cool night air.

CHAPTER FORTY-FOUR

NOAH

The man standing only feet from the orphanage wasn't Sheikh Omar—and he didn't appear to be one of his men, either.

No, this was someone unrelated to the sheikh. More commanding in his presence.

This man walked with the authority of someone who gave his allegiance to no one—and didn't care who he burned down to get what he wanted.

Noah's hands tightened around the stock of the rifle, his heart steady as he peered down the barrel.

The tremor in his fingers was back. This was bad timing, but he couldn't let it get to him. Not now.

The door to the orphanage opened, then Jack stepped out, a gun already in his hands. But as Jack's eyes collided with the man in the street, he stopped short.

Not who Jack expected.

The man swiveled toward Jack.

Click.

Noah froze as the cold metal barrel of a gun pressed into his neck. A rough, familiar voice gritted out in Arabic, "So, Yusef. You show your true face at last."

Noah nearly hung his head.

Checkmate.

He was now completely at the man's mercy. Lowering the rifle, Noah then lifted his hands, turning slowly. The sheikh himself stood behind Noah, a rifle in his own hands. Two of his men flanked him.

"Sheikh Omar," Noah said with a grim smile. "I can explain—"

"Save your words, Yusef. The presence of Sharif al-Rashid is evidence enough of your betrayal."

Noah raised a brow. *Al-Rashid?*

Of course.

Prescott must have contacted him.

"I have nothing to do with that." Noah held the sheikh's eyes. "The man who has been chasing the American woman—the man who wants to help al-Rashid cover up his crimes—he's the one who must have told al-Rashid to come here."

The sheikh gave a brittle laugh. "You expect me to believe such tripe? How would al-Rashid know the precise time to be here if not for you?"

No way around this. He couldn't give a better explanation than the truth. Noah grimaced. "*That* ... is coincidence."

"Yusef—" The sheikh's tone was one of fatherly, patronizing scolding. "Yusef, you cannot expect me to believe such lies." His gaze hardened.

Noah's pulse beat hard at his throat. He kept his hands up, kept his composure steady, but everything inside him screamed for time. *For Ginger. For Alex. For just one more second to explain.*

He doesn't understand.

The sheikh stepped back. As he did, one of the sheikh's men moved in, lifting his rifle. The butt of it slammed against Noah's head and jaw with such force that Noah gasped in pain, a painful crack rippling through his senses. His mouth tasted blood, and one knee crashed down against the earth.

The man who'd struck him grabbed him by the collar, dragging Noah before he could recover. The tops of the nearby buildings blurred with the dark sky and the glistening stars, his boots scraping against dust and stone as he tried to get a footing until the sheikh's men dragged him in front of the orphanage steps.

A distant cry reached his ears—Ginger.

The sheikh's man tossed him to the ground in front of al-Rashid.

Al-Rashid barely blinked. His boot moved, almost lazily, nudging Noah's leg aside.

Running footsteps approached, then warm arms wrapped around him. "No! No, stop!" He caught the scent of his beautiful wife before he saw her, before he felt her tears on his neck.

"Who is this?" Al-Rashid demanded, looking at Noah with the disdain that Noah had seen men use when finding rats in their quarters.

"This man belongs to you, Kamal. Your faithful servant. Did you think you could fool me?" The sheikh moved closer to al-Rashid, his steps heavy.

"Why would I hire an English dog to do my bidding?"

Noah focused on Ginger—her hand still gripping his shirt, her knees pressed into the dirt beside his face. Her breath stuttered against his neck. "Get out of here," he hissed, turning just enough to meet her eye. "Get out of here, *rohi*."

"No, I won't leave you," she said, voice shaking. "I didn't come all this way to lose my husband to spineless men who would kill women and threaten children."

"Do you enjoy being their fool, Omar? The way these English dogs make you their puppet?" Al-Rashid sneered, louder now, for everyone to hear. His Arabic was flawless, clipped and precise, the kind Noah had only ever heard from the most influential families.

Straining with effort, Noah drew himself up on one knee, not fully down but not standing either. His rifle had been stripped away, and the skin around his neck stung from where the sheikh's man had grabbed him. Ginger hovered just behind him, her hand on his shoulder, an anchor. A reminder of what he was fighting for. Who he was.

"I'm no one's dog," Noah said quietly in Arabic. He didn't look at the sheikh.

The sheikh stepped closer anyway, his sandals slow and deliberate in the dust. "No," he said with bitter mockery. "You're just a liar. A liar with many names."

Noah's jaw tightened. He wasn't going to apologize again. Not here. Not to this man who had already made up his mind about him.

"I gave you shelter," the sheikh continued. "I treated you as a guest. And you bring this into my house—" He jabbed a finger toward al-Rashid. "You dishonor me, and now you expect me to believe it was all by chance?"

"I don't expect you to believe anything," Noah said, his voice low. "But it's the truth."

"Then your truth is as useless as your weapon," the sheikh snapped as he motioned to one of his men.

The man stepped forward and, with grim efficiency, drove his boot into Noah's ribs.

Pain knifed through Noah's side and he folded, air collapsing from his lungs. He coughed and spat into the dirt, forehead pressed to the ground.

Ginger screamed. She lunged—then was caught mid-motion by another figure.

Fahad.

He appeared out of the shadows like smoke, wrapping his arms around her, spinning her back behind him with a low command in Arabic. "No!"

"But he—" Ginger choked out.

"I know," Fahad said, his voice calm, kind. "I know, *habibti.* Let me watch your back." He placed himself between her and the sheikh's men.

Noah gasped for breath, pain rippling through his body.

He'd never imagined he'd be back here once again—unarmed, humiliated, kneeling in front of two men who had the power to destroy everything he loved.

His eyes flicked toward Jack still at the edge of the scene, just barely restrained by Alastair's presence at his side. Thank goodness for Alastair. He was always cool under pressure, able to restrain Jack when necessary.

Tension coiled in Jack's stance like a bow pulled tight, his body half-turned, holding someone back until she pushed past him anyway.

"Stop!" she commanded, breaking away.

Alice Darby.

Noah hardly recognized her.

The last time he'd seen her, she'd been in pigtails. But it had to be her. The resemblance to Jack was uncanny. If Noah had expected some sort of relief at retrieving her, it didn't come. They may have beaten Prescott here, but the man was still out there and hadn't shown his face.

And he has Alex.

Al-Rashid's eyes hardened as they sized Alice up, his dark and striking features fierce. "There she is." His voice was soft.

Gentler than Noah had imagined it could be. "The woman who was never meant to survive. You stole from me, Alice. I do not forgive betrayal."

Alice's shoulders heaved. "Stop hurting these people," she repeated. "You want me, Kamal? I'm right here. I'm done hiding. I won't have any of these people die for me."

Jack stepped forward, sliding in front of her without hesitation. His gun was still in his hand, steady. "I don't believe we've been introduced," he said coolly.

"Ah," al-Rashid said. "You must be the infamous Jack Darby. I've been told about you. You're the one who led us all here, yes?"

"And you're the man who's been trying to cover his tracks with blood."

Al-Rashid gave a small shrug. "Justice, Mr. Darby, is always subjective. Was it justice when our lands were parceled out like spoils of war?" He flicked a glance at the sheikh. "Ask Sheikh Omar about British justice." He held out a hand toward Alice. "Come, woman."

Alastair was steps behind him and came to Alice's other side, grabbing her arm. "Best be on your way, Sharif. As you can see, Alice is already out of your hands. And you're vastly outnumbered."

Noah studied the sheikh, better able to see what he was up against now. A half-dozen men hung back in the distant shadows, faces hidden by keffiyehs—al-Rashid's.

And who knew where Prescott was and how many Blackwell operatives he planned on bringing tonight.

The sheikh had come with eight men, who now stood in a semicircle behind him.

Alice put a hand on Alastair's. "Let me go, please."

Don't do it, Alastair.

But Alastair was too much of a gentleman not to. He did as asked, and Alice stepped away from him. Then Noah frowned. Where was Kit?

He'd seen her exit the orphanage with Jack, but in the midst of everything, he'd lost track of her. Now he didn't see her at all.

Alice appealed to Jack with wide eyes, a determined look on her face. "Prescott will never let me leave his company, Jack. You know this. He'll never stop hunting for me. And I deserve any punishment I get. I deserve to pay for all the wrong I've done."

A movement behind him—the sheikh flinched, taking a step toward Alice.

His certainty was brittle. Crumbling.

"Are you really going to allow Alice to hand herself over to this butcher?" Noah asked, locking eyes with the sheikh now. "You made an agreement with me. And with Jack. You promised to protect the girl. You said your honor mattered."

"Sheikh Omar," Fahad said gently, his arms tightening around Ginger. "You know what kind of man Kamal is. You know what he's done. Help us, *ya sidi*. We are not his allies. We've come to rescue the girl, not harm her."

The sheikh hesitated.

Fast footsteps approached.

A scuffle of sound from the far edge of the orphanage. Several heads turned.

The sheikh stilled.

Al-Rashid's hand went to his pistol.

Noah shifted, trying to raise himself upright, heart jackhammering in his chest, preparing himself for yet another confrontation.

A shape emerged from around the corner. Two figures, smeared in blood and soot, stumbled out of the shadows.

Alex.

He was dragging someone—no—carrying her. Her arm was slung over his shoulder, her leg trailing, blood dark against her pale skin.

Ginger cried out, pulling away from Fahad with an unstoppable strength. "Alex!"

The pain in Noah's ribs, the throbbing in his jaw, the sting in his throat all seemed to fade away as one clear thought surged through Noah's mind.

He's here. He's alive.

* * *

Alex

"W\ʀᴇ ᴀʟᴍᴏsᴛ ᴛʜᴇʀᴇ," Alex managed to Ruby, his words short and choppy as the people on the street in front of the orphanage came into view. He'd been running, half-carrying Ruby for what seemed like ages, with her directing him on where to go. "Hang on."

His dragging feet almost stumbled to a stop at the sight.

He'd hoped Uncle Jack might be there—Ruby seemed to think the chance might exist.

But what he saw instead chilled him through.

Mama. Papa.

They were here?

How? When? How had they got here?

His heart squeezed so tightly in his chest that an ache pulsed out from it, spreading to his ribs, and he gasped for breath.

Worse still, his father was bleeding and appeared to have been beaten. Men with rifles stood only a few feet from him.

God, no! His academic, language-loving father.

What is he doing here? Playing soldier?

Ruby's shaking had become violent by now—either due to shock or pain, maybe both. Mama was already running toward them, though. Mama, her beautiful red tresses gleaming in the moonlight as she tore toward him without a thought for anything else.

Alex tried to ignore the arrow to his heart at the sight of her. *I love her so much.* He wanted to choke on a sob like a young boy, throw his arms around his mother, allow himself to be held by her.

He wanted every inch of the comfort he knew he'd find in her embrace.

But Ruby was desperately injured, and he couldn't think of himself right now.

As Mama drew even closer, he set Ruby down, crouching beside her. "Don't worry," he said, grasping her hand. Her skin was slick and sticky with blood, despite his best efforts. He'd only stopped to tie a tourniquet and bandage the wound to staunch the blood flow, but Ruby needed much, much more than he could help with.

Ivy would have known what to do.

The thought left him almost as quickly as it had come. He couldn't think about Ivy right now. And his mother would be more helpful than anyone right now.

"Mama!" he shouted, his voice feeling hoarse. "Help me!"

She practically threw herself toward him, catching him by the shoulders. "Are you hurt?" she asked, hands to his face, searching his eyes.

"No, no—it's not me. It's her. Her name is Ruby … help her."

"Alex, get away from her," a clear, strong voice called out.

Alex looked up to see Uncle Jack coming closer. "She's a liar and a manipulator. Works for Prescott Federline."

Alex stood slowly, his gaze shifting from Ruby's writhing, ailing figure to Uncle Jack. *I no longer know what to believe.*

"Actually, she doesn't," another male voice announced, stepping from the shadows.

Theo?

Harsh electric lights flooded the street, coming from the roof of the orphanage.

Alex dropped back, covering his eyes, barely able to see.

The light illuminated almost as much as it cast shadow, long and heavy onto the dusty street. Several British policemen came out from inside the orphanage, following a well-dressed man in a linen suit that seemed incongruous to the dirt and blood and grime caking Alex's skin.

Alex's heartbeat slowed, and for several moments time seemed to stand still, the silence perfect. Consuming. Blocking out everything.

His mother's lips moved, her head bent over Ruby, already assessing, trying to heal.

His father, half-kneeling in front of an Arab man, had his hands lifted in surrender, but his eyes were locked on Alex. Behind him, Papa's friend, Fahad, had a steady hand on Papa's shoulder.

Uncle Alastair—*Uncle Alastair*—stood in the background, holding on to the arm of a dark-haired, thin nun.

Uncle Jack, half-turned, stared at Theo, opened his mouth suddenly. "Kit, no! Al-Rashid isn't worth it!"

Another woman Alex didn't recognize stepped from the shadows, gun raised. Her long blond braid gleamed in the electric light, her face cold and ruthless. The bullet ripped through the air with a singular, sickening crack, then the man standing in front of Papa fell, a cloud of blood spraying in the air.

The courtyard exploded.

A few men shouted something in Arabic—outrage and fury in their voices that sliced through the night.

Then the gunfire started, deafening, echoing off stone walls, cracking through the dark like lightning in a canyon.

Alex didn't move.

He should've dropped. He should've ducked or run or done literally anything else—but he didn't. He stood frozen on the street, numbly watching the scene unfold, Ruby's blood sticking warm and wet to his sleeve.

Everything was happening too fast.

A muzzle flashed near a wall by the orphanage, and a woman screamed. *Mama?*

Uncle Jack had bolted back into the chaos and gripped someone tightly in his arms, while Uncle Alastair shielded the other woman with his body, hiding behind a nearby motorcar.

And Mama, of all people, dragged Ruby off the road, away from the gunfire, half-carrying, half-hauling, leaving a smear of blood across the packed dirt, all while screaming, "Alex! Alex! Run, Alex! Get down!"

His feet felt as though they'd grown roots.

His heart stuttered—then seemed to stop entirely as one of the men holding a rifle pivoted, swinging toward him. The barrel caught the moonlight, pointed straight at his chest.

Oh God.

"Alex!" Mama screamed.

But before the shot fired, something else happened. A blur of motion. A rush of shadow cut across the chaos. Moving fast. Moving with purpose. His father?

Alex barely recognized him at first. Not like this.

There was no hesitation. No flare of fear in his eyes. Just a pistol raised and ready—God, when had he drawn it? The last Alex had seen, he'd been disarmed and kneeling. *Bleeding.*

One clean shot flashed and cracked through the doubt. The

rifle clattered to the ground as the man aiming at Alex dropped like a sack.

Alex stood motionless, ears ringing.

The man's body sprawled in front of him, blood seeping into the dirt in a dark-crimson puddle. The stench of powder choked the air. His father—*his father*—had shot a man at close range and didn't so much as blink.

His father stepped forward, calm, controlled, his stance rigid and grounded. One hand still on the pistol, the other lowering just slightly—not in hesitation but readiness.

He positioned himself between Alex and the next threat, shoulders squared like a wall.

"Get down," his father said, his voice low and cold. Completely unrecognizable. "Now."

Alex dropped.

Gravel bit into his palms, breath sawing through his chest. He blinked fast, trying to focus, trying to see anything but the twisted, ruined dead man just a few feet away. Hard shadows fell across his father's face, his eyes lethal and deadly.

This wasn't the man Alex had grown up with.

Not the one who took them to church on Sunday or made notes on their essays. The one who'd taught him to tie his shoes and had marveled for days over a broken piece of pottery he'd dug up in a field near home.

That man didn't exist right now.

This was someone else.

"Papa?" The word left his mouth before he even realized he'd spoken.

His father didn't turn. His stance didn't falter. "Stay down, son."

Alex could only stare at him. At the back of that broad frame. The calm in his grip. The way the moonlight touched his shoulders as if he'd been carved from it. *He saved me.*

All the doubts Alex had carried—about who his father really was, whether the past had been a lie, whether he'd ever known the man who raised him—collapsed under the weight of that one moment.

That one bullet.

He was safe.

Even here, in the bloodied streets of Jerusalem, far from Penmore—he was home.

CHAPTER FORTY-FIVE

JACK

"Give me one good reason why I shouldn't punch you in the face right now," Jack growled, his anger barely restrained as he glared at Theo.

Beside Theo, Alain Roche shifted in his chair. They'd been at this since before dawn, and Jack was tired.

Sick of bullshit.

"I did what I had to do," Theo said with a shrug. "I'm not asking for your apology."

"You gave the microfilm to Prescott. *And* you may have let him get away."

The truth was none of them knew what had happened to Prescott. That was almost *more* unsettling than the certainty of him being alive.

"Technically that's on Ruby. I wasn't even there when the car exploded."

"You saw the car though—and no sign of a body."

Theo's gaze flickered with coldness. "The car was an inferno by the time I reached it. The microfilm would have melted. A body would have turned to ash. Prescott is almost certainly dead. Alex doesn't even know what he saw after the explosion. I don't know what you're so worried about."

"I almost died trying to keep that microfilm out of Prescott's hands." Alice spoke up from the corner of the room, her glare liquid fury. She hadn't said much this entire time, but every time she spoke, it felt like a jolt to Jack. Like he'd entered a strange new world that his sister was not only a part of but where she'd become a competent and fearless adversary to anyone who stood in her path.

Roche raised both hands. "Captain Knight decided it was better for Theo and Ruby to remain undercover and deliver the microfilm to Prescott before we lured him to the orphanage. It was his decision."

Captain Knight. Better said, *MI5*. Which Theo and Ruby apparently were. Along with their friend Felix, who Jack had throat-punched back in Cairo.

Roche and Theo had explained the situation to Jack after they'd cleared the streets of the dead bodies of al-Rashid, his men, and some of the sheikh's men. The sheikh had survived but had been arrested.

So had Kit. She'd been arrested for shooting al-Rashid.

Roche hadn't said if she'd be quietly released or made a scapegoat. Jack had a sinking feeling he knew which it would be.

None of it made Jack feel any better. He didn't care if Ruby and Theo had been ordered to infiltrate Prescott's organization by Knight. Didn't care that they'd been working this case for months, since Kit had first sent out an SOS to MI5.

He just wanted to forget.

"I'm not sure what you think you accomplished here," he said to Roche, "but all I see is a whole lot of nothing. Al-Rashid is dead. He'll never face justice for his crime and, if I know the government—and I do—what he did will get buried under fifteen inches of classified files, never to be released. Prescott, on the other hand, might still be out there. Absent of a body and proof of his death, I'm not willing to say he's out of the game. But you wouldn't go after him even if you thought he was alive, would you? Because you know before you do, he'll dig up every last skeleton in the closet of every person you care about and blackmail you with it. This is easier for you."

"Maybe al-Rashid's death is meaningless to you, but I see it as a satisfactory result in all this," Roche said with a grim smile. "The best possible outcome. Now we can all carry on with our lives."

"Sure," Alice said with a quirk of a dark brow. "Maybe you can. Meanwhile, Jack and I will just hold our breath hoping Prescott doesn't shoot us in the back someday. The man has as many aliases and friends as the British mandates have problems. He's a ghost—on paper he doesn't even exist. And I know more about Blackwell than most."

Roche closed the leather folio in front of him and leaned forward. "Then I suggest you become a ghost too, Miss Darby. I'll see you both out."

Alice and Jack exchanged a look.

That was it, then. They were being dismissed. Case closed.

"I'd like to say good-bye to Kit before we leave," Jack said in a tone that brooked no objection.

"Certainly," Roche said pleasantly.

With one last glare at Theo, Jack pushed his chair back, its legs scraping the floor as he did. He stood and left Roche's office, Alice by his side.

If he'd gained anything from this whole experience, it was that: Alice, by his side.

They'd still have years of hurt to overcome.

Prescott to face—and maybe even his organization to dismantle, brick by brick.

But they had each other again.

When they stopped by the door that led to the cells, Alice reached over and squeezed his hand. "I'll let you talk to her alone," she said, then leaned over and planted a kiss on his cheek. "See you outside?"

Jack nodded. "Go straight to Alastair's car. I don't trust Prescott not to rear his head."

Alice rolled her eyes and smiled. "I didn't miss the bossy older brother routine, that's for sure."

Managing a warm look for her, Jack swallowed hard. This would be hard to get used to. He hadn't been an older brother for way too long. And Alice was a woman now.

He followed Roche toward the cell block. At the end of it, in the dim, cold light of dawn, Kit sat on a bench in a cell, shirt still splattered with al-Rashid's blood. She stood when she saw him.

Jack went up to the bars and let out a slow, exaggerated sigh that was heartfelt and yet not enough. "Kit Federline."

"Jack Darby," she said, coming closer. She gripped his forearms, then set her forehead against a bar.

Jack swallowed hard, moving over so that his forehead dipped against hers, making what little contact he could with her.

His voice stuck in his throat and then he managed, gruffly, "Why didn't you come back?"

She was slow to answer, the sound of her breath thick. Warm against his cheek. "I thought about it. But then you were married before I could blink. And … that seemed better for you. Maybe what you needed. I was never what you needed, Jack. We were never good for each other."

How could she really say that? He had *wanted* her, *loved her* more than anything. Her words sounded hollow. Like an easy excuse for never loving him enough.

"That marriage ended though. And you still stayed away."

"Jack ... do we really have to do this now? What difference will it make?"

He stared at her, blinking slowly.

Difference? It made all the difference, didn't it? Everything he'd ever wanted to say to her, all the times he wished he could have told her ...

But he had told her, so many times, how much he loved her. Yet that had never been enough for her. And maybe that was what he'd failed to realize all along. He'd been holding on for so long to something that really had died years ago ... not her, but the youthful fantasy of loving her.

"I should have kissed you when I saw you at Fahad's house. Held you close and *left you there*," he murmured.

"Do you really think I would have stayed?" she asked with a chuckle.

Kit pulled back and looked at him, searching his eyes. "Besides, Jack. We've both moved on from each other by now, haven't we? I was engaged in Baghdad, you know." Her eyes glistened. "My father had him killed."

Moved on?

He'd been with other women, yes.

Loved another woman.

And even with Ruby, there had been a spark there to explore —something he'd been sure could blossom with time.

Ruby.

He couldn't think about her.

He needed to deal with Kit first. Kit ... who was alive, who had run from him over and over again.

Kit ... who would never love him in the way he'd dreamed. Kit, who, maybe, he didn't really even know at all anymore.

And in the meantime, the woman I'd started to care about is in the hospital and I've ignored her.

He'd been a fool for Kit. But he wasn't an ignorant boy anymore.

"I'm not sure if you ever move on from what we felt for each other when we were kids, Kit." *Or what I felt for you.* He forced himself to take a step back from her.

"But you were right. Time has never been our friend. And I can't keep living my life with your ghost hovering at the edge of my soul. I almost forgot who I was because of it."

Sadness flitted through her gaze. "I understand." Smiling sadly, she shrugged and stepped back. "And right now I'm at the mercy of the British authorities. I can just see the paper headlines now: *American heiress murders Arabian lover in crime of passion.*"

"Maybe. Or maybe they'll hush the whole thing up and release you when they're bored of you."

Kit nodded. "Either way, you won't be waiting for me."

His heartbeat slowed.

He wanted to tell her no.

Wanted to say, *"Of course I'll wait. I'll wait forever, Kit,"* just the way he had as a youth.

But he knew better now. Knew what he would sacrifice if he did.

I have to let her go.

"No," he breathed. "I won't."

"Good," she said.

CHAPTER FORTY-SIX

GINGER

The last thing Ginger had expected was work triage before dawn on the streets of Jerusalem, but somehow all roads always seemed to lead back to that. Fortunately, she hadn't been alone—a local doctor had rushed to the scene after hearing the gunfire bringing much-needed supplies with him.

Then he'd helped her get Ruby to the local hospital, where Ginger had pleaded for the opportunity to help with the operation to remove the bullet from Ruby's leg. The doctor had been skeptical about her credentials but had allowed Ginger to assist as a nurse—a blow to Ginger's pride, but not a battle worth fighting that morning. Ruby was more important. She'd have to spend several months recovering, but she was alive.

Thank goodness.

Ginger didn't know her and, the truth was, much as it hurt to lose any patient, right now she'd cared more about saving Ruby for Alex's sake. Alex had nearly thrown his own life away saving Ruby from Prescott—if she'd died after all his efforts, he might not have ever recovered from that.

Ginger left the operating room and went down the hallway to the patient room where the local doctor had put Noah and Alex. Her husband and son, both carrying minor injuries, were a sight for sore eyes despite their bandages.

Both stared at her, identical eyes tracking her movements with identical expressions.

Father and son.

How could Alex have ever doubted it?

She closed the door to the room, then leaned back against it, exhausted.

"She's fine," Ginger said to Alex first, recognizing the anxious look in his eyes. "She'll be just fine, thanks to you."

Relief settled Alex's expression, and he sank further back into his chair. "Thank goodness." He scratched a cut above his eyebrow, gloomily as he looked from his mother to his father. "I'm sorry, Mama. Papa. I shouldn't have left Penmore without telling you. Maybe none of this would have happened." He stared at his shoes. "I didn't know you would have the means ..."

Noah cleared his throat and met Ginger's gaze, then leaned closer to Alex and set his hand on his shoulder. "A lot of what happened during the war and when we were first married is ... complicated history. We should have told you about it sooner. Including the fact that my work was primarily in intelligence. There's a lot we still need to tell you."

Alex lifted his face, his eyes shining with tears. "I might have killed a man, Papa. Or at the very least wounded him gravely. I thought I saw Prescott get out, but I don't know. I might have just hoped I—I ..."

Ginger's throat clenched. She knew the burden of that horrible guilt. "If Prescott died, you should know your actions might have saved others, Alex."

"But, *a life*—"

Noah nudged him gently. "Death—especially when it's

violent—is always ugly. No amount of philosophizing can change that fact. And the days to come will be difficult. But you're not to blame for what happened, either. And we will never think less of you for it."

Ginger began, "But, Alex—"

He stiffened, ready for his mother's inevitable scolding.

Ginger's throat filled with tears. "I'm so proud of you, son." She hurried over toward him, then threw her arms around him.

She hadn't anticipated Noah stepping quietly from his seat, but when he did and wrapped them both tightly in his arms, the weight of years seemed to lift.

Maybe she didn't need a grand hospital in the country to prove her worth—she could save lives from anywhere. And maybe she didn't always need to prove herself, either. This morning had demonstrated that.

The medical community could be damned. For twelve years she'd fought against a tide determined to belittle what she had built, and nearly let its pressure grind the love out of her work. She would not waste herself in endless battle. Yet her time away had reminded her she still had fight left, if she chose where to spend it.

Alex was safe. Ivy and Victoria were tucked away in Cairo, beyond harm. Soon she would gather them, return to England for Clara, and go home.

Her family, and the community that needed her, were all that mattered.

The rest—the councils, the journals that dismissed her, the men who tried to silence her—could rage at the sea of change. She would stand where she was needed, as she always had, with no apologies and no regrets.

CHAPTER FORTY-SEVEN

JACK

The hospital hallway smelled faintly of alcohol and antiseptic, and Jack waited by the closed door, his hand on the knob.

In Baghdad, he'd opened a different door—to Ruby, to his heart.

He'd promised Ruby he wouldn't leave.

But everything had changed. Gone so far off the rails in a way he couldn't possibly have anticipated.

Theo and Ruby's true loyalties, the sting operation … Kit.

None of it made it any easier.

Come on, Darby.

Don't be a coward.

He hesitated just another second, then opened the door.

Sunlight filled the room. Ruby lay back in the bed, reading a newspaper, pillows behind her head. She looked paler, frailer than he remembered her. More natural, too, without any rouge.

Still beautiful.

"Jack." The paper crinkled as she set it down. She offered him a hesitating smile. "You're here."

Jack shut the door quietly, then stepped toward her. "I wanted to see how you were recovering."

"I'm—" Ruby gasped for breath. Then her lower lip trembled, and she looked away, her gaze traveling to the window. "I spent part of the morning in surgery, woke up here, and had breakfast. And all that time, you know what I kept thinking about? How I was lying there on the ground, shot and bleeding, and you didn't even come over to see if I was going to live. I was right there, Jack."

Her words gutted him.

She's right.

And it wasn't that the thought hadn't crossed his mind. But when the shooting had started, Kit had been in the crossfire, right beside him. And Alice too. Ginger had seen to Ruby—and then Jack had been carted off the streets by Theo and Roche before he'd even had a chance to go check on her.

"I probably deserve it," she whispered when he didn't respond. "You thought the worst of me after Baghdad, I'm sure."

"I did," he said, coming closer. He rubbed his newly shaved jawline. He'd gone to Fahad's to change and shave after leaving Kit in the prison because he'd come here first, and Ginger had told him Ruby was asleep, still under the effects of the ether.

But maybe he shouldn't have. He should have stayed here, by her side, so she wouldn't have woken up alone.

"I did think the worst, Ruby," he said more softly. He pulled up a chair and sat at her bedside. "And the truth is, you lied to me from the moment we met. I talked to Theo—I know why you did it, but it's still hard for me to swallow."

"I only lied about who was pulling the puppet strings. Everything else I told you was true." Ruby's eyes were big and expressive. "Including my name."

Which one?

But he knew. He knew when she'd finally shared the truth. "Ruby Weber?"

She nodded.

"But you weren't a thief either." He smirked. "So that's another one."

"No, I was." She grimaced. "Just not when you met me. Everything about my family—that's true. And Felix, Theo, and I were all stealing, trying to scrounge up the money to help them. Then Felix met Maxwell Knight—and he said … he said if we worked for him, he'd get the British government to help my family."

Jack stared at her, wishing that the information made him feel better about all this.

She'd been desperate, sure. But he still couldn't shake the feeling that everything had been a lie.

He raised a brow. "So you didn't set up that whole ruse in Lydda to get me to trust you? All the while planning to report back to Theo, then clobber me over the head and steal the microfilm after seducing me?"

"No!" Ruby drew back, blinking quickly. "It wasn't like that. Not at all." She folded the paper, setting it aside. "Theo didn't—doesn't—like you. Didn't like that you wanted to do things your way. He was going to try to force you to tell us what you knew about Alice's disappearance in Lydda, but I didn't think you'd trust us. So I decided to ditch him and actually help you, the way you needed and deserved. But I still had to check in eventually—so I did after we arrived in Baghdad. And when I did, I found out Theo had already got to Baghdad ahead of us."

She took a shaky breath. "He found me late that night—after he'd taken the microfilm. Forced me to leave with him. Knight was furious with me and threatening me." Ruby squared her shoulders. "But I was even angrier. So I sent Knight the message that I was done. I'm not working for him ever again after this job. Not after what they did to you in Baghdad."

"It won't be that easy, you know. And your family still isn't safe."

"So I'll go to the Americans. Someone else." Ruby shrugged. "I'll figure it out. Even if I have to do it alone. I won't quit until I get every last member of my family out of Germany."

Jack smiled at her bravado. She was a tough woman. And she'd saved Alex from Prescott—which he had to admire.

But she was also a little naïve about the world she'd gotten involved in. She had no idea what she was up against.

Who she was up against.

If he was alive, Prescott Federline wouldn't forgive the woman who'd double-crossed him.

And Knight wouldn't simply allow a valuable spy to walk away.

Noah himself had confessed that he worried Knight would keep coming after him, especially in light of what had happened with Hower.

The worst part was, it made Jack *want* to wrap his arms around her and shield her.

"What about Theo and Felix?"

"I don't know," she whispered, looking away from Jack. "They both came to see me this morning. They're furious with me. Knight sent Theo a message saying we were a *package deal*—whatever that means."

Jack closed his eyes, letting silence settle between them.

When he looked up at her at last, her eyes were downcast and quiet tears trailed down her cheeks.

Jack's heart squeezed, then he reached over and slid his hand over hers, his fingers curling tight.

Somehow that only made her cry harder.

"Hey," he said softly, then slipped onto the empty space beside her. He set his hands on her shoulders. "Hey, look at me."

"I'm so sorry, Jack," Ruby said, her gaze watery. "I never wanted to lie to you. And I really didn't expect you to be …" She drew a shallow breath. "I didn't expect to like you so much."

"Like me?" Jack grinned.

She gave a broken, tearful laugh. "Jack … I think I'm falling in love with you."

He didn't move. Didn't breathe.

In love?

"I know it's crazy," she went on. "And we barely know each other. You don't have to forgive me. And I know I don't deserve you, but—"

He cut off her words with an impulsive kiss.

Her eyes widened, then her mouth softened against his, returning his kiss with a quiet, appreciative moan.

The kiss lingered for a few moments, her tears wetting his cheeks, her lips salty from them. Then he pulled away and set his forehead against hers. "Sorry—I didn't expect to do that."

She smiled, then gave him a quick kiss. "You never have to apologize for kissing me, Jack. You're a good man."

"By the way," he said in a low voice. "I still owe you some money for smuggling me into Iraq. That might be able to help at least a couple members of your family make it out of Germany."

She smiled sadly and shook her head. "I can't accept it, Jack. I won't. I don't need your money. Not now. I don't want you to think your money is all I'm after. I need you to believe in me—and you'll never believe in me if I take your money."

"We have a deal. You have to let me—"

"No," she said more firmly. "No. I won't take it. I'm sorry. My mind is made up."

Is she serious?

The idea that she was willing to sacrifice like this … he didn't know what to say. To think.

"But your family needs it. You need it."

"The only thing I need right now is for you to never question my motivation for anything I do. I broke your trust in a way that I'm not sure how to rebuild, and you have to let me do this on my own. That's what I need."

He sighed and cupped her face in his hands. "Ruby, you deserve a lot more than you give yourself credit for. And, for the record, I like you too. I spent a decade spinning circles in the desert, and then you came around and made me feel … less alone. You gave me hope. And I meant what I said in Baghdad."

He searched her eyes, then kissed her again. "I'm not ready to walk away from you, Ruby Weber. And I don't intend to. I understand the position you were in, and I can forgive that. But you have to promise never to lie to me like that again."

She sniffled, his words provoking a fresh wave of tears. "I won't, Jack, I promise." She threw her arms around his neck, her tears splashing against his collarbone. "I promise."

Jack held her tightly, breathing in the scent of her, letting himself melt into her warmth.

She might not need him.

But he needed her.

EPILOGUE

JACK

The sun shone brightly on the grassy lawn beside Alastair and Lucy's Cairo home, and Jack sipped his lemonade, watching from the verandah as the others played a lazy game of croquet. Noah and Ginger would be leaving in the morning with Alex, catching the first train to Alexandria, then taking a steamer back to England. They'd been away from home, the hospital, and Clara for too long.

Victoria and Ivy were, shockingly, not going with them.

While here, Victoria had announced she intended to explore a move back to Cairo. Reestablish herself, on her own two feet, alone. Ivy would stay with her for several months, then return to England to attend Roedean in the fall.

Jack wasn't sure why Victoria had made such an abrupt about-face, but he couldn't say he disliked the idea—it would be nice having a friendly face nearby.

He'd decided to stay in Cairo for now. Even accepted a job at a nearby dig in Giza. He and Alice had too much to work out between them and she would be safest here, continuing to stay at one of Alastair's safe houses most of the time.

"Did you find something to spike the lemonade with?" Ruby's laughing voice came from several feet away.

He grinned and stood straighter. "Is that what you think I came up here for?"

She shrugged, limping closer with a cane. She had a long way to go for a full recovery, but she made progress every day. "It's a good guess."

Jack swung her into his arms, and she squealed with a laugh as her cane clattered to the ground. He dipped her back, hovering inches away from her lips. "I don't need alcohol, sweetheart. I've got you."

He kissed her and she melted into it, her arms tight around his neck. Being with her here felt so right.

So good.

When he pulled back, he set her down gently, then lifted her cane and handed it to her. "I just came up for a quick break in conversation. Glad you missed me though. I'll be right back down."

"All right. But don't be too long." Ruby pressed a kiss to Jack's cheek, and he smiled at her as she walked away, returning to the group.

His heart felt so unusually light. After everything, the idea that he could experience something like this again felt as if he'd entered strange, unchartered waters—ones he was willing to risk. For her. For them.

Jack set his hands on the rail of the verandah, the laughter of Alex and Ivy carrying from the lawn as they continued their game. Only steps behind them, Ginger sat at a table with Alice, their gazes focused on the pair. Both women wore similar expressions—curved smiles at the sight of young love, too innocent to realize how obvious it was to everyone but them.

Noah sat with Alastair, who smoked his pipe, a satisfied gleam in his eyes. Nearby, Lucy busied herself giving instructions to one of the servants, though Jack had seen her just moments ago speaking with Victoria.

As though she'd been summoned, soft footsteps beside him revealed Victoria approaching from the stairs. She gave him a warm smile, but something else flickered in her eyes as she stopped beside him. *Uncertainty, maybe?*

"You're a hard man to catch alone," she murmured with the same silky tone that had once captivated him as a much younger man.

"What can I say? My popularity has never waned." He winked teasingly.

She chuckled. "Neither has your arrogance." Her chin raised higher, then she stood shoulder to shoulder with him, her gaze focused on her daughter. "Being here in Cairo has been interesting. Reminded me a lot about the woman I used to be—the mistakes I made."

He gave her a sidelong glance, his heart warming. "We all made mistakes. But we learned our lessons, didn't we?"

"Sometimes." Victoria shrugged, her expression sobering. "Jack, there's something I need to tell you. Something I should have told you years ago—about Ivy's father."

Ivy's father?

Jack frowned. Victoria had never spoken about that. He had been fairly certain Ivy wasn't Stephen Fisher's, but other than that, he didn't venture to make guesses.

He set his hand on top of Victoria's, though. "You know you can always tell me anything, Tori."

Victoria's smile faltered and she looked away, back at Ivy. "She's yours, Jack."

She spoke the truth softly—and it shattered everything.

AUTHOR'S NOTE

When I first approached Jack Darby's story, I had originally envisioned presenting my readers with his prequel adventures before World War I. (Somewhere in a dusty drawer is a copy of it, featuring characters later brought up in *A Spark in Ashes*—including Prescott Federline, Alice, and Kit.)

I've always known Jack's history, but after *Whisper in the Tempest* what I kept receiving was a request for a happy ending for him. Of course, that posed a problem. I didn't really know how I wanted to handle Jack's story after the war. He's long been one of my favorites, but that doesn't mean he's been spared from suffering. (Authors often put their favorites through quite a bit of pain, sadly.)

His story isn't over, but for now I hope he's at least on a slightly better path than where we left him at the end of World War I. Where he'll go from here? Only time—or more books—will tell.

This was a difficult book in a lot of ways. A little too relevant to current events, unfortunately, and filled with political waters that can be very difficult to wade into. As a student of history, I truly believe that there's a level of nuance that often gets over-looked in favor of weaponizing more convenient facts or soundbites. I never aim to make a statement in my books (though my characters may have opinions, I try to keep them accurate to their perspectives), mostly because I want to do my best to present the history without bias.

Three things inspired me in my research for the creation of this story, and two of them are conspiracy theories—that T.E. Lawrence and Faisal Hussein may both have been victims of murder rather than dying by accident and heart attack. Is there any truth to those claims? Who knows. I'm definitely not a conspiracy theorist. But they were great fodder for fiction, so I decided to include them, and Noah's journey being pulled back into espionage is directly influenced by the T.E. Lawrence theories.

The third source of inspiration was the well-documented fact that the Nazis, later in the 1930s, began to court Arab nationalists. These overtures were fascinating to develop into a plotline, so I decided to nudge the timeline forward just a bit.

At the end of the day, I think one thing is clear: the history and painful conflict that has endured for centuries in this region of the world is complex and multi-faceted, filled with countless *what ifs*. I hope that I can at least continue to bring some of it to my readers through beloved characters whose stories bring it to life, and through new characters who offer fresh perspectives.

NEWSLETTER AND NEXT BOOK

I hope you enjoyed Jack's story! Thank you so much for reading; my readers really are what make this possible and I am so grateful for you! If you enjoyed this book, I'd love it if you took the time to leave a rating or review at your favorite book retailer. It truly goes a long way.

And if you'd like to stick around and see more of my work and find out more about the characters from the Windswept Saga, I encourage you to join my newsletter on my website or Facebook Reader's group! I have freebies and giveaways, exclusive content and, of course, you get to hear all about upcoming book news, my life, and my small army of children.

ACKNOWLEDGMENTS

This book owes so much to so many people—I could never make any of these happen without a small army of people to help.

To Susanne Lakin—thank you, thank you, thank you, for your flexibility, your encouragement, your honesty, and for always inspiring me to keep going, even when the words just don't want to come.

I would be completely unable to make this happen without the fact-checking and accuracy of Robin Seavill, who is brilliant and so much fun to work with. Thank you.

Julie Deaton, I am going to miss you so, so much. Thank you for this wonderful journey the last few years. You are the best.

And to my beta readers, my family, and every single one of my readers that wrote to ask me for Jack's story. You're the reason I keep going and I hope I can keep putting out books that bring you joy!

newsletter or Facebook Reader's group! I love hearing from readers and have some great offers lined up for my subscribers.

ABOUT THE AUTHOR

Annabelle McCormack writes historical romantic fiction and contemporary romance packed with sprawling adventures, epic love, and soulmates who just can't stay away from each other (even when the world is falling apart). If there's a sweeping love story with high stakes and deep emotions, she's probably writing it—or at least dreaming about it while chasing down her next cup of coffee.

When she's not wrangling words, she's wrangling five home-schooled kids, a couple of dogs, and an unreasonable amount of books in Maryland. If life had more hours (and less laundry), she'd be traveling, painting, or becoming a professional pastry chef. For now, she's content with baking, reading, lifting heavy things at the gym, and plotting her next great escape—er, novel.

Visit her at www.annabellemccormack.com or http://instagram.com/annabellemccormack to follow her daily adventures.